W9-ASD-825

Neil White was born and brought up around West Yorkshire. He left school at sixteen but studied for a law degree in his twenties, then started writing in 1994. He is now a lawyer by day, crime fiction writer by night. He lives with his wife and three children in Preston.

NEIL WHITE

THE DOMINO KILLER

sphere

SPHERE

First published in Great Britain in 2015 by Sphere

1 3 5 7 9 10 8 6 4 2

Copyright © Neil White 2015

The moral right of the author has been asserted.

*All characters and events in this publication, other than those
clearly in the public domain, are fictitious and any resemblance
to real persons, living or dead, is purely coincidental.*

All rights reserved.
No part of this publication may be reproduced, stored in a
retrieval system, or transmitted, in any form or by any means, without
the prior permission in writing of the publisher, nor be otherwise circulated
in any form of binding or cover other than that in which it is published
and without a similar condition including this condition
being imposed on the subsequent purchaser.

A CIP catalogue record for this book
is available from the British Library.

Hardback ISBN 978-0-7515-4951-5
Trade Paperback ISBN 978-0-7515-4952-2

Typeset in Meridien by M Rules
Printed and bound in Great Britain by
Clays Ltd, St Ives plc

Papers used by Sphere are from well-managed forests
and other responsible sources.

MIX
Paper from
responsible sources
FSC® C104740

Sphere
An imprint of
Little, Brown Book Group
Carmelite House
50 Victoria Embankment
London EC4Y 0DZ

An Hachette UK Company
www.hachette.co.uk

www.littlebrown.co.uk

Acknowledgements

I write alone. I don't share my plots or send out works in progress, looking for hints or advice. Instead, I keep everything in my head as I pace and fret, shape and reshape, until I present a completed story to my editors and agent, like a nervous schoolboy.

My editor, Jade Chandler, and my desk editor, Thalia Proctor, have always been gentle with me, as has my agent, the wonderful Sonia Land at Sheil Land Associates. They give me their ideas and suggestions, pointers as to where I could do things better, always thorough and constructive, so I lock myself away again. More fretting, more pacing.

For the reader, you see the finished book, the end of my endeavours, but I know the changes, the improvements, the advice and small tweaks that make it appear as it does on the shelf or your ebook reader. For the help of my editors and agent, I am eternally grateful.

As for the people who have to listen to my fretting, my worries, my occasional tantrum, I can only apologise. I'm always glad of the process, the highs and lows, as it's all part of just that, a process. Those who can only watch don't get the same from it, but their patience does not go unnoticed, and for that I am thankful.

One

He paced. It was hard to stay still. He'd been in this moment before, but those times had been different. He'd controlled them, planned them out. He wasn't in control this time.

The wind rustled the leaves above him, like whispers, providing a cover for the thump of his heartbeat and the nervous rasp of his breath. The sun had gone; the park was in darkness, just the glow of street lights in the distance. He closed his eyes for a moment. He couldn't think about what he had to do. Just do it. There was no choice.

He needed to summon what had driven him before, to shut out everything else.

It began like heat, his blood flowing more quickly, his fingers stretched outwards with tension. His thoughts became flashes; bright, stark images that made him want to shield his eyes. And the sounds. They started like scratches, something he could barely hear, but they got louder as the images grew brighter, a constant murmuring so that he had to clamp his hands over his ears to stop the pain. It became a compulsion, and the more he shut them out, the harder they seemed to come at him, wave after wave of need that drove out all other thoughts until he had to do something to satisfy it. An unstoppable force, willpower alone not enough.

This time it was different. So different. Cold-blooded and brutal. But deep down it was the same need. He shouldn't feel bad about that, because he knew he couldn't help himself. There was no hatred for the man he was waiting for, but killing him would get back something he needed.

Memories flooded through him as he stood in the darkness. Skin soft under his hands, struggling, writhing bodies; his memories like white light, everything bleached out, only the desperate cries making it through. Later, there were the tears, the screams. Ripples, that's what they were.

His breaths came faster.

This time there'd be no blankness, no surge of adrenalin as he finished, no glow of anticipation at what lay ahead. It would be just a swing of the hammer and everything would be remembered.

The park was empty: he was alone amongst the grass and trees on the very edge of the city, with the dark brood of the moors ahead. Tarmac paths cut through it, flowerbeds running alongside filled with bright colours. The paths ran towards a wooden shelter that nestled underneath birch and sycamore trees, the wood painted black, a brass plaque proclaiming it as IN MEMORIAM for those who fell in the last war. Black scrawls showed where bored teenagers made a claim for the living, their nicknames written in marker pen.

He settled behind the tree, leaning against the bark and looking down at the floor. The police would want to know where he'd waited. The soles of his shoes were imprinted into the soil between the huge roots so he brushed at it, to make them indistinct. He needed a cigarette, but the glowing tip would give him away.

There was some movement. The steady *click-click* of shoes.

He peered out from behind the tree. There he was.

His fingers dug into the bark as he put his head back. He let out a quiet sigh. The man looked uncomfortable as he walked slowly along the path, looking around, a bunch of calla lilies wrapped in green paper held in one hand. That was the sign:

the flowers. The clicks of the man's footsteps became louder. He was dressed smartly, as though he was on his way home from whatever job he did, his shoes shiny black, his suit dark grey, brightened by a yellow tie.

The man didn't sit in the shelter straight away. He paced around, fiddled with his tie, preened, looked about, as if checking that he was alone. That was why the park had been chosen, so he was told: no one used it at night.

Eventually, the man stepped into the shelter and sat down, the flowers across his knees. The wooden bench creaked beneath him and there was the hiss of a breath freshener. The man's shoes tapped out a fast rhythm, as if he was nervous. He should be.

He felt in his pocket, just to remind himself that it was the right way. A hammer. Quick and easy. He had a knife in his other pocket in case he needed it. The hammer should be enough, though. It was heavy, the rubberised grip reassuring, but the weight of the metal head made him shudder.

He crept out from behind the tree, his clothes brushing against the bark. He gripped the shaft of the hammer. A bird flew from a branch above him but it didn't distract him. His shoes squeaked on the grass, making more noise than he wanted. He zipped his jacket up to his neck and slipped on the mask, a ghoulish Halloween mask he'd bought for this, so that if it went wrong he might avoid identification, but he knew it was going to be all right. He had the size advantage, plus the element of surprise.

He paused at the edge of the shelter. He could still walk away. The man inside would get to go home. Then he thought of why he was doing it. His mind became more focused, the view ahead like looking along a tunnel, bright light ahead.

This was it.

He rushed into the shelter, pulling the hammer out of his pocket. The man's eyes widened in surprise, then in shock, but it didn't stop him.

The first swing caught the man on his arm and he yelled in pain. The flowers fell to the floor, the petals crushed under his rubber soles as he stepped forward for another blow, the man leaning back now, trying to protect himself. It was no good.

The next swing made him crumple, the hammer finding his skull.

From then it was frenzied, his mind taking nothing in. Everything was white. His arm rose and fell, liquid struck him, covering the mask, hitting his eyes and making him blink, the shaft of the hammer slick with blood. The sound of wet thuds broke the silence of the park but still he carried on. His breaths came as grunts, and he didn't stop until his hammer struck tarmac, with nothing left of his skull to stop its path.

He stood ramrod straight and looked up at the sky. The white light receded and his chest rose quickly as he sucked in air. His arm ached.

Once his breathing returned to normal, he looked down. The man at his feet was unrecognisable. The lilies were stained deep red, as were his shoes and trousers. The man's head was just pulp, the tarmac now a red pool. How could a body contain so much blood?

He wanted to know who this man was. Why was his death so important? He gritted his teeth and reached into the man's pocket, the metallic smell of blood making him gag. He took his wallet. He was about to step away when he noticed the watch. It looked expensive. He unclicked it and pocketed it.

He stepped out of the blood and moved away, walking backwards all the time, then he turned and ran for his car.

Two

Joe Parker wiped his eyes as he locked his car door. Just before six o'clock in the morning, it was no time to be parking up in a town centre, even if it was close to the police station. There were threats in the shadows. As a defence lawyer he couldn't use the police station car park, so he left the car on a side street flanked by shops protected by steel shutters. There would still be those who stalked the streets in the early hours, looking for unlocked doors; this was the regular nightshift for those wanting something for nothing.

He yawned and looked around. The coffee he'd gulped down before he set off was starting to take effect, but thirty minutes earlier he'd been in bed and hoping that the next sound he heard would be his alarm.

Police station visits were disruptive. Either they took place during office hours and wrecked his plans for the day, so that an evening or weekend was lost to catching up, or they were at some God-awful time of the night. But the best way to get a client was to be there at the beginning of the case, so if he got a call, he always turned up.

This visit didn't seem anything special. A burglar, so he'd been told. He must have been caught inside the premises, whatever they were, because a cold forensic hit, like DNA, would have resulted in a daytime arrest, when there would be the resources to deal with him. He would have to say sorry and hope for a sympathetic judge, or keep quiet and buy himself a few weeks to come up with some lies.

Joe jabbed the button on the intercom and drawled, 'Joe Parker from Honeywells,' when the speaker fizzed into life. A loud buzz told him that it was time to push. A short corridor led towards another door, where another buzz allowed him into the custody suite.

Wherever Joe went, custody suites were the same. A high desk, so that prisoners couldn't leap over easily and attack the sergeant, and a large space in front, enough room for the brawlers to carry on their disputes with whoever had handcuffed them. Most prisoners were led in meekly, but there had been a few occasions when Joe had stepped into the cell corridor to avoid the flying fists and feet as someone protested their arrest. They always started the same way, with the steady rumble of the police van and then shouts as the rear doors opened. The worse they behaved, the harder the ride in, with the driver aiming for speed bumps and plenty of stamping on the brakes, so that the prisoner's anger had turned to rage by the time the doors were thrown open. Metallic clatters announced the struggle into the station, and then there'd be the strangled obscenities as a tangle of uniforms and dirty clothing tumbled into the custody area.

This morning it was quiet, and Joe preferred it that way. He'd seen enough fights – they were no longer exciting, and being a witness ruled him out of a case. The money wasn't good in criminal law, so there was no point in cutting yourself out of a case just because the human drama became more interesting. Lawyers learned to look away.

Someone banged on a cell door and shouted something, but it was strangled rage. The sergeant ignored it, just part of the soundtrack of a night behind bars. The noise would get louder before it stopped.

Two plain-clothes officers were waiting for Joe: the duty detectives. Any hope they'd had of spending the night catching up on paperwork had been ruined by whatever his client had done. They didn't make to shake Joe's hand and he didn't proffer.

'Is he mine?' Joe said, tilting his head back towards the source of the screams that echoed along the tiled corridor.

'No. He's just someone too drunk to know when to take heed of an instruction to go home. Your guy is very quiet.'

'So what have you got?' Joe opened his folder, a pen poised over a notepad.

'Mark Proctor,' said the taller one, the scruffier of the two. His tie was a little looser, his mauve shirt faded from too many washes. The shorter one liked his shirts tight and well-pressed, clean and rigid, like his posture.

'They told me burglary on the phone,' Joe said.

'That's right,' the tall one said. 'Broke into the vehicle compound and stole his car back.'

Joe raised his eyebrows. 'The police compound?'

'That's the one. We subcontract it these days; use an old mill towards Royton.'

'So he went in to take his own property?' Joe said. 'That makes it a tricky burglary.'

'Unless it was never really his.'

'I'm intrigued,' Joe said, but the weariness in his voice hinted that he was far from that. 'So how did you catch him?'

The smaller one puffed out his chest and put back his head. Joe knew his type. It wasn't in his nature to cooperate. Joe preferred the taller one, who seemed like he just wanted to get through his shift and go home.

'He set fire to the car,' the smaller one said finally.

'Unusual, after all the effort he put into getting it back.'

'That's what we thought,' the other man said. 'His car flashed up as uninsured when he passed a traffic patrol so the

7

car was seized. It was taken to the compound, and within an hour, he'd climbed over the fence. Once he was inside, he just opened the gate and took it, all on camera. A mile away, he was caught running from a burning car. So we're guessing it's stolen.'

'If it's only a guess, looks like he'll be staying quiet,' Joe said.

The smaller one took a deep breath through his nose and stepped closer to Joe.

'Don't bother,' Joe said. 'I've had all the intimidation before. I'll do my job, you'll do yours, and somewhere along the line it will be decided whether there's a case.'

The taller one tried not to smirk as his colleague jabbed his finger towards a small door. 'Get in there. I'll fetch him.'

Joe smiled, his first of the morning, and opened the door into a small space in front of a glass screen. His client would appear on the other side.

Defence lawyers couldn't be trusted to have too much privacy with a client; some have provided more than legal advice to get their clients through the night. Tiny holes in the glass would allow them both to talk, just, but Joe knew the detectives would be waiting outside the door to hear what was said when voices were raised.

The door closed behind him and Joe sat down, mild claustrophobia settling in. There was only just enough room for his chair, and the glass screen prevented him from using his notepad comfortably. Joe understood: if he was tempted to drag out the hours, just to frustrate an investigation, it was going to be uncomfortable.

The sound of voices drifted in from the corridor that ran behind the space on the other side of the glass. Joe pulled out the form he would complete with his client and waited.

The civilian jailer was first, obscuring the client behind him. Joe smiled a greeting and then yawned. He needed another coffee.

Joe was still looking down, sorting out his paperwork, when his client sat in front of him, the small space filled by the sound of his forearms slapping on the desk.

'Hello, I'm from Honeywells,' Joe said, his voice quiet as he looked at his papers. 'I'm Joe Parker.'

'I'm Mark Proctor. Thank you for coming.'

When Joe looked up, everything changed.

His vision swam and his throat clammed up. His mouth dropped open and his pen fell to the floor. He gripped the desk to steady himself and clamped his eyes closed.

He took deep breaths to fight back the rise of bile. Sweat from his hands made the desk damp. It couldn't be. Not after all this time. He was making a mistake. Too many years had gone by.

'Are you all right?' the voice said on the other side, a finger tapping on the glass.

Joe knew that he wasn't, but he had to pull himself together. He couldn't lose his grip. Not now.

He looked up again and nodded. 'I'm fine. Just a migraine. It'll pass.' He bent down for his pen. He swallowed. 'Just give me your details for the forms and then we'll start talking.'

His handwriting was shaky as he took them down, but that didn't matter. All that counted was the information.

'Tell me what you were doing with your car,' Joe said, trying to keep his tone even, but as he looked through the glass, he was transported back. A woodland path. A hooded figure. His darkest secret.

'Who says it was me?' Proctor said.

Joe tapped the notepad with his pen, making sharp blue points in the paper. 'They do,' Joe said, and he pointed towards the door.

'They're just going to have to prove it then,' Proctor said. 'Unless you can come up with a story for me.'

'I don't do stories,' Joe said, regaining his composure. 'Either talk or stay quiet, that's your choice, but don't expect me to come up with an excuse for you.'

Proctor shrugged. 'Fair enough. Can we get on with it, then?'

Joe banged on the door. The detectives answered immediately. They'd been right outside.

When Joe was back in the openness of the custody suite, he reached for his handkerchief and wiped it across his brow. He wasn't sure he could do this. But he knew he had to.

For Ellie's sake.

Three

Sam Parker was one of the last detectives to arrive at the park. He'd had to leave his car on the nearest main road so he was panting as he arrived at the scene. The access road was clogged with police vehicles, the team assembled ahead in white forensic suits, stark and bright against the dark stone walls. The uniformed officers were at the top of the road, keeping away the ghouls, but there was a regional office for a newspaper at the junction and Sam could see a camera lens poking through an open window.

There would be more officers arriving soon, vans filled with those used to search in a long line, a sweep with sticks and dogs. They didn't reveal much usually, not in a public space like this. It was partly cosmetic, to show that they were doing something, one less fault to pick up on later.

The day hadn't really got going. A light mist hung over the park, the dew evaporating in the early morning sun, but the Murder Squad was assembled. There was another horror story to decipher.

The park was a retreat, accessed through a metal gate, a cluster of trees and gently rolling lawns, a children's playground in the middle. Sam knew it from visits with his own children. The Pennine hills were behind, the rural vibe spoiled by the occasional rumble of a lorry from the haulage yard next door. The allotments running alongside would get busy later, as the curious gave in to the urge to tend to overgrown plots so that they could peer over the fence at the activity in the park.

Charlotte Turner put her hands on her hips as Sam approached. They'd formed an unofficial partnership, the newest recruits to the Murder Squad, even though Sam had been on the squad for a couple of years now. Above them were egos and reputations, pressed shirts and puffed chests, so they looked after each other, made sure their contributions were recognised. It was the little things, like suggesting in the team briefings that the other had thought of something, even though it was pre-planned, taking it in turns to remind people they were there.

'Not eager for the action?' she said, her eyebrows raised but her eyes shining her smile. She tapped her watch theatrically, her hood down, her long dark curls stark against the pristine white of the forensic suit.

'I had children to say goodbye to,' he said, as he ripped the plastic bag containing the forensic suit he'd grabbed from a crate. 'So what do we have?'

'Another day in paradise,' she said. 'Someone beaten to a pulp.'

Sam looked around. It wasn't the best part of Manchester, but it wasn't the worst, more tired old cotton-town than inner-city concrete. The park was a magnet for gangs of kids at weekends, with poor lighting and dark corners. Fences along one edge bore the multicoloured scrawls that the artists proclaimed as art, whereas in reality they were just names that shouldn't go beyond the cover of a school exercise book.

'Any idea who it is?' Sam said.

'No, not yet, except it sounds like someone who shouldn't have been here,' Charlotte said. 'I haven't been to the body yet, but the uniforms first on the scene said that it was some-one in a suit. There were crushed flowers in the blood.'

Sam frowned. 'A romance gone wrong, around here? It's not a cruising place, is it?'

'I don't think so. The door-to-doors might give us more of an idea, a bit of local knowledge, but nothing has come up on intelligence.'

Sam pulled on his paper suit. As he snapped his face-mask into place, he said, 'Who's the SIO?'

'Brabham.'

Sam rolled his eyes. 'Looks like we'll be getting more work then.'

Before Charlotte could respond, Brabham walked over.

'Just in time,' he said to Sam. 'Ready to go?'

'As I'll ever be.'

Brabham was the DCI most detectives wanted to avoid. He was known for loving the cameras but ducking the difficult issues. Whenever there was a high-profile arrest or conviction, he was first to the microphones on the police station steps. His favoured look was a shirt, sleeves rolled to just below the elbows, as if he'd been dragged to the cameras straight from an interrogation. Behind his back, people scoffed that he'd created the look on the way to the exit. If cases went wrong, he sent someone else along, disowning the bad results as if he'd never been involved. He was an expert in presenting himself, though, always smart, his tan just right, his hair dark and well-groomed, his shirts tight enough to show the work done in the gym.

They walked along the grass together in silence. The crime scene investigators ahead were working on the path, where small numbered stickers were being photographed. Blood spots, Sam guessed. There were more white suits ahead.

Sam pointed to the streets visible alongside the park. 'That might be a good place to start. Even if it was too dark to see anything, any screams or shouts might give us a quicker time of death.'

13

They slowed as they reached the group of crime scene investigators clustered around the body. More photographs being taken, more numbered markers pointing out spots of blood on the path, and what looked like footprints, some tread pattern visible.

Sam let out a long breath.

It was a man's body, there was little doubt about that, from the clothes and hands and the size of the feet. From the neck down, he looked respectable. Dark suit, patent black shoes, yellow silk tie. From the neck up, however, there wasn't much to see. Blood had congealed on the concrete in a wide pool and the head was distorted, like a punctured football, caved in, the dull grey of brain matter showing through the gleaming white of his skull.

'Another one,' Sam said.

'What do you mean?' Brabham said.

'Nothing really,' Sam said, realising he'd just sparked Brabham's interest. A series would make the news. 'We've got another murder at the moment, that's all. A teacher stabbed by the canal in Mossley. Respectable middle-aged man, on his own in a quiet spot one evening. Discovered by a dog-walker in the morning.'

'But stabbed?' Brabham said. 'They might not be connected. This is different.' And he pointed towards the dead man.

'It certainly is,' Sam said, looking at the blood and brains pooled on the floor. 'And it's going to get messy when they take him away. What do we know so far?'

'About him? Nothing much,' Brabham said. 'There's no wallet in his jacket, so it could be a robbery gone wrong.'

'Do you think so?' Sam said, gesturing to the bouquet. 'Robbers grab and run, they don't stamp and kill. Robberies are spontaneous. This seems different.'

'Why do you say that?'

'The flowers,' Sam said. 'He was waiting in a park for a romantic meeting and ended up dead.'

'He could have been robbed as he was waiting?'

'So why didn't the person he was meeting call it in? Even if it was extramarital, there would have been something – a scream or an anonymous call.'

'Those were my thoughts,' Brabham said, nodding to himself.

Sam tried not to roll his eyes. That was Brabham's other skill: adopting ideas as his own.

'Why here, though?' Charlotte said. 'His suit doesn't look cheap, so he could afford something better than here.'

'The wedding ring,' Sam said, pointing. 'Look around. We're a hundred yards into the park. He wasn't meeting his wife here, that's for sure. It wasn't about the romance; it was about the privacy, as seedy as it is.'

'The robbery could be a disguise, then,' Charlotte said. 'A jealous husband?'

'Or even his own wife,' Brabham said.

'Which makes it well planned,' Sam said.

'Why do you say that?'

'Frenzied makes it look random, spontaneous, but if he was lured here it was exactly the opposite: planned.'

Brabham nodded to himself. 'That makes the victim even more important. Who is he and why was he here? And we know which way the killer went.' He gestured along the path they had just walked alongside. 'Footprints heading away, where the attacker had stepped in the blood. And it was dripping from something. If it's the victim's blood, that suggests a weapon. If it was on his hands, he'd have wiped it on his clothes.'

'Unless the victim got some strikes in first,' Sam said. 'There might be some of the attacker's DNA on those spots.'

'This is going to get expensive if we don't get lucky,' Brabham said. 'Analysing each swab to see who the blood belongs to will take some approving.'

Sam knew how budgets were stretched, and getting authority for forensic submissions got harder with every case. Murder trumps everything, but money spent on one case means less for another. Policing wasn't just about feet on the beat.

'Any missing persons reports yet?' Sam said.

'Someone's checking,' Brabham said. 'But if he's married, his wife might have put it down to another dirty stop-out.'

'If there's no call from a worried wife, don't you think it helps to rule her out?' Charlotte said. 'If she was behind it, wouldn't she be play-acting the frightened wife, sitting at home and calling it in?'

'Not if he's given himself an alibi,' Brabham said. 'Working away, that kind of thing. His fingerprints might help, or DNA, but he might not be the sort to get into trouble. When we find out, though, I want you to go through his life, every detail, however small.'

Sam was pleased with that. His area of expertise had always been financial fraud, picking through the fine detail, looking for patterns. In cases like this, with husbands playing around, changes in behaviour gave up the secret.

'I'll start with those,' Sam said, pointing towards the flowers. 'I'll go round the florists, see who sold some of those flowers yesterday. What are they?'

'Calla lilies,' Charlotte said, and then, 'Why can't men ever identify flowers?'

Sam smiled as he pulled down the zip on his white suit and pulled out his phone. He took a photograph of the paper that the flowers were wrapped in. 'I'll think about that as I ring round.'

Brabham nodded his approval as he turned to go.

Identifying the body was the most important thing, although finding the answer just meant that someone somewhere was about to receive bad news, and be left forever wondering what her husband was doing in a park, holding a bunch of flowers.

16

Four

Joe sat in his car outside his mother's house. The police station was fresh in his memory. The smells from the custody suite – sweat and bleach – were still on his clothes, but that wasn't what lingered. It was something much worse.

It was the sneer Mark Proctor wore throughout his police interview, always looking at Joe, not at the officer, as if he knew what Joe was thinking. Surely he couldn't know – he wouldn't have asked for Honeywells if he knew. No, it was something else, as though he harboured a secret, as though he was the only clever one in the room.

But it all came back to something else, and that was Joe's memory of Proctor from years before.

He stepped out of the car and walked slowly up the path to his mother's front door. He wasn't sure what he hoped to find when he got there but he felt the need to go back to where it had started.

His mother still lived in the home he'd grown up in, a once happy family home, a semi-detached behind a low garden wall where he'd lived with his parents, his older brother Sam, and his younger sister Eleanor. Or Ellie, as she'd preferred it.

As he walked up to the door, the familiar sights calmed him, flooding his mind with images. Playing in the road with Sam; chalking arrows onto the pavement so he could follow. Falling out with neighbours over lost footballs and those slow walks to school. All of that innocence was lost when Ellie died. From then, the house seemed to be in shadow, always an unhappy place; even Ruby couldn't brighten it.

So Joe had run away. First to university, then to a series of flats around the city, rented from landlords who crammed people into every tiny space they could create, until he bought his own place. Anywhere but home.

He knocked on the front door, and watched as his mother's shadow grew larger behind the frosted glass panel. She opened the door warily, the chain still on.

'Joe?' she said, surprised. 'Is everything okay?' And she unlocked the chain to let him walk in.

'Morning. I was passing and I fancied a cuppa,' he said, trying to sound casual. It was if he was thinking through fog, only able to see a short distance ahead.

His mother smiled. 'I'll make you one,' she said, and shuffled back along the hallway to the kitchen at the rear of the house.

Joe knew that she had a hard day ahead. She'd finally listened to his concerns that she was drinking too much, that Ruby, the baby of the family, needed looking after. Ruby was fifteen, at that age when being allowed to make her own decisions invariably led to bad ones. His mother had sunk into a routine of drinking that started earlier and earlier each day, and one day, when Joe had caught her reaching for a glass before Ruby had left for school, he'd told her that enough was enough.

So for his mother, each day was about not being left with nothing to do, the silence too easily filled by the sound of vodka pouring into a glass.

When Joe followed her inside, he felt the stifling heat of her radiators, the heating turned on even though it was early summer. The cheeriness of breakfast TV drifted from the living room and, when he looked in, his sister Ruby was sitting with

18

her legs over the chair arm and a bowl of cornflakes in her hand.

On another day, he might have suggested that she used the table. Ruby had always been allowed to do what she wanted, treated like a precious doll. On this day, it didn't seem important. After what the family had been through, eating breakfast sprawled in an armchair didn't seem like much of a big deal.

'Hi, sis,' he said.

'Joe, what are you doing here?' she said, her mouth full.

Concern flashed across her face, perhaps expecting a long lecture. Their father had died when Ruby was young, so Joe and Sam had tried to step into the breech whenever his mother couldn't cope. Which was often.

'I just wanted to say hi,' he said, and went into the room.

'So you're not here to have a go at me?'

'No, I'm not,' he said, and sat on the sofa. It sagged under his weight, and he wanted to sink into it. He closed his eyes for a moment, but the lack of sleep made his head dip and his legs twitch.

Ruby giggled. 'You look like you've been out all night.'

Joe paused as his mother brought him a cup of tea. He raised his cup. 'That's how it is sometimes.'

Ruby shrugged and finished her cereal, putting her bowl on the floor. 'So what do you really want?'

Joe thought about that. The truth was that there wasn't an answer.

'Let me walk you to school,' he said.

Ruby rolled her eyes dramatically and swung her legs over the chair arm. 'This *is* a lecture. What have I done now?'

'I just want to spend some time with my baby sister,' he said. 'There's not enough of that.'

Ruby frowned. 'Okay, if you must,' she said, and stood up. She went upstairs to finish getting ready, leaving the bowl for someone else to clear away.

19

Joe looked around the room. It had hardly changed since he'd left home years earlier. A gas fire with fake coals sat beneath a wooden fireplace with glued-on mouldings. The wallpaper was thick and with two designs, a flowered border separating the two. He'd tried to persuade his mother to change the look, to go for something more modern, but she said she didn't want the fuss. Joe knew the real reason, though: she didn't want to move on.

The real reason for his visit was the large picture above the fireplace. His little sister, Ellie. Like Ruby, she'd been a tangle of long limbs that had not yet learned to be graceful. On Joe's eighteenth birthday, she'd taken a short cut from school, along a wooded path that cut out the long sweep of the road. The path twisted as it wound through the trees, so that for a hundred yards a person would be out of view from the road near the school or the ginnel that opened out near the house. Ellie had been told not to use the path, but Joe knew that she did.

Joe had woken in a good mood on his birthday. He'd opened some cards in the morning and the family were due to convene later, his uncles and aunts and cousins coming together from the different parts of Manchester, some of them from even further afield. His father had promised to take him to a nearby pub, wanted to be the person to buy him his first legal beer. Joe had appreciated that. His father hadn't been the expressive type, but the placing of a pint glass in front of him would somehow be symbolic, the passage from boy to man.

As he looked, Joe pictured the scene again, as he did often. His birthday cards over the fire, presents in the corner of the room, his uncles and aunts and cousins and longstanding family friends all standing around and talking too loudly.

He'd come straight in from college; his A levels were looming – the last stop before university – so he'd spent the day in revision classes. The backslapping had started the minute he got home.

Nearly an hour passed before anyone mentioned Ellie. It was his mother who raised the alarm. Joe had swallowed and said nothing, just grimaced at the first churn of worry as he knew something had gone wrong.

His route home had taken him past the entrance to the wooded path. As he got closer, he saw Ellie ahead, her school bag swinging, wearing headphones that would blot out any shout he thought about making. She had turned into the path. She would be home a long time before him. She might have wanted it that way, so she could take in his delight at the gathering. If it had been another day, she might have walked home the long way. The safe way.

Joe had seen him. A figure in a grey hoodie, loitering, making as if to tie his shoelaces, his foot hoisted up onto a street sign. He looked up as Ellie walked towards him. Once she'd gone past, he strolled down the path after her.

Joe hadn't thought anything of it, wouldn't have carried on walking the long way if he had. It was just a man, a jogger, perhaps, stretching before his run. The man had seen Joe, caught his gaze. A blond fringe coming down from the hood, his face boyish almost, with pale and unblemished skin. The man had seen that someone had noticed him, so how could he pose a threat? Joe watched the man walk down the path. As Joe passed the entrance himself the man was a long way down it, Ellie already around the bend and lost to the trees.

Ellie hadn't been there when Joe arrived home, but the fuss he'd received made him forget about her. She could be unreliable. She had a boyfriend she didn't talk much about and sometimes went there after school. Ellie liked attention, and the focus would be off her for a few hours.

The police car came later. Joe had been upstairs, playing on a computer game he'd been given. He had known what it meant as soon as he heard the screams. *Ellie.*

A police officer had been holding his mother as Joe made his way down the stairs. His father was slumped in a chair, his arms around his head, muffled *no, no, no, no* coming out.

The questions came later.

Ellie had been found partially undressed in the woods, her books scattered in the undergrowth, her underwear dragged down her legs and torn. Her school blouse had been ripped and deep bruising around her throat gave away how she died.

Joe could have stopped it. He'd seen the man follow her. If he'd gone, Ellie would still be alive. He would have been close enough to hear her screams. He could have rescued her, but he hadn't. He'd let her walk along a shadowy path with a predator following her; he'd let her walk to her own death.

So when the police asked, he had said nothing, too scared to say what he'd done.

The face of the man had imprinted itself on his memory, though. He saw it whenever he thought about Ellie, however pleasant the memory was. Ellie as a young girl cooing over dolls, or annoying him deliberately by pulling faces at him when she thought no one could see her. Just the silly stages of childhood he was supposed to reminisce with her about, but he couldn't. He never would.

And he'd seen the man's face again that morning.

He'd been taken by surprise – at the police station for something innocuous – and then suddenly his mind had flashed back through the years as if rushing down a time tunnel. A memory was awakened that Joe knew to be true as soon as he saw him. A certainty that was whole.

Joe had seen the man who'd murdered his sister.

Five

He woke. He was in a chair in the workshop at the bottom of the garden, a blanket over him. Sweat drenched his forehead and his hair was plastered to the back of his neck. He looked around the workshop, hardly breathing, his eyes darting, certain he wasn't alone. He listened: were there people outside his door? The murmurs of police or the soft clump of careful feet?

No, it was quiet.

He threw off the blanket and stretched, went to the window. A net curtain hung over the bottom part of the frame, a mix of yellow from nicotine and grey from age, making him invisible to those outside. The glass was covered in cobwebs and mould. He rubbed at it to get a view outside. A light was on in the house but he wasn't ready to go up there yet.

He fumbled in his pocket for a cigarette. The packet was crumpled, squashed against him in the chair, but there were still three left. He shuffled across the room, wiping his eyes, his skin tired and drawn, to the small Calor gas stove in the corner. When he lit it, the air was filled with that familiar smell of bottled gas. He bent down to light his cigarette and closed his eyes as he drew the first long lungful of smoke before placing a kettle onto the gas ring, shaking it first to check whether there was water in it.

There was a heater next to a wall. It needed a few pushes of the button to make it come on but it lit suddenly with a whoosh. The day would get warmer outside but it took a while to make its way into the workshop.

He went back to his chair and sought the warmth of the blanket once more. He looked at his fingers. Nicotine-brown.

The workshop had been standing for a long time. Pebble-dashed sides and single-glazed windows, the roof corrugated iron, it was filled with tools along one wall: chisels, small files, gardening equipment further along. It had been his wife's father's haven before he died, and his own retreat ever since he'd moved in. There were memories here, times of reflection.

He smiled and took another long drag. As he took his cigarette from his mouth, he thought he saw something ingrained in his fingers. Something red lodged into the fine ridges of his fingerprints.

He wiped his hands on his trousers and looked back towards the window. The light that filtered in was murky, struggling to make shadows across the floor. There were large candles spaced around, for those moments of reflection, so that the workshop came alive with warmth and flickering light. They were unlit. Not yet. Later.

His thoughts were interrupted by the shrill whistle of the kettle on the gas ring.

Ruby came downstairs in her school uniform. Her dark blue skirt was shorter than it ought to be, her legs covered by grey socks that went over her knees. Her tie wasn't much more than a stub under the knot. She collected her bag, which had been discarded in a corner by the stairs, and shouted, 'Bye, Mum,' as she went through the door.

Joe's mother appeared in the kitchen doorway and said, 'Bye, love,' and then to Joe, 'Good to see you.'

Joe smiled. 'I might come round later,' he said, and then went to follow Ruby.

Just before he got out of the door, his mother called, 'Are you all right, Joe? I mean, really all right?'

He nodded and waved. 'I'm fine,' and then joined Ruby on the street.

She was waiting with her arms folded, looking sullen. She gave a slight shiver. The day's warmth hadn't really got going and a light breeze fluttered her hair.

'Come on,' Joe said, and started walking.

'So you're not here to lecture me?' she said, as she caught up.

'Should I be? Anything you want to confess?' When she didn't respond, Joe turned to her. 'I'm only teasing you. Nothing's the matter, I promise.'

Ruby unfolded her arms and linked her arm in his, in that unselfconscious way that teenagers have sometimes.

The normal route to Ruby's school was to turn right further along and follow the long curve of the road until it ended near her school. The quick way was to turn left and into the darkness of the path. To the spot where Ellie was killed.

Ruby was silent as they walked, but she faltered as they got to the entrance to path, as if she knew she ought to keep going because Joe was there, but really her habit was to turn left.

'Come on, take the short cut,' Joe said, pointing to the wooded path. 'You'll be fine with me here.' He crossed the road and Ruby followed.

A canopy of trees cast deep shadows over the tarmac path, which sloped steeply to a small wooden bridge over a stream.

Joe was soon swallowed up by gloom. The morning sun was lost, except where it streamed through in the gaps between the branches, making spears of light. Their footsteps were in time with each other, the regular *thump-thump* broken only by the occasional rustles from the bushes and the loud chirp of a bird high up in the trees.

Joe's nostrils filled with the crisp smell of damp grass and weeds. This was the part of the path that Ellie had never reached. A peaceful haven, the noise of the streets soon lost.

As they walked, Ruby said, 'What was Ellie like?'

'Why do you ask?'

'Because I never knew her.'

Joe wondered what to say as he thought about Ellie again. He remembered their fights, how she used to scream at him to come out of the bathroom, or when he'd chased her along the landing, flicking a towel at her legs because she'd shouted out that he had a girlfriend. Her younger days, when Ellie had dreamed of being a nurse and would make him pretend to be injured so that she could wrap his wounds in toilet paper, red felt tip marking out the blood on the make-believe bandages. Long trips in the car, with Ellie talking in his ear, a stream of nothing for the sake of just something to say, with sensible Sam ignoring her, looking out of the window.

'She was a lot like you,' Joe said.

'I wish she wasn't,' Ruby said. 'It's not fair.'

'What do you mean?'

'Because I know that I'm supposed to be her replacement, and it feels like I disappoint everyone because I don't quite live up to her.' She paused. 'Mum says things.'

'What like?'

'We'll argue about something, or I'll say I won't do something I don't like, and it's all, "Ellie would have done it", and I want to scream at her that I'm not Ellie. I'm me. Ruby.'

Joe stopped walking. Ruby stopped too, her arm dropping from his.

'It's been difficult for Mum,' Joe said. 'She lost Ellie, and then Dad, and I know it's made it tougher for you. Just don't be too hard on her. I remember the Mum she was before Ellie died.'

'What was she like?'

'She was different. She was warm and fun and had time for us. If we had homework to do, she'd help, as if she enjoyed it. I remember I had to make a Roman helmet for history, and she made this fantastic one out of gold card, with red wool cropped and stuck on for the plume. I'm sad for you that you don't know that woman. She won't always get it right, because losing Ellie broke her, changed her so that she could never go back to the woman she was. Just try to understand her.'

'I do try,' Ruby said. 'But why can't my life be about me? Ruby Parker, not Ellie Parker.' And with that she turned to carry on walking.

Joe watched her go for a moment. He understood what she meant, but it was impossible not to think of Ellie. She was right.

She turned back towards him. 'Come on, I'll be late.'

Joe smiled and caught her up.

They talked about her school day ahead as they clumped across the wooden bridge over the stream, and then the path curved towards her school and became stones and mud, the banks of trees higher on each side, barriers between the housing estates that bordered it.

They were close to where Ellie was found. Bluebells grew in clusters and ferns made the route through the trees a tangle. There were some tracks, made by school kids seeking short cuts to the housing estate further along, and probably used by Ellie's killer to escape.

Joe's gut tightened and his jaw clenched.

This was the reason he'd come and he felt a burst of guilt. He hadn't walked with Ruby to spend time with her. Instead, he wanted to imagine Ellie on the ground so that he could feel the anger that was never far beneath the surface. He'd learned how to bury it so he could cope with his own guilt for allowing her to walk down the path to her death, but he needed that anger again.

Ruby was still talking, and Joe knew that she was doing it on purpose, filling the air with talk of her own life as they passed where Ellie's ended. Ruby's desperation to be seen as her own person was evident, and she was right, that she was born as a replacement for the girl the family had lost.

Joe resisted the urge to stop where Ellie had been found, her clothes dishevelled, her knickers torn and pulled down, her skin covered in scratches and bruises. When they got to the end of the track, Ruby turned to go towards her school.

'Thank you,' Joe said.

'What for?'

'For letting me spend time with you. You should come down to the apartment more.'

Ruby shrugged. 'I might.' And then she was walking, her bag over her shoulder as she made her way towards school.

Joe sat on the street sign and watched as the kids filled the pavements – some in cliques, others just walking alone, all of them getting ready for whatever their adult lives had in store for them.

He looked along the road, seeking the spot where his younger self had been all those years earlier, as Ellie's murderer rested his foot where Joe was sitting now.

Joe's fists clenched in his pockets. He'd got the anger he'd been looking for, the reminder about why he did the job.

Ellie's murder had driven him into criminal law, and his brother Sam into the police force.

Sam had chosen his career out of a desire to seek justice for Ellie, and his admiration for how the police had helped the Parker family on that dark day and the weeks that followed. Joe followed his career because it was the one area of law where he stood the greatest chance of seeing her killer again. It was why he called round the Manchester police stations every morning and kept on eye on who was appearing in the remand courts, always wanting to know whether a child rapist or murderer had been arrested. There was always a chance he would kill again, and perhaps this time be caught.

And Joe had promised one thing to himself, and to Ellie: if he found her murderer, he would kill him.

Six

Sam rushed towards the station doors. The crime scene had been taken over by the forensic teams. The results would take a while to come through, but there were still enquiries to be made. The first step was identifying the victim.

The squad operated out of a station in a small town that served as the last stop before the moors, in an old Victorian building awaiting sale – glazed red brick and high windows – on one of the roads that headed out to the Pennines. The radiators clanked in winter as they fought hard to heat the place, and although most of the rooms were empty he preferred it to the newer stations. He'd worked from enough modern buildings to know that what they made up for in comfort they lost in atmosphere. Sam preferred the older stations, where the cells told the history of the city with knocks and chips in the doors and graffiti scratched into the tiles.

The day would be all about procedure, the first few hours of a murder inquiry the most important. The scene had been preserved and the results had to be collected. Roles would be assigned: exhibits officer, disclosure officer, family liaison officer. Before then, people were following their own ideas, hoping to find something to raise at the briefing.

As he approached the doors, a woman stepped towards him. He hadn't noticed her; she must have been waiting in the shadows created by the station entrance. Young and tall, smartly dressed in a dark blue trouser suit, she said, 'Are you on the murder team, about the dead man in the park?'

Sam paused. It might be a witness. 'Yes, I am. Can I help you?'

'It is a man, isn't it?'

'Who are you?'

The woman reached into her pocket and produced a business card. She passed it over and said, 'Lauren Spicer. I'm a reporter. Just avoiding the pack at the scene.'

'We have a press officer for media enquiries, you know that,' Sam said, and headed towards the door.

Lauren stepped in front of him. 'It's good for your career to talk to me,' she said. Her gaze was direct, her smile cocky.

'How so?'

'Because I can make sure your cases get all the attention.'

'You speak highly of yourself.'

'I'm good,' she said. 'Look at me now. Do you see any other reporters hanging out here? I'm just trying to stay ahead of the game.'

'And you're the one not getting any quotes,' Sam said, and stepped around her. 'Speak to the press officer,' he said, and he went inside.

When he walked into the Incident Room, one of the detectives at the desks by the window looked up and said, 'Who's the hot stuff you were chatting up?'

'Just a reporter taking short cuts,' Sam said. 'What are you doing?'

'Looking at incident logs, checking for any reports of a husband who hasn't returned home, or of someone seeing a man covered in blood, but it's quiet so far. Nothing from last night. You?'

'Flowers,' Sam said, as he went to his usual terminal in front of the window. 'They were bought from somewhere, and it's likely to be somewhere local.'

31

He glanced outside as he waited for his computer to boot up. The reporter was still there. She looked up at him and waved. He turned away.

The room was quiet but wouldn't be for long. He looked at the pictures on the wall: photographs from open cases. Three murders that were about to be pushed back. One an old man found beaten to death in his flat, his battered skull bleeding out in front of his three-bar fire. Another was a woman found strangled in her bed as she read a book. The theory for the first was a burglary gone wrong and the second killed by her ex-husband, except the man's new lover had given him an alibi they couldn't disprove.

The third one was the case he'd mentioned to Brabham earlier. A teacher, Keith Welsby, stabbed and left sitting at a picnic table by the canal in Mossley. A quiet man who sought out a deserted spot one evening. No known motive. Another case to end up in the Cold Case Unit, one more unexplained death to be dusted down occasionally until it faded from memory.

Sam returned to the current case and searched for florists on the internet, starting with the ones in the city centre. Although the victim might have worked out of one of the many business parks on the edge of Manchester, it seemed sensible to start in the middle and work outwards, following the road towards the park. And if they knew where he bought the flowers, it would help them work backwards and follow his route back to where it started.

The results of his calls were better than he expected. Perhaps Monday nights weren't big on romance. Most of the shops sold calla lilies, but only three had sold some the day before. Even better, only one had sold some to a man in a suit.

Sam grabbed his coat and headed for the door.

When he got outside, Lauren Spicer came towards him again. 'Have you got some news for me?'

'Nice try,' Sam said. 'And don't follow me. I'm chasing something from a different case.'

She accepted his lie with a shrug and went back to leaning against the wall.

It was a short drive to the florist's, a small shop on a corner along a road that was mostly given up to buses. Buckets of flowers brightened a drab exterior, the signs made dirty by passing traffic.

The bell over the door tinkled as he went in. A young woman with blonde hair shaped into a bob came from the back room, secateurs in hand. Sam pulled out his identification. 'DC Parker,' he said. 'Greater Manchester Police. I called earlier.'

She smiled. 'I guessed when I saw you. Come through.'

Sam followed her into the room at the back. His nose twitched. The air was thick with scent. It was part sweet, part fusty, almost stagnant, the fragrance of the flowers competing with the smell of damp stalks. There were rolls of paper on a shelf. It was the same as the paper on the flowers in the park, green with silver dots.

'I'm Debbie,' she said, sitting on a stool and reaching for a coffee. 'What's it all about?'

'I just need to know about the man who bought your lilies yesterday,' he said. 'Does he come in often?'

'No. I haven't seen him before.'

'How did he seem?'

Debbie looked into her coffee as she thought. 'Nervous, but a lot of men are like that. He knew what he wanted, though, which is less usual.'

'What do you mean?'

'When men come in, they usually look around and seem a bit lost. If I didn't help them, they'd just grab the first bunch they saw. So I help them. I ask them who the flowers are for and the occasion. This man came in and was very specific. Calla lilies. Nothing else. No discussion.'

'What did he look like?'

'Average, really. In his forties. I remember his hair, though. It looked dyed, just a bit too dark, and he was wearing an earring. He was a bit, you know, oldest swinger in town.'

'How did he pay?'

'Cash.'

Sam was disappointed. A credit card would have given up a name.

'I can show you him, if you want,' Debbie said, and pointed to a monitor with a video player whirring beneath it. 'We were losing money from the till so I got this last year. He's on it. I looked for him after you called. He was easy to find because I was just about to close up.'

Sam suppressed his smile, it seemed inappropriate somehow.

'Yes, that would help,' he said, his tone more neutral than he felt.

Sam brought his chair forward as Debbie pressed a button on the machine. The screen flashed and then it showed images of the shop from different angles.

On the screen, a man entered. The shot from above the door didn't show much of his face, just the swirl of his hair where he'd tried to cover a bald patch. It got his patent shoes, though, and the tie looked the same. The man walked straight to the counter and placed both hands on it. Sam concentrated on the image in the top right of the screen. Something was bothering him about the image, but he couldn't quite work it out.

The man spoke to Debbie, who went out from behind the counter and to a bucket in the corner of the shop, just behind the window displays. She lifted out some lilies and held them up, as if seeking his approval. The man didn't even look. He nodded his agreement as he rifled through his wallet, pulling out two notes and handing them over as Debbie wrapped the flowers in paper.

He didn't say anything else. No attempts at conversation. He just paid and left, the flowers in his hand.

Sam tried to see where he went, hoping that he might go to a car, but he walked out of shot. He kept watching, though. If he'd been in a car, he would set off shortly, and he'd gone out of the shop and turned right. The direction of the park was left. He would pass it in his car.

Four minutes passed before Sam saw it, guessing from the way the car seemed to be pulling away from a parking space rather than merely driving past. A light saloon, silver or maybe light blue, possibly a Mondeo.

'Can I take that?' he said, gesturing towards the video.

'Yeah, sure,' she said. 'I've got some spare tapes.'

'I'll be back to take a statement. I hope you don't mind.'

'Is it to do with the murder case?'

'Why do you say that?'

'Because I saw all the police at the park before.'

'I'm afraid I can't say,' Sam said.

'Which confirms it,' she said, her eyes wide. 'Is he the killer? Should I be worried?'

'Thank you for this,' he said, ignoring her question and left the shop, the tape in his hand.

He'd got their first break.

Seven

Joe was late getting into work.

His time with Ruby had put him behind schedule and when he walked into the building his client was sitting in the reception area, looking impatient.

Honeywells didn't like its criminal clients. It was mainly a commercial and civil firm, but had maintained a criminal practice out of a promise to the firm's founder. Even so, the criminal clients used a separate entrance, and it was a struggle at times; Joe was the only lawyer in the criminal department, helped by Gina, his legal clerk.

The firm was spread over two buildings, with its Georgian pillars and high sash windows overlooking neat public gardens. Joe's clients used the first entrance, where the reception was plush but without vases of flowers or items of decoration; they were just something else to steal or get smashed. There was a time when a solicitor's waiting room was a place of reflection, nervous clients waiting for their appointment. A lawyer's stock had fallen since those days. Now, it was just another place to carry on their battles. Fights had broken out more than once.

Joe's practice was changing, though. He was starting to attract clients who couldn't get legal aid but didn't mind paying hugely inflated fees, his reputation growing after some high-profile cases. The other departments were sending clients his way too, but mainly driving cases or the errant sons of wealthy clients.

They rankled Joe, because his client base had always been those who somehow got lost somewhere in their lives. The drunks, the druggies, the thieves and fraudsters. Joe wasn't so naive that he thought that all of his clients were victims of their backgrounds. Too many preferred the small victories of criminality over an honest living. Like those who peddled drugs for status, or the builders who persuaded lonely pensioners that their roof was about to cave in, and then marched them down to the bank to withdraw thousands of pounds to pay for some lead flashing around the chimney stack. Joe had little time for those, but he did his job just the same.

His new clients were different; they seemed to think they were too rich to be guilty. Even the nastiest criminal knew that a prosecution was part of the price they paid for their lifestyle choice. His newfound wealthy clients thought the law didn't apply to them in the same way, because the outcome of a case was just another thing they could afford. Like a new watch or a sports car, and all done with Joe's help.

But they filled the tills so that Joe could still do the other criminal work.

Joe smiled a greeting at his client, who was sitting in reception with a file of papers perched on his knee.

That irritated Joe straight away. There are two types of clients to avoid: those who turn up with jumbles of papers in a carrier bag, usually a sign that they think somewhere in the mess of papers is proof of some higher conspiracy, and those who insist on carrying the papers around in files of their own. It was the client's way of saying that he was in charge, that he was watching Joe.

His client returned the greeting but checked his watch at the same time. Joe spotted the gesture. There was no need to check, because there was a clock above the reception desk.

'I'll be ten minutes,' Joe said, and then trotted up the stairs.

Gina was waiting for him when he went into his office. She raised her eyebrows and tapped her watch.

'Sorry,' he said. 'I had to see Ruby.'

She must have detected something in his voice, because she said, 'Everything okay?'

'Just an early start,' he said, and threw the file onto the desk, the papers he'd completed at the police station.

Joe depended on Gina. A former senior detective, she became his paralegal once she retired from the Force, Joe wanting her keen mind and an eye for the truth. She'd been one of the best cops he'd come across, too good to see out her working years pottering around in her garden.

He took the file Gina was holding and went to sit down. His secretary, Karen, appeared with a cup of coffee, as always. He didn't like being waited on, but the partners in the firm liked to emphasise what they saw as the great divide: lawyers on the well-paid side and everyone else just glad to have a job.

Joe took a sip and stared straight ahead. He was thinking of Ellie's murder, not the file. He'd been so certain about Mark Proctor earlier but now he was starting to doubt himself. He knew what a defence lawyer like him would make of it: a fleeting glimpse, from a distance, many years earlier. It wouldn't get anywhere as a case. So how could he be so sure? Was it because he wanted to see the man so much that he latched onto the first vague likeness?

Gina pushed some letters over the desk towards him.

Joe looked up and realised that she'd been talking to him. 'Sorry, what was that?'

'We're still getting letters from that man in Full Sutton,' she said. 'You know, who killed his wife and dumped her in a suitcase but wants an appeal. Are we taking it on? We could do with something high-profile again. It doesn't matter if we get anywhere, provided we make some noise about it.'

'I'll have another look at it. Later, after today's trial.'

Gina considered Joe for a few moments, and then went to close the door. As it clicked shut, she put her hands on her hips and said, 'What's going on, Joe?'

'Nothing, like I said. Just tired.'

'I've known you too long. You're avoiding my gaze.'

Joe looked up at her and stared into her eyes. 'I'm fine,' he said, and tried to sound jovial. It was a poor attempt.

Gina thought for a moment, and then said, 'Okay. But just remember that you can talk to me.'

'I know, and thank you.'

Gina left the room. Joe turned in his chair and looked out of the window. He didn't need to read the file. There wasn't much to this client's case. He'd blown double the drink-driving limit but was trying to say that the machine must have been faulty because he'd only had one bottle of lager.

Joe didn't believe him, even if his wife was prepared to back him up. She was sugary-sweet and relied on the flicker of her eyelashes to get people to like her. It didn't work. Joe had to get rid of the case before she took to the witness box, because ten minutes of her insincerity would convict her husband.

So it was a day of the usual picking away at the technicalities of road traffic law, hoping that he'd pick up on an error and help something unravel.

He told himself that it was the system that was wrong and that he would be unsuccessful if the police carried out their procedures correctly, but it was a hypocritical stance, he knew that. The truth was he preferred defending those from the wrong side of life's luck, and unfortunately they were the people who always got things wrong.

But it wasn't his client in reception that was souring his mood, no doubt tapping his feet with impatience, feigned outrage spurring him on. No, it was the man he'd seen in the police station.

He wished he could tell Gina, but she was the last person he could speak to. It wasn't just her thirty years in the police force that Joe cherished. No, it was much more than that, because Gina had been in charge of the investigation into Ellie's murder. Even though her killer hadn't been found, Joe remembered how she'd treated the family, with kindness and respect.

How could he tell her that he'd seen her killer all along? It might have led to his capture but Joe had trapped himself into a lie, that he hadn't seen Ellie as he walked home. Guilt consumed him because he could have saved her, should have shouted out to her, warned her not to go down the path, but why should he have realised that she was in danger? It was just another day, just some guy walking the same way.

Only one person knew: Sam, his brother, through a confession a couple of years earlier. He had no wish to expand that circle of confidence.

He stood up, pushing the chair back. He had to get to court. But once he was done there, he was going to find Mark Proctor. Joe needed to know more.

Eight

Sam drove slowly towards the crime scene, leaning forwards over the wheel, scanning the cars along the side streets, just long rows of terraced housing. There were no driveways, so street parking was precious and cars lined the pavements, jammed close to each other.

He was looking for the silver or light blue Mondeo he'd seen on the footage from the florist. He couldn't guarantee it would be here, because no keys had been found on the victim, but the killer might have arrived in a car too. Would someone covered in someone else's blood have wanted to run around the streets clicking a key-fob, trying to find their victim's car?

Every time he saw a silver or light blue car he turned down the street to note down their number plates, until he'd driven along all the residential streets that were close to the park. There were three possible contenders for the car he'd seen on the CCTV footage.

He headed back towards the park, pulled into an empty space, and called Comms to get details of the car owners. The reply came within a minute. Two of them lived on the streets where their cars were parked, so he discounted those. The other one was from Oldham, ten miles away. And he had a name.

'Will you send me his DVLA photograph?' he said, and he gave his email address.

As he waited, he watched the group of police officers still working at the crime scene. Brabham and Charlotte were out of their forensic suits, Brabham giving instructions to a group of uniformed officers.

Sam's phone beeped as the email came through. He looked at his screen and gasped. He got out of his car and rushed up the hill. Brabham turned round as he got close.

'I've got him,' Sam said, breathless.

Brabham's eyes widened.

'Henry Mason,' he said. 'He lives in Oldham. His car is parked just down there.' And he pointed. 'He bought calla lilies yesterday afternoon. I have the footage from the shop. I've watched it and the person on the footage matches Mason's DVLA picture.'

'We're getting somewhere,' Brabham said.

'There's something else, too,' Sam said. 'Was the victim wearing a watch?'

Brabham frowned. 'He's been taken to the mortuary,' he said, before calling over one of the crime scene photographers and asking her to scroll through the pictures on her camera. 'No, he wasn't.'

'He was on the footage,' Sam said. 'I knew I'd seen something but it took me a while to work it out. Big garish thing, metal.'

'Makes it look more like a robbery,' Brabham said. 'Sometimes these things are simpler than you think. And you know where you're going next? To break the bad news.'

'Me?'

'If it's a simple robbery, we don't have to suspect whoever he lives with. Just give her the news and I'll send along an FLO to sit with her. Take her with you,' he went on, nodding his head at Charlotte. 'I need to keep an eye on things here. And get his computers. Let's see who he's been talking to. We need to know who he was supposed to meet.'

Charlotte smiled at Brabham but Sam recognised irritation in her eyes.

As they walked to his car, Sam said, 'Come on, spill it.'

'It's nothing,' she said. 'I just feel that I shouldn't be sidelined for the hand-holding parts, breaking the bad news. That's his job.'

'He's a ducker. There's no glory at the widow's house. This is where the TV cameras are.'

'At least I don't have to put up with him looking at my chest all morning.'

'That obvious?'

'I'm sure he thinks I take it as a compliment.'

'We'll do our job and report back. You're a good copper. Let's make sure we do something to make him notice.'

'Thank you,' she said as they climbed into Sam's car. 'Do you know anything else about this Henry Mason?'

'The florist said it seemed like he knew what he wanted. He asked for calla lilies, and I watched the footage; he didn't even look up when she picked some out.'

'Perhaps his girlfriend likes calla lilies.'

'But if it was a long-term thing, and he knew that she liked calla lilies, would they really meet here, in a park at night? They'd have a routine – a pub or somewhere quiet.'

'What are you thinking?'

'I'm wondering if it's something else, like a sign.'

'What, a blind date?'

'Something like that,' Sam said. 'He's certainly a player. There's the smack of a mid-life crisis. Dyed hair. Earring.'

Charlotte sighed. 'Right, let's go break some bad news. Always the worst part.'

'Assuming he's the body in the park,' he said. 'We know he bought lilies, and we know his car is still around here. Perhaps he did the killing. There's not much left of his face, remember.'

'All the more reason to get to his house,' Charlotte said. 'It sounds like Henry Mason is either our victim or our murderer, and we need to find out which.'

Charlotte stayed silent as he drove. As they got closer to Oldham, Sam said, 'Everything all right?'

She looked out of her window for a few moments before saying, 'I'm thinking of moving on.'

'What, from the squad? How come?'

'Because I'm sick of being the coffee-girl. Half the people on the squad do it for the machismo, for the pub tales. I'm thinking that I'll have to go somewhere else to move up.'

'Have you spoken to anyone about this?'

She shook her head. 'I'll do it in my own way.'

'But if you went, I'll be stuck with them.'

'You'll never be like them, though, and that's the main thing.' As they drove from the motorway and into Oldham, she said, 'How are things at home? How's Alice?'

Sam didn't want to say too much. He kept his home life private, even from Charlotte, his closest friend on the Force, but he knew it was a pointed question. A year earlier, Sam's job had brought peril into his family and put Alice's life in extreme danger. Alice wasn't coping well. Part of her wanted him to give up his job, but she knew as much as he did that it was more than just what he did. It defined him.

But Sam saw her sometimes, looking out of the window at the sound of his car engine, as if she'd been looking out for him. Once he got inside, it would be different; she'd be watching the television, or walking into the kitchen, but he knew what he'd seen.

'She wishes I wasn't doing this job,' he said.

'She's not the first to think that,' Charlotte said, before glancing across to Sam. 'Don't sacrifice too much for the job. It will end one day. The ones who miss it are the ones with nothing else in their lives.'

'You've soon got old and wise.'

Charlotte laughed. 'Too many nights sitting in feeling pissed off. Look, we're nearly here.' And she pointed out of the windscreen.

Oldham was an old mill town on a high plateau just before Manchester gave way to Yorkshire. It was gritty and tough, lost industry never properly replaced, with the occasional mill building, high chimney and huge brick block, like relics on the horizon. It was a hard place to live, divided by racial tensions, and made harsher by the bitter winds that howled in from the Pennines during winter.

Henry Mason's address was on an estate of new houses close to the main road, on the site of what had once been a factory. It was picture-perfect modern living, the estate fenced, all the driveways wide, the windows leaded, the flowers and gleaming photograph frames glimpsed on all the window sills hinting at ordered lives.

They went to get out of their car when Charlotte's phone rang.

Sam waited for her to finish the call, which seemed to consist of Charlotte listening wide-eyed.

When she hung up, he said, 'What is it?'

'That was Brabham. The victim's fingerprints were taken, before you came up with the identification, hoping to find him that way. Guess what: it turns out we've been looking for him.'

'I don't understand.'

'You know the Keith Welsby case we've been getting nowhere with – the teacher stabbed by the canal, and all we had was a bloody fingerprint found on a knife nearby? Well, it seems that the fingerprint belonged to Henry Mason.' She pointed at the house. 'The dead man was a wanted man.'

45

Nine

Joe was on his feet in court. The police officer who'd stopped his client and then carried out the intoxilyser test at the police station was in the witness box.

The defence was that the machine was faulty so that the alcohol reading couldn't be relied upon. Joe had picked and probed at anything he could think of, despite the prosecutor's objections, trying to find a defect in the procedure. His client would think he was getting value for money if he put up a fight. It wasn't the outcome that mattered to get a reputation; it was the showboating along the way.

So far, his questions had fallen flat and his concentration wavered. His client was making notes next to him, his script becoming smaller and more jagged. Joe's mind kept flashing back to the man at the police station, Mark Proctor. The spark of recognition had been like a flash, the years gone in an instant, the memory of Ellie's killer looking towards him as if it was the day before.

The sound of rustling paperwork interrupted his longest pause yet. The magistrates sounded restless, whispering to each other.

Joe turned back to the policeman, a tall traffic officer whose fluorescent green coat rustled as he stood ramrod-straight in the witness box. He'd seen a Porsche coming up behind him, but the driver seemed especially reluctant to overtake. The more the officer slowed down, the more the Porsche did, until there was no choice but to go past. And the driver did, weaving in his lane as he took the next exit, even though it wasn't the one he wanted. Once at the station, he'd provided a breath sample that tested double the drink-driving limit.

An expert witness was sitting at the back of the courtroom, listening to the evidence in the hope he'd pick up on something. He'd provided a report, once he'd trawled through the historical data from the intoxilyser and exaggerated blips into potential major faults, the pages padded by technical information intended to justify his fee. He pretended to be neutral, there to assist the court, but it was the defendant he sat with before the case started, and it was the defendant who was paying him. Everyone has a price.

'So at the station, on the intoxilyser, you asked Mr Pollard to provide the first sample of breath?' Joe asked.

'Yes, your worships,' the officer replied, turning to nod an emphasis to the magistrates, the equipment on his belt jangling.

'And he didn't delay or cause any problems?'

'No.'

'And he provided a long, steady breath into the tube, exactly in accordance with your instructions?'

'Yes.'

'And he'd provided a sample at the roadside, hadn't he?'

'Yes.'

'Exactly in accordance with your instructions?'

'Yes. Just as I asked.'

'So the second breath sample into the intoxilyser. Talk me through that one.'

'He put his mouth around the tube, but he seemed more reluctant.'

'Had you told him that the first sample was over the limit?'

'Yes. I remarked on the reading.'

'So his reluctance to provide a further sample only came after you told him that the first was over the limit?'

'Yes. I presumed that he knew he was in trouble.'

Joe glanced at the magistrates and smiled theatrically. 'Or perhaps he was just surprised, given that he'd only had one bottle of lager.'

It wasn't a question, it was a comment, and the prosecutor was rising to his feet. Joe put out his hand. 'If it helps my friend who prosecutes, I will add a lilt to the question.' He turned back to the officer. 'So, this hesitation. How long did it last?'

'A while. I was watching the clock on the machine count down from two minutes and I thought it was going to time out.'

Joe blinked and glanced across at the expert witness. He was scribbling in his notepad. There it was. The slip.

It was time for the fake.

'The machine wasn't counting down from two minutes, was it?' Joe said.

'Yes, it was. I was watching it.'

'Are you sure you were watching it closely?'

'Of course I was. I watched it tick down.'

'Definitely two minutes? You have no doubts about that?'

The officer looked towards the magistrates and spoke clearly. 'Absolutely none.'

Joe had what he wanted. The officer had made a mistake and then stood his ground, turning a possible mistake into a cast-iron certainty. Joe wanted to get through the rest of the case quickly, to leave the intoxilyser clock in the minds of the magistrates.

He didn't call his client to the witness box. He had what he wanted and it would just give the prosecutor a chance to ask awkward questions, looking for a slip.

The expert did the rest. Blinded everyone with how the

machines can sometimes be wrong, giving plenty of examples, even though they were mainly examples of where he'd blinded other courts. But the clock was the clincher.

'Does the machine have a set period in which the second breath sample must be given?' Joe asked.

'Yes,' the expert said. 'The machine purges itself and then counts down. If the sample isn't provided in time, the machine times out.'

'And what is that set period?'

'Three minutes.'

'Not two minutes?' Joe said.

'No, three minutes. I have the operators' manual in my briefcase if you need it confirming, but it counts down from three minutes, not two.'

'And if it counted down from two minutes?'

'The machine wasn't working properly.'

There it was. The prosecutor hunched forward over his file, thinking how to deal with the problem, but there was nothing he could do. There was no expert for the prosecution, and why would there be? The prosecution case was that Joe's client was telling lies about how much he'd had to drink, and backed up by bad driving and alcohol on his breath, it was a good one to make.

Until a police officer had made a simple and honest mistake, and Joe was ready to exploit and magnify it just because his client was wealthy enough.

His client walked out of court with the air of a man who had almost been the victim of a gross injustice. Joe hoped that at least when his client was alone later that day he would reflect that he'd got lucky, nothing more, but Joe doubted that.

Joe watched him go, his wife holding his hand, the expert witness walking with them.

He turned to the prosecutor and said, 'Sorry about that.'

'Sorry? What for?'

'You know what I mean.'

'Don't be, Joe. I'd have done the same. That's the game.' He collected his paperwork and his laptop and followed Joe's client out of the courtroom.

Joe followed more slowly. By the time the courtroom door closed, there was no one left on the corridor. Joe went to the window and looked out over the city centre, or at least the sliver of it that he could see, the view ahead along the glass fronts of designers stores, the taxis and traffic of Deansgate further up. He thought back to the police station again, to Mark Proctor. Ellie's death was the reason he'd become a lawyer. Helping wealthy clients avoid road traffic laws was just about paying the bills.

He pulled his phone from his pocket and took some breaths to calm himself. He'd written Proctor's number on a scrap of paper.

Proctor answered on the third ring. 'Yeah?'

'It's Joe Parker from Honeywells, your solicitor from last night.'

A pause, and then, 'Oh, hiya. What do you want?'

'I need you to come into the office, just so that we can get your story straight for when you go back to the police station.'

There was another pause, and Joe fought the impulse to fill the silence. He had to sound casual.

'Yeah, okay then. What time?'

'We can do either three or four o'clock. Which suits you?'

'Three,' he said.

Joe thanked him and hung up.

He tapped his phone in his hand as he remembered his promise to himself. He'd made it at the time and reminded himself of it whenever he thought about Ellie. It was one he intended to keep and had dreamed of getting the chance.

The promise? To kill the man who murdered his sister.

Ten

Sam looked at Charlotte in surprise. 'Henry Mason was wanted for the murder we were already working?' he said. 'And now he's been killed? What is it, some kind of gang feud? Look at this house, the area. Remember his clothes. He doesn't seem the type.'

'He was hanging around in a park after dark, a few miles from home,' Charlotte said. 'That isn't normal behaviour. He was up to something. We need to find out what.'

'And what the connection is with a dead teacher.'

'Exactly,' Charlotte said. 'Let's see if there's anyone in.'

As they both got out of the car, they put on their jackets. The day was warm, but if they were breaking bad news, it didn't seem right to be casual. Sam was in a white shirt, a blue tie against the charcoal grey of his suit. The heat made his collar damp.

They approached the door slowly, putting off the moment when they changed someone's life for ever. The house looked silent as they got close, with no bright flickers from the television or signs of movement.

They exchanged quick glances before Sam rapped on the door. He looked around. There was no one watching. They were in an unmarked car and they could have passed for salespeople or religious doorsteppers.

'I'll speak to a neighbour, see if anyone else lives here,' Charlotte said.

Sam stepped back and looked up at the house. 'There's a dead man in a park around ten miles from here, connected to another dead man. What about the occupants here? There might be more inside. We've got grounds to force the door.'

Sam was about to aim a kick at the area around the lock when there was a sound nearby. He stopped and looked up. A man in a dark blue suit was coming from the house next door. He stopped when he saw Sam and Charlotte.

'Everything all right?' the man said.

Sam pulled out his identification. It was time for a change of plan. 'DC Parker, Manchester Police. Does Henry Mason live here?'

'Yes, he does. Is he in trouble?'

'Does anyone else live here?' Sam said, ignoring the question.

'His wife, Claire, and their two sons. Or at least they did.'

'What do you mean?'

The man looked around and then walked towards them. 'There was a screaming row last week,' he said, leaning in before raising his hand in apology. 'We're not nosy, you understand, but it was hard to miss it. The night was warm and our windows were open. Theirs too.' The man frowned. 'Is everything all right?'

'I don't suppose you have a key?' Sam said.

'No, I don't, but I know where they keep one: under the pot at the back. The alarm password is 1234. They told us in case the alarm goes off when they're away.'

'Thank you,' Sam said. 'Sorry to keep you.'

'It's all right. Just being neighbourly. If you need anything else, just call. You know where I live.'

Charlotte went to get the keys that were hidden where most people hide them as the neighbour took his time in deciding to set off, until his curiosity was beaten by his need to be some-where else.

When Charlotte came back to the front of the house, she was holding a set of keys. 'Thank God for good neighbours,' she said, as she tried a few. When she found the right one, she took a deep breath and went inside. There was the frantic beep of the alarm until Sam pressed in the numbers. Then there was silence.

They were in a wide hallway with stairs ahead, the floor wood-lined, modern and shiny. There was a living room to one side. Sam pushed at the door. It opened onto a room that seemed almost golden: light brown carpet and yellow striped wallpaper. The sofa and chairs echoed the stripes, with gold trim on the cushions. A chandelier hung from the ceiling, but the ceiling was low so Sam had to dodge it as he moved across the room. He didn't want to touch anything in case he made it less than pristine.

A set of doors led to a dining room, the table shiny dark wood, with glasses set on coasters and napkins folded inside.

'Intense,' Charlotte said. 'And there are children in the house.' She pointed to photographs on the mantel over the fire.

They were studio shots of two young boys, nervous smiles under dark fringes, their best shirts worn for the occasion. There was just one happy family picture, taken on holiday, Sam presumed, the whole family grouped around a restaurant table. Henry Mason was in a red T-shirt, his tan deep, the mus-cles on his arms taut, his hair deep black. He was the man on the video from the florist's. The woman in the picture had blonde hair that was pinned back by sunglasses, her smile bright and wide.

'It must be an effort to keep it like this,' Sam said.

'Appearances matter, it seems,' Charlotte said. 'We need to check upstairs, to make sure we've no more dead bodies.'

Sam went first, walking slowly upwards, unsure what they

would find. The stairs and landing were like downstairs, neat and clean with a tall vase of dried flowers at the top of the stairs and family photographs on the walls.

He took a pen from his pocket and held his breath as he used it to push open the door to the first room, so that he wouldn't remove any forensic traces. It creaked open into a boy's room, action toys in a box in the corner. It was empty.

'Nothing here,' Sam said.

'No, here neither,' Charlotte said, looking into another child's bedroom before pushing open the bathroom door with her foot.

They faced each other as they stood in front of the door to the main bedroom. Sam used his pen again to push open the door. It swished along the pile of the carpet as it opened, revealing an ornate metal bedframe with a silky bed cover. There were photographs on a dresser and a large wardrobe, but there was no one inside.

'At least the body count has stayed low,' Sam said.

'I'll take this room,' Charlotte said. 'If there's a lady of the house, the contents of her drawers might make you blush.'

'Thank you for sparing them,' Sam said. 'I'll have a look around downstairs.'

He listened to Charlotte opening drawers as he went downstairs and into the living room. Whenever someone is killed, secrets and private lives are revealed.

Sam went straight towards an oak bureau in the corner of the room. It was three drawers deep, with cupboards on either side. The top drawer was filled with placemats and napkin rings. It was the drawer below that held the document envelopes. He peered inside. Bank statements, bills, papers relating to the house, like insurance and mortgage details.

He checked the mortgage documents first. The first one was a letter from the building society: they were behind on their payments.

Sam rifled through the bank statements. They were ordered but they told the same story: things were not going well financially.

Charlotte came back into the room.

'Anything unusual?' Sam said, looking around.

'No, nothing. And you'd have been fine up there. The vibrator count was low.'

'Less fun down here,' Sam said. 'There's money trouble. I wonder if he went to the wrong kind of person for help.'

'But why would his fingerprint be found in blood at another murder scene?' she said. 'They might be in money trouble, but people like this always are. Their life is all about how other people see them, a family to be admired. Affording it is something else entirely.'

Sam was about to start looking at entries for a month earlier, any purchases or cashpoint withdrawals that might put him near the other murder, when a car sped into the cul-de-sac, braking sharply on the driveway.

Charlotte raised her eyebrows. Someone had passed on the news that they were at the house.

A car door slammed. Angry footsteps were followed by the front door opening so quickly that it banged on the wall in the hallway. The woman from the photograph burst in. She didn't look as radiant as she did in the pictures. Her hair was shorter and her eyes flared with anger.

'Who the hell are you, and why are you in my house?' she said.

Sam pulled out his identification. 'I'm DC Parker, Greater Manchester Police, and this is DC Turner. Claire Mason, I presume.'

'What's he done now?'

'Henry?'

'Who else?'

'Please sit down, Mrs Mason,' Sam said, his voice softer.

'No, I won't sit down. Tell me what the hell is going on.'

Sam stepped forward and took hold of her hand. He looked her in the eyes and gave a smile loaded with regret. 'No, please sit down.'

That's when she knew.

Claire Mason slumped onto the sofa, her hand trembling in front of her mouth. Charlotte sat next to her and held her other hand.

Claire stared straight ahead. She hadn't asked any questions, even though Sam could tell that she was full of them. Eventually, she looked up at Sam and said, 'How?'

Sam gave her a regretful smile and said softly, 'We've found a man in a park near Stalybridge, murdered. We think it's your husband.'

'What, so you might be wrong?'

Sam didn't answer. There was a chance they might be, but they didn't think so. The clothes matched the footage from the florist and so did the pictures in the house.

Claire wailed and put her head in her hands. Sam and Charlotte waited once more, until she looked up and said, 'What was he doing in Stalybridge?'

'It looked like he was meeting someone,' Sam said. 'Do you know anything about a meeting?'

'Meeting someone? Who?'

'That's what we're trying to find out,' Sam said. 'Does he know anyone in that area?'

'No. He works on the other side of Manchester,' she said. 'That's where his showroom is, near the airport.' A pause and then, 'Why do you think he was meeting someone?'

Sam swallowed. This was the hard part. Any chance of his memory being fondly held was about to end and Claire's life would become about bewilderment, but they had to get the answers. A delay in a murder case can allow forensic evidence to be scrubbed away.

'He was carrying flowers,' Sam said. 'We've got footage of him buying them and they were found at the scene.'

'Flowers?'

Sam nodded.

Claire started to shake her head, anguish replaced by disbelief. 'Why would he have flowers?'

'Mrs Mason, do you know whether your husband was seeing someone else, or planning to see someone else?'

'No, of course not,' she said, anger taking over. 'Why would he? No, not Henry.'

Charlotte leaned forwards. 'Mrs Mason, we are going to have to look through everything. We need to find out more about Henry's lifestyle. We need computers, phones, anything.'

Claire seemed as if she was about to object, but she nodded eventually and slumped back on the sofa.

The family liaison officer would arrive shortly, because the hard job of telling their sons would come next. Then they would go about the task of disassembling Henry's life, to find that secret he was hiding from his wife, the secret that eventually cost him his life.

Eleven

Joe drummed his fingers on the green leather inlay on his desk. Legal texts dominated one wall, a collection of law reports he never looked at but were there to impress his clients.

His office was laid out like an Edwardian drawing room, with richly coloured wallpaper and a wooden fireplace. There was a more sympathetic meeting room on the ground floor, with a low table and comfortable chairs, a box of toys in one corner for those times when the whole family came along, but he didn't want this client to feel comfortable. He wanted to unsettle him. The room was silent, apart from the regular tick of the clock. It helped him focus.

His phone flashed red. He paused for a moment, wondering if he was doing the right thing. But he had waited so long for this.

He answered, listened to the message and said, 'Show him up.' Then he called Gina. 'Could you come to my room in five minutes. I've got a client I want you to meet.'

Joe took a deep breath as he listened to the clomp of Mark Proctor's footsteps along the landing. His door opened slowly.

Joe stood up and said, 'Come in, Mark. I can call you Mark?' There was a slight tremble to his voice. He sounded like he was trying too hard.

As he came into the room, Proctor looked around cautiously, as though he was expecting someone else to be there. His tongue flicked onto his lip and he wiped the palms of his hands onto the front of his black jumper. He smelled of cigarettes.

He considered Joe for a moment and then shrugged. 'Yeah, fine, whatever.'

Joe gestured to the seat in front of him. 'Sit down.'

Proctor followed his direction and looked around again. 'So why do we have to do this now?'

'Because you might remember more now than in a month's time, when you have to go back. It means we have our witnesses ready if you're charged.'

'There won't be any witnesses,' Proctor said matter-of-factly, turning back to Joe.

'I'd rather be ready than not,' Joe said, feeling a sense of panic. 'My caseworker will take your instructions, but I thought I ought to introduce myself properly. I wasn't myself last night.'

Proctor reached into his pocket for a packet of cigarettes, staring at Joe all the time.

It was a test, Joe knew, to see whether he objected, to determine who was in charge. Some clients saw the relationship with their lawyer as being about power, about who had it and how far the lawyer would go for them. There were too many lawyers in prison cells who'd got the balance wrong. Joe wanted to concede some power to Proctor. He pointed to an ashtray on a shelf near the fire.

Proctor smiled, the first one, although it was more of a sneer. 'I thought you were going to puke last night.'

Joe returned the smile, surprising himself that it came so easily. 'So did I. It must have been something I ate.'

'You lawyers like to eat too rich.'

'So tell me about the break-in at the compound,' Joe said, not wanting idle conversation.

'How do they know it was me?'

'You were caught near the car, after it had been set alight.'

'It doesn't make it me.'

59

'There will be CCTV.'

'Good. Let's see it. We both know that CCTV is never good.'

Joe didn't disagree with him. 'Why were you running away from your car, which had been set alight not long after it was stolen?'

'Stolen?' Proctor said, his eyes wide. 'So I'm the thief in this, not the people who decided they could just take my car without asking, and who were never going to give it back to me unless I handed over cash?'

'And proof that it was yours.'

'I could prove that all right.'

'You sound like you agree with them, that you took it back because you were angry with them.'

'Yeah, I can see how it looks that way, but it isn't, because that's just them guessing. You're the lawyer, so you know how it is; they've got to prove it, not me.' He leaned forward, warming to the conversation. 'Maybe I'm the victim here. They take my car from me because it's got no insurance – big deal – but it's their job to keep it safe so that I can collect it. I'm a scapegoat, that's all, because their compound isn't secure. I might have a claim.'

'And the fact that you were running away from where your car was burning?'

'Coincidence, that's all. I see a burning car and I know I'm in a bad neighbourhood, so I run. How was I supposed to know that it was my car? Sometimes you end up in the wrong place at the wrong time. That's just bad luck, isn't it?'

Joe didn't know if it was some kind of a hint or message, a reference to Ellie. Did Proctor know who Joe was? No, he was reading too much into it. Joe met Proctor's gaze but there was no taunt there.

'Tell me about yourself?' Joe said.

'What do you want to know?'

'Your story. We've all got one.'

'It's insignificant, some might say,' Proctor said. 'Born and brought up in Ancoats. A brother and a sister. I left home and got married. No children. Like I say, insignificant. Invisible almost.'

'Is that how you feel, invisible?'

'No. That's how others see me.'

'Are you close to your family?'

'What's this, the psychiatrist's couch?'

'Just building a picture,' Joe said. 'I might need to talk about you in court.'

Proctor curled his lip as he thought about that. 'Not really close,' he said. 'My brother Dan works down south somewhere, a big shot in events management. My sister Melissa thought she was something big, going off to university and marrying some high-flyer. Now? She works in a pub near Piccadilly, wiping up beer stains.'

'Which pub?'

He paused, as if he wasn't sure he wanted to answer, but said eventually, 'Mother Mac's.'

Joe fumbled for his pen and was about to start going through the forms when there was a light knock on the door and Gina walked in. Joe looked up and watched them both carefully. He wanted to see whether Proctor had ever been in Gina's thoughts when she was investigating Ellie's murder, or whether Proctor had kept watch on the investigation and knew who she was. He was looking for a flicker of recognition from either of them, just to show that he was right.

Gina strode into the room and smiled. 'Hi, I'm Gina Ross,' she said. 'I'm Joe's caseworker.' She walked over and stood behind Joe, ready to take over. Joe looked up at her. She looked back to Proctor. There were no suspicions.

Proctor was impassive. He looked at Joe, then Gina, then held out his hands. 'Let's get this started.' He lit his cigarette.

Gina was about to object to Proctor smoking but Joe held up his hand. 'No, it's okay,' he said.

Gina didn't say anything but turned around to open one of the windows. There was a sudden rush of traffic noise.

Was he getting it wrong? Gina had led the investigation into Ellie's death, so Proctor must know who she was, but there'd been no reaction.

But Joe was so certain, everything about his first reaction to Proctor told him that.

Joe stared at Proctor's hands, one clasped around the wooden chair arm, the other resting on his knee, smoke curling upwards from his cigarette. His fingers were long and skinny, nicotine staining two of them brown.

They were the hands that had wrapped themselves around Ellie's neck. Those fingers had ended her life, squeezed out everything that was so special, and his leering face had been the last thing she'd seen. Those hands had destroyed a family. And for what? To satisfy an urge?

He should tell Gina. Why not tell the police? There might be the chance of new evidence, some forensic trace that couldn't be detected all those years ago but would be brought back to life by advances in science. There might be people connected to Proctor that would remember things he'd said, whose own suspicions would be fleshed out.

But he didn't want that. Joe had never wanted that. His desire to find Ellie's killer had been about one thing: putting his own hands around the murderer's neck to let him know how it felt when your life slipped away. He wanted to see that knowledge in Proctor's eyes and for him to recognise Joe from that day, so he knew it was about payback.

Joe stood up quickly and said to Gina, 'I'll leave you to it.' He looked at Proctor and forced out a smile. 'Good to meet you again, Mark. If you've got any problems, speak to Gina, but you tell her all you can.'

And with that, Joe rushed out of the room.

He shut the door behind him and leaned his head against it. His heart was thumping hard and his collar was damp. He took deep breaths and then pushed himself away from the door. Consumed by his own certainty and years of dreams of avenging Ellie's death, he couldn't stay confined in there any longer. He needed air and space, room to think, so he stamped along the corridor, just to get outside.

But he knew one thing: he was going after Proctor.

Twelve

Claire Mason stared at the floor, her jaw set, tears streaming down her cheeks. She glanced across to the photographs of her sons. 'How am I going to tell them?'

Sam didn't answer. Instead, he said, 'How have things been between you and your husband?'

Claire glared at him, swiping her hand across her face to take away the tears. 'What has that got to do with anything?'

'Your husband was found in a park in Stalybridge. We need to know why he was there. I know this must be hard for you, but we need to find out what happened. When did you last see him?'

'A couple of days ago.' She spoke quietly.

'Why that long?'

'We'd had a row.'

'Enough to make you leave?'

'Things haven't been good recently, that's all. It can't have anything to do with whatever happened to Henry.'

'Why do you say that?'

'Because it was just something between him and me. Something private.' She jabbed her finger towards the framed photographs. 'Those boys will spend the rest of their lives thinking about Henry, wondering what the hell had gone wrong. I am not going to soil his name by discussing our private lives.'

'But if it catches his killer?'

'It won't bring him back!'

'Where did you stay?' Charlotte said.

'Am I under suspicion?' Claire said, incredulous.

'We've got a jigsaw to build,' Charlotte said. 'We need to take all the pieces from the different parts of his life to recreate his final week. Somewhere in that jigsaw might be the answer to how he was killed. But we need every piece.'

'I stayed with my sister, Penny. You'll be wanting her details, just to prove I was there.' She curled her lip as she said it, but then gave her sister's address. 'I'll need to call her, to tell her.'

'No, don't, let us do that,' Sam said.

'But who's going to pick up the boys? They'll be out shortly.'

'There'll be someone along to sit with you. You'll be able to go to the school and meet them. You don't want them finding out from someone else.'

Claire nodded. Her attention had switched to protecting her children.

Sam exchanged glances with Charlotte, who said, 'Did Henry know a man called Keith Welsby?'

'I don't know,' Claire said. 'He didn't tell me everything.'

'Do you know him?'

Claire thought for a few seconds before shaking her head. 'No, never heard of him. Who is he?'

Present tense, Sam noticed. No slip-up at the dead teacher. If Claire had been somehow involved with Keith Welsby, she'd know he was dead. Sam didn't think she could fake not knowing so soon after finding out about her husband.

Unless, of course, she'd known about that too.

'He worked at St Hilda's Catholic School,' Sam said. 'He was murdered a month ago.'

'What's that got to do with us?'

'It's just something we need to find out.'

She shook her head in exasperation. 'No, no connection.

We're not Catholics, our children don't go to that school, wherever it is. I've never heard of the man.'

'Did your husband keep a diary or calendar?'

'There's one on the back of the kitchen door, but there's not much on it.'

Sam went through. It was hanging from a hook, hair appointments and school inset days scrawled on it in black ink. He turned the page to the month before, to the night of Keith Welsby's murder. There was an entry: *H away, car show*.

Sam took the calendar back into the living room. 'Do you know where he went then?'

Claire looked at it. 'Something in Birmingham. A trade show or something. He goes every year.'

And a good alibi, Sam thought. All he had to do was show up, check in and slip back to Manchester to kill Keith Welsby. The place would be busy, and a trade show and hotels means booze. Recollections get muddled, times get forgotten.

'Where did he stay?' Sam said.

'A Travelodge somewhere. His boss sorted it; you'll have to ask him.'

A car pulled up outside, followed by a knock on the door. When Sam answered, it was Eddie, a detective from the squad.

'Hi, Sam. How is it in there?'

'Like you'd expect. You the FLO?'

'Yes,' Eddie said. 'Brabham likes my soothing tones.'

Sam was pleased. Quiet and unassuming, Eddie played the hand-holding role well, but he was sharp. Experienced, heading towards retirement, he'd spot anything untoward, any whispered telephone conversations. After all, a family liaison officer isn't just there to comfort the bereaved. They're looking for clues all the time, teasing out confidences.

'Anything happening?' Eddie said.

'No,' Sam said. 'She's defensive, so there are some secrets, but his death appeared to be a shock.'

'But the secrets could be connected.'

'Don't let her speak to her sister. We're heading there next. You know how it works with false alibis: they breakdown in the detail. Let's see how her sister's account squares up with Claire's.'

Sam went back into the living room and made the introductions. Charlotte got to her feet and lifted the large plastic sack containing Henry's laptop and the family desktop computer. They'd seized them as Claire cried out her grief. If there were secrets to be found, the computers were the best place to start.

Charlotte said her goodbyes, Sam too, as Eddie ushered them out, reassuring them both that he had it under control. If there was going to be a revelation that would solve the case, Eddie was the one who wanted to tell everyone.

When they got back in the car, the computers on the back seat, Charlotte said, 'What do you think?'

'There's something going on. Whether Claire Mason will say anything is a different thing. She's tough. We need to go back to the Incident Room with something. At the moment, we've got two murders that are connected, but I can't think of anything that connects them.'

'So let's get these computers dropped off at headquarters and see what big sister has to say.'

Thirteen

Joe's hands were balled into fists as he walked quickly along the street from his office.

He was still certain about Proctor, the spark of recognition as keen as it had been at the police station, but the lack of anything between Proctor and Gina had thrown him. Gina had never mentioned any suspects, so that wasn't a surprise, but Joe had expected something from Proctor. There'd been press conferences, appeals for information. Gina had been on television; there was no way Proctor wouldn't have known who she was.

But Joe knew deep in his gut that he was right. He had to decide what to do with this knowledge, but needed to be surrounded by noise. His apartment offered only silence, and in the quiet he would be alone with his thoughts. He didn't want that. His thoughts frightened him. He wanted to feel the buzz of the city.

Joe loved Manchester. He had been brought up in its suburbs but it was the noise and strut of the city centre that enthralled him. From the swagger of its musical history, embedded into the bars and clubs squeezed into grime-soaked railway arches, to the dirty scars of its industrial past, Manchester dragged its memories with it. The centre had once been squalor, with families squeezed into small rooms to serve the factories that turned the canals black and the air thick with smoke, but now glass and steel towered over ornate Victorian buildings, the distant skyline interrupted by the vast brick mills that once hummed with the sound of cotton looms.

Joe loved everything about the place, even the threatening undercurrents, the surliness, all against the backdrop of rumbling cabs and the electric screech of the trams.

A pub on the other side of St Ann's Square was often a magnet for him. Inside it was dark, the wooden bar dominated by rows of glasses hanging from a rail. Men stood along it in small clusters, mostly in suits, talking out the working day, although the solitary ones wobbled on their feet, the day coming to another soaked and lonely end.

Joe ordered a pint of bitter and sat down at a table. Old photographs of the city hung on the wall next to him and the daylight glowed through the doorway against the dimness of the bar. The pub calmed him usually, the stresses of a day in court forgotten in the slow pleasures from a pint glass. Today it wasn't having the same effect. He took a drink but it tasted sour. His fingers tapped out a rhythm on the scuffed wooden table.

He was about to walk out and leave his drink behind when someone pulled out the chair opposite. It was Gina.

He was surprised. 'You weren't long with Mark Proctor.'

'His decision, not mine,' she said. 'He seemed like he wanted to be elsewhere.'

'Am I this easy to find?'

'You were only ever going one way,' she replied. 'Can I join you?'

He wanted to say that he'd rather be alone, but it wasn't true. 'It looks like you already have,' he said.

Gina went to the bar to get a drink. She returned with a glass of wine and put her suit jacket over the back of the chair. As she crossed her legs, her skirt rode up, revealing toned and bronzed legs. Two men at the bar glanced over. Gina was fifty-three and she looked great.

'You all right?'

He closed his eyes as he fought the urge to tell her about Mark Proctor, about his long-held promise to kill Ellie's murderer. She would stop him, tell him to call the police, but that didn't seem enough. He'd never wanted an arrest. He wanted revenge.

'Yes, sorry,' he said. 'Just not feeling myself today, that's all.'

'Mark Proctor said he thought you were going to throw up last night.'

Joe didn't respond, so Gina said, 'What is it, then? A bug or something?'

'Must be.' He smiled, although it was thin, never reaching his eyes. 'I'll be fine, don't worry. What did he say about his car?'

'Nothing much. He wouldn't go into details. I probed but he didn't seem keen on sharing. If the police want to interview him again, he'll need to stay silent.' She frowned. 'It's a weird one, though. Why would he break into a compound to steal back his car, only to torch it?'

'You're the ex-detective,' he said. 'Why do you think?'

'Because he had something to hide? His car was pulled over and impounded because it was uninsured. If there was something in the car he didn't want to be found, why not just get some insurance and remove it?'

'What was his car worth, though?' Joe said. 'A couple of grand? He'd rack that up in fees at the compound fairly quickly, so he'd never get to keep the car. It might just have been spite, nothing more, that he wouldn't let them have it.'

'He could have just walked away from it,' Gina said. 'They wouldn't get their money at all then. It would become just scrap value.' Then she laughed. 'But since when did our clients do anything sensible? They wouldn't be clients if they did.'

'Don't you think that Proctor is different to our normal client?'

70

'Why do you say that?'

'I don't know . . . ' Joe paused. 'There's just something about him that I can't quite work out.' He took a drink and stared at the table.

'So what's on your mind?' she said.

'Perhaps I'm just feeling reflective.'

'You don't do reflective, Joe. You work hard and then you have fun. You're a two-mood man. This is something different. You came here with the look of a man determined to get drunk.' She raised her eyebrows. 'I'd like to think it's your love life, but you don't have one, as far as I know.'

That made Joe smile, despite himself. Gina played the part of a scolding big sister. 'I do all right,' he said.

'Whatever happened to that pretty prosecutor? Kim?'

'She made up with her fiancé. She's getting married next month.'

'That's a waste,' Gina said. 'I thought you were good together.'

'We were all about bad timing,' Joe said. 'I see her at court. We're friends, but that's all it will ever be.'

'Yeah, yeah, I've heard the mantra, that you don't do infidelity, even where you're just the bit on the side.'

'It's more complicated than that,' he said. 'I'm at a difficult age.'

Gina laughed. 'I wish I was at the same difficult age. Try mine.'

'I'm thirty-five,' he said. 'It seems like everyone is either attached or has children.'

'Is having children that bad?'

'No, of course not, but I can't just drift into their life and then out again. Uncle Joe shows up for a few weeks and then he's gone.'

'God forbid you actually fall in love with someone,' she said. 'And you're not in here because you're moping about your

71

love life. I brought that up. It's something else.' A pause. A tilt of her head. 'Talk to me.'

Joe took another drink, the beer going down too easily, leaving foamy rings on the glass. 'I've been thinking about Ellie today, that's all.'

'You think about her all the time. Why has it brought you down today?'

'Sometimes it just does.'

'Okay, I think I understand,' Gina said. 'I've never lost a brother or sister like that, but I can imagine how it never goes away.'

'It's not the pain,' he said. 'That fades in time, like a nerve that hurts only when something jabs it unexpectedly. No, it's the anger that never fades. The injustice, that whoever killed her is still out there, that he hasn't paid for what he did.'

Gina flushed. 'I'm sorry about that. I've gone over and over it so many times in my head, but honestly I can't think of anything we missed.'

Joe reached out and put his hand over Gina's. 'I've never blamed you for not catching him. Not once.'

'Thank you, Joe, but I blame myself, only because I can't change it, and you deserve for it to be so different.'

'There is one thing, though,' he said. 'Time has passed and I can handle things better. I want you to be honest with me about something.'

'Go on.'

'Was there ever a suspect? I know you've always said that there wasn't, but I don't know if you were holding stuff back, just to make me feel better, or because the police say things like that.'

Gina sighed and shook her head. 'We looked into a few who lived locally, but some had alibis, and the others? Well, we needed evidence and there wasn't any. No eyewitnesses, no forensic evidence.'

'Nothing at all?'

'Whoever killed her got lucky.'

'So if something new came up, like a name, would there be anything to link it with? Any scraps of DNA? You remember how it was with the Yorkshire Ripper, that once they knew who he was, they realised they'd spoken to him.'

'Not that I remember,' Gina said. 'The investigation started as a blank sheet and pretty much stayed that way. We spoke with some of the known sex offenders, just hoping they would feel guilty enough to confess, but there are so many out there and we couldn't chase every one. It would frighten people if they knew, but at times it felt like there was a predator on every corner. Over forty thousand people on the register, Joe. Over two thousand in this county alone. How the hell could we trawl those? And they're just the ones we've caught. All we could do was knock on a few doors and hope that someone said something incriminating, but that never happens. We don't even know if it was a sex attack.'

'She was dragged into the bushes and her knickers torn off, for Christ's sake, Gina!'

'Hey, calm down, Joe. I'm only telling you what we know, and that is we're pretty sure she wasn't raped. There was no semen on her, no injuries down there. Her torn knickers could have been a distraction.'

Joe closed his eyes. He wanted to say that it had to be a sex crime, because he'd seen a man follow her, the man Gina had spoken to minutes before, but he stopped himself. Gina had confirmed what he suspected, that there was no point in telling the police about Mark Proctor. If there was going to be justice, he had to do it his way.

'Ellie became just another number,' Joe said. 'Another dead child.'

'It feels like you're blaming me.'

'I'm not, I told you.'

'Thousands of kids go missing every year,' she said. 'We ended up putting them into categories. Which ones were probably runaways. Which ones were probably dead. Most turn up again, even if they end up in short skirts working for some shitbag under the railway arches, or giving handjobs in exchange for cigarettes. The others will be buried somewhere, and we know we'll never find them. Some can never be found. Girls like Ellie are the exception, not the rule, because we know what happened to her.'

'That would be worse, if she'd been taken and not found,' Joe said. 'I would have spent all my life looking for her. At least we had something we could learn to deal with.'

'What made you think of her?' Gina said.

'Just one of those moments where she jumps back into my life,' he said, and drained his glass. 'I'm going now. If I stay, it will turn into a long session, and I don't want that.'

As he manoeuvred his way out of his seat, edging around the table, Gina touched his hand. 'Joe, if you need to talk, you know where I am. I know when something's on your mind. You don't hide it well.'

He swallowed. He found it hard to look her in the eye. He gave a quick smile and a nod.

'Thank you,' he said, and went for the door.

Once outside, it was as if he couldn't hear the noise of the city any more. He could see nothing beyond Mark Proctor. He'd always promised himself what he would do if he found Ellie's killer. Now that he'd found him, he was letting Ellie down by not following through on it.

Fourteen

Sam pulled up to the kerb outside a detached house in the south of the city, close to a boutique-filled crossroads just a short drive from the motorway. A brand-new Mini stood on the curved tarmac driveway, underneath the kinks and curls of a twisted hazel tree that cast a shadow over a half-circle lawn. The roar of a plane broke the peace and calm as it passed close overhead, on its way to the nearby airport.

The front of the house was clad in roof tiles, so it looked as if there'd been a surplus when it was being built, but the size of the plot shouted wealth. If Henry Mason's lifestyle had been aspirational, his sister-in-law had reached her goal.

'Nice,' Charlotte said, peering through the side window. 'I bet she'll make us take off our shoes.'

'Somewhere like this?' Sam said. 'Too well mannered.' He climbed out. Charlotte followed.

The driveway crunched under their feet, announcing their arrival, but no one appeared. They weren't just checking out the movements of Claire Mason. They wanted dirt on Mason, to work out why he hung around in parks with flowers, and his wife's relatives may be more amenable to slating him than his wife.

The doorbell was a loud chime, and there was a long pause before the door opened. The chain stayed on and wary eyes appeared in the crack.

'Mrs Hadfield?' Sam said, raising his identification. 'DC Parker, Greater Manchester Police. This is DC Turner.'

The door was closed, to allow the chain to be taken off, and then it swung open to reveal a woman who was doing her best not to be in her forties. As she smiled, her teeth shone back too brightly, and her jumper revealed a cleavage that was too sprightly to be natural. Sam didn't feel bad about noticing; it was meant to be that way. Her eyes were red.

'I'm sorry, come on in,' she said, and set off walking down the hallway. She was in jodhpurs and pumps, and as they followed her into the kitchen Sam glanced into one of the rooms. There were exercise machines and mirrors. The kitchen was large, with a central plinth containing a hob and a large silver duct hanging over it. The black granite twinkled and matched the shiny floor tiles that glinted in the spotlights in the pristine white ceiling.

'You're here about Henry, I presume,' she said.

'That's right,' Sam said, confused about how she knew.

'I've just seen it on the news,' she said. 'And call me Penny. I can't believe it. How's Claire?'

'The news?' Sam said.

'Yes, didn't you know?' A flat screen TV attached to a wall was playing. Penny picked up a remote control and rewound the footage. After a few seconds, Brabham appeared, giving an impromptu press briefing outside the station.

Sam sighed. Brabham just couldn't help himself. Sam hoped Claire Mason had been able to collect the children from school.

'It's simply awful, isn't it?' Penny said. Her accent sounded affected, as though she was trying too hard to enunciate. 'Sit down please.' She gestured to a gleaming white table in front of a large window before she walked over to a glass-fronted cupboard and took out two thin white cups. There was a pot of coffee bubbling in the corner. She looked down as she filled both cups. When she brought them over to the table her smile was fixed back on. As Sam and Charlotte settled down, Penny fetched a small jug of milk. She was the perfect host.

'Is this where Claire has been staying?' Sam said.

'What do you mean?' Penny said, looking surprised.

'We know there've been marital problems and Claire has been staying away from home,' Sam said. 'And there's a bag with clothes in over there.' He pointed to a holdall in the corner of the kitchen.

Penny sagged in front of them. 'Yes, she has, just for a few days.' Her voice lost some of its confidence. 'The boys, too.'

'What's behind it?' Sam said.

Penny scowled. 'He's a man, what do you think?' she said, and glanced at Charlotte.

'If you mean Henry, we need more than that,' Sam said. 'If we don't expose Henry's life, we might not find out who killed him. Or why.'

'It doesn't seem fair to Claire.'

'Neither is letting Henry's killer stay free. This is no time for secrets.'

'Claire was here all night,' Penny said. 'You can scrub her from your list of suspects. She came home with the children and stayed in. We drank wine and talked. Paul, my husband, will confirm it, if you want. Call his office. We annoyed him because the boys were running around and when he gets back from work he likes to relax.'

That was when Sam realised what was missing from the house: a heart. It was all appearance over warmth. No children. Just a large empty box filled with things to make it resemble a magazine article.

'What did you talk about?' Charlotte said. 'And how did Claire seem?'

'She was angry,' Penny said. 'She's always been there for him and then he does – well, did – what he did.'

'Which was what?'

77

'It's such a cliché, you know, but Henry had always been like that. He was jealous of us, but Paul has worked hard for everything. It didn't bother us that they didn't have as much money. I just wanted to spend time with my sister and my nephews, but I couldn't because they argued whenever I went round. He thought I was judging them, but I wasn't, and he tried too hard to match us. He took out loans and mortgages they couldn't afford, so Claire had to go out to work too and all their money went on childcare. They just about got straight, but as soon as we moved here Henry decided he needed a bigger house.' Penny shook her head. 'It's no one's fault that we've got more money than them and he shouldn't have felt bad about it, but he did, and it ate away at their marriage. He accused Claire of not loving him enough, of not respecting him. He said that she should look up to him because he was the man of the house but all she saw was failure.'

'Would you describe him as a bully?' Charlotte said.

'No, just weak, but Claire loved him. At least she did, until he ground her down, and then *it* happened.' Penny pulled a face when she said it.

'It?' Sam said.

'Like I said, Henry was a cliché. Hair dye, jewellery that had more show than value. It was no surprise when something went on with the babysitter.'

'When was this?'

'A couple of months ago, but Claire only found out a fortnight ago, when she tried to get her to come round and she wouldn't.'

'So what happened?'

'I don't know, Claire wouldn't go into details, but I know that she'd been trying really hard with Henry. They'd been doing that date-night fad, you know, where you set aside a night to pretend that you're young lovers again. Henry had never really been interested but he went along with them, but Claire said he'd been getting a bit weird.'

'What do you mean, weird?' Sam said.

'Look, it's not my place to say. Things that go on between a husband and wife should stay private.'

'She told you.'

'I'm family.'

'And Claire's husband has been killed.'

Penny let out a long sigh. 'I suppose you could say kinky. Claire said he'd become more forceful.' She shook her head. 'No, that's not right. That isn't how she described it. It was more about hurting her. It wasn't about her enjoyment any more, it was just about his, and he liked hurting her, almost as if he resented her, and he talked about how he'd preferred her when she was younger. Can you imagine how that made her feel? So they have this date night but it doesn't go well. He drove Molly home, the babysitter, and something happened. I don't know what exactly, but that's why Claire walked out.'

'What else had Henry been getting up to?' Charlotte said.

'That's all she told me. He was always in his study, looking at his computer. I don't know what things he'd been getting into, but my sister loved him, and that was all that counted.'

And betrayal is a powerful emotion, Sam thought. Was it strong enough to provoke murder?

Fifteen

Joe quickened his pace as he walked through Piccadilly Gardens. It had once been a sunken patch of green used by the homeless and the junkies, a place to walk around, not through. It had been smartened up now, with shiny paving slabs and manicured grass, but still the menace lurked on the pavements. Youths patrolled their small patches outside the shops, mainly newsagents and convenience stores, to catch the commuters rushing to the nearby railway station, looking to barge and intimidate.

Where Joe was headed wasn't much better. In an alleyway not far from the Gardens was Mother Mac's, what purists would call a real pub, what others would call an example of why everywhere else had moved on. He'd never been there before, but he knew of it, a haunt for City fans and Irish Loyalists.

Joe was looking for Proctor's sister. He'd mentioned where she worked, and she was a link to Proctor's past. If he was going to carry through with his promise, he needed to be sure he was right. He was starting to doubt himself. He'd dealt with so many trials where identification had become confused. He knew too well the mantra about how a mistaken witness can be a convincing witness. Joe was sure he'd got it right, but his legal instincts told him he needed more than that. He'd lived for so long with just a flash of memory, the glance backwards.

He needed to know about Mark Proctor, his history, his background, so that when he took his vengeance for Ellie, he wasn't making a mistake.

As Joe turned into the narrow street that led to Mother Mac's, litter flapped around his ankles. The walls on either side were smeared with graffiti and sealed off by metal grilles, or else hummed with air-conditioning units that cooled the chain-pub on the other side of the block. Mother Mac's was on a corner, with green railings over the windows. As dreary as it was outside, it didn't improve much when he went inside.

The bar was old wood, with four alcoves of worn-out seating that seemed to merge with the carpet. Tankards hung from the ceiling and a quiz machine flashed and beeped in one corner. The tables were scuffed, the chairs old and uncomfortable. Joe knew he stood out in his suit, most of the clientele were old men in worn-out shirts, seeing the world through rheumy eyes and murky pint glasses. There was no free Wi-Fi in this place. One red-faced man held the floor with his beer-soaked opinions, drawing bored nods from anyone pretending to listen.

There were two women behind the bar. One stood with her arms folded, challenging, trying to keep charge of her customers. She was younger, with a pierced nose and a dark tattoo curling up the back of her hand. The other woman was nearer forty, her ginger hair pulled back tightly, high pale cheekbones and pretty, but she looked weary as she changed a bottle on the optics.

'Bitter please,' Joe said, when the younger woman approached him. She was suspicious of him as she poured, no word spoken yet. He knew she wasn't the right woman.

When she put the glass on the bar, he said, 'I'm looking for Melissa.'

The woman by the optics looked round but the woman serving said, 'Who's asking?'

'I am,' Joe said. 'You heard me.'

A man further along the bar put his glass down and looked across. He planted his feet further apart, staking out his territory. He was wiry-thin, his knuckles prominent like his cheekbones, his face hollowed out with the look of a man who kept fit in a boxing gym.

'I'm a solicitor,' Joe said. 'I'm looking for Melissa Proctor.'

'There's no Melissa Proctor here,' the woman said.

'I was told there was.'

The man further along said, 'I think you got your answer, pal.' There was menace in every syllable. 'Have your drink and go.'

Joe was in the mood for him, tension still wound up tightly inside him, but he wouldn't get what he wanted by brawling. 'I'm not here to cause any trouble,' he said.

The man smirked and looked round to a group of men sitting by the quiz machine. 'That was never my concern.'

The woman by the optics put the empty bottle on the bar and said to the man, 'It's all right, I've got this.' She turned to Joe. 'What do you want to talk to me about?'

'Melissa?'

'That's right.'

'I'd rather do this somewhere more private,' Joe said, and he gestured towards an empty alcove surrounded by pictures of old Manchester and a flag exhorting people to SUPPORT OUR TROOPS.

She shrugged and came round to join Joe.

Away from the harsh lights of the bar, Melissa seemed more relaxed. She was slim and tall, elegant in her own way, at least as much as you can be in tight jeans and pumps. Blue eyes that glinted when she smiled, her teeth even and white.

She sat down opposite Joe and said, 'Don't pay any attention to the customers. They look after each other, that's all.'

'Yeah, it has that feel.'

'Never any fights,' she said. 'They just get suspicious of

82

outsiders. Worried they might be police or something. Maybe even United fans on a wrecking mission.'

Joe looked down at his suit. 'Do I look like a football hooligan?'

'You'd be surprised,' she said, smiling now. 'So what can I do for you?'

He handed her his business card. 'My name's Joe Parker.' As she scrutinised it, he said, 'I need to speak to you.'

She tapped it on her knuckles. 'Is this from Peter? We've agreed everything, the flat has been transferred, there's nothing he can do.'

'Peter?'

'My ex-husband. Has he changed solicitors to you?'

'No, I'm sorry, it's nothing to do with him.'

She looked confused. 'What do you want to know?'

'It's about your brother, Mark.'

As soon as he said it, her jaw set and the warm gleam in her eyes turned cold. She started to stand when Joe reached across the table and held out his hand. 'No, please don't. I need to talk about him.'

'I've got nothing to say.'

'You might be able to help.'

Her eyebrows shot upwards and her head tilted. 'Help? You're kidding me. He'll get no help from me. Ever.'

She stormed back behind the bar, suddenly finding plenty to do.

Joe watched her go. He hadn't achieved much, except he knew now that Mark Proctor wasn't attracting much family loyalty.

He left his beer and didn't look behind as he left the pub, the creak of the door and clink of glasses replaced by the deep rumble and fumes of a passing bus. But he knew he'd be back. Whatever family secret engendered such hostility, it was one worth knowing.

Sixteen

Sam and Charlotte were walking towards the babysitter's house, hoping to find out exactly what had gone on with Henry Mason that was so bad that Claire had walked out. They'd called the FLO, who'd got Molly's address from Claire.

'We go back to the station after this visit,' Sam said. 'We've followed a trail but we can't keep away from the squad all day.'

'Agreed,' Charlotte said. 'I just hope this might give us something to go back with.'

That was always the hope. The first day of a murder investigation was always like this: poking around lives, hoping for the quick answer. Most often, things slowed down until the forensic hits started to arrive and versions of events given by the guilty at the start of the case began to unravel.

The address was a small terrace on the other side of Oldham, one in a long line of gleaming redbrick houses broken only by the regular pattern of a door and one window. Cars blocked both pavements and speed bumps did their bit to slow traffic down, but the steep slope made it a magnet for young men trying to recreate car chase scenes. Parking was hard to find, so Sam had left his car a few streets away.

Charlotte knocked softly on the door. It was answered straight away by a woman in her early thirties, in black jogging bottoms and a T-shirt, her mousy hair tied loosely.

Sam identified himself and asked, 'Molly Benson?'

'No, I'm not Molly. What do you want with her?'

'We need to speak with her.'

'Is it about Henry Mason?' Before Sam could say anything, she said, 'People were talking about it on Facebook. I can't believe it. I really can't.'

'Is Molly in?'

The woman thought for a moment but then stepped aside.

The door opened straight into the living room, where a leather sofa was pushed against the rear wall. The back room held a dining table, visible through the open door, with the stairs going from a small door in the corner of the room.

'She's only just come in,' she said. 'I'm her mum, Hazel.' She went to the stairs and shouted up, 'Molly! Someone to see you.' As footsteps sounded through the ceiling, Hazel said, 'I'm not going to say I'm sorry about Henry, because I didn't like him, but I'm sorry for Claire and the boys. I work with her. She's my manager. She's a nice woman.'

As Molly arrived in the living room, panting, Sam and Charlotte exchanged glances. Molly was a child. She was still wearing her school uniform of black trousers and white shirt, although the shirt wasn't tucked into her trousers and the top button was undone.

'It's the police,' Hazel said. 'About Mr Mason.'

Molly's eyes widened and she went to sit down. She looked up at her mother, who sat on a chair opposite. Charlotte sat down next to Molly as Sam leaned against a wall.

'How old are you, Molly?' Charlotte said.

'Fourteen,' Molly said, her voice quiet and nervous.

She was a young-looking fourteen, Sam thought. If something had gone on with Henry Mason, he couldn't have made a mistake about her age.

'Have you heard about Mr Mason?' Charlotte said.

'He's been killed, Mum said.'

'That's right. So we need to find out what we can about him, to work out why someone would do this.'

Molly fidgeted but didn't respond.

'What did you think of Mr Mason?'

Molly looked at her mother, who nodded for her to continue.

'I used to think he was all right, because he was funny. When I babysat for him, he'd drive me home and tell me jokes. But then, well, that thing happened.'

'What happened?'

Molly blushed. 'We weren't going to tell the police.'

'It's all right, it's different now,' her mother said.

'It happened the last time he drove me home,' Molly said. 'He seemed different. Like, way more intense. He was telling me how pretty I was, and how he liked seeing me so grown up now. And he started asking me about boyfriends and things.'

'Did you tell him?'

'There was nothing to tell. I tried to laugh it off but he kept on. Then he stopped.'

'What do you mean, stopped?' Charlotte said.

'I hadn't realised but we'd gone a longer way home and we were down this quiet street. He turned off the engine and got real intense, like way more than before. He stroked my leg and I didn't know what to do. I clamped them together, but he carried on. Then. . . ' She looked at her mother again. 'Then he got his thing out.' Molly's blush deepened. 'He tried to make me touch it but I wouldn't. So he did it himself. Once he'd, you know, finished, he zipped himself up and set off driving. He didn't say anything after that, until we got here. Then he said I shouldn't say anything because he'd get into trouble, and it wouldn't be fair on his boys.'

'When did you tell your parents?'

'When Claire asked me to babysit again a few weeks later. I

started crying, because my parents wanted me to babysit so that they could go out too, and it seemed like I was spoiling their night. I had to tell them.'

Sam looked across at Hazel, who was sitting forward, her jaw set. 'Is that right?'

'Yes, exactly.'

'What did you do?' Sam said to Hazel.

'I called Claire and had it out with her,' she said. 'It would make it hard at work but no one touches Molly like that or does what he did.'

Molly looked up. 'Mr Mason's murder, is it anything to do with what happened to me?'

Sam thought about that and guessed at the anger inside the house when they'd found out.

Hazel must have guessed at his thoughts, because she said, 'My husband works at Dewhursts. He's been on the night shift at the factory all week. I know you'll want to check. He's either there or in bed.'

'And you?'

'Here, watching television.'

Sam scribbled down details of the programmes she watched, to check the listings. He knew it would come to nothing, though. Henry Mason's murder seemed to have some planning to it, the meeting in a park, so Hazel wouldn't get her alibi wrong. All she had to do was record the programmes and watch them when she got in. Who would ever know?

'Will I have to go to court?' Molly said.

'I hope not, but you've helped,' Sam said.

'Have I?'

'Yes, very much.'

Sam and Charlotte said their farewells, Sam leaving his business card behind. Once they were back in the car, Charlotte said, 'That changes things. Henry Mason liked them young. Very young. His world is starting to look a bit murkier.'

'Could that be our motive? An angry father? Molly might not be the first person he tried it on with.'

'And Molly's father?'

'We'll call Dewhursts from the station. Right now, it's time to report back. Let's see how everyone else has done.'

Seventeen

Joe was waiting at the end of the alleyway that led to Mother Mac's. It gave him enough of a view in case Melissa Proctor turned the other way but with a busy street to lose himself in if she came directly towards him. He didn't mind waiting. He'd been waiting ever since his eighteenth birthday. A few hours in a dirty back street would be no hardship.

More than an hour passed before he heard the door go at Mother Mac's. Joe peered along the alleyway, wondering if it would be one of the daytime boozers, and was relieved to see that it was Melissa. She was heading his way, looking down, sorting out the contents of a small handbag.

He slunk back behind a long-defunct doorway, now just a backdrop of fly-posters advertising upcoming gigs. He wanted her to reach the main street before she saw him. If she saw him too soon, she'd retreat into the sanctuary of the pub.

As she came onto the street, Melissa was looking through her purse for money and didn't glance towards Joe. He stepped out of the doorway, ready to follow. Her purse went back into her handbag as a black cab rumbled along the street, the yellow light shining. Her arm went into the air.

The cab pulled into the kerb to pick her up. As she opened the door to climb into the back, Joe came up quickly behind her and followed her in.

Melissa sat in the seat with a jolt, her eyes wide with alarm. 'You?' she said. 'What the fuck are you doing?'

'I need to talk,' Joe said.

A voice from the front said, 'Everything all right back there?'

'You know where I work, you kept my card,' Joe said. 'You know you'll be safe.'

Melissa frowned, her lips pursed, before she said, 'This ride is on you.' She leaned forward and said, 'Ancoats, Blake Mill.'

Joe settled back in the seat as the taxi set off.

Melissa's arms were folded. 'This had better be good. Do lawyers normally chase down people like this?'

'No, not normally,' he admitted. 'This isn't a normal situation.'

Melissa stayed silent as the cab turned into the streets that would take them towards Ancoats. Joe let her stay that way, because for as long as he wasn't saying anything, he wasn't upsetting her.

Eventually, Melissa said, 'So are you helping him, or working against him?'

Joe almost laughed. 'Both. Your brother is my client, but I need to know more about him, good or bad.'

'Not much good, plenty of bad,' Melissa snapped.

'Explain?'

Melissa went silent again. The converted mills and apartment buildings were getting closer, the short journey to Ancoats nearly over.

'Melissa?'

'You don't know much about him, I can tell,' she said.

'That's why I'm here.'

'Are you single?'

'Yes.'

'Good. Take me for a drink tonight and I'll tell you all about dear sweet Mark.'

'A drink?' Joe said, confused.

'Yes. Not too tricky to understand, is it?'

The taxi made a right turn and the driver said, 'Here okay?'

'Yes, thank you,' Melissa said, and then to Joe, 'Collect me here at seven. I'll tell you all you need to know.'

'But how do you know I haven't got plans?'

'If you'll loiter down alleyways for me, you'll break plans.' Her look softened and a smile crept across her face. 'Perhaps I'm just after some intelligent company.'

With that, Melissa climbed out of the cab and walked towards an apartment building, seven storeys of a converted mill looking towards the murky brown water of the Rochdale Canal.

'Where to now?' the driver said.

'Castlefield,' Joe said, and then sat back in his seat. He'd just been asked on a date by Mark Proctor's sister. How the hell had he been dragged into that?

A thin blue carpet lined the corridor to the Incident Room and most of the doors from it opened into empty rooms, where old notices fluttered against walls that bore the scars of yellowing sticky tape.

The station had once been the heart of the small town on the edge of the city, until Manchester swallowed it up and someone decided that the community no longer needed a heart. It housed one of the Major Incident Teams because it meant the team could grow or shrink, depending on the case. Sam liked the sense of history, although it did feel as though the building was slowly crumbling around them, from the clanking radiators to the flickering strip lights. It was too cold in winter and too hot in summer, but Sam had grown to see it as his home as far as his job was concerned.

As Sam and Charlotte walked into the Incident Room, everyone looked round. There were more people than usual;

it looked like a second murder had helped Brabham pull in some new recruits. It was warm, though, too many people squeezed into a room that had been heated up by the sun for most of the day. It smelled of stale cigarettes and sweat and dried-out coffee cups.

Brabham was at a desk in the corner, so he could see everything that was going on. As they walked over, he said, 'Glad you could join us.' He looked at Charlotte when he said it, and she blushed. 'What have you got?'

Sam spoke up. 'Henry Mason seemed like an ordinary guy but he had a few secrets. All the trappings of a good life – nice house, nice family – but I'm guessing it wasn't exciting enough for him. He tried it on with the fourteen-year-old babysitter and his wife left him.'

'When?'

'It happened a couple of months ago, but his wife only found out two weeks ago.'

'That's two areas for suspicion,' Brabham said. 'His wife and the babysitter's family.'

'I'm not sure there's much in either.'

'Why do you say that?'

'Claire Mason was angry that we were in the house and didn't know who we were,' Sam said. 'If she'd been involved, I reckon she would have been there playing happy families. And she was protective towards her sons, keeping her husband's behaviour quiet to protect them. I can see how she might have left Henry, but kill him? No, I'm not convinced.'

'What about the babysitter? Who are her parents?'

Charlotte spoke up. 'Hazel and Paul Benson from Oldham. We didn't see Paul, he was at work, just started his shift at Dewhursts. Hazel works for Mason's wife.'

The detective closest to them tapped on his keyboard. 'Auburn Terrace in Werneth?'

'Yes, that's him.'

More taps on the keyboard. 'He's got some form for violence. No domestic warning markers, and they go back a few
years, but he's been handy with his fists.'

'Working-class guy from Oldham who got in a few scraps
when he was younger, most likely,' Charlotte said.

'But still worth a look,' Brabham said. 'Call Dewhursts, check
when he was there. Did you ask about Keith Welsby?'

'Yes,' Sam said. 'Claire Mason hadn't heard of him, but
we've dropped off Mason's computers at headquarters. They
might reveal something.'

'We need to link Mason and Welsby,' Brabham said. 'That's
our focus. Have you got any ideas?'

'Their ordinariness,' Sam said. 'Welsby was a teacher. Unassuming. Quiet. Unremarkable, even. Yet both he and Mason
died loitering in quiet places at night.'

'Perhaps their ordinariness is their cover?' Brabham said.
'They might have dodgy connections we don't know about.'

'Mason's house didn't seem like something from the criminal underworld, though,' Sam said. 'There were some debts,
house clean and ordered, but nothing too extravagant. You
know what the high-flying criminals' houses are like: they
can't put the money in the bank so they spend it. Jacuzzi bath-
rooms, cars that are too good for the neighbourhood, grand
ornaments. Mason's house was just – what's the word? – aspirational.'

'Were his debts greater than he would let on?' Brabham
said. 'Loan sharks?'

'Loan sharks don't kill,' Charlotte said. 'They threaten and
frighten, and perhaps maim, but murder? No.'

'That depends on the level of debt. They could also go after
Mrs Mason for it.'

'But what about Keith Welsby?' Sam said. 'Mason's bloody
fingerprint was on the knife. And it fits with it being Mason.'

'I don't understand.'

'The knife used to kill Keith Welsby was left at the scene, a fingerprint on it. Our theory was always that the killer panicked and threw it away, aiming for the canal, because it was caught in a bush overhanging the towpath. Who'd panic more than someone unused to crime? We just need to work out why Mason would murder a private, unassuming teacher.'

'Private can mean secretive too,' Brabham said. 'Just because he stayed quiet at work doesn't mean that he wasn't hiding a nastier side. Was Welsby after Mason and Mason got the better of him, and last night was about payback?'

Sam shook his head. 'Everything we found out about Keith Welsby suggested that he was a likeable teacher who led an ordinary life. We found nothing at his house. This is something different.'

'Explain.'

'I don't know, just a gut feeling. For reasons we can't yet fathom, a car salesman is implicated in the murder of a teacher he didn't know. At least that's the theory. Because of that, the car salesman himself was murdered. There is some kind of circle here but I don't think it's complete yet.'

'Not a circle,' Brabham said. 'They topple into each other, like a chain.' His eyes brightened. 'No, like dominoes.'

'But there are only two deaths. Hardly dominoes, sir.'

'But that's how they run, isn't it? For now, you keep on the family. Go through Mason's Facebook page, and Welsby's. Look for a connected friend. Speak to every friend and see if they know the other. You've got an evening of breaking bad news so share it out amongst you. If someone doesn't seem keen on talking to you, chase it.'

'Perhaps Mason found Welsby already dead and panicked,' Sam said. 'That's the other scenario that could fit. He's where he shouldn't be, because he's seeing someone else, so he doesn't ring it in. He might have been the witness to that murder, and his murder is just to eliminate witnesses.'

'There's something in that,' Brabham said. 'It doesn't really matter whether he committed that murder. We just know there's a connection. If we can find that, everything else should follow.'

Sam went to his usual desk, Charlotte with him.

He pulled out the bank statements taken from Henry Mason's house. Claire had agreed to him taking them, but he could have got them anyway. Claire's permission just saved him some time. 'I'll go through these, to look out for a pattern, like regular large cash withdrawals or debits to debt companies.'

'I'll do the Facebook stuff,' Charlotte said, and then, 'What do you think about Brabham's notion, this domino thing?'

'It's meaningless,' Sam said. 'There are two murders. That's not a domino effect.'

'That's what I thought,' she said.

As they both set about their duties, Sam smiled to himself. This was his favourite part of any investigation: the trawl. The information was here somewhere. It was just a case of finding it.

Eighteen

Joe checked his watch as he arrived in Ancoats. Ten minutes to seven, right on time. He'd left his suit behind and was in jeans and a shirt, a linen jacket over the top.

He was tense, pacing as he waited, his fingers tapping his thumb. Melissa had made it sound like a date, but Joe wasn't interested in that. She was Proctor's sister and he wanted information about him. He had no interest beyond that.

Ancoats was a curious mix. Once the industrial powerhouse of Manchester, when the Rochdale Canal brought cotton to the huge mills and warehouses along its banks, the area had been densely packed with cramped housing and foundries. The residents were either killed by cholera or developed bad lungs from the constant smoke in the air, which made it impossible to see from one side of the district to the other, the high mill chimneys and rows of terraced housing just vague shadows in the dirty distance. It bred poverty and gangs – the world's first street gang came from Ancoats, the Scuttlers, hoards of young Victorian teenagers identified by their neckerchiefs and haircuts, the fringe slightly longer on the left.

Most of the area was flattened in the sixties, the slums bulldozed into history, but it was only in recent years that something properly habitable was put up in its place, as the mills were either converted into plush flats or razed to allow new apartment buildings to pop up in their stead.

But it seemed like someone had lost interest. The apartment blocks and converted mills overlooked fenced-off wastelands and a small narrowboat marina, the cobbled streets leading to some of the older Ancoats houses. Young men carrying open cans of beer passed professionals in snug suits and sharp shoes, each resenting the other, the area never quite reinventing itself enough. It was history and industry and inner-city blight fused with upward mobility and hipster living.

He checked his watch, debated whether he should leave, that there must be a different way, but then he saw her.

Her hair was down. The streetlight behind her made it glow and silhouetted her elegant stroll. She was in three-quarter-length pants and simple flat shoes, her handbag soft brown leather. When she got close, Joe saw she was wearing glossy lipstick and the fatigue from earlier in the day had been powdered away.

'Where are you taking me?' she asked.

'Is there a pub nearby? I just want to talk.'

'I was hoping for something nicer.' Before Joe could respond, she added, 'I don't get taken out much. If you want the family history, at least pretend there's a nice evening ahead.'

'I know a tapas place in town. Will that do?'

'Sounds lovely. How do I look?'

He softened. 'You look nice,' he said.

'Thank you,' she said, and she smiled, much warmer than it had been earlier.

They hung around the main road, looking for a black cab. Joe kept his hands in his pockets and his concentration on the road, not ready for the small talk. He wanted information but he was unprepared for how to deal with someone so close to Ellie's killer.

The silence was awkward in the taxi and the restaurant was quiet, not much of a Tuesday-night crowd, even though it was close to Castlefield. Joe had been there one weekend and had queued for a table. Now, they got a table in the window, the waiter trying to make the place look popular. Joe ordered a bottle of Chenin Blanc but Melissa took control of the food ordering.

Joe was about to ask about Mark Proctor when Melissa said, 'So how long have you been single?'

'A couple of years now.'

She raised her eyebrows. 'A catch like you?'

That took Joe by surprise.

She blushed. 'I'm sorry, I didn't mean to come on to you like that. It's just, well, I've had my fair share of men who lie about their relationships. I hope you're not one of them.'

'I'm not,' he said.

'So what happened?'

He wondered what he could say. The truth was simple: he'd thrown himself into his work so much that his fiancée looked for affection elsewhere, except she hadn't looked far. They both worked at the same law firm, Mahones, and when he caught her with one of the partners he walked out and ended up at Honeywells. The break-up was about hurt and self-loathing. The one thing he did remember was the white heat of infidelity, so he promised himself he'd never be with anyone attached, he would never inflict that pain on someone else.

He opted for something simpler. 'It just didn't work out.'

The food arrived, nine hot clay bowls containing meatballs and potatoes and seafood and vegetables. It meant he had her as a captive audience for a bit longer but he couldn't turn the conversation straight to Mark. As Melissa spooned some onto her plate, she asked, 'So don't you want to know about me?'

'It sounds like you're going to tell me.'

Melissa put down the clay bowl and scowled. 'You came to me,' she said. 'You want to know about my brother but all I'm getting is attitude.'

'But that's all I want, information about your brother.'

'And all I want is an evening out.'

'I'm sorry,' Joe said, feeling guilty. She was right: he was treating her badly. Whatever her brother had done, it wasn't her fault. 'Tell me about you.'

She frowned as she reached out for a squid in tomato sauce. 'I'm an Ancoats girl who went south for a while. My ex-husband Peter, well, he was different to me. We met at university in London. I was doing an Art History degree but I was self-conscious of my background, a working-class girl, because I was eighteen and trying to broaden my horizons, shake off my past. I didn't want to be the *northern lass*.' And she exaggerated her northern accent when she said it. 'Then I met Peter at an art gallery. A nice guy, good-looking, funny, and for me, an Ancoats girl, he was a guy I'd never find at home.'

'But you came back to your family,' Joe said, trying to turn the conversation back to her brother.

'It wasn't for them. I was lonely. I couldn't get a proper job down there, a graduate job, and all my university friends had gone their own way. I was just living Peter's life, turning into the wife who waited for him to come home. If we went out, it was with his friends, his circle. I became pregnant for something to do, to make my life mean more.'

'And did it?'

'Just made me more lonely. So I gave him an ultimatum when Carrie, that's my daughter, was three: move north with me, or stay in London alone.'

'Which did he choose?'

'North, at the start.'

'But it didn't work out?'

'He got a job easily enough – he works for a bank – but settling in the north wasn't for him. He's a nice guy but he hadn't lived anywhere like Manchester, so it was alien to him. Too gritty, too earthy. Too frightening. We bought an apartment in Ancoats. For me, it was coming home. I thought Peter would like it because it was up and coming, everything made new again, but it wasn't enough. My loneliness was swapped for his. Two years ago, he went home.'

'And your daughter?'

'Carrie's with me. She goes to London once a month, for a weekend. She's at a friend's house tonight, staying over. Fourteen now.' She shook her head. 'It flies.'

'But still you didn't get the graduate job,' Joe said. 'Mother Mac's doesn't seem the kind of place for an Art History graduate.'

She laughed, spearing a meatball onto her plate. 'The people in there are honest, they look after each other, and you never get any fights, not like the fancier places in town. Unless City are playing, it's just somewhere for men to stare into a glass and reflect on their lives. I like it.'

Joe smiled, but then he stopped himself. He'd started to relax into the evening and realised he liked her. No, more than that. He was starting to feel the beginnings of something, a connection, a need. He couldn't think like that. She was Mark Proctor's sister, and there were times when he got a flash of him, from the gleam in her eyes to the slight blush to her cheeks. Every time he thought that, anger simmered and took away his smile.

Melissa snapped him from his thoughts when she said, 'I'm talking too much and you're doing too much listening. Your turn. Tell me what my brother's been up to.'

Joe put down his fork and dabbed at his mouth with his napkin. 'I can't say too much just yet. He's my client, but I need to know more about him.'

Melissa put down her own cutlery. 'But why? I can't just tell you everything about him and get nothing back.'

'Come on, you know how it is. Client confidentiality.'

'What sort of lawyer are you?'

'Criminal.'

'So he's in trouble, right?'

More than he realises, Joe thought. 'I can't say.'

'So how can I help you if you won't tell me what it's about?'

Joe thought about that and realised he wanted information more than he wanted to protect his client, and Melissa didn't seem the sort of person who'd sell him out. But family bonds can be tight.

'Are you close to Mark?' he said.

Joe got his answer from the flash of anger in her eyes. And there was more than that. Something deeper.

'You won't be getting a character reference, if that's what you're after,' she said.

That was the answer he needed.

'He's accused of burglary,' Joe said. 'His car was seized so he broke into the police compound and stole it back.'

Melissa's laugh was bitter. 'That's a new one.'

Joe didn't return the laugh.

She put her plate to one side. 'Something is troubling you,' she said. 'I don't know much about lawyers, but I can't think many would come out for dinner with a client's sister, one he hasn't spoken to for years, in connection with a burglary. What do you really want to know?'

'What's he like?' Joe said. 'As simple as that. I want to know about the real Mark Proctor.'

'But why? There's something you're not telling me.' Her eyes narrowed. 'This is something personal.'

'Very.'

Melissa thought about that. 'He's dangerous,' she said eventually.

Joe closed his eyes as he felt a rush of adrenalin. There it was: the answer, a sign that he'd been right.

'Is he still doing all that grief counselling stuff?' Melissa said.

'Grief counselling?'

'Didn't he tell you? He used to be a volunteer for a victims' charity, but he was getting too involved. That's why we fell out.'

'Explain.'

'He gets off on misery, that's what.'

'When was the last time you saw your brother?'

Melissa's frown turned to a scowl. 'Nine, ten years ago. Maybe more. Carrie was only a toddler. I didn't even go to his wedding.'

'That's a long time. What happened?'

She took a drink and looked round for their waiter. When she caught his attention, she held up the empty wine bottle to indicate she wanted another. Then she turned back to Joe. 'He killed my cat. It sounds stupid when I say it like that, but that's what he did.'

Joe's eyes widened but Melissa shook her head.

'Don't start thinking that it's a psychopathic thing, the early stages of a monster,' she said. 'It wasn't about the cruelty. It was about me.' She took a deep breath and then wiped her eyes. 'Look at me, for Christ's sake. It was more than twenty years ago when it happened. Our parents bought it for me when I turned sixteen. Barney. A lovely ginger tabby. He'd sleep with me, wait for me, sit on my lap when I watched television. He was just over a year old when I found him at the bottom of the garden. His neck had been broken. I was heartbroken, devastated.' Melissa stopped to wipe away another tear. 'This is anger, because Mark was so protective of me. He bought me things to make up for it. He sat with me, was everything a big brother should be, but then, years later, we argued. Peter and I had moved back to Manchester and he was doing his grief-thing. But he didn't have a proper job. I used to ask him about it, because he was still living at home then and my parents wanted him to leave. He was turning thirty and I suppose I was trying to help them, showing him how sad he looked, but he freaked out, became angry, really angry.'

'What did you say to him?'

'Just that it was time for Mum and Dad to be on their own. He went on about family, how we have to look after each other, that he was good for my parents, and that he'd been good to me. He said he'd been such a comforting hand when Barney was found, and he was. He comforted me, fussed around me, and then he said. . . ' Melissa paused again to wipe her eye. 'He said that he'd been so good that I hadn't even noticed the scratches and red marks on his hand.'

'Did he actually admit to killing Barney?' Joe said, surprised.

'Not in so many words, but it was easy to work out. I asked him what he meant by that, and his reply gave me the answer.'

'Tell me.'

'He said that sometimes it's good to enjoy the ripples more than the splash.'

Joe thought about that for a few seconds before he asked, 'What do you think he meant?'

'That he gets off on being the comforter, the wonderful and sensitive Mark Proctor, so sometimes he has to create the splash so that he can enjoy the ripples, be the one people turn to.'

Joe put his cutlery down. 'Do you think he could go one stage further?'

'A stage further?'

'Kill a person.'

'What, for the attention?' She blew out. 'I don't know. For all his charm, there's coldness in there. He killed my cat because he wanted to enjoy my distress. Anyone who can do that is capable of anything.' Melissa frowned. 'You said this was personal and now you're talking about my brother killing someone. Is there something you should tell me?'

Joe wanted to spill out the words – that her brother had killed his sister – but he held back. He'd spent his adult life holding back. 'Client confidentiality,' he said.

Melissa nodded but she seemed suspicious. It made the rest of the meal pass more quietly, more awkwardly, so that when they finished their food Melissa said she was tired.

They went outside.

'Thank you for a lovely evening,' she said. A taxi crawled along the street. Melissa held her hand in the air and went towards it, pausing only to reach for a scrap of paper and a pen in her handbag. She scribbled down a telephone number. 'Call me, if you want. Or text.'

Joe looked at it. 'Thank you.'

Melissa went to climb into the taxi but paused. Joe was holding onto the door. She went as if to kiss him, leaned in towards him.

He turned his head so that her kiss landed on his cheek.

Melissa smiled ruefully at that and climbed in, the taxi door slamming. Joe didn't look up as the taxi set off. Instead, he thought about what she'd said about Proctor. Dangerous.

Then realisation of something else came like a slap to his face. He'd enjoyed her company. He'd felt close to Proctor's sister. How could that make sense? But it wasn't to 'Proctor's sister'. It had been to Melissa. He shouldn't think of her in the context of her brother. She was her own person. Good company, witty, attractive, intelligent, some fight in her.

He looked up as the taxi rounded the corner, tucking her phone number into his pocket. He couldn't see whether she was looking back.

Then something occurred to him. If Melissa hadn't seen Proctor for all those years, how did he know she was working at Mother Mac's?

Nineteen

He threw his phone to the other side of the room. Why were there no messages, no emails? Why the silence?

The day had been long and frustrating. He'd made a quick trip into the city centre, and then spent the rest of the day pacing around, the TV flickering in the corner, the sound turned down.

He clicked off the television and the room darkened, with the only light coming from a reading lamp in one corner. He needed his memories.

He left the house and went along the uneven path, grass growing between the paving slabs. The door to the workshop was kept locked and he was the only one with a key. He remembered the day when he'd come home and found it open, the lock smashed: tools moved, his radio taken, his toolbox stolen.

The workshop door scraped on the concrete as he opened it. He clicked on the light, stepped inside and locked the door from the inside.

The air felt cold and dust floated in the glare of the light bulb. His steps were loud until he reached the thick red rug covering the concrete floor. It made his special place feel warm.

There was a chair at one end and around the space there were small tables, a thick candle on each one. He closed the thin curtain in front of the window and reached into his pocket for his lighter. Once each candle was lit, he switched off the bulb. This was the lighting he preferred, the flames like small angels dancing.

The chair creaked as he sat down. He needed his box.

He checked his phone again. Nothing.

His impatience grew. He went to the messaging app, the one he'd installed at his suggestion. It was their way of keeping in touch. No records kept. No phone logs. All of it deleted instantly.

Still nothing. The hot burn of anger swelled inside him.

He typed, *Where is it?*, and jabbed at the SEND button.

He didn't always respond straight away. Impatience mounting, he typed, *I did what U asked. Now 4 me.*

Ten minutes went by before a light flashed on his phone. He opened up the app: *The Green at Worsley. 8pm. Tomorrow.*

His tongue flicked across his lip as he waited. His breaths shortened. The workshop seemed to contract around him. Then the light on his phone blinked again. He opened the app and groaned when he saw it.

His box. Blue metal. His treasures inside. His memories rushed through him like a film on fast forward. Smooth skin, soft white, unblemished. Wide eyes. Angry eyes. Some fighting. Others too scared. The last breaths.

Tomorrow.

He couldn't wait that long. He tugged at his belt.

Joe was deep in thought as he headed back to his apartment. *Dangerous.* That was the word Melissa used.

But what should he do about Mark Proctor?

As he walked, his mind toyed with all the possibilities. He recalled his promise to himself, that he would kill Ellie's murderer when he got the chance, but as the evening breeze fluttered his hair and he was assaulted by the everyday sounds of the city, he wondered whether he could go through with it. Was ending Mark Proctor's life worth giving up all this for? He knew what Gina would say, that it wouldn't bring Ellie back, but it didn't stop the searing heat of revenge from burning him up.

His apartment block loomed ahead. He stalled, wondered whether he was ready to face the solitude, when someone stepped from the shadows of the high wall.

He jumped, startled, until a voice said, 'Hi, Joe.'

It was Ruby. And she was carrying a bag.

'I want to stay with you for a while,' she said.

Joe groaned. He didn't need this.

'Go home, Ruby.'

'No. I'm not going back.'

'But what if you can't stay here?'

'It's warm tonight. I'll sleep outside.'

'Come inside,' Joe said, irritated. She'd given the answer she knew would get her what she wanted.

They were both silent as they walked through the apartment building, and once inside Joe's apartment Ruby slumped into a chair, the leather creaking loudly. She threw her bag onto the floor. Joe went into the kitchen and put his keys on the counter. He filled the kettle. If nothing else, it gave him a few minutes to decide what he was going to do about her.

'I'm hungry,' Ruby shouted.

Joe rolled his eyes. She should have stayed at home if she expected its comforts. He opened the fridge: a carton of milk, half a block of cheese, two bottles of wine and a potato.

He closed it again. 'Fancy a takeaway?' he shouted through.

'Chinese, please.'

Joe grabbed a menu from a collection he kept next to the microwave and took it to her.

Ruby was lounging, her long legs dangled over the chair arm. He tapped her foot to tell her to put her legs down and passed her the Chinese menu. 'You choose and then we talk,' he said. 'I've eaten.'

She shrugged in that exaggerated way that teenagers have, her lips set in a scowl, and started reading the menu.

Ruby made the room look untidy straight away. It didn't have much warmth, there were no plants or flowers, no photographs apart from one of Ellie, and blinds covered the window rather than curtains. It was tidy, though. His records and CDs were stacked neatly, the few books he had were in an oak bookcase, and there was nothing lying around. No magazines or old cups. Ruby seemed to bring some chaos into his apartment that he didn't like.

Joe went to the record player and selected an album, a Robert Johnson collection, country blues from the thirties: just a man playing scratchy music on an old guitar. When Ruby's scowl deepened as the hiss of the vinyl filled the room, he knew why he'd picked it: he was setting down a marker. This was his apartment. If she had any notion she could stay, Ruby would have to learn to let someone else have their way.

She tossed the menu onto the glass coffee table. 'Chicken satay,' she said, before sitting back and folding her arms.

Joe sat down on a chair by the window. He pulled on the drawstring to close the blinds and turned the volume down so they could talk. 'Why are you here?' he said.

'Because I can't stand living there any more. I've had enough.'

'Why have you had enough?'

'She's an embarrassment. She fusses round me all the time, or has a go at me when I haven't even done anything. Do some revising, or don't stay out late, or where are you going. I can't breathe in there.'

Joe raised an eyebrow. 'And you think you will here?'

'Yeah, you're cool. You hang out with criminals and gangsters. Whatever I do shouldn't worry you.'

'You think?' he said, his tone incredulous. 'I don't "hang out" with them. I represent them in court and then I come home. I don't drink with them, I don't go to their parties, and they sure as hell don't come here. I've seen how they live, and because of that I worry more about you, because I've seen how easy it is to get dragged into it. If you think I'm going to let you doss here and just live your life how you fancy it, you can forget it. Do you think I got to be a lawyer by messing around and staying out late? No. I worked hard, so I expect you to do the same if you want to make something of yourself.'

'God, you sound like Mum.'

'Perhaps we're both right.' He paused. 'What do you want to do with your life?'

'I don't know. Maybe a lawyer like you.'

'And you think that's your choice?'

'Yeah, of course.'

'Not without hard work. This is the hard realities of life coming at you now, Ruby, and that's what's annoying you. You can't face up to them. If you don't, you won't get any choice about what you do.'

'Why are you being so mean?' she said, tears jumping into her eyes.

'I'm being your big brother and looking after you,' he said, his voice rising.

'No, you just don't want me here,' she said, and stood up and grabbed her bag. 'I'll go somewhere else.'

Joe reached out and grabbed her arm. 'No. Stay. For now. It's okay.'

Ruby paused before saying, 'Thank you.' She grinned. 'Can I have prawn toast too?'

He sighed. 'Of course you can. I'll make up a bed.'

And with that, Joe had taken responsibility for his little sister.

Twenty

Sam sat back and stretched, rubbed his eyes. It had been a long day. No one left early on the first day of a murder investigation but the desks were slowly emptying as lines of inquiry dried up. The detectives who'd stay on the phones during the night had arrived. Sometimes calls came in during the early hours, when people caught the late news, or when long-held secrets spilled out when the caller reached the end of a bottle.

'I'm done,' Charlotte said, yawning.

'Yeah, me too,' Sam said. 'Did you find anything?'

She shook her head. 'Just a few hours delivering bad news. I'll keep an eye on his Facebook page tonight, see whether anyone posts anything suspicious, but so far it's just been people in shock. Henry Mason is just what we thought: an ordinary guy.'

'Any of Mason's friends know Keith Welsby?'

'No, none. If there's a connection, no one's pointed it out yet.' She stood up and took her suit jacket from the back of the chair. 'What about you?'

'The same. I've gone back through the bank statements and it reads just like a couple trying to keep a lifestyle afloat with money they don't really have, but what's strange about that?'

'No unusual payments?'

'What do you mean?'

'I don't know. He was going through a mid-life crisis, with

a thing for young girls. Any large cash withdrawals or cheques cashed? Blackmail or something?'

'What, you think that might have some link with Keith Welsby?' Sam said.

'He was a teacher. Was Henry Mason after one of his pupils and Welsby found out? Did a pupil confide in him, and rather than confront Mason, Welsby decided to blackmail him? Mason stopped the blackmail by killing him?'

'That's a good theory for explaining Welsby's death, but how does it lead to Henry Mason's murder?'

Charlotte let out a long tired breath. 'Oh God, I don't know. My head is mashed. I'll have a think about that overnight.'

Sam logged off. 'I'm done too. We'll see what the morning brings.'

He picked up his jacket and left the station with Charlotte, into the dark car park, the floodlight broken, as always.

He was about to climb into his car when his phone rang. It was Alice.

'A development?' Charlotte said.

'No, family. Have a good evening.' He pressed answer. 'Hi.'

'Your mother called. Ruby's left. She's gone to Joe's.'

'What the hell?'

'Yeah, I know, but she sounded pretty upset.'

'Okay, I'll go over. I won't be late.'

He hung up and wiped his eyes. The day had been long enough. He could do without Ruby making it longer.

Joe wasn't surprised when the buzzer to his apartment sounded and Sam's voice came over the intercom. He pressed the button and gave Sam a few seconds to get through before opening the door.

Ruby looked up, her mouth open.

'I didn't call him,' Joe said. 'He might just be worried.'

She stayed silent as the sound of footsteps echoed in the

111

corridor outside. When Sam burst in, he was out of breath. Ruby looked up and folded her arms.

'What's going on?' Sam said.

'I'm staying with Joe,' she said.

'No, you're not.'

'Stop me.'

Joe held his hands in the air. 'Hey, hey, everyone calm down.'

'I'm not here for an argument,' Sam said.

'So stop arguing,' Joe said, and then, his voice weary, 'We've been through it. She can stay here for the moment, tonight at least.'

Sam thought about that, before he sighed and pointed towards the door that led to the balcony. 'We need to talk.'

Joe led the way. As he pulled on the door, Ruby said, 'Can I use your shower? I'll get out of your way if you're going to talk about me.'

'Help yourself,' Joe said. 'Fresh towels in the basket in there.' And then he stepped out of the living room and into the cool evening breeze.

The hush of the apartment was replaced by the noise of the city. The clink of glasses and echoes of laughter drifted over from a restaurant on the other side of the canal – an open-air place that thrived on sunny days – and the roads provided a steady hum of tyres.

Sam put his hands on his hips. 'So how long are you going to let her stay?'

Joe placed his hands on the rail and stared into the night. The canal twinkled, the willow trees in silhouette against the steel gleam of the water and the glare from the restaurant behind.

'Not long,' Joe said, his voice distant. 'What use am I for personal guidance?'

'What about Mum?' Sam said. 'We can't leave her on her

own up there. Caring for Ruby is just about the only thing that keeps her stable. If we take that from her, who knows what will happen.'

'I'm not doing this because of Mum,' Joe said. 'Ruby turned up. What could I do? Send her away into the city? You know what it's like out there. Ruby is headstrong and she'd sleep on the streets to spite us. At least this way we know where she is.'

'But we can't take her away from Mum.'

'Okay, let her stay here tonight at least. I'll persuade her to go home tomorrow.'

'And if she doesn't?'

'We'll worry about that tomorrow.'

Sam fell silent again as he looked at the scene from the balcony. 'We should look out for her more. I feel like we're letting her down.'

'No, circumstances have let her down. We do what we can. Go home, look out for your own girls.'

'Okay, thanks,' Sam said. He looked back into the apartment, where Ruby's bag was discarded on the floor. 'If you need any help, you know where to find me.'

Sam turned to go, but Joe reached out and grabbed his arm. Sam stopped.

'What is it?' Sam said.

Joe wondered how much he could tell his brother. Sam was a policeman and he knew Joe's secret, the only person he'd confided in. Sam would stop him, tell him that there was a different way to go about things.

But what about the promise he'd made to himself? If he walked away from that, Proctor would walk away from it too. It had driven him through his career, the steady gnaw of revenge, how he wanted just one chance to even things up.

Joe knew he needed to be stopped, or he would lose everything he had. His apartment. His job. His life. The view he treasured. He would come out of prison in sixteen years or so with no future. All he had to do was say the words and Sam would know what to do.

Joe closed his eyes for a moment. When he opened them again, he let go of Sam's arm and said, 'Thank you for coming. Ruby will appreciate it when she's older.'

Sam's eyes narrowed, but he said, 'No worries, Joe. Look after yourself.'

Joe stayed on the balcony and listened as Sam left. When Sam appeared on the paved canal bank below, Joe watched as his outline grew faint in the dusk light and, once he rounded the corner and went out of sight, Joe turned back into the apartment. Ruby was back in the living room, drying her hair with a towel. As he watched her, he felt everything change. She'd come to him for help when things had got bad at home. He was her big brother, and he and Sam were the nearest things to a father she had. He'd never thought about being arrested for killing Ellie's murderer, but he'd never been confronted with him. Now the time to act had arrived, he realised that it wasn't just about the material things but his family too. If he went to prison for killing Proctor, wouldn't that mean that Proctor had stolen something else from them? If he acted on his promise, Ruby would lose him, and she'd lost enough in her life.

There had to be another way. He didn't have to kill Proctor to get his revenge. All he had to do was make Proctor pay for it. The problem was the lack of evidence against him. He had to think like a lawyer, not a brother seeking revenge. If he tipped off the police, Proctor might be able to get rid of evidence. No, he had to do more than that: he had to find evidence. Joe had waited many years to get Ellie's murderer. He couldn't stand to watch him walk away from it.

Joe was going to get Proctor, but he would do it his way.

Twenty-one

The workshop had been his sanctuary all the through the night. He'd curled up with his memories, wrapped up in a large blanket. He tended to his candles, his flickering angels, replacing those that burnt out. He'd been listening out for the crash of the door, the sound of heavy boots, but nothing so far. His wife knew not to disturb him, this was where he lived with his secrets, but the police wouldn't care about that.

Things were changing. He sensed it like a scent in the wind. He'd given something up: a small bit of control, because he'd been directed to act. It had spoiled everything. So he'd watched the flames dwindle on the large church candles, the wicks like sand in a timer, burning to pools of wax, everything distorted and messy.

The morning announced itself with a chill, the walls slick with condensation, his breaths coming out as a slight mist. He gathered his blanket around his shoulders. The night had been long.

He blew out the remaining candles and let the morning light take over, muted by the curtain still over the window. He blinked as he opened the door, the creak loud, and pulled his blanket tighter. As he walked up the path to the house, birds sang the welcome to the new day. He didn't feel their brightness.

Everything was quiet in the house. The burglar alarm

buzzed. A tap dripped. Other than that, there was nothing. It was too big for just the two of them but Helena wouldn't leave. The place was filled with memories. He didn't mind that. Cause and effect, that's what memories are, the impact of an event embedded into the mind. And more than the mind. Every room took them back to when they met. Her sorrow. How she'd held onto him as she sobbed.

Cause and effect. Ripples.

Helena was still in bed. The alarm would sound soon and she'd go through her morning routines. They'd talk, just polite pleasantries, like two strangers forced to share a space. But he needed her. Her presence was like a diversion. It made his life look normal. She concealed him.

She would be getting ready to go to work shortly. He didn't want to be there when she got up.

He left the house, blinking at the morning sun. His eyes felt heavy. He had to get his control back.

And at that thought, he felt the first simmer of anger. If nothing else, he could hit back at those who could hurt him. If his life was changing, so must the lives of others.

Joe was impatient as he waited on his balcony. He'd been ready for fifteen minutes but Ruby was still taking her time. The morning was underway outside, the streets already clogged, the trains and trams busy over the bridges. Where was she? It was school she was going to, not a night out.

His fingers drummed on the balcony rail, impatient to get the day underway so that he could find out more about Mark Proctor. Even the view failed to calm him, as it usually would.

There was a noise behind him. The swish of the balcony door. Ruby was there, a canvas bag slung over one shoulder. She was wearing make-up and her hair looked like it had been curled. He was about to say something, knowing that she was dressed like that because their mother wasn't there to tell her otherwise, but he didn't want to fall out with her. Was it really that important?

'Come on,' he said. 'Let's get you to school.'

He was silent as they walked through the apartment building, and in the lift on the way to the underground car park. He passed a few people in the building who were leaving for work. Some of them cast a suspicious eye over Ruby, a dolled-up schoolgirl leaving an apartment complex with a single man. Joe didn't have the energy to disabuse them of their suspicions.

As they walked through the car park, Ruby's shoes clomped loudly, the soles thick and heavy.

'What's wrong with you today?' she said.

'Nothing,' Joe replied, and pressed his key fob to open the car door. 'Just not used to being a taxi this early.'

Ruby climbed in with a slump and her arms were folded by the time Joe joined her.

He turned towards her. 'I'm sorry, but this is one of the reasons why you have to go home. What if I'd been called to the police station? How would you get to school then?'

She shrugged. 'Get the bus.'

'Do you want to get the bus now?'

Ruby paused, and then shook her head.

'Exactly,' Joe said, and started the engine.

Ruby sulked and looked at her phone, as if she was messaging someone. He turned off the engine and put his forearms on the wheel. He looked across at her.

'What?' Ruby said, without looking up.

He sighed. 'Nothing. Just looking at you, all grown up. It's gone so quickly.'

'Stop it, you're getting all weird,' she said.

'You know that if anything happened to you, we'd be devastated. That's why I need to know you're safe. I don't know if I can do that as well as Mum.'

'Devastated?' Ruby said, and lowered her phone. 'I'd want

much more than that. I'd want you outside the town hall with candles.'

'It's not funny,' he said.

'So stop saying stupid stuff. We're going to be late.'

Joe turned the engine back on and reversed out of his space. He drove up the ramp, towards the bright sheet of daylight, and turned onto the road as if to go towards Ruby's school. Just as he joined the slow-moving traffic, there was someone ahead staring straight at his car, standing, rooted to the spot, his hands in his pockets. Except he was against the sun so Joe could only get the outline, like a cutout figure.

Joe lowered his sun visor to get a better view, just to make sure, but by the time he could see with less glare, the person had gone.

Ruby turned to look. 'Who was that?' she said. 'He looked like he was watching us.'

'No, I'm sure he wasn't,' Joe said, unconvinced.

'I saw him before.'

'When?'

'When I was getting ready. I could see him near the corner, looking up at the apartment.'

'Why didn't you say something?'

'Because there are a lot of apartments. He could have been waiting for anyone.'

Joe's hands tensed around the steering wheel. Who was waiting outside his apartment building? And why?

Twenty-two

Sam had already been up for nearly two hours. He didn't want to wish away the childhood of his two daughters, Emily and Amy, but he longed for them to acquire adult sleeping patterns.

He'd opted to get up so that Alice could get some sleep, but it left him needing coffee. The girls were at the breakfast table, chirping away to each other and munching on cereal. He could see them through the glass in the door, but he enjoyed listening to them more. Aged two and four, it was the last precious few months before school started; Emily spoke garbled nonsense as Amy used her younger sister as a sounding board for whatever she had planned for the day ahead. It would all change when Amy started school. Sam had seen what happened then, from the moans of his colleagues. Regular birthday parties meant weekends lost in play centres, and then the arguments over homework. What lay ahead was an end to this magic, and he knew he would miss it.

It was different for Alice. Sam knew she was feeling cooped up in the house and that she was thinking of going back to work once Emily started school, or even a college course. Anything but stay at home all day, was how Sam interpreted it. He understood completely. He needed to work. Alice deserved that too.

There was the steady thump of feet on the stairs, and then Alice came into the kitchen. Her hair was dishevelled and there were lines on one side of her face where she had been lying on a crease in the sheet.

'I'm tired,' she said in a drawl.

He looked up and down her body in an exaggerated way. 'But sexy,' he said. And he meant it. She'd cut her blonde hair into a much shorter style, elfin-like, which suited her sharp features: the cute point of her chin, the outline of her cheekbones, her eyes wide and blue. He'd fallen for her the first time he saw her, a sudden rush of adolescent desire, and the wonder had never left him, that someone as beautiful as Alice would be with him.

It drew a smile from her, and she went to him and put her arms round his waist. She buried her face into his chest and he kissed the top of her head, enjoying the feel of her body against his. He reached round her to put his cup down before putting one arm around her shoulders, the other on her bottom, the silkiness of her short nightdress creating static on his hands.

'So what have you got on today?' he said.

'Much of the usual,' she said, her voice muffled. 'I might take the girls into town.'

'You'll never get these times back, you do know that.' He started to lift up her nightdress, wanting to feel her naked skin under his hand.

She laughed and pulled away. 'Easy, tiger,' she said, and reached round him to flick on the kettle.

Sam smiled. 'I've got to go anyway.'

'We could meet up later. My parents could have the girls for an hour.'

'The first days of a murder case are hectic,' he said, but when her smile faded he added, 'I'll try though.'

'I'd like that,' she said.

He kissed her and then opened the kitchen door to say goodbye to Emily and Amy. They shrieked and waved and then he was gone.

It felt suddenly quiet when he got outside. The calm of his suburban street, a bulb of a cul-de-sac. He said hello to his neighbour, who was climbing into his four-wheel drive, ready for the journey along the flat streets. His neighbour waved back. Sam had lived next door to this man for six years and didn't even know his surname.

As he sat in his car, getting ready to set off, he remembered how Joe had been the night before: distant but somehow trying to reach out. Joe had touched his arm, as if to ask him to stay, but then held back, the moment gone. Something wasn't right.

He pulled out his phone and texted Joe: *Everything okay?*

Sam waited for a reply, under the pretence of looking for some music to put on in the car. After a few minutes, Joe replied, *Need to talk.*

Sam had been right. He texted back, *Meet me at the station.*

He turned on the engine and set off, disquieted by the uneasy feeling that the day was going to become stranger than it had started.

Twenty-three

Joe waited for Sam outside the police station. His car window was open to let in some sounds; he didn't know what lay ahead for the day and wanted to savour it. All he could hear was the steady hum of traffic noise. All those cars filled with people who had started the day with no worries. He was jealous of them, and longed for how he'd felt just a couple of days earlier, when Mark Proctor had been just a hooded figure in his past. A ghost, a shadow. Becoming real had changed everything.

He thought about leaving and not telling Sam anything, but movement in his rear-view mirror caught his eye. Sam's stride was purposeful, his jacket over his arm.

Joe clicked the unlock button and carried on looking forward as Sam climbed in.

'Is this about Ruby?' Sam said.

Joe thought of how to answer that. This was the moment when he could still walk away from it and leave Sam out of it. He looked at Sam and saw the weary contentment in his eyes. The early mornings, the family routines, the very ordinariness of his life. Joe didn't want to take that away from him.

But Sam needed to know. Ellie's murder had shaped Sam's career as much as it had determined his own.

Joe shook his head. 'No, it's not about Ruby. Nothing as simple as that.'

'So go on, talk to me.'

Joe spotted Sam glance at his watch.

'It's about Ellie,' Joe said.

'What do you mean?'

'Go back a couple of years. Do you remember how I told you that I'd seen a man follow Ellie down the path where she was found and that I'd done nothing about it, hadn't told anyone?'

Sam's jaw clenched. 'Of course I remember,' he said. 'How could I forget that my own brother had kept quiet about my sister's murderer just because he was scared he'd cop for some blame?'

'I was scared,' Joe said. 'I was just a kid.'

'You were eighteen that day. You'd become a man, or at least that was the theory.'

Joe closed his eyes for a moment and put his fingers to his forehead. 'I didn't come here to have an argument.'

'So what is it?' Sam said. 'Did you wake up this morning with some kind of delayed guilt trip?'

'And whatever happened to understanding human frailty?' Joe said, his voice rising, his eyes opening again. 'Maybe you've been in the police too long. Not everything is black and white. People do stupid things or make wrong decisions. I should know, I deal with it every day. Yes, I got it wrong, but let's just say that knowing I could have stopped my little sister getting murdered isn't exactly a great feeling.' He banged his hand on the steering wheel. 'Forget it. Go on, go inside.'

Sam went for the door handle, but just as he pulled on the lever Joe reached out and grabbed him by the forearm.

Sam looked round. 'What is it?'

'The man I saw,' Joe said, taking a deep breath. 'Do you remember what I told you I would do if I ever saw him again?'

'Yes, I do. You said you'd kill him.'

Joe stayed silent.

Sam's brow creased. Realisation grew in his eyes. 'You've seen him?' he said, his mouth dropping open.

Joe paused, knowing that once he said the word, everything would change for Sam. But he deserved the truth.

'Yes, I have.'

Sam sat back in the car seat and looked out of the window. Joe let the silence grow. After a few minutes, Sam turned back to him and said, 'Where?'

'At a police station early yesterday morning. He'd been arrested for burglary at the car compound. His name is Mark Proctor.'

'Are you sure it's him? It was a long time ago.'

'I know all of that, and it was a fleeting glimpse from a distance, and his hood was up. I know exactly how I would defend him if he were arrested. There is no way he'd be charged; a novice lawyer could get him off, but I knew it was him straight away. His face has been burnt into my memory. There is no way I'd get it wrong. I was certain, absolutely positive. It wasn't just a sighting. It was an emotion too, the knowledge that he was in front of me, talking to me, oblivious. Ellie's killer, after all these years.'

Sam put his hand to his forehead and closed his eyes. His look of weary contentment was gone, replaced by something much deeper, the pain of what had been done seventeen years earlier. When he opened his eyes again, he said, 'So what are you going to do?'

'Yesterday, I thought I could kill him.'

Sam snorted in derision. 'Don't be so stupid. What good will that do?' When Joe didn't respond, Sam added, 'You'll throw away your life just to take away his. And don't forget he'll die an innocent man, because you won't be able to prove that he killed Ellie. None of us can. So all your noble act will do is make you a cold-blooded killer, murdering an innocent man, and no one will care what you believed.'

'Like I said, that was yesterday.'

'And today?'

'I just want to make it right, but the system is all skewed. He'll never pay for what he did, and for as long as he's alive, someone else is at risk. What if he's done it again? People like him often do.'

'Do you think I don't know that? Do you think I don't know how the system is twisted, because it always seems to be in favour of people like this guy, this Mark Proctor, whoever he is. People like you exploit it, for profit. That's how it's always been.'

'This is different. This isn't about you and me now. It's about Ellie.'

'Don't turn the guilt onto me,' Sam snapped. 'If you'd shown more courage all those years ago, we might not be having this conversation.'

'I know that,' Joe said. 'I think about that all the time. So let me put it right.'

'You've given me his name,' Sam said. 'The minute I go in there, I report it.'

'No, not yet.'

'Why not?'

'Because it's too early. Gina told me how little evidence there was. Do you think your Cold Case Unit will be interested in my recollection? Of course they won't. It's too vague, too late, I know that. So we need more than just his name. We need to investigate him so that they take it seriously.'

'How come this is becoming a "we"?'

'Ellie was our sister,' Joe said. 'Let's work together on this one, find out more about him. I'm looking into him from my side. You find out what you can from yours. Once we get enough, take the lot to the Cold Case Unit.'

Sam reached for the handle and threw open the door. 'How do I know that you're not just trying to find out about him so that you can carry out your threat, that you're not sure about Mark Proctor so you want me to shore up your doubts?'

'You don't,' Joe said.

Sam slammed the car door and marched towards the police station entrance.

Joe's fingers were white with tightness as he gripped the steering wheel and stared after his brother.

He started the engine, his jaw clenched. There was someone else who needed to be told about Mark Proctor, and this would be even more difficult.

Twenty-four

Sam's mind was reeling as he walked through the station, Joe's words spinning in his mind. Until that moment, the day had been all about the murder of Henry Mason, the tense start of another investigation. Now, everything had changed. It was about Ellie's killer. Could he have been under arrest so recently? Could it be so convenient?

He was sure Joe was wrong. Joe spent his working life finding doubts in certainties, but yet saw no doubt when there must be uncertainties. It was so long ago. People change. They get older or fatter or greyer. Sometimes they change hardly at all, but seventeen years? How could he be so sure?

The Incident Room was busy when he walked in, dragging him back into the day, like someone turning up the volume slowly, the meeting with Joe fading slightly. The atmosphere was filled with that hushed clamour, everyone on the phones but trying not to disturb each other.

Sam walked over to the terminal he used by the window and logged on, throwing his jacket around the back of the chair.

Charlotte was sitting opposite. She threw a newspaper onto his desk. The *Manchester Press*. 'Have you seen the front page?'

Sam looked down and said, 'Oh yeah,' without taking it in.

'Try reading it this time.'

Sam sighed.

Charlotte folded her arms. 'Everything all right?'

He looked to her as his computer whirred itself awake. 'Sorry, I'm a bit distracted.'

'What is it?'

Sam couldn't say what was really on his mind. 'It's about Ruby,' he said, deflecting. 'She's staying at Joe's for a while and I'm worried about Mum.'

'Teenage girls can be worse than boys,' Charlotte said. 'Check out the paper.'

Sam looked down again, but he read it this time. THE DOMINO KILLER was emblazoned on the front page, with pictures of Keith Welsby and Henry Mason underneath, along with a blank rectangle containing just a question mark.

'What the hell?' He checked the byline. Lauren Spicer, the reporter who'd been hanging around the day before. 'Who's leaked?'

'It wasn't me, and I'm guessing it wasn't you,' Charlotte said. 'But look who's giving the quotes: our dear Chief Inspector Brabham.'

Sam read quickly. Brabham was quoted giving a summary of what had been said at an earlier press conference, except he scoffed at the suggestion of the name Domino Killer, telling the reporter that 'giving titles to people who kill gives them notoriety'.

'He was the first person to use the name,' Sam said.

'Exactly, but it gets his face in the paper. Look at his suit today.'

Sam looked over. Brabham was always smart, but today his suit looked new, tight to his body, and Sam thought he could see creases in his shirt where it had been folded in its wrapper.

'What, you think Brabham leaked a name so he could deny it?' Sam said.

'Have you heard anyone else use the name?'

'But it doesn't even make sense. There are only two deaths. That's not a domino effect.'

'It doesn't have to make sense,' Charlotte said. 'It just has to keep his profile high.'

Sam rubbed his eyes. He felt tired already.

'Here, I'll get you a drink,' she said, and grabbed the mug from his desk, rings around the inside from coffees drunk but not washed away properly.

As soon as she was out of sight, Sam's mind flashed back to what Joe had told him. He typed in the name 'Mark Proctor', and the entry from two nights ago came up.

It was the only entry against his name. His life before his recent arrest was invisible. No history, no intelligence, just the report from a bizarre incident two nights earlier, when he broke into the police compound to take his car back, before setting it alight.

Sam read the confidential report, the one completed by the officer in the case but never seen by the defence. Mark Proctor was a respectable man. A financial adviser. Married. No convictions. Why would he be breaking into the compound?

Sam knew there was only one answer: he had something to hide.

He went to the witness statements next, already uploaded onto the police server.

It had been a routine stop. Proctor had been driving home when he passed a traffic patrol car. They have cameras that scan oncoming traffic; if a car flashes up as not being on the insurance database, it's pulled over.

The statement was brief. Proctor hadn't said much; just waited until the recovery truck arrived and then walked off as his car was taken away, his ticket in his hand.

A few hours later, the car was ablaze and Proctor was in the back of a police van. Joe had turned up and his client had said nothing. And now Joe was convinced that he was responsible for Ellie's murder.

Sam needed to find out more about Mark Proctor, if for no

other reason than to persuade Joe that he had nothing to do with Ellie, so that he didn't do anything stupid.

Then something occurred to him. The murder of Henry Mason. Proctor had been driving his car at around that time. It was tenuous, but it gave Sam an excuse to look further into it.

He went back to the witness statement and found a mobile number listed on the back of it.

Sam picked up the phone and dialled. It rang out for a while, until a sleepy voice said, 'Hello?'

'PC Wilkins?'

A pause, and then, 'Yes?'

'Sorry to disturb you at home. It's DC Parker from the Major Incident Team. We're looking into a murder the night before last, and I understand you stopped someone in a car.'

There was the rustle of bedclothes and then the voice became clearer. 'I stopped a few people in cars. I'm a traffic officer.'

'This was a car you impounded.'

A short laugh. 'The guy who pinched his own car back from the compound? Yeah, a strange one, that.'

'What can you tell me?'

'Not much. Just a routine stop. He tried to charm us at first, you know, all the "yes officer, no officer" stuff you get, best buddy act, but it didn't get anywhere with me. I've heard it all before.'

'How did he come across?'

'Nice guy, if I'm honest. All we want is to do our job and get no grief, and he didn't give us any.' A pause, and then, 'There was one thing, though.'

'Yes?'

'All the time I was speaking to him, he was pleasant and friendly, understood that I was just doing my duty, but as I pulled away, once the tow-truck had taken the car away, I spotted him in my mirror, and he was staring as I went. Just like that, his arms by his side, staring. It seemed a bit weird.'

Sam frowned. 'Okay, thank you.' And he hung up.

Before he had chance to think any more about it, Charlotte arrived and put the cup on his desk. 'We've had a development,' she said.

He clicked off the screen. 'Go on.'

'They've found some suspect web searches on Henry Mason's computer: Lolita. Underage babes. Preteen. All the nasty stuff you'd expect.'

'Any images?'

'Not yet, but you don't come across search terms like that accidentally; he'd gone looking. Is that behind the fractured marriage: he'd been looking away from home but for someone younger than his wife?'

'Younger than all wives, by the sound of it,' Sam said. 'But it didn't look like that in the park. You know how paedophiles work. They do everything in secret, gain the trust of their victims. They don't hang around in parks with flowers, like someone on a date.'

'We've got the job of digging into that side of his life.' Charlotte said. 'At least we get a trip out of the office. We'll speak to the people he worked with, his friends, see if we can find a darker side his wife doesn't know about. Drink that and we'll go.'

Sam raised his cup in agreement, but his mind was a long way from a man battered to death in a park. He was thinking about Mark Proctor, and what he could do to track him down.

Twenty-five

Joe was nervous as he walked towards his office. This was the moment he'd been putting off: admitting the secret he'd held for so many years to the one person who should have known all along.

He turned round to look at the scene around him. The gardens, the rhododendron bushes blossoming over the metal railings, the slow bustle of people, men and women in dark suits, some carrying coffee, others grabbing a last cigarette before the office confines stubbed out their habit for a few hours. White sash windows in brick fronts. This was his day, the scene that greeted him most mornings, but everything seemed different somehow. And it was because of Mark Proctor. This was where he became real, all of his details in a slender file. His address. His signature.

He looked up at the building. Gina was watching him from a window.

Marion greeted him in the usual way as he breezed past. 'Can you call Gina and ask her to go to my room,' he said to her and then took the stairs two at a time. When he got to his room, he leaned back against the doorjamb, his heart pounding. As he heard her footsteps in the corridor, he stepped away from the door.

When she came in, she held up two files and said, 'Your clients for the morning: an assault outside a restaurant, some road rage thing, two men who wouldn't walk away. And I've arranged a prison visit for you later. Someone who reckons he was fitted up by someone to take the blame for a murder.'

'I'm not interested.'

Gina frowned. 'You all right, Joe? I saw you walking in. You looked agitated.'

'We need to talk.'

'What's going on? When you get like this, it's usually bad news.'

'This isn't about me,' he said. 'It's about Ellie.'

'Ellie? I don't understand.'

Joe took a deep breath. This was it. Once he said it, there was no going back.

'You said yesterday that there were no suspects for Ellie's murder,' he said. 'I want to know the truth. You weren't holding back to protect yourself, or the investigation?' Joe tried to bore into Gina's eyes, to gauge her response. 'I don't mean lines of inquiry; I mean actual suspects. Anyone you think might have done it but just couldn't prove it?'

Gina flushed, her eyes angry. She took a deep breath before speaking slowly and deliberately. 'You're accusing me of lying to you about Ellie's murder. I've never done that. She was your sister so I'll let it go, but don't ever accuse me of lying again. We've known each other too long for this.'

'Thank you, I believe you,' he said.

'Ellie's case was one of the most frustrating investigations I've ever been involved with,' Gina continued. 'It was a horrible crime, sick and depraved, and whoever killed her was bound to do it again. It wasn't just that, though, because all murders are horrible, a waste of a life. Ellie's youth just made it more so. No, it was the emptiness of the investigation, that there were no good leads at all. It was impossible to track down any cars in the area because it was just after school closing time, so there were cars everywhere. There were people everywhere, it seemed, except down that path where Ellie was murdered. I'm sorry, Joe.' A pause, and then, 'What's this about? Why now?'

Joe thought about how to phrase it, and realised that there was no other way than directly. 'There was an eyewitness. Me.'

Gina opened her mouth as if to say something but stopped and cocked her head. 'What do you mean?' she said eventually.

'I saw him. I was walking home from college and Ellie was walking in front of me. She was some distance away. She had her headphones on and I didn't want to walk with her anyway. It was my eighteenth birthday; walking with my annoying little sister wasn't on my list for the day.'

'Joe, I don't understand.'

'I watched her head into that wooded path, where we'd always told her not to go. There was a man there, in a hooded top. He looked at me and then followed Ellie down the path.'

Gina's mouth hung open, her eyes wide in disbelief. 'Joe?'

'I faltered. I should have followed her, because I felt uneasy, but then I told myself that she'd be all right. She was so close to home. Why would she be at risk?'

'I can't believe you're telling me this.' Her hands were on her hips. She was shaking her head, her cheeks flushed. The steady tick of the clock filled the tense silence until she slammed her hand on the desk, making Joe jump and look at her. 'You should have told me!'

'Do you think I don't know that?' he said. His throat tightened and the sharp sting of tears made him blink. 'Don't you think I wish I'd done it differently, that I hadn't been such a coward back then, more worried about being blamed than finding her killer? But it wouldn't have brought her back. I was just a kid; eighteen was just a number. I was scared, and because I stayed quiet then, I've been tormented by it ever since. Nothing you can say will hurt me more than my own thoughts.'

'What about the fact that you might have allowed him to kill again?' Gina said, her voice rising. 'People like Ellie's killer don't do something like that as a random act, a one-off, an experiment. They build up to it, spend years fantasising about it, and once they act on it, they do it again and again until they're caught. Even if Ellie was the first, she won't have been the last.'

Joe didn't respond to that. It was something he'd considered through all of those years: that his silence had cost the lives of other people. It added to his guilt.

'Whatever I could tell you couldn't have caught him, though,' he said.

'Is that the best you can do?'

'I asked you if there were any suspects and you said no, so it wouldn't have narrowed anything down.'

'But it might have helped with an appeal,' Gina said, exasperated. 'Anything helps, you know that. If you'd have told us what he was wearing, or his age or his build, or just about fucking anything, someone else might have seen him. They might have come forward with a better description, or even a name.'

'All right, I get it,' he said. 'I messed up, I know that. I've always known that.'

'It's not just that,' she said, tears in her eyes now. 'You've made me feel insignificant, because I tried to look out for you. I felt guilty that I couldn't find Ellie's killer; it was my responsibility to do that. All the time, you were keeping this from me.'

'It was our tragedy, not yours,' Joe said, but as soon as he saw the colour rise in Gina's cheeks, he wished he could take the words back.

'I feel like I don't know you,' Gina said, shaking her head. 'I feel let down, betrayed, and lots of other emotions I can't quite work out.'

'Gina, I'm sorry. But it's not about us any more. This thing has driven me. There's a darkness in here that you haven't seen.' And Joe slapped his chest with the palm of his hand. 'Do you know why I became a criminal lawyer? Because it was the one career I could have where I might see him again. Like you say, they don't stop at one. I've dreamed of revenge ever since, to feel my own hands around his neck. This is why I'm telling you now.'

'Let's hope you never meet the guy then. For your sake.'

Joe didn't respond. He didn't raise an eyebrow or give a shrug, nothing to give away the truth, but Gina guessed it from his silence.

'You've seen him,' she said, her hand going to her mouth.

Joe nodded.

They both stayed silent as Joe let Gina take it in. She stared at the files on the desk, tapping her index finger against her thumb, until she looked up and said, 'Who is he?'

'Mark Proctor.'

Gina burst out in a laugh. 'Mark Proctor. You're kidding?'

Joe shrugged.

'You're serious?' she said. 'He's small-time. The police are just angry that a car was stolen from their garage. They had to get someone, and by making it Proctor they're hoping he's too worried about himself to make a fuss about the police losing his car. The most they can show is that he didn't have any insurance.'

'What did you make of him?'

'Quiet, but friendly enough. Just unlucky to be caught up in a situation. There was no suspect in Ellie's case, and the name of Mark Proctor never came up. I would remember him, the name at least. Definitely no Mark Proctor.'

'I knew it was him as soon as I saw him.'

She shook her head. 'That's not enough. Think like a lawyer. What would you say to a witness saying the same as you?'

Joe didn't have to say it. They both knew the question: have you ever been on the street and about to say hello to someone, only to realise at the last moment that it wasn't who you thought it was? It was the slam-dunk question in any recognition case: say no, and the witness isn't believed, because everyone's done it; say yes and the witness has admitted that mistakes in recognition are made. Heads we win, tails you lose.

'That's why I'm going after more.'

'What the hell are you talking about, Joe?'

'I'm going to find out more about Proctor. We can both do it. Work with me, Gina. I want to present evidence to the police, because a name won't be enough. My evidence won't be enough.'

'You should have done more for me, all those years ago.' She shook her head. 'What are you hoping to find that the police won't?'

'I know his sister.'

'You what? How the hell do you know her?'

'I looked her up and took her out last night. Gina, I need to know more about him, to dig deeper with her, find out his secrets, follow him.'

'Joe, it's no good. You've left it too late. And for us.'

'What do you mean?'

'What do you think? Have you any idea how angry I am? I feel betrayed. I've tried to look after you through the years. I don't do maternal, but for you, I wanted to protect you. But now?' She shook her head. 'You've broken everything. Goodbye, Joe.'

She walked towards the door. As she passed Joe, he reached out and grabbed her arm. 'What do you mean, goodbye?'

'What do you think I mean?' she said, pulling her arm away.

'I quit. I need some time on my own. I'm sorry, Joe, but I can't look at you. Not right now.'

And with that, she went.

Joe went to the window and looked out. Gina rushed out onto the street. Her hand went to her cheeks to wipe something away. Tears, he presumed. As she went into the park, he lost sight of her behind the leaves and blooms.

He grabbed the court file and headed for the door. He needed to get rid of his client and then he was going after Proctor.

Twenty-six

Sam could feel Charlotte's gaze on him as he drove. He was turning over the news about Mark Proctor in his head but none of it made any sense. Joe's recollection had to be wrong. And what if he helped? Joe reckoned he wanted to bring Proctor before the courts, but that isn't what he'd said before he knew his identity. He'd only ever thought about killing him. Was Joe using Sam to shore up his doubts so that he could carry out his threat? That would drag Sam into a conspiracy.

'You're quiet,' Charlotte said.

He smiled, but it was thin. 'Just some personal stuff I'm dealing with.'

'If you need to talk, remember your friends.'

His smile grew at that. 'Thank you.'

They pulled into the car park outside police headquarters, negotiating the security barrier and then parking in the furthest spot, giving themselves a long walk.

The Force headquarters was on a business park close to the city centre, just about on the spot where Manchester United first started out as a football team for the nearby railway yards. Now, it was surrounded by office complexes and accessed by a bland route of tarmac and roundabouts, livened by sculptures that aimed to fool those who had to work there that it was bright and cutting edge. Sam didn't see it quite like that.

Once there, you were stuck, far away from anywhere worth a walk, staring through huge windows and willing the clock forward.

Sam preferred the location of his squad, in their run-down old station close to the clatter and noise of a small town on the edge of the city. He enjoyed the chance to get away for his lunch, hearing people, just something different from the daily trudge through cruelty and murder; something ordinary, mundane. Being locked away in a glass box on a business park would chip away at his soul.

Something had been done to make it seem like an upgrade. Over-priced art dominated the entrance and quotes by figures from history lined the walls, meant to be inspirational, although Sam noted that it was always the top brass that benefited from high-priced improvements. The exterior was like an out-of-town hotel, windows interrupting the concrete exterior at regular intervals, but at night it lit up like a blue police lamp. It was supposed to be a beacon to the rest of the city, reassurance that the police were there. Sam saw it more as an acceptance that the police had been forced into retreat, sheltered behind concrete bollards so that a van couldn't drive up to it and blow the place into small pieces.

'It's definitely nothing about the job?' Charlotte said, as they skipped up the steps towards the large glass entrance, an image of Robert Peel bearing down on them. 'Don't exclude me so that you can be the hero.'

He stopped and grabbed the sleeve of her jacket. She turned to look at him, surprise in her eyes. 'I'm not hiding anything from you,' he said. 'Like I said, it's personal. I'm fine, though. Just something I've got to work out.'

'Okay, I'm sorry,' she said. 'Come on, let's get this computer sorted.'

They were there to see the computer examiner, the man who had the job of analysing the contents of Henry Mason's hard drives. He'd already found some search terms that suggested he liked girls who were too young. Sam was hoping for more, because the internet gave up a person's secrets, those places they look when they think no one is watching.

They made their way through the large atrium, with tables where people ate their lunch, more like a motorway service station than the old-style police canteens that served glorious food for next to nothing. The tables were busy with people taking a break, the offices overlooking it just glass cubes.

The corridors were carpeted and new, so everything felt plush as they went, following the directions of the security guard at the front of the building, until they knocked on the door of a small office and went inside.

'Tony Davies?' Sam asked.

A man sitting at a desk in the furthest corner of the room looked up from his monitor and said, 'That's me. You here about Henry Mason?'

'That's us,' Charlotte said, and turned to Sam. 'I called ahead.' She walked over, Sam just behind.

Tony was a small man with bushy eyebrows and a shirt with coffee stains on the front. He spoke quickly and nervously, so that he almost had a stammer, his words trying to come out too fast.

'I haven't found much else,' he said. 'I've been all over his drives, everywhere. There's nothing encrypted or saved, no hidden folders.'

'So he doesn't keep any kiddie porn?' Sam said.

'No, he doesn't keep it, but that doesn't mean he doesn't look. Why would anyone save it on their own computer now? It's all out there on the internet, if you know where to look. But that's the thing: you've got to know where to look. The ones we get now are just hoarders.'

'So what does the computer tell you about Henry Mason?' Sam said.

141

'Computer savvy,' Tony said. 'Internet cleaners, all the malware protection, and his clean-up software was set at a really strict level, so that whatever he looks at on the internet it can't be recovered. But he tried a different browser and it didn't clean up as well.'

He reached behind and picked up a disc. 'This is all the emails from the last six months, plus all the files from his documents folder. There's nothing in his pictures except for family photos and cars.'

Sam took it from him. At least it gave him something to look through, to take his mind from what Joe had told him.

'I looked through his other folders, because people sometimes hide things in program folders, but nothing seemed out of place.'

Sam looked at Charlotte, frustrated, but then Tony said, 'There is one thing, though.'

When Sam turned back to him, Tony was smiling. This was the postscript, the silver lining.

'What is it?'

'Online chat. I found fragments of conversation in the internet cache. Just snippets, the occasional sentence. It was sexual, though.' And he passed over a printout with words appearing randomly, interspersed by symbols.

'It's where the software has tried to overwrite the data but not got everything,' Tony said.

Sam skimmed through the printout. It contained long paragraphs of symbols and random letters, but occasionally a phrase or word would appear. It was sleazy, with words like 'fuck' and 'cunt' appearing like someone had tried to delete the expletives but ended up deleting everything but.

'Who was he speaking to?' Charlotte said, glancing over Sam's shoulder.

'This is where it gets interesting,' Tony said. 'No site name, but I have a username: vodkagirl.'

Someone young but up for fun, Sam thought.

'But that's only any use if we know where the username is from,' Charlotte said.

'You're the detectives. But look at the fifth page. I've circled a word. It appears twice.'

Sam turned to that page and he whistled. Surrounded in red pen was the word 'meet'. They had something.

'Come on, back to the station,' Sam said.

They walked back to the car with more urgency. Henry Mason's story was beginning to unfold.

Twenty-seven

He drove aimlessly, wanting to avoid the stillness of his house. He was waiting for the message. His phone was on the passenger seat. At every junction, every red light, he glanced across, looking for the flashing light that told him that there was news, but it was never there.

So he kept on driving, thinking all the time of his box and revisiting his past. He needed his things back, his precious memories. Without the physical items, all he had was what was left in his head, but it was harder to pin down the memories without something to prompt them.

He'd been outside Joe Parker's office when Gina had stormed out. He'd parked further up the road, deciding what he should do, when she'd walked past him, wiping her eyes, looking down. He remembered her from years before. She'd hardly changed. Pretty then, pretty now. He'd watched her from time to time. He did that with all those involved as he kept watch on his past. He'd breathed death into their lives and watched it spread. It was an intoxicating power.

He checked on Joe Parker most of all. He remembered him from the day he'd taken Ellie. He didn't like the word 'killed', because it was more than that. He'd been waiting for Ellie that day. She always took the short cut and he'd decided that day was going to be the day. His first. That made her special. The demand for it had been like a siren in his head, making him want to clamp his hands over his ears.

He'd tried to satisfy it in other ways, with thoughts of her when he was on his own, but the need was still there even when he thought he'd got rid of the desire. He tried abstaining, to get used to the steady burn of what his mind said he craved. It didn't change anything. He realised then that it hadn't been about Ellie.

But Joe had seen him. As soon as he stood up to follow her, he couldn't resist one look back, and there he was, the brother.

He'd followed her anyway. He could always back out. Or maybe it had been a sign, that somehow fate would help him and stop him from acting.

Fate had worked differently. Joe had ignored him. He'd taken the longest route and let Ellie walk to her death. So as the canopy of trees got bigger, and the lighting dissolved into shadow, he'd gone after her. Joe Parker could have saved her. Ellie's own brother had let her down. Everything that followed was down to Joe Parker.

But Ruby was his jewel. A new life born from the misery he'd created; the new life that followed on from the old.

He pulled up close to the woodland where Ellie had died. There were memories there.

Things were changing. He could feel it like a shift in the breeze. And if he couldn't stop whatever came next, he had to make sure people remembered him. Hurt those who hurt you. That had always been his way.

Sam threw his jacket over the back of the chair. The Incident Room was as it had been before; there was no excited buzz that you get with a development, a break in the case. Charlotte sat down and pulled her chair up to Sam's.

'Where do we start looking for this vodkagirl?' Charlotte said.

'Just search the name and see what turns up,' Sam said, and typed it into the search bar.

'Nearly sixty thousand results,' Sam said.

'Try adding "Manchester",' Charlotte said. 'If they were planning to meet, she has to be local.'

Sam typed in then sat back confused. 'Fifteen million hits now.' He went back to the previous search and started to scroll through.

There were links to photo-sharing and social-networking sites, and as they browsed there was nothing that seemed to have any connection to Henry Mason. They were either based overseas or sites that had no real chat facility.

They were on the eleventh page when they clicked on a link that took them to a site called No One Tells.

A lurid homepage of silver lettering on a purple background filled the screen, with photographs in a list. There were some faces, but mainly they were bodies, or body parts, or just a blank square where someone had been unwilling to be identified.

'It's some kind of dating site,' Charlotte said.

'Hardly a dating site,' Sam said. 'Dating sites are full of hope, people looking for shared interests, a good sense of humour and all that. Look at the descriptions here. "Likes it rough". "Loves oral and being dominated". This is somewhere for married people to find affairs. It's just sad and desperate, pages and pages of failed marriages.'

'It fits Henry Mason, but it might not be our site.'

Sam went to the search bar and narrowed the display to women from Manchester. Fifty pages of profiles were shown, with around sixty people on each page.

Sam clicked on a few profiles and the difference from a normal dating site became more obvious. It was a fuck-site, as simple as that. There was no need for anyone to turn up with wine and roses. Just a spare couple of hours and an anything-goes attitude.

'This is making me feel grubby,' Charlotte said.

'There're a lot of people out there looking for someone else,' he said.

He found vodkagirl's profile on the twelfth page, trapped between a woman in her fifties staring into a webcam, glasses down her nose, and a woman who looked like she was wearing a dog collar, the studs gleaming in the picture. Sam clicked on vodkagirl's picture.

After a few seconds, a user profile came up. Sam and Charlotte both leaned closer.

The picture was a silhouette, a young woman backlit, her face in shadow. Her hair was light and long and wavy, her shoulders bare and skinny. It was her profile that caught their attention, though. More particularly, the opening four words: *I'm not really eighteen.*

Sam felt a chill. The site wasn't just about adults.

The words were ambiguous, because it could mean that she was much older, but the rest of the profile made it clear that she was still at school but looking for a man, a real man, to teach her about the world. And her location said she was from Manchester.

'She's underage,' Sam said. 'That fits in with what we know Mason liked, the search terms.'

'It's not as simple as that,' Charlotte said. 'If he met an underage girl, why would he end up dead? And what about Keith Welsby, the teacher? On its own, this dating site link is significant, but a fingerprint connects two dead men. That's the connection we need to explore.'

Sam sighed. Charlotte was right. Vodkagirl was a red herring, just something that Mason was doing before he was killed. His life might have been full of things like that. He'd been murdered for reasons they couldn't fathom, and on the way they'd learned that he liked young girls.

'So do we ignore it?' Sam said.

Charlotte tilted her head as she thought about that. 'What does your gut feeling tell you?'

'Does that beat logic?'

'Sometimes,' she said. 'I trust your instinct.'

'I don't think we should ignore it,' he said. 'If Henry Mason was on this site and chatting to this vodkagirl, he was talking about a "meet", which fits in with what we know about his murder. If we can work out whether it connects with the other murder, we've got something to work on.'

'So let's carry on,' Charlotte said. 'But if there is any connection with Henry Mason, we need to find him on here, and Keith Welsby.' She raised her eyebrows. 'Let's look into the murky world of No One Tells.'

'We'll try there,' Sam said, and pointed to a link to a support page.

'How come?'

'They will have some record of vodkagirl's use of the site. In the internet frauds I did before I joined this squad, the IP addresses used to create online accounts got people. This might be the same, so we might be able to track her down, whoever she is. Or even show that Mason was chatting with her.'

When he looked at the support page, there was just an email address, with all queries to go through there. He started to type:

My name is Detective Constable Sam Parker from Greater Manchester Police. Can someone from your site please contact me as a matter of urgency, in connection with an inquiry into child pornography.

He added his direct line number.

'Not strictly true, but close enough,' Sam said as he clicked SEND. 'If I'd said it was to trace a site user, they'll tell me to get a warrant. This will get a quicker response.'

He browsed the site for a few minutes before his phone rang. The screen on his phone showed a London number.

'What did I tell you?' he said, and picked up the phone. 'Good afternoon, DC Parker speaking.'

'You asked someone to call,' a voice said, the accent southern, the tone hesitant. 'I'm David from the No One Tells website.'

Sam glanced at Charlotte as he spoke. 'Thanks for calling, David. I'm afraid there's a problem with your site. It's being used to facilitate child abuse.'

A pause and then, 'I don't believe that.'

'I'm afraid so. One of your user profiles even states that, more or less. We need to know who's been visiting the profile.'

'I can't disclose that kind of thing,' David said, wariness in his voice now. 'The name of the website is No One Tells, and that includes us. We promise discretion.'

'I don't want to cause you any trouble,' Sam said, 'but I could get your site closed down until all the user profiles are examined. Trace them through their IP addresses.'

'You can't do that.'

'This is a serious investigation.'

'No, you actually can't do that. We use a server based in the Philippines to stop this exact thing. All our traffic goes through there, and everything is held there, all the user data. Like I said, the site is called No One Tells. That includes us.'

David fell silent, and Sam let it fester. All he could hear was the slight nasal rasp of David's breath. After a moment, David said, 'What's the user name?'

'Vodkagirl.'

Sam listened to the tapping of a computer keyboard as David navigated the site. Then there was a sigh. 'I see what youmean,' he said. 'We keep an eye out for things like this, and you aren't allowed to register yourself unless you say you're over eighteen, but she's used the profile to mask it. It won't cause you problems for much longer, though.'

'What do you mean?'

'A user request was sent this morning to close down the profile. We say on the site that it can take two weeks to process it, but it's really in case they change their mind. People were registering and then deregistering all the time, guilt trips and postings, depending on their mood. I can take the profile down now.'

'No, don't do that,' Sam said. 'We need to know who she is. What IP address does she use when she logs on?'

There was a pause before David said, 'I can let you have that, I suppose, seeing as her account is a fraud. We don't allow underage people on here. I'll contact the server. Everyone else is off-limits.' He sighed. 'Look, there are other ways to go about this.'

'Tell me.'

'Have a good look around her profile.'

'What do you mean?'

'I've nothing more to say. Good luck with it. The profile will be gone in fourteen days, and I'll email you with her own IP address.'

'Wait, wait,' Sam said.

A sigh and then, 'What is it?'

'How do you make your money?'

'Easy. The profile is free, and you're allowed to contact five people. You start with a seven-day trial period. After that, if you want to send messages, you've got to buy credits. If you want to contact more than five people, you've got to buy credits.'

'Do a lot of people go on to buy after those first five contacts?'

David laughed. 'There are a lot of desperate people out there.'

'And how will it look on the bank statement?'

'TSJ Publishing,' David said. 'Named after my kids.' And then he hung up.

Sam went back to the bank statements piled on the desk next to his monitor. He thumbed through until he reached the month leading up to Henry Mason's murder. He ran his finger down the columns until he found what he was looking for. He jabbed the bank statement. 'There,' he said. 'TSJ Publishing. A twenty-five-pound payment. I'd presumed it was a magazine subscription. We've got him. Henry Mason was a member and he was buying credits.'

'To chat to vodkagirl,' Charlotte said, nodding.

'So it's about time we did the same,' he said. 'Let's find out about Henry Mason's secret life.'

'Are you going to set up a profile?' Charlotte said.

'Why not? It's a way of speaking directly with someone who had contact with our victim. I'll let Brabham know, so I can monitor it from here.'

'Are you going to tell your wife?' Charlotte said, a glint of amusement in her eye. 'You're going to have to use a personal email. You can't use a police one.'

'I've got an old Google email I never use,' he said, smiling. 'I'll join with that.'

Charlotte watched over his shoulder as he filled in fake details. Six feet two, gym instructor, thirty years of age. 'You need to be careful,' she said. 'You might get a few requests yourself.'

'Reality would chase them away again,' he said. 'I need a username.'

'Make it geographical.'

He typed in 'manchester-guy' and pressed the enter button. The site whirred away for a few seconds, before it flashed up an acceptance page.

'I'm in,' he said. 'I'm about to enter a dark world.'

'Just make sure you cancel once we've checked it out,' Charlotte said. 'You might have emails you can't explain at home.'

Sam navigated to vodkagirl's page and pressed the SEND A MESSAGE button. It flashed up a box.

'How should I start it?' he said.

'Sound hesitant, like you're curious but nervous. It will put her in control, so she thinks.'

'It might not even be a "she",' Sam said.

'So *he'll* get off on the power trip even more.'

Sam started to type.

Hi. I saw your profile. You sound interesting. I'm not used to this kind of thing. Is it okay if I message you?

They both watched the screen for a few minutes, but there was no response.

'Leave the page open and let Brabham know what you're doing,' Charlotte said.

'Good idea,' he said.

As he walked over to the other side of the room, his mind went back to what Joe had said: that the person locked up a couple of nights before was Ellie's killer. He checked his watch. It was nearly lunchtime. He needed to look into what Joe had said. Once people started to drift out, he'd take a look to see what he could find out.

He'd been fighting it all morning, but he was feeling that same burning need for revenge that had fuelled Joe through the years. If Mark Proctor had killed Ellie, he was going to find out. He didn't trust Joe's motives, but if Joe was right, Sam was going to catch him.

Twenty-eight

Joe rushed out of the court building, leaving his client with the Probation Officer. For Joe, the hearing had been about getting it finished. His client had paid Joe to defend an assault allegation, expected some fight, some enthusiasm. Instead, Joe had bullied his client into pleading guilty on a promise that he would avoid prison. It was a promise Joe couldn't keep, it was out of his control, but it got the case finished early.

He called the office as he headed towards Deansgate, to see whether Gina had returned. She hadn't. He tried her phone. It was switched off. He didn't want that. He needed Gina with him.

She was right, he shouldn't have kept the secret, but he had, and there was nothing he could do to change that.

His focus was on Mark Proctor. He had to find out more. Melissa's number was in his wallet.

He stopped as he dug it out. The traffic noise was getting louder so he hung back as he thought about calling her. He closed his eyes for a moment. He felt conflicted. Melissa was Proctor's sister, bound up in all the hatred he felt for him, but he couldn't deny that he'd felt something else the night before. And he'd seen something in her eyes that told him she felt the same. He'd fought against it, though, because it was some great irony that he desired the sister of his own sister's killer, as if the whole situation was meant to taunt him.

He paused as he looked at her phone number. Then her parting glance came back to him.

He called the number. She answered straight away.

'Hello?' she said. Her tone was tentative.

'It's Joe Parker,' he said. 'Can I see you?' There was a pause, so he filled it with, 'I can come to the pub.'

'I'm not working today.'

'Oh, I'm sorry,' Joe said, his cheeks flushing, angry with himself. It had been a bad idea.

'No, don't be,' Melissa said quickly. 'Come to my flat, if you want.' She gave him her address.

Joe hung up and stared at his phone. He thought about whether he was doing the right thing, but then he remembered why he was doing it; it was about Ellie, not Melissa.

The journey didn't take long. He looked up at her apartment building as he climbed out of the taxi. A converted mill, seven storeys of red brick and bright white windows, solid and imposing, one of a few similar blocks still standing in Ancoats.

He straightened his jacket before he pressed her numbers on the keypad. There was a short delay before the control panel fizzed and a cautious voice said, 'Joe?'

'Yes, it's me.'

'Take the lift, fifth floor, and turn left. I'll wait for you.'

A buzzer sounded and Joe pushed at the door and went inside.

The entrance was grand, the inner workings of the mill used to great effect. Iron pillars were painted black and the walls scrubbed of the years of dirt and dust so that the old brickwork shone back bright and clean. Thick oak beams ran across the ceiling, and fastened to one was some old machinery, a black metal wheel hanging down, the look spoiled by the need for health and safety, with black and yellow tape across the edge. The history of the building was evident in every scar of the bricks, every groove in the stone flooring, blunted only by a carpet along the corridors that led away from the entrance.

He took the lift to the fifth floor. Melissa appeared in a doorway further along. She was smiling as he got closer before she turned to go inside.

Her apartment was bright and open. Like the entrance, the walls were exposed brick, broken by paintings on white canvas, just plain squares with a splash of colour on each. There was a kitchen area overlooking a sofa and two big chairs that faced each other across a gnarled wooden table, as if an oak tree had been sliced up and Melissa had ended up with the part with a huge knot along one side.

Joe was drawn to the window. It was almost as high as the room and looked out over the slow movement of the canal. He went to it and looked out.

Melissa appeared behind him, a bottle of beer held out for him. 'It's the view that sold it to me,' she said. 'They've bulldozed most of the Ancoats I knew, but the water stays the same.'

'I chose my apartment for the same reason,' he said. 'Something about the water keeps the city attached to its past.'

Melissa sat down in one of the chairs, a wine glass in her hand. She caught him looking and said, 'I don't make a habit of afternoon drinking, but I'm a bit, you know, nervous.' She drew her knees onto the cushion and her legs underneath her. She was in tight jeans and a T-shirt, clothes for a day off, but Joe felt it again, an unexpected longing.

He looked away, tried to shut it out.

'So is it more about Mark?' she said, her hand twirling a stray strand of hair that was hanging down.

'I need to know more about his past.'

'Will he know you're here?' she said. 'You can't keep secrets from your client.'

'No, he won't.'

'I don't want him to know where I live.'

'Why not?'

'Because we don't speak and he doesn't deserve to see his niece.'

Joe couldn't think of anything to say. There were so many thoughts rushing through his head that they all seemed to get jammed together, not one of them formed enough to make it out.

'He killed your cat,' he said eventually. 'Did he do anything else like that?'

Melissa frowned. 'What kind of defence lawyer are you?'

'I told you, this is personal.'

'But you make it sound like you think he's a psychopath in waiting, that he murdered small animals before moving onto people.'

Joe didn't respond.

Melissa put her glass down. 'What's going on, Joe?'

'I can't tell you. Not yet.'

'When?'

'When I know for certain.'

Melissa shook her head. 'You talk in riddles, Joe Parker.'

'I want to speak to your parents?'

'Not a chance!'

'I need to know about your brother, that's all. His history. There'll be things about him they'll know that you don't.'

Melissa shook her head. 'Not my parents.'

'So you won't help me?'

'You haven't given me a reason to yet. There's so much you're not telling me.'

Joe wanted to tell her, because if he did, she'd understand. She'd tell him about all those moments that they'd always thought strange, because knowing that Mark was a murderer would put it all into context. It would give him the nod that he was right, might even lead him to other people who knew him. To catch Mark Proctor, he had to unravel him and find the beast within.

But he couldn't tell Melissa. Not yet. Family loyalty might still run too deep.

'What do you want from me, Joe?'

'It's complicated,' he said. 'So damn complicated.'

'I thought you were here because you felt something, about us. About me. Did you feel something?'

He swallowed, his cheeks flushed. 'I'm here about your brother.'

'So how can it be complicated?'

He put his head back and stared at the ceiling, oak beams running across the room. He'd headed straight for Melissa and got nowhere. Was there another reason he was there?

There was the sound of movement across from him. Melissa's feet made soft noises on the floor but Joe didn't look up.

He closed his eyes when her hand touched his leg. It was as if she was kneeling in front of him and her hand was just rested on his thigh, but she started to caress his leg with gentle strokes, caring more than sensual, until her hand went higher, towards his hips, her body rising. Her knee parted his and he became aware of her perfume, lightly floral, and the soft gasps of her breaths.

'What are you doing?' he said, his voice low.

'Taking charge,' she said.

Her first kiss was gentle, almost a brush, until he reached for her, the need for her taking him by surprise, his hand going to her hair, pulling her into him, so that her body pressed against his, the sound of their clothes sliding against each other in static crackles. In that moment, he lost sense of everything. Where he was, what he'd been thinking of, Proctor and Gina, what he planned to do. Right then, he was consumed by the quickening of her breath, the beat of his heart, his fingers gripping her hair.

Melissa pulled away. Joe was breathless, his vision blurred.

She stood in front of him. She flicked the button on her jeans and slid them over her hips, kicking them off until she was only in her knickers and T-shirt.

'They're so restrictive,' she said, and smiled, but it was her eyes he noticed. Her gaze was smouldering, direct.

She straddled him in his chair. She pushed against him, the thin silkiness of her panties almost a non-existent barrier.

The image of Mark Proctor flashed into his brain, that final look before he followed Ellie into the woods.

Joe pushed Melissa off and slid out from under her. He stood up and went to the window, his hand in his hair. 'This isn't right,' he said, breathless. 'Not right at all.'

Melissa looked up at him, hurt, embarrassed. She gathered her clothes in her arms and ran to her bedroom.

'Get out!' she shouted, before slamming the door.

Joe didn't go. Instead, he punched the wall in frustration, grazing his knuckles. He'd messed up his best link to Proctor. 'Fuck!'

Twenty-nine

The Incident Room was quiet as Sam sat at his desk. He twirled his seat around and tapped his pen on the desk. Charlotte had gone out for some lunch but Sam had turned down the opportunity to go with her. He wanted to find some solitude so he could make a call. He was still reeling from Joe's news earlier and wanted to find out more. The only people who could help were those on the Cold Case Unit, but he didn't want to be overheard nor use his mobile; whoever he called to resurrect Ellie's case, he wanted them to see that it came from an internal number.

He went back to his computer and scrolled through the phone directory to find the right number to call. He made a note and was about to reach for his phone when Brabham came into the room. He walked straight over to Sam.

'How are you getting on?'

Sam filled him in on Henry Mason's use of the No One Tells site. Brabham curled his lip.

'Is Keith Welsby connected to it?' Brabham said.

'Not that I can find out,' Sam said.

'So why is it relevant? The two murders are connected. Dominoes. If you go down that line alone, you won't discover the link.'

Sam wanted to say that two murders hardly made for a

domino effect but he knew that it wouldn't sway Brabham. He'd spotted a headline and gone for it. Instead, Sam said, 'But it's the secret life Mason had in the final month of his life. Don't we need a full picture of Henry Mason?'

'No, we need relevant evidence to find out who killed him, not to destroy his character. Do you think his widow will thank you for laying bare his secrets?'

'We don't know it's irrelevant yet, though.'

'But it's not connected to Welsby,' Brabham said. 'That's what we need to find.'

'So what do I do about it?'

'Keep tracing Mason's friends and associates. We need that link, because I can assure you of one thing, Parker, that if this is a domino effect, we all know what happens next.' He raised his eyebrows. 'Another one falls.'

Brabham walked away, seemingly happy with his wisdom. Promotion didn't always favour the wise, Sam thought.

His phone buzzed: Alice. *I've got lunch. On the OTH if you want some daylight.*

OTH. Old Town Hall, a small concrete amphitheatre created by its demolition, where curved steps stared through the portico that remained. It was one of the reasons why he didn't want to be based in a new glass and brick block on some business park. The area was still old Manchester, although without the smoke and grime of a hundred years earlier. It was where he escaped to on sunny days, eating his lunch as he watched the sun glint off the canal surface nearby, listening out for the general putter of the barges. Tall chimneys and the occasional large old mill building were visible through the gaps in the trees, redbrick monstrosities that built the city.

He grabbed his jacket and headed outside.

Alice was sitting on one of the concrete steps, watching Emily and Amy run and skip. He was pleased to see them. He needed to talk to Alice; he always felt that way whenever he had a problem to share, because she seemed to know the right thing to do. She'd always been good like that, a soft and gentle hand when he needed it, or a firm push whenever that was more appropriate. It was how she'd been when Ellie died that had made him realise how they were going to stay together: understanding, patient and comforting.

As he stepped into the open concrete space, there were shrieks of laughter and then the sound of running feet. Emily and Amy wrapped themselves around his legs and he felt some of his shadows lift. He ruffled their hair and somehow made his way to Alice without them letting him go. She looked up at him, shielding her eyes from the sun. She was in a white shirt and jeans, a polka-dot silk scarf knotted around her neck. She looked elegant and stylish, and not for the first time Sam realised how lucky he was.

Alice smiled as Sam bent down to kiss her. 'I hope your colleagues are watching.'

'So do I,' he said, which widened her smile. 'I'm glad you stopped by.'

He sat next to her and the girls went back to chasing each other in the circle between them and the old stone façade. She reached behind her and produced a sandwich and a coffee in a paper cup. He took a bite, and said, 'It's been a strange old morning.'

'How so?'

'It's about Joe.'

'It often is,' she said.

'This is different,' Sam said, and went to tell her about his meeting with Joe earlier.

When he'd finished, Alice put her hand to her mouth. 'So Joe is certain about this man?'

'It seems that way.'

'How do you feel?'

'Confused. What if he's wrong?'

161

'It doesn't matter if he's wrong or right,' Alice said. 'You've got to look into it.'

'It's not as simple as that. Joe has always said that if he ever found this man, he'd kill him.'

'He won't though, will he? Not Joe. He's not the violent type. Or is he? Perhaps I don't know him as well as I think I do.'

'He told me that he just wants to build a case against this Proctor so that he can't get away with it. I'm worried that he's just having doubts so he wants me to make sure he's right before he carries out his threat. That would make me look like a conspirator, because they'll find my traces on the police computer.' He sighed. 'What do I do?'

Alice reached for his hand. 'Imagine you're not involved with the case. What would you say to someone with the same predicament?'

'I'd tell them to go to the police, that to handle it properly is the only way to do it.'

'So you know the answer,' she said. 'You just wanted me to help you say it.'

'Yes, I know. Thank you.'

'It's not your job to keep your brother out of trouble. It's up to him what he does, but if you really want to help Joe, let him know you've told whoever has the case; it might just be enough to stop him doing anything rash. He'll be upset and angry with you, but one day he'll wake up in his own apartment, with a lazy day ahead to do whatever he liked rather than going down to breakfast with the rest of the prisoners, and he'll be glad for it.'

He gave her hand a squeeze. 'You're a wise one, thank you,' he said. He took a last bite of his sandwich and checked his watch. 'I'm going to have to go back in. It's good to see you, though. We should make the effort more often.'

As he headed back to work, pausing first to cuddle his daughters, the police station seemed a much darker place.

He snatched up the receiver and dialled the number he'd found before, scribbled onto a yellow Post-it note.

It rang out just twice. 'Cold Case Review Team,' a voice said, clipped and formal.

'It's DC Parker from the Major Incident Team,' Sam said, nerves making his voice tremble. 'I want to ask about an old case. Seventeen years or so. We've had a tip-off about a suspect.'

'Which case is it?'

Sam paused before he said, 'Eleanor Parker.'

There were a few seconds of silence before the voice said, 'Are you a relative?'

That would stall everything. Victim's relatives are treated differently than when speaking cop-to-cop, but there was no point in pretending. 'Give me a break here,' Sam said, lowering his voice. 'She was my sister, but the tip came through the job. I'm passing it on, not looking into it.'

A pause, and then, 'You know I can't tell you anything, but tell me what you've got and I'll see what I can do.'

'Mark Proctor. It was an anonymous tip, from someone who thought I ought to know.'

There was a sigh and then the tapping of fingers on a keyboard. 'This case has been dormant for a long time,' he said. 'They all get looked at every six months, usually looking at the suspects or connected people, to see whether there has been an update, some new pattern, or whether any new forensic advance might help. I'm looking at the last review notes.' A pause, and then, 'I'm sorry, but Eleanor's case goes away again each time. There were no real suspects and no forensic evidence.' Another pause, and then he said again, 'I'm sorry.'

'Just bear that name in mind, that's all. Mark Proctor.' And then Sam hung up.

He sat back in his chair and thought about where he went next. He should be on the No One Tells site, looking at user profiles, looking for Keith Welsby, but he was lost in memories of Ellie. Like so many times before, he tried to recall Ellie that final morning, but he never could. Before she died, the day had been all about Joe and his eighteenth birthday. He'd felt cheated ever since, that he'd been deprived of that one opportunity to say goodbye.

The sound of laughter filtered in from the corridor as Charlotte came back into the room, two male detectives with her, flirting with her. Charlotte went along with it, the looks up and down, but when she turned towards Sam she looked weary.

When she sat down, she said, 'You could have saved me.'

He smiled. 'Sorry about that.'

'So what next?'

Sam thought of Brabham and his order to look for the connection with Keith Welsby, not just to dissect Henry Mason's seedy secret life, but a niggle in Sam's brain told him that there was some relevance there somewhere. He just had to find it.

Or was it something else, that the men who'd contacted vodkagirl were similar to the man who'd targeted Ellie? That was enough to focus his mind.

He turned back to his screen. It was time to go hunting.

Thirty

He pulled up his hood as he lingered at the end of the woodland path. The school day was ending and he was waiting for Ruby.

The place was the same as it had been all those years before. No one noticed him because so much time had passed. When someone died, people looked out for lurkers and everyone held their little ones a bit closer. If they'd looked out for them beforehand, they could have stopped him. They all had to share some of the blame.

He'd expected to feel more, though, going back. Perhaps a tremor of excitement, some nervous energy at the revisit to the same spot, but there was nothing except a sense of familiarity.

His emotions had always been like that. Empty, distant, apart; he'd never felt the same joy other people professed to feel. Everything was clinical, as if it didn't really mean anything. Perhaps it never had. He only felt himself come alive when he was killing, when his nerve endings tingled, his mind sharp and focused. That's what people talked about in the true-crime books he'd researched to try to understand himself. But it'd still felt hollow somehow, until he'd realised that it was the effect on the living that gave him the most pleasure. He observed the bereaved like butterflies trapped under glass. Ellie had been just a vehicle, a way of creating an effect; it was the ripple of her death through the living that excited him.

Being at the same spot didn't have the same resonance. Back then, it was as if he'd been looking through a fisheye lens, just the centre in focus and the rest blurred. His footsteps had been loud, hers too, no other sounds. He was zoned in on her, everything about him that day sharp, everything about Ellie so clear. Her legs fighting against him, the undergrowth rustling. The sound of her school blazer against the ground, her hair snagging on a small twig, the thud of her heels as she kicked against the ground, the creak of his fingers as they gripped her throat.

Then he was gone, running through the trees, heading for the estate on the other side, where he could get lost in the small passageways until he ended up in the large car park where he'd left his car.

They'd called it random, but that was wrong. Ellie had been chosen. He'd followed her and learned her routines. He'd even spoken to her, just to ask directions, gave her a smile. She had been tall and awkward but her innocence smouldered, her eyes large and warm, her smile quick and easy.

That was how he worked. He drove around. He watched. He asked for directions, flashed a smile as he leaned across the passenger seat. He saw how shy they were when they leaned forward.

He wasn't alone, though. He'd spotted others as he travelled around. There was always someone watching from a distance, the long-held desire they didn't act on, as if watching was all they needed to do. If he saw it, he took it.

It was strange how his first had led to something so beautiful: little Ruby, grown up so tall, just like her sister. From his act, new life was born. If he asked Ruby to choose, she'd want Ellie to die so that she could live. Who wouldn't? Everyone begs for their own life in the end.

He'd watched Ruby from a distance as she grew up. Her first day at school, her dress too short for skinny legs, only just sticking out from the hem of her red coat. Sports days. Her move to high school. He'd experienced them all, just the man watching from a distance, a shadow amongst the trees or in a parked car. He'd created her, in his own way; she was his responsibility.

He was shaken from his thoughts by the stream of schoolchildren. Some disappeared into cars parked nearby; others boarded the buses that queued up further along the road. His eyes scanned the pavement as he looked out for her.

He waited twenty minutes, until the crowds thinned out. Ruby always came this way. He knew that from all the times he'd watched her.

He got up from the sign where he'd been leaning and headed towards the school, his hands thrust into his jacket pockets as he walked up a slight rise. Most of the cars were gone. She must have walked a different way.

A sudden burst of anger flared inside him, but then he saw her.

She was scowling, standing with her arms folded, a long canvas bag hanging down to her waist, heavy with schoolbooks.

He smiled as he approached her, disarming, friendly. She didn't look his way. She'd taken her phone out of her pocket and was scrolling through something.

As he drew alongside her, he said, 'Hello, Ruby.'

Ruby looked round, surprised, and then she said, 'I saw you this morning. Hanging around my brother's apartment.' She sounded petulant.

'Yes, sorry, I'm a friend of Joe's,' he said. 'I've been looking for him. Have you seen him?'

'He's coming soon. Supposed to be, anyway.'

He checked his watch. 'I'm going to have to go, sorry. Can you tell him I came looking?'

'Yeah, sure.' He set off walking. Ruby shouted after him, 'Who shall I say was looking for him?'

He turned as he answered. 'Mark,' he said, walking backwards, waving. 'Tell him Mark Proctor came looking.'

When he turned back again to go to his car, his cheeks were flushed and he couldn't stop his grin.

Yes, Joe Parker, he'd known it was you all along. He'd always known. That's why he'd asked for you.

He laughed to himself. Sometimes the smallest of ripples cause the biggest effect.

Thirty-one

Joe tapped on Melissa's bedroom door.

He was confused. He wanted to know about Mark Proctor but he wanted Melissa too. He'd felt it the night before and it had felt so right not long before. But thoughts of Ellie and Proctor had taken away the moment.

Melissa didn't answer. He'd been expecting another expletive, a demand that he leave, but there was just silence.

He pushed open the door. Melissa was sitting on the bed, still in her knickers and T-shirt, her jeans on the floor by her feet.

'Did you expect to find me in here crying?' she said, and looked up to him. 'Is that the game? Get me on the hook and then play with me?'

Joe went to the bed and sat next to her. He looked at her legs. Her skin was pale and her hairs soft. He ran his finger over her thigh, expecting her to pull away, but she didn't.

'There's no game,' he said.

'It's been a long time for me,' she said, not looking at Joe. 'I don't know what the rules are now, but I thought I sensed something in you, that you wanted me, and I liked it. I haven't felt wanted by a man for a while. I misread it. I'm sorry.'

'You didn't read it wrong,' he said. 'And there are no rules. You just go with what feels right.'

'And it didn't feel right for you?'

'Like I said, it's complicated.'

'Because you're my brother's lawyer?'

He gave a small laugh. 'Something like that.'

She turned to him. 'You need to talk to me about Mark.'

Joe was unsure. If he told her, it would change everything. How could he go from this closeness, such as it was, to 'Your brother killed my sister'?

'I will, I promise. Just be patient with me.' He put his arm around her shoulder and kissed the top of her head. Her hair smelled of soft fruit, the remnants of whatever shampoo she'd been using before he arrived. 'If I make you wait, you'll have to see me again.'

'Do you want to see me again?' Her voice was a soft murmur, her head resting on his chest.

'Yes, I do.' And when he said it, he knew that he meant it.

She sat up straight. 'What time is it?'

'Nearly half three,' Joe said.

Her head drooped. 'Shit.'

'What is it?'

'I'm sorry. Carrie will be back from school in fifteen minutes. We can't be found like this.'

School?

'Oh shit, I've got to go too,' he said.

'What is it?'

'My sister is staying with me, just for a couple of days. I need to collect her. I'd forgotten all about it.'

'Not used to the parenting lark?'

He grinned. 'Something like that.'

Melissa stood up to pull on her jeans. He went as if to go, but he paused as he admired her body, enjoying her slender legs as she wiggled herself into her jeans.

She caught him looking and blushed. 'If you want to see them again, come round again. Now go.'

Joe grinned and did as he was told.

Once he was back on the street, he texted Ruby: *Running late. Go to Mum's. I'll collect you.*

A message pinged back: *Too late. On the bus to yours.*

Joe cursed and jogged to the main road, pacing back and forth until a black cab rumbled towards him.

Ruby was walking towards his apartment building as he climbed out of the cab, playing on her phone, hunched over the small screen, tapping something in. 'Hi,' she said, without looking up.

'Ruby, you need to go home.'

'Let me stay a bit longer,' she said. 'I need a break.'

Joe let her into the apartment building and endured her silence as her attention never wavered from her phone. Once in the apartment, she dropped her school bag, heavy with homework, on the floor and sat down on Joe's favourite chair.

Joe put his hands on his hips, splaying his jacket. 'Can you see now why it's easier for you to be at home? I can't always drop everything.'

Ruby didn't look up from her phone when she said, 'Yeah, well, because you didn't make it, I had to put up with your creepy friend.'

A chill ran through him. 'What do you mean?'

'After school. I was waiting for you and this creepy guy came over. He said he was looking for you but he had to go. What was he doing waiting outside a school? Ugh.'

Joe went over to her. He knelt in front of her. 'Who was he?'

She shrugged but didn't take her eyes from her phone. 'Just some random guy.'

He snatched her phone from her. 'Who was he?'

She was about to object but something about the glare in his eyes told her that it was something serious. 'I saw him outside

171

the apartment this morning. Told me to tell you that he'd been there. Said he was called Mark Proctor.'

Joe clenched his fists and closed his eyes as blood rushed to his brain.

This changed everything.

Thirty-two

Sam was looking at vodkagirl's profile again, trying to find some kind of hint. He was still logged in but she hadn't replied. Then he noticed something on the top of the page. A logo of a thumb.

He clicked on it and the logo changed to a thumb with a gold star on it.

Sam sat back. 'What did I just do?'

Charlotte looked over. 'I take it you're not into the social media thing,' she said.

'No, not really. I prefer real life.'

'You've just *liked* her.'

'I did that already. I sent her a message.'

'No, this is something different.' When Sam frowned, she said, 'The site makes money from people making contact with other users. How did you say it worked, that the first five contacts were free but after that you paid for them?'

'Something like that. You buy credits.'

'Think about it, Sam. People aren't going to pay money to send a slew of messages to random strangers, hoping for a response. But what if that person has already hinted that they like you? You might buy some credits to send a message then. You've just told vodkagirl that you like her. It's the site trying to stimulate conversation, because chat pays.'

'Can I tell if anyone else has liked her?'

'Hang on.' Charlotte got closer and took the computer mouse from Sam. She moved the cursor over the thumb icon and it flashed up that 112 people had liked vodkagirl's profile.

Sam groaned in dismay. Over a hundred men responded to the ambiguity of her not being eighteen. The hint was obvious, and there were a lot of men too eager to chase it.

'It must be here somewhere,' Charlotte mumbled, before clicking on a heart symbol underneath the profile picture. A list of thumbnail images appeared, with links to user profiles underneath.

Charlotte grinned. 'It had to be somewhere. The site makes money from online chat, not meetings, so there had to be a way for people to connect with each other. Shared interests, you might call it.'

'Why didn't the guy from the site tell me this?'

'Because it's called No One Tells. He did tell you to search the site, though, to find it for yourself. Now you've done that, you can try to contact these people. You've got seven days before your trial period ends. You need to move quickly.'

Sam thought about that as he looked at the list of profiles. He had to be careful. The whole point of this site, as far as he could see, was for people to find extramarital sex; if he called at their houses, they would clam up, claim they had been the victim of a hoax. No, he had to appeal to their need for discretion. To their fear of being found out.

Geography seemed the obvious filter. Sam made three columns on a sheet of paper. One was for those from the Manchester area, the middle one for anyone within a fifty-mile radius, and the last being further afield. Sam had to assume that most users told the truth about where they lived: sneaking out for a sleazy liaison would be tricky if it involved a hundred-mile trip. It was simply a case of going to each profile and looking at the town or county given, and checking whether they gave away any information that could identify them.

He drafted a message to send to them all:

My name is DC Samuel Parker from the Major Incident
Team in Manchester. I am investigating a case that may
have links with the website of which you are a member, No
One Tells. I need you to contact me as a matter of urgency,
and if you don't, I'm afraid I will need to call at your house
to discuss the case. I understand the need for privacy so
please contact me through the police switchboard or by
using my police email.

He knew it was blunt, but he was banking on the fear of
being found out outweighing the reluctance to call. He needed
to find out about vodkagirl, to see if there was any connection.

'This is only going to work if the person logs in,' Sam said.

'See if there's a different way to make contact?'

Sam went through the user profiles again, until he saw
something.

'There,' he said.

Charlotte leaned in.

'Someone's put their email address into their profile,' he
said.

'Cheap as well as perverted,' she said. 'Going for the direct
contact rather than paying through the site.'

'Except he's slipped up, because that looks like a work email,
not some Hotmail account. We can trace him.'

Sam smiled. Charlotte was right, someone had made a mistake, because the email gave up his name. He went by the
username of cashlover, but his email address identified him as
B. Carter.

Sam put the email address in an internet search bar and on
the first page it identified him as Bruce Carter from a Manchester management consultancy. Bruce's smile beamed out
from the About Us page of the company's website.

'Shall we pay him a visit?' Sam said.

'Why not?' Charlotte said, and logged off her computer.

Just before Sam did the same, he scrolled through the rest of the profile pictures. Most were blank or were of people who thought they were handsome enough to be a magnet. Near the bottom, there was a profile picture showing a Mercedes, nothing else, apart from two letters on a sign behind the car, large and red on a white background. R and D. From Richards Garage, the showroom where Henry Mason had worked.

He grinned. They'd just found Henry Mason.

Thirty-three

'Where was he?' Joe said, gripping Ruby by her arms. 'I need to know everything.'

'You're hurting me.'

'Tell me!'

'Outside school.'

'And what did he say? Exactly.'

'Just what I said. He told me to tell you that he'd been there. And he told me his name: Mark Proctor.'

Joe let go and put his hands on his head. Ruby looked scared. She rubbed her arms and grabbed her phone from where Joe had thrown it.

'Why are you freaking out?'

'Get your bag, we're going.'

'But I want to stay here.'

'You said he was outside the apartment this morning.'

'Yes, hanging about by the corner, just behind the wall,' she said, and she pointed towards the window. 'He was looking up.'

'Come on, we've got to go,' he said, and went to the door.

'Where?'

'Just somewhere.'

'I'm not going home.'

Joe gritted his teeth and went for her. He grabbed her by her arm and pulled her hard towards the door. She screamed and yanked backwards. Tears flashed into her eyes.

'What are you doing, Joe?' she said, her lip trembling.

Joe spoke slowly and deliberately. 'Get your bag. We've got to go.' He jabbed his finger towards the door. 'We're not arguing about it. We're doing it.'

Ruby paused for a moment, before reaching down for her bag and rushing past Joe, her shoulder brushing against his, jolting him.

Joe locked his apartment and followed her. She folded her arms and walked with her head down. She took the stairs rather than the lift, avoiding the awkwardness. When she burst into the underground garage, her fear had been overtaken by anger.

'I didn't know you were such a bully,' she said. Her words echoed.

Joe stepped closer to her. She didn't back away.

'The problem with people your age is that you think you know it all,' he said. 'You think that you've got the world all worked out. Let me tell you something: you haven't. You get older and you realise that working out the right thing to do isn't always that easy, and that sometimes, just sometimes, you've got to let someone else lead the way. So for your sake, let me.'

Her lip trembled and she looked up, blinking fast. 'You're scaring me.'

'Good. If that's what it takes to get through to you.' He spoke more softly. 'You remember a couple of years ago, when that man took you in his van.'

That made her cry. 'Of course I remember,' she said.

'That's not happening again. I won't let it. No one will hurt you, Ruby, never again.' He reached round to unlock his car. The flash of the lights and the click of the lock were bright and loud. 'So get in the car.'

Ruby did as she was told, slumping in the passenger seat, her bag on her knees, wiping her eyes before folding her arms across her chest.

Joe drove up the slope and away from the garage, looking out for Proctor as he went. He wasn't there. As Joe got onto the main road, he pressed hard on the accelerator.

He drove impatiently, getting too close to the cars in front, swearing at those who got in his way. Ruby kept on looking across to him but he wasn't going to slow down. His head felt like a pressure chamber, blood pushing against his skull, his cheeks flushed and angry.

They were both silent until they reached the calm of Sam's cul-de-sac. He braked hard. 'You're staying here for a while.'

She looked out of the window and shook her head. 'I'm not staying with Sam.'

He got out of the car and rushed round to the passenger door. He yanked it open. 'You need to get out. Here or home, your choice.'

Ruby let out a sulky breath before climbing out.

Joe went to the door and knocked loudly. Alice smiled as she opened the door but her smile quickly disappeared when he said, 'Ruby needs to stay with you for a while.'

'Joe? What do you mean?'

'Just that. I'm sorry. There's something I've got to do. Keep her safe.'

He ran back to his car.

'Joe!'

He didn't answer. He knew where he was going.

Thirty-four

Sam checked his watch as he waited in the car park of the management consultancy where Bruce Carter worked.

They were by a small business complex in a village close to the Pennines: glass and brick blocks squeezed into a space created by a bulldozed factory. Close to the motorway, it was perfect for those businesses that wanted cheap premises but whose employees worked at other locations. Sam guessed Bruce Carter saw himself as some kind of gunslinger, heading into businesses to help them raise themselves from the mire.

Charlotte had found the consultancy website on her phone, with Bruce's page open, so they could compare the picture with whoever came out of the office. There were many cars on the car park, but Sam had singled out four that were probably driven by middle-aged management consultants. He was right. A silver BMW was registered to Bruce Carter.

'We could just go in,' Charlotte said.

'No, he'll clam up. As far as he's concerned, whatever he did on that site was a secret. He just wasn't good at covering his tracks. If he knows he can talk to us in confidence, he might open up.'

They waited another thirty minutes before anyone appeared.

'There he is,' Sam said, checking the picture on Charlotte's phone before climbing out of his car. Bruce Carter looked round, startled, as Sam approached him.

'Mr Carter? I'm DC Parker from Greater Manchester Police. This is DC Turner. We'd like a word.'

Bruce looked surprised. 'Is everything all right?' He swallowed. 'Is it my wife? Is there a problem?'

'No, Mr Carter. It's about your use of a website called No One Tells.'

Bruce paled and reached out for his car to support himself.

'You're cashlover, right?'

'What is this?' he said. He sounded like he'd lost all the moisture in his mouth.

'You're not in any trouble,' Sam said. 'We just need some help.'

'If I'm not in any trouble, then I've nothing to say.'

He reached for his car door handle but stopped when Sam said, 'I'll head to your home then. I've got your address from your car registration. Your wife might be able to help. It's in relation to an important investigation.'

'You bastard.'

Sam remained impassive.

Bruce stared at him for a few seconds before looking at his watch. 'There's a pub along the road towards the motorway.' He pointed out of the village. 'The Frightened Horse. I'll meet you there.'

'Thank you.'

'But just you.'

Sam looked across at Charlotte, who scowled. 'I'll see you there,' Sam said.

Bruce got into his car as Sam and Charlotte walked back across the car park.

'I'm sorry,' Sam said.

'Why doesn't he want me there?'

'Because he wants it to be all man-to-man. He'll know that you'll see him for what he is. He's probably hoping that I'll be some sort of kindred spirit.'

181

'I'll let this one slide,' she said. 'Just don't turn it into a long session. Sitting alone in a pub car park wasn't in my plans.'

The journey didn't take long. The Frightened Horse was a stone pub on the way to Saddleworth Moor, with an old slate roof that dipped in the middle and small white lattice windows that would let in little light. The building was designed to keep out the elements, not welcome them in. It was wild around it, just a barren spread of heather and wild grass matching the clouds gathering in the sky above.

It was quiet when he stepped out of the car. There was just the coolness of the breeze and then the slow crunch of his footsteps over the unmade car park.

The door jammed on the stone floor as Sam went in, making everyone look around. The warmth hit him straight away. The layout was more like a cottage than the pubs he was used to, with a room straight ahead with tables filled by people eating and a smaller room to his left, where Bruce Carter sat at a small table by an open fire. He was clutching a whisky. He hadn't wasted any time.

Sam ordered an orange juice, and went over to him. As he sat down, Bruce said, 'Am I a suspect for anything? Because I spoke to a friend who's a solicitor, and he said you can't talk to me like this if you want to arrest me, and I don't have to help if I don't want to.'

Sam sat down on the chair next to him. There was no one else in the small room. 'It's not me you're scared of though, is it?' Sam said. 'You're scared that whatever you get up to might leak out.'

Bruce didn't answer that. He took a quick sip of whisky. His wedding ring clinked on the glass as he put it back down.

'Tell me about No One Tells,' Sam said.

'Come on,' Bruce said, scoffing. 'What do you think it's about?'

'Sex, away from your marriage.'

'So why did you ask?'

'Because I want to know what attracted you.'

'Can't you guess? I've been married twenty years. Got four beautiful children, nearly all grown up now, but the spark goes. Nothing unique in that, I know. I'm a different person to who I was twenty years ago. We both are.'

'Do you love your wife?'

'I don't know,' Bruce said. 'I've thought about it and I just don't know. I like her, and wouldn't want to hurt her, but do I feel any excitement? I like my life, because we've got a house and the kids are happy, but I can't remember the last time I felt thrilled about anything, felt that surge you get when you want something so much. Every day just sort of rolls into the next. Call me shallow, but that's just how it is. So I went looking, and I'm not alone.'

'How would you feel if you saw your wife on the site, looking for the same things as you?'

'Honestly?' Bruce said. 'Relieved, probably. It would be like us accepting it was over.'

'So why vodkagirl?' Sam asked. 'Is the problem that your wife has got a little too old?'

Bruce tensed and his cheeks flushed a little more. 'I contacted lots of people, the local ones.'

'But she was different, wasn't she?'

'Different? How?'

'Not eighteen.'

'That could mean anything.'

'So what were you trying to find out?' Sam said. 'That she was over eighteen, or under?'

Bruce stood up too quickly, almost knocking over his drink. 'I'm not a child molester,' he hissed.

'Sit down, Bruce.'

'I don't have to put up with this.'

Bruce went as if to leave, but Sam gripped his wrist. 'You

made contact with someone you thought was under eighteen, with sex in your mind,' he said. 'That bothers me. Perhaps even enough to seize your computer to look for kiddie porn. How would your wife like that?'

'You bastard.'

'I'm just doing my job. So sit down and answer my questions. You can talk to your solicitor friend if you want, but I know you're not interested in your legal rights; just about keeping your secrets from your wife.'

Bruce stared down at Sam for a few seconds, before he pulled his hand away and sat down, slumping against the back of the seat.

There was a shout from behind the bar: 'Everything okay over there?'

Sam cocked his head at Bruce and raised his eyebrows, until Bruce said, 'Yes, everything's fine.'

'So talk,' Sam said.

Bruce took another drink and simmered for a while. Sam let him think about his answer. He was there to find out about vodkagirl, not about Bruce.

'I was curious, that's all,' Bruce said at last. 'I can feel myself getting old, and I just wondered what it would be like to be with someone who was the same age as I was when I was last single. It sounds pathetic, but I just wanted to know that I was still attractive to someone young, and being under eighteen doesn't mean under sixteen.'

'How old did she tell you she was?'

Bruce reddened and said nothing.

'Don't make me go to your house and seize your computer, so we can examine your chat threads.'

'Fourteen,' Bruce said, and looked down.

'A child.'

'Yes, I know that,' Bruce said, and he reddened again, except this time it was through shame, not embarrassment.

'Did you meet her? Or make any arrangements to meet her?'

'No, it never got that far. Deep down, I knew it was wrong. I wanted to prove to myself that I could still be attractive to someone younger. When it came to the thought of meeting her, I felt uncomfortable. I haven't met anyone from the site; just chatted. There was something else too.'

'Go on.'

'There was something not right about it; everything seemed too good to be true.'

'How so?'

Bruce frowned and took another drink. 'We chatted a few times, used a messaging app on my phone, and she would get all flirty and confide her fantasies, but they were extreme. Too far-out for a girl that age. Perhaps I'm naive, but you can't really know what turns you on at that age. You might think you do, but you haven't tried anything so it's just all talk. She said how she liked strong men, those who saw what they wanted and took it. That's why she liked older men, success-ful men. She wanted to hear stories, things I'd done, shameful things, so she could show me how it wasn't bad, because what-ever turns you on is good.'

'She wanted confessions?'

'Something like that. She said violence turned her on, because it was a strong man seeing what he wanted and taking it. She complained about how people see abuse as a bad thing, but it was really just a man's strength and that's what built the world.' Bruce shook his head. 'It wasn't right. I've never abused any child. It's wrong, I know, because it shatters innocence, taints their view of the world, despite her own experience. But she wanted to know of things I've done, said it would turn her on, that it would be something special between us. A shared secret, and we could meet and it would be explosive.'

185

'You said "despite her own experience",' Sam said. 'What do you mean?'

'She said she was abused by her teacher,' Bruce said. 'A couple of years earlier. They'd flirted for a while but then one afternoon he got her to stay behind for some extra tuition. He forced himself on her. It sounds tacky, but it was in the class storeroom. He ripped her blouse and tried to take her virginity, but she said it changed her, because afterwards he hardly spoke to her and it upset her. She wanted to understand it, even if it was only through descriptions of things I'd done.'

'And did you tell her anything?'

'I had nothing to tell,' Bruce said. 'I've never done anything like that, and as we exchanged messages I knew I never would. I was stupid, yes, but I wasn't interested in a child and her fantasies, so I stopped messaging.'

'Did she chase you?'

'No. I told her I'd never done anything like that and it was as if I'd switched off the light. She wasn't interested any more.'

'Thank you,' Sam said. He drained his drink. 'If I need to speak to you again, I know where to find you.'

'You're not going to say anything to my wife?'

'You said you didn't arrange to meet this girl. You haven't committed a crime.'

Bruce let out a long breath.

'But don't talk to underage girls again.'

'I won't, I'm sorry.'

Sam rushed out of the pub. Charlotte had moved to the driving seat and she'd started the car before Sam reached it.

As he climbed in, she said, 'Excuse me for being impatient,' and set off quickly, sending gravel up behind them. 'What did cashlover have to say?'

Sam frowned. 'A strange one. He admitted contacting her, but was curious more than anything. He backed off when he realised what he was doing was wrong.'

186

'Did you believe him?'

'Yeah, I think so. He seems like a man who's looking for some thrills before his body lets him down, some colour in all the greyness of his life. But this is the weird thing: there was more to this profile than just sex.'

'What do you mean?'

'He said she seemed too grown up, too sure of herself sexually, even though she said she was only fourteen.'

'You can get all the information you need on the internet now. It doesn't mean you have to understand it.'

'I think it was more than that. He said it was as though she was trying to tease out his confessions. Said it would turn her on if she knew his dark secrets, that it would be a bond between them, a shared secret.'

Then he remembered something.

'Wasn't there someone going around trapping child molesters like this?' he said. When Charlotte looked across to him, he added, 'Somewhere in the south. There was a TV programme about him. He was going online with fake profiles, chatting to men, pretending to be thirteen or fourteen, and arranging meetings. When they turned up, they were ambushed with cameras, the footage going online.'

'What, you think this might be similar?'

'All we know is that Henry Mason was hanging around in a park, flowers in his hand, and his internet chat says he was talking about a "meet" with someone whose internet profile said that she isn't eighteen. And we know Henry Mason likes them young. It all fits.'

'Except the person he was speaking to wasn't underage at all,' Charlotte said. 'It's a honeytrap, a lure for people who like young girls too much. Remember the profile? It was so corny, all that stuff about looking for a man to teach her about the world, along with some shadowy picture of a willowy frame with long hair. If you think about it again, I've never seen a

187

more obvious hook.' She frowned. 'There's still one problem with that theory.'

'Which is?'

'What is vodkagirl trying to get? Money?'

'You're thinking blackmail?' Sam said.

'What else do you do with secrets you're so keen to get?'

'But if she was blackmailing Henry Mason, he ended up dead, and there's no money to be squeezed out of a corpse. And how does that link in with Keith Welsby, the teacher?'

Before Sam could say anything else, his phone rang. It was Alice.

'Hi,' he said. 'I won't be long.'

'Ruby's here,' Alice said. 'Joe dropped her off, told her she had to stay here.'

'Why? What did he say?'

'Not much, but he wasn't right. He seemed wound up like I've never seen him.'

'Did he say where he was going?'

'No, but something's wrong.'

'I'm on my way,' he said, and clicked off. 'Damn!'

'What is it?'

'Sorry, Charlotte, but I've got to go home. We'll try to work out how this all fits and then we'll go to Brabham in the morning. But there's family stuff going on I've got to sort out.'

And in the meantime, he thought, he needed to find Joe. Sam remembered Joe's long-held promise to kill Ellie's murderer. Was that moment getting closer?

Thirty-five

The light was fading as Joe sat in his car close to Proctor's house. He was slumped in his seat so that he couldn't be seen. His fingers tapped out a fast rhythm on his knee.

Proctor lived in one of the poorer parts of the city. They were once grand houses, Edwardian four-storeys with stone bay windows and front gardens bordered by millstone walls, but they'd mostly been converted into flats and bedsits. The pavements were cluttered with wheelie bins and takeaway wrappers were strewn across front gardens. A group of five men loitered on a wall, smoking and talking, watching the day drift along.

Joe didn't know them but they were just like so many of his clients. Scrawny, their T-shirts hanging from their shoulders, the skin on their forearms mottled and with crude black markings where boredom had ended with homemade tattoos, words badly scratched into their skin. A cigarette was passed along the line, but the way each cherished it told Joe that it contained more than just tobacco.

He was prepared to wait it out. He had to. Nothing was happening. The street had got busier, people talking over walls, going from house to house, except no one visited Proctor. So Joe had sunk into his seat, grinding his teeth, trying to calm himself, but all the time the blood raged through his brain, flushing his cheeks, his head filled with the pressure of barely contained rage.

Joe tried to think of a plan but it eluded him. He was being driven by emotion. He'd waited for this moment but never really expected it, so all he could do was let his feelings guide him. He knew one thing though: Proctor had ramped up the pressure. He'd decided to target Joe by seeking out Ruby. He wasn't going to let that go.

Joe closed his eyes for a moment. He rubbed his forehead with his fingers. Everything that had become stable about his life seemed to be in tatters. Gina was gone and now Proctor was tormenting him.

He opened his eyes and tried to refocus. He couldn't think about himself. He took a deep breath and flexed his fingers. He was ready.

Sam burst into his house. 'Alice?'

She came from the living room. 'Sam? What the hell?'

'Where's Ruby?'

'I'm in here!'

Sam went through to the living room. Ruby was lying on the floor, helping Emily fill in a colouring book. Amy was kneeling and watching. Emily and Amy both grinned their greetings but didn't leave Ruby; she didn't visit often. Ruby rolled her eyes and said, 'Hi, big bro.'

'What's going on?'

'Not here,' Alice said, pointing towards the girls.

'In the kitchen, Ruby.'

She groaned and got to her feet, stomping into the kitchen, Alice with her.

'You're as bad as Joe,' she said, once the door closed.

'What happened?' Sam said.

So she told him about Mark Proctor and how Joe had reacted.

Sam leaned back against the wall and let out a long sigh.

'Sam, is everything all right?' Alice said, and put her hand on his arm.

His smile flickered. 'Yes, fine,' he said, and then to Ruby, 'I think Emily and Amy need you.'

Once she'd left the kitchen, Sam said, 'Has everything been all right tonight? No visitors?'

'Don't, you're scaring me.'

'Has there?'

'No, it's been quiet.' Alice scowled. 'Tell me.'

He put his arms around her and pulled her in close. She was surprised at first, holding back, but she let him wrap her up.

'Do you remember after last year, when I almost lost you,' he murmured. She stiffened. 'I let danger come into our house, my job brought it your way, and I promised I'd never let it happen again.' He kissed her hair. 'I intend to keep that promise.'

Alice pulled away. She wiped her eye. 'I don't want to think about that time.'

'I know, and I'm sorry, but do you remember the man I was telling you about this afternoon? The man who Joe thinks killed Ellie.'

'I remember. What about him?'

'That's the man who spoke to Ruby at school today. That was his way of saying he knows who we are and where we live.'

Alice's hand went to her mouth. 'No one's been here.' She closed her eyes and forced out more tears. 'I'm worried, Sam.'

Sam cursed himself. He'd dealt with it badly. 'Don't be. I think he's just trying to unsettle Joe.'

'But he's a murderer, according to Joe.'

'Yes, and if he is, I'll catch him.'

'Are you sure we're safe?'

'Positive.' He took her hand. 'But I'm not leaving you tonight. I'm home now. My case can wait until tomorrow.'

'But what about Joe?'

'I'm not leaving tonight.'

191

'He looked so angry, Sam. He was different. You need to find him, before he does something stupid.'

'I'll call him.' And Sam took his phone from his pocket.

'And if he won't talk to you?'

'Then he's on his own.'

Thirty-six

Joe's phone buzzed in his pocket. He looked at the screen: *Sam*. He thought about not answering, he didn't need a sensible voice, but then he remembered Ruby.

'Hi,' Joe said.

'What's going on?' Sam said. 'Where are you?'

'Everything's fine.'

'It doesn't sound like it. Mark Proctor was waiting for Ruby outside school, for Christ's sake,' Sam said. 'Proctor knows you recognised him. But how could he know?'

'What do you mean?'

'In the day or so since he became your client, he's been able to work out Ruby's movements?' Sam was incredulous.

That hadn't occurred to Joe.

Joe could accept the coincidence of Proctor being in the police station. He'd done something wrong and Joe had become high profile as a criminal lawyer. He could understand why Proctor might ask for him. But as he thought about it, Sam was right. Proctor had known who he was all along. He knew all about Ruby and where she went to school; he knew where Joe lived.

'He's been watching us,' Joe said. A cold shiver ran through him.

'What do you mean?'

'Just that. He must have been watching us for a while. That's why he asked for Honeywells when he was arrested: he knew who I was and he wanted to taunt me.'

Sam was silent for a moment. 'Who have you brought into our lives?'

'Fuck off,' Joe said, and ended the call. He turned off his phone. Sam would ring back, full of apology, but he wasn't in the mood for hearing it.

He looked across at Proctor's house. It seemed even gloomier in the light of early dusk. The paintwork was faded and there were no splashes of colour. No bright curtains, no hanging baskets of flowers. It was as if Proctor wanted to fade into the background and be invisible, even to his neighbours. There was a car parked on Proctor's drive, a car-hire logo in the back window: a temporary, replacement, Joe guessed, for the car Proctor had burnt out.

It was just after eight before anything happened.

Proctor came out of the front door and looked around. Joe's stomach tightened. There it was, the furtive look, Proctor's hunched shoulders. The same as years earlier. Joe wound down his window and listened out. There was no one talking; just the clunk of a car door and then the sound of an engine.

Proctor's car reversed out of the drive and then turned away from Joe. That was good. He wouldn't have to do any lengthy manoeuvres to turn around. He turned on his engine and started to follow.

Proctor headed towards the motorway. Joe kept him in sight, tucked in behind a lorry but able to see far enough ahead to keep the hire car in view. Eventually Proctor turned off at the Trafford Centre, a huge shopping mall on the edge of Manchester. Joe stayed with him but wondered whether all the effort was just to watch him shopping.

Joe followed Proctor into the covered car park, the world thrown into semi-darkness. Proctor was moving quickly, ignoring spaces, as if he knew where to head for. Joe found a space where he would have a view of the exit and waited. He knew that if he followed Proctor into the shopping centre, the other man would spot him. Instead, he would sit tight, wait until Proctor left. He put his head back, impatient and edgy, not knowing how long he'd be there.

The next thirty minutes dragged. Joe had to stay alert, but the only thing to distract him was the occasional group of shoppers returning to their cars.

Then there was movement ahead. Proctor's car heading for the exit, Joe temporarily blinded by the headlights.

He turned on the ignition and set off after him, the screech of his tyres echoing as he cut across empty parking bays to make sure he didn't lose him.

Joe caught sight of him near the lights. Proctor was four cars ahead. The lights changed to green and the traffic crawled forward. The driver of the car in front was distracted by something he was being shown so he was slow to react. Joe was going to pip his horn but he didn't want to make Proctor look in his mirror. Instead, Joe cursed and pulled into the inside lane, making a car behind brake, and accelerated hard through the lights.

They changed to red before he reached them but he didn't care. The traffic to his right had started to move but Joe put his foot down and rushed through, getting ahead and within a couple of cars of Proctor.

They both rejoined the motorway and began the steady circuit of Manchester. Proctor wasn't going home; the route was taking him the wrong way, so Joe wasn't surprised when he turned off towards Worsley, an area of wealth and gentility squashed between the grittier parts of Eccles and Salford.

Proctor didn't go far. They'd driven just a couple of hundred yards when he pulled into a space at the side of the road. Joe didn't slow down, not wanting to look obvious, so he

195

drove further along until he found his own space. As he turned off his engine and looked back, he caught a glimpse of Proctor disappearing over a bridge over the canal, just his hood visible.

Proctor had chosen a pretty location to visit. Restaurants and estate agents lined the road that ran alongside a canal. The area was open and with views towards large houses with Tudor-style eaves and trees that drooped their branches over the water. A small wrought-iron bridge crossed the canal, lined with cobbles, leading to a path running between two houses, lit by Victorian lamps. Canal boats were moored up at the side of the water and the nearby motorway provided a soothing hum.

Joe walked slowly. He didn't know where Proctor had gone but he would have to come back this way, and Joe didn't want a confrontation in a dimly lit pathway.

The path led to a large space of grass brightened by patches of daffodils that caught the glow of the street lights. It was a large open semicircle with a village-green feel. Joe peered around the corner and then ducked back when he saw movement in the distance. There was a structure ahead, a brick shelter or monument perhaps, the detail lost in the night, but in the middle of it was Proctor, in a hooded top, his hands thrust into his pockets.

Joe took a deep breath. He shook his head, almost laughed out loud. This was his proof that he couldn't carry out his promise. Proctor was somewhere dark, alone and isolated, but still Joe hung back. He had the chance and he couldn't take it. He wasn't like Proctor. He wasn't a killer.

A few minutes passed. People were starting to notice him. A woman walking a small dog had crossed the bridge but turned back when she saw Joe. A teenage couple had walked through and headed across the green, where there was a steady stream of headlights heading towards the motorway.

Joe looked round again. Proctor was still there.

He pulled back, closed his eyes. He wondered whether he should go back to his car. What could he say if Proctor walked round the corner and saw him?

But then he thought of something else: Ellie had been attacked along a quiet path. Was Proctor waiting to do the same? Had he come here to attack another young girl? This was Joe's chance to make a difference and catch him in the act.

There was a noise. A shout. Footsteps.

As Joe looked round, someone was running across the green, footsteps thumping. Joe looked back towards the small stone structure. There was something on the floor.

Joe tried to keep his footfall light, but the early evening was quiet and every footstep seemed to announce his arrival. When he got closer, he dodged behind a tree and moved a branch to one side to get a view. He scoured the area for movement. There was nothing.

Then Joe gasped. Proctor's hood was on the floor.

He moved closer still, and there was the bright sheen of skin in the dim lighting. A face. It wasn't just the hood. Proctor was down.

Joe ran towards him. He skipped up the stone steps, his body tense, ready to run in case it was a trap. His foot slipped. There was something dark and wet on the floor, sticky like blood. He grimaced and looked back down again. It was hard to make out much in the dusk, but he could tell that it was a person on his back, his arms by his side.

Joe gasped. It was the person he'd been following; he recognised the hooded top, but there was blood all over it now. There was a deep wound in his neck, just below his ear.

The metallic smell of warm blood wafted towards him. He turned away, fighting the urge to vomit. Once he'd controlled his breathing, he bent down over the body and put his ear to the man's chest. There was no heartbeat. He remembered something he'd seen in a film, so he grabbed his phone and held the glass screen over the man's mouth. There was no misting.

Joe clicked on the flashlight on his phone to turn it into a small torch. He shone it towards the man's face, then immediately turned away, gasping.

The wound in the neck was deep and wide. Blood soaked the ground beneath his head. There was more blood coming from under his back and there was a large red circle in his chest. The ground around him was awash with blood, splashes of it dripping from the side of the bench nearest to the body. Joe looked at his hands. There was blood on them.

His mind swam with panic. He'd followed the person to this park. People had seen him loitering nearby, his footprints would be in the blood. How the hell could he explain all that?

There was something else too: the dead person wasn't Mark Proctor.

Thirty-seven

Mark Proctor looked down at his hands. They were steady. No trembles or shakes. It had been an interesting evening but not entirely a surprise.

He fumbled with his keys and went into his house. There was music playing in a back room, some radio station turned up too loudly. Helena knew he hated that; the inane chatter, that Americanised drivel, the constant stream of badly written commercials.

'I'm back,' he shouted.

The music carried on.

'I said, I'm back,' he shouted louder.

There was a pause before the music was switched off. He preferred the silence, to let the sounds of the house take over. The tick of the clock, the clangs of the radiator, the hum of the fridge. They gave the house life and shouldn't be drowned out by bad radio.

He walked along the hallway, pausing only to straighten a picture that had become askew, and into the small room. Helena was there, her hand around a glass of wine, a scented candle burning on the hearth. She looked up at him, wide-eyed. 'You're late.'

'I got held up,' he said. 'I went to see a new client and Greg borrowed my car to meet someone.' He nodded towards the glass. 'Wine?'

'Yes, I'm sorry,' she said. 'It was just something to do.'

'Is there anything to eat?'

'I didn't know what time you were due back, so I haven't made any supper.' She put her glass down with a heavy clink. 'I can make you something, if you like.'

'Yes, that would be nice,' he said, and backed out of the room. She knew not to put the music back on.

He threw his jacket over the banister and went upstairs to the small study. The door clicked closed and the room felt like a haven. He put his head back against the door and closed his eyes. He needed to work out what to do next. The computer was the obvious start.

As the computer booted up, he took the camera out of his pocket, slipping out the memory card and putting it in the drawer on his oak desk. Once the screen was showing, he went to the email software. No emails.

He opened the messaging app on his phone. He was angry, but he needed to keep that at bay; acting through anger leads to mistakes, and he didn't make mistakes. He typed:

I sent my assistant to collect my box, I was busy at the time,
and he hasn't returned yet. What's going on?

He clicked SEND and sat back. The noise of Helena in the kitchen drifted through the house: water filling a saucepan, some chopping of vegetables.

He thought again about the memory card from the camera and then glanced across at the A4 binders on his desk, the public face of his business. They contained the accounts he showed if he visited an investor. That was his business, persuading people to forget about the banks and trust him, because his accounts showed his successes, five-yearly investment plans that paid out big.

The sight of his accounts made an idea begin its slow journey

200

to fruition, from a niggle to a growing realisation and then to an absolute certainty that it was the right thing to do.

His real accounts were locked away in a small safe in the corner. He went to it and pulled out an old ledger, hard-backed. He slid the bolt on his study door and settled back into his chair. He opened it to reveal his spidery handwriting, a list of names and numbers, showing monies in and out, along with a running balance. It was the only number that mattered because his scheme was a simple one: people paid him money and he did his best to make sure he didn't have to give it back.

A smile was all it took. A shake of the hand, words spoken earnestly, promises that sounded plausible, with recommendations passing through whole families. They loved his balance sheets, those annual summaries of the progress of their investments that he used to get them to make another investment. Give him twenty thousand pounds, and after five years it's grown to thirty-two thousand pounds. Give them back two thousand and they trust him to invest the remaining thirty for another five years. So it goes on, every five years, small sums given back and the rest reinvested. It was brilliant because they trusted him. He dropped off calendars at Christmas, held small parties for them, and their relatives couldn't wait to join; he'd never let anyone down.

It was all a sham. He paid out using the new investments and enjoyed a good life, fobbing them off with loose change every five years. It was laughable. They thought they had a couple of hundred grand in the bank, when all they had done was give him a chunk of their money many years ago and believed his promises ever since.

The banking crash had made it difficult. People got scared and wanted their money back, but there wasn't any left, so he'd relied on a lot of charm. But he'd ridden it out, putting off those who wanted their investments back by promising a decent return if they held firm. Less than before, but still better than the banks, because he knew where to look.

That wasn't the difficulty, though. The hard part was attracting new investors, because people just didn't have the money like they used to. He needed a new surge of capital, and as he looked at the memory card from the camera, he knew that he had it.

Thirty-eight

Joe sat in his car, running his hands over his hair, panicking, looking around, wondering who was watching. He'd just left a dead man whose blood was still warm. His fingers were trembling. Should he have done more? The man could have been saved.

No, the man was dead. His eyes were open, staring, and there'd been no breath coming from him. The man was beyond saving.

He looked at his palms and his vision swam. There was blood dried into the ridges in his palms and fingers. It will be in his hair and his clothes, just small traces of the victim's DNA on everything he touches.

He slammed the steering wheel with his hand. Fuck! He shouldn't have touched him, should have thought about evidence, but he'd reacted naturally. A man was on the ground and Joe had reached out to him, a human reaction.

He had to get away. Where could he go? There was one person who might help him. It might be too late for that, but it was the only person he could turn to.

Gina.

He set off quickly, his mind trying to make sense of it all.

The man had been alive just minutes before, Joe had seen

him. So it could only mean one thing: that the killer had been waiting for him, striking as soon as he had the chance.

So who was he? Joe had been certain it was Proctor. It was a hire car, like Proctor's, the same make and model and colour. The man was wearing the same hoodie Proctor had been wearing earlier.

Then he remembered the Trafford Centre. The car park. A switch? A pre-arranged meeting that Proctor had been suspicious about, so he'd got someone to go along on his behalf?

But if it wasn't Proctor, who was it, and why was he murdered?

What about the body? It might not be discovered until the morning; the evening was setting in and midweek didn't seem the right time for the green to attract the local teenagers. He had time to get rid of the traces.

But where was his morality? There was a dead man and Joe had witnessed his last movements. He should help. Except he knew the answer straight away, that as soon as he said that he'd been following the victim, suspicion would fall straight on him. Everywhere the police looked, he would be the prime suspect. He'd been seen loitering nearby, conspicuous in his courtroom suit. If they asked his family, they would say that he'd rushed off after he'd found out that Mark Proctor had spoken to his little sister. Sam would tell them that he'd once vowed to kill Mark Proctor.

Joe shook his head, gritted his teeth in frustration. What could he say? He thought he was following a man he'd once vowed to kill, right up until the point where he was murdered in a park by someone he couldn't describe? He could see every investigative trail point back to him: he'd made a mistake, that in the gloom he'd mistaken the man for Proctor and carried out the promise he'd always made to himself. And there were traces of the man's blood on him. It was a strong case, and he would become that cliché, the murderer who protests his innocence all the way through his life sentence.

He punched the steering wheel in frustration, making his horn sound, and screeched out loud.

There was only one thing Joe knew for certain, one thing that kept his anger under control: he hadn't killed the man. He had no reason to feel guilty. But he had to keep on the move until he got to the bottom of everything.

He drove to Gina's but parked a few streets away. It was too soon for the police to be interested in him, but he wasn't taking any chances. He walked the rest of the way, looking around as he went along the slow curve of a suburban street. If there was a threat, he wanted to see it coming, even though he knew he looked suspicious.

Gina lived in a modern house on an estate, with wide lawns and cars parked on driveways rather than garages. It was non-descript and boxy, with the streets busy with children every weekend. He was relieved to see that her living-room light was on.

Joe paused before he walked up her drive. Gina used to be a detective. If she suspected he'd done something murderous, would she help or turn him in? He wasn't sure he could trust her. But he remembered her true nature from when she was a detective. She'd been almost a mother figure to him as the family grappled with Ellie's murder. She wouldn't turn her back on him now, he was sure of that.

He took a deep breath and approached her door. He knocked and checked his watch: after nine. The curtain in the living-room window moved and then went back. At first, Joe thought she'd decided not to answer the door, but then there was the rattle of the security chain.

When the door opened, Gina just let it swing and walked back into the house.

Joe followed, closing the door behind him. When he went into the living room, there was no television on. There was a wine glass on the floor, as good as empty. From the way Gina slumped into her chair and pulled her knees up to her chest, Joe guessed that the glass wasn't her first.

'So that's it,' she said, raising her hands.

Joe could hear the slow growl of anger in her voice, along with the drawl made by the wine. 'What do you mean?'

'I'm retired,' she said, and bent down for her glass. She drained her wine and said, 'At fifty-three, I'm all washed up, just thirty years alone in these walls to look forward to. Thank you, Joe Parker.'

Joe didn't sit down. 'I'm not here about that.'

'What, me leaving isn't even worth talking about?'

He looked up at the ceiling and let out a long breath, tried to stay calm. 'I'm sorry, Gina. What more can I say? I let you down.'

'No, you let Ellie down.'

Joe glared at her. Gina raised her hand in apology. 'Yeah, a low blow, I know, but that's how I'm feeling.' She pushed herself out of her chair before weaving towards the kitchen. 'So what is it then? Have you come here to apologise?'

Joe listened to the opening of the fridge door and then the glug of the wine being poured. When she returned, she was carrying two glasses.

'Too late for sorry,' she said. 'I've quit.' She handed him a glass. 'But I don't get drunk alone.'

Joe sat down and took a drink. The wine was cold and fresh and just what he needed.

'I've come here for your help,' he said.

Gina pointed with the hand that was holding the wine glass, so that the wine spilled onto the chair arm as she jabbed her finger towards him. 'You had my help once before, but you weren't being truthful to me, so it all came to nothing. You betrayed me, Joe. It feels like you cheated.'

'This is different,' he said. 'Whatever's happened in the past, you're my friend, and I've come to you because I don't know who else to turn to.'

Gina took a drink and stared straight ahead. After a few seconds, she said, 'Go on, tell me.'

So he did. About Mark Proctor speaking to Ruby and about how he'd followed him to see where he went. When Joe got to the part where he found the man dead in the park, Gina's mouth dropped open and she put her glass down.

'What do I do?' Joe said.

She left her chair and kneeled beside him. 'What the hell have you done, Joe?'

'Nothing! I told you how it happened.'

'What if I don't believe you, because you have to admit it looks pretty coincidental? You wanted to kill Mark Proctor. You followed him, and someone you thought was Mark Proctor is dead. Show me your hands.'

'Don't you think I know that?' he said.

'Show me your hands!'

Joe put his glass down and held them out. Gina turned them slowly, looking intently at his fingers. 'There's blood on them,' she said, her voice quiet. 'And your shoes. I can see it on the edge of the sole.'

'I know that,' he said, jerking his hands away. 'I went to the guy, to see if I could help. I trod in his blood.'

Gina thought about that. 'What would you tell a client to do?'

'Not cooperate,' he said. 'Let them find me.'

'So you're not going to call the police or hand yourself in?'

He shook his head.

'But how does that look?' Gina said.

'Guilty, that's how it looks,' he said, with resignation. 'You've got to believe me. There's no one else I can turn to. Yes, I made a mistake in the past, but I was hiding what someone else had done, not what I'd done.'

'No, you were hiding what *you'd* seen,' she said.

Gina looked at his hands again and got to her feet. She went over to her phone, which had been charging on the table in the corner. She unplugged it and placed it on the chair arm.

'Leave,' she said.

'Gina, don't do this.'

'Leave and go back to your apartment. Do whatever clean up you want. If you're lying, your clothes will have blood spray on them ...'

'They won't, I didn't kill him. It's contact only.'

'Then save them, to prove that. Call me when you get to your apartment, but make sure the call is a long one. Make it twenty minutes. I'll answer and leave the line open. I'll tell the police I tried to make you hand yourself in. The record of the phone call will be there, and it might just help you. That glass ...' And she pointed at Joe's wine glass. 'It's going in the dishwasher and I'm going to wash the carpet where your shoes have been. As far as I'm concerned, you were never here.'

'And then what?'

'I'll make some calls and see if anyone has discovered the body. If he's been found, you're on your own. Don't come here again. Don't drag me into it, because I don't know whether you've done it or not. I want to believe you, but you've lied to me before and for a long time. Everything points to you, Joe, and I'm not going to jail if you've lied again.'

Joe nodded slowly, dread creeping through him. 'And if the body hasn't been discovered?'

'I'll tell them. I was a murder detective, and whatever you've done or haven't done, there's a body and a crime scene that will be degrading by the minute.'

'And what will you tell them?'

'That you called me and you told me what you just have.'

He let out a long breath and got to his feet. 'I understand.'

'This is goodbye, Joe.'

'I know that.'

Gina didn't move as he left the house.

He had to get back to his apartment. From there, he had no idea what he was going to do, but he knew he had to keep moving.

Thirty-nine

'Has Joe called?' Alice said.

'Not yet.'

'So what do we do?'

'I'm not doing anything.'

'But if you think he's going to harm someone, shouldn't you help?'

'He's a grown man,' Sam said.

'And you're a policeman, who promised to protect people.'

Sam didn't respond.

Alice's eyes widened. 'So that's it?' she said. 'You don't mind if he carries out his threat, because what if this man did kill Ellie?' She shook her head. 'You're better than that.'

'So what do I do? Warn the police that my brother is out there on some murderous rampage? Go to Proctor's house myself to warn him? I don't want Joe to do anything, because he might have the wrong man or might get caught.'

'So it's fine as long as he gets it right and gets away with it?'

Sam took a deep breath. 'I'll shed no tears.' He lifted his phone and held it out to her. 'Call the police. Tell them your concerns. They might find Joe.'

Alice didn't move.

'You feel exactly the same as me,' he said.

Before Alice could respond, Ruby came in. 'What are you two arguing about?'

'Nothing for you to worry about,' Sam said.

'Is it about me staying over?'

Sam softened. 'Of course not. You're family. You've got the sofa, though.'

She shrugged. 'That's fine. What are you doing now?'

He glanced at Alice. 'I'm going to do some work.' He put his laptop onto the dining-room table and turned it on.

'So what sort of work?' Ruby said.

'You really want to know? I'm going on a dating site for married people,' he said. When Ruby's mouth dropped, he added, 'All in the name of research.'

'Research?'

'Yes, a case I'm working on. But you're not watching.'

'What is it?' Alice said.

He logged onto the No One Tells site and turned his screen round to show her. Alice raised an eyebrow.

'Yes, you're right,' she said, and tilted her head to hint that Ruby should go into the other room.

Once Ruby had left, she said, 'I'm worried about Joe, that's all.'

'So am I. But he's an adult.'

'So what's this?' she said, and pointed to the laptop.

'I've created a fake profile so I can lure someone in. It's to do with the case I'm working on.'

Alice examined the thumbnails that filled the screen. 'People never stop looking for the special one.'

'It's not that kind of dating. It's for affairs, not romance.'

'People finding happiness amongst the sadness.'

Sam was surprised. 'I thought you'd be more damning than that.'

'Don't worry,' she said, reaching across and patting him on the hand. 'I'm not thinking of joining. I just try to be more relaxed about life now. Promise me one thing, though.'

'What?'

'If you ever think of it, tell me first. If we can't sort it out, I'd rather know so we can move on, not sink into this kind of desperation.' And she nodded towards the screen.

'Is that what it looks like, desperation?'

'Have you got a better word for it?'

When Sam realised that he didn't, he said, 'I'm about to have a taste of their world. I could do with your help.'

'How so?'

'Because I want to know what to say. There is someone on this site pretending to be an underage girl to lure in paedophiles. I sent a message earlier.'

'I'm not sure I want to. The underage part sounds too sleazy. And don't you need to be careful? You might be accused of being a paedophile.'

'I'm trying to lure her into a trap, to find out why she's doing it.'

'Is it a her?'

'I doubt it,' he said.

Alice frowned. 'So you think it's a man posing as a young girl to lure in abusers?'

'Something like that, although there are still some things I don't get. I just don't know how it fits in with everything. You ready?'

'Okay, I'm right with you.'

Sam logged into the site and his profile page came up. He'd added a couple of pictures he'd found on the internet, of men who took their photographs too close to the webcam, so they were dark and out of focus.

Alice read the description he'd given himself. 'Strong, silent type, likes to dominate?' she said, and gave a small laugh.

'I can be in charge,' Sam said, and then grinned. 'If it's all right with you, that is.'

'Just type.'

Sam went to the inbox and saw there was a message. It was from vodkagirl. She'd replied. It just said, **Hi.**

When he clicked the message, it opened a chat window. 'Right, here goes,' he said, and typed, **Hi to you. I like your picture.**

Alice raised an eyebrow as Sam clicked the SEND button. He winked and sat back. If she wasn't online, he'd have a long night of staring at a screen, but within a few seconds the words **vodkagirl is typing** popped up, and then a few a seconds later the words appeared: **What do you like about my picture?**

'Tell her it's her body,' Alice whispered.

'She can't hear us,' Sam said, and typed, **Your body. It's nice.**

'Nice?' Alice said, shaking her head. 'You're damning her with faint praise.'

A few seconds later the reply came in. **Not too young for you?**

Sam sat back as he thought about that. He didn't want to sound too eager, but equally he didn't want to waste any time. He needed to know how the person worked.

Is there such a thing? he typed, adding a winking emoticon.

A smiley emoticon popped up in the chat window, and then, **Why do you like young bodies?**

Sam glanced across to Alice. She was curling her lip in distaste. 'Yeah, I know,' he said. 'It makes me want to take a shower or something.'

'What are you going to say?' Alice said.

'The opposite of what I think,' he said, and then typed, **So untouched, so taut, so much promise but unfulfilled.**

There was a long pause before the reply came back: **I like you. When do I get to see some of you?**

'You're not going to do that,' Alice said, her voice stern.

'I know that,' Sam said. He thought back to what Bruce Carter had said in the pub earlier, about her saying that she liked men who grabbed what they wanted. 'I'll try something else,' and he typed, **Eventually, but that's not how I work. I'll let you know when you're in charge. I've got a lot to lose.**

How come? was the reply.

My job, Sam typed.

But why do you do this if you would lose so much?

Because I go after what I want, and nothing stops me, he typed.

The chat window fell silent.

'You've frightened her away,' Alice said.

'I hope not,' Sam said quietly. 'I need to know what's behind this.'

He stared at the screen as the minutes ticked away, and then the words **vodkagirl is typing** popped up again.

Sam tensed as he waited for the message. When the words appeared in the chat window, he cursed.

Gotta go, they said. **Talk later.**

And then the chat window changed to **vodkagirl is offline**.

'Looks like I'm playing the waiting game,' he said, almost to himself.

'Just don't enjoy it too much,' Alice said, and the look of reproach in her eyes told him that she was only half-joking.

Forty

Joe looked around as he got close to his apartment, his stomach lurching every time he heard the rev of an engine, expecting to see a police car hurtling towards him. By the time he reached the metal footbridge that would take him to his apartment building, he was almost running.

He'd left his car unlocked on a quiet side street in Salford, just on the other side of the canal. He didn't expect to be a suspect so soon but he wasn't taking any chances. Someone might wreck any forensic value by stealing it. Right then, needing to buy a new car wasn't his biggest worry.

The streets were quiet. The rush-hour traffic was gone and the pavements were clear of those who wanted a drink before they went home, the lawyers and bankers and office workers who spilled into the nearby bars. The city centre had turned into that lonely and dangerous place, the workers gone home and replaced by drunks and muggers.

The familiar sounds comforted him. A tram ran overhead and two large river barges were docking. Cars streamed away from Deansgate – taxis feeding the bars underneath the railway arches, all glass and techno music no one listens to at home. He checked his watch. It was half an hour since he'd left Gina's.

There was no one waiting outside his apartment building. He hadn't expected there to be, not yet, but it was a relief just the same. His key fob got him inside, but Joe knew it would create a log too, another chance for an alibi gone, but that was just the way it was. He'd let the situation get away from him. He sucked in deep breaths and he could almost hear the loud echoes of his heartbeat in the small chamber of the lift.

Once in his apartment, he leaned back against his door and slid down. His apartment was silent. The computer was off. No ticking clock. Even the central heating was quiet. It was just an empty apartment. He put his head in his hands.

He'd watched a man walk to his death, oblivious. Joe tried to think of whether he'd seen or heard anything else. The killer had been nearby and Joe must have missed him by moments. He'd seen him running away but where had he been hiding before he struck? Was there any trace of him in his memory? He closed his eyes and walked himself through the scene again. The way the victim had walked slowly and carefully, as if he was unsure what he was doing there. The woman walking the dog. The young couple. No one else. There were houses nearby, though, and bushes and large trees. There were plenty of places to hide.

But he'd seen him run away. That was where he had to start.

His brief feeling of hope was extinguished by the smell of the blood as it came back to him.

That got Joe back onto his feet. He had to get moving.

Joe stripped off his clothes and put them into the washer. Gina was right, the lack of blood spray on his clothes might be enough to convince someone of his story, but his instinct as a defence lawyer was kicking in: they'd have to prove he was there first. He rushed through his apartment to the bathroom. Once in the shower, he scrubbed his fingers and hair to get rid of any traces of blood and let the water run for a few minutes more once he was out, to flush away what was left in the drains.

He remembered Gina's instruction: call her. He dressed in jeans and a baggy old jumper and went to his balcony. The air was cool as he slid the door open. A light breeze ruffled his hair.

Things were looking bad for him; the police would have no trouble in making a case against him. But he couldn't think like that. The best thing he could do was find out who'd killed the man and why.

He called Gina. She answered on the first ring but didn't say anything.

'Gina?'

She paused before she said, 'Like I said, I'm going to put my phone on the table and then hang up after twenty minutes. There'll be a record of a call long enough for you to tell me all you know.'

'And then what?'

'I call it in.' She sighed. 'I'm sorry, Joe. Whatever it means for you, there is a murder victim not too far away. I can't ignore that.'

'I understand,' he said. 'Can I call you later, to find out what's happening?'

'No,' she said. 'You're not dragging me into this.' A pause, and then, 'Goodbye Joe.'

'Goodbye,' he said. 'And I'm sorry.'

Her phone went quiet, apart from the clunk of it being put on the table.

He leaned over his balcony. The slow rumble of a train mixed in with the clink of glasses from the bar on the other side of the water. The ordinary sounds of an ordinary night.

He picked up his phone and listened. All he could hear was the faint murmur of Gina's television. He wanted to shout, to bring her to the phone so that he could make it all right with her, but he knew that moment had passed.

He had one last look around and then he headed for the door. It was time to keep moving.

Forty-one

Mark Proctor didn't need a torch as he made his way through the old building, he'd been through it so many times. It was in complete darkness lower down, the windows blocked out, but as he climbed higher the occasional broken windowpane let in the faint strains of street lighting. He'd learned to ignore the bats that swooped through the building whenever he disturbed them, the scrape of his soles on loose stones making the frantic flap of tiny wings fill the night. He felt them like a breeze around his hair.

He couldn't sit in the house any longer. Everything was changing, so he craved solitude. Usually, the scene would calm him, take him through all the years he'd visited the derelict block, but he was clenching and unclenching his fists. This time, it felt like goodbye.

After three flights of stairs, he arrived at his favourite place. This was where he watched and observed. There was an old mattress in one corner, propped up on the side, blankets behind it, next to a broken window over which he'd placed a piece of roof tile. It was held in place by a bent nail, so that he could turn to release it. He removed it and peered through. It was just the usual scene. Streets and apartment blocks, the flickers of the headlights on nearby roads.

He stepped away and went to the opposite corner, where he'd wedged a piece of tarpaulin in a hole in the roof that he'd created. It went a small way to keeping out the rain but it still made it through, slowly rotting the wooden flooring. Not that it mattered. The place had been deserted for years and he couldn't imagine anyone developing it soon.

He pulled at the tarpaulin and blinked at the stars that burst into view. The view from the window wasn't enough. He wanted to feel the night, not just gaze at it. He reached up into the gap and wedged his elbows onto the tiles. It was getting harder all the time, unfitness getting the better of him, but by hoisting himself upwards and then sliding forwards onto his stomach, he was able to tumble into the bottom of the V where the two roofs met.

The canal and roads were far below him, the people just small figures on the pavement. He leaned back against the roof, the tiles digging into him, the night air cooling his light coating of sweat.

How had it all got to this? All of these years, it had been him in charge. Now, someone was getting the better of him. That wasn't how it was supposed to be.

A friend had been murdered, someone who needed a quick injection of cash, and had accepted Proctor's offer of payment in exchange for collecting something. Proctor had set off before him once they'd swapped cars, and had been waiting further along. He'd watched as the man stepped out of the shadows and crept towards the brick folly, a nearby light catching the glint of metal. There'd been a frenzy of movement and then the man was running and his friend lay on the floor. As the man bolted back to his car, Proctor saw his face. The man's identity changed everything.

He wrapped his arms around himself. It was going to be a long, cold night, but he needed to take one last look and enjoy a final night of calm. In the morning, it was time to hurt those who'd hurt him.

*

219

Joe got a taxi to Melissa's apartment building.

He'd texted her first, just to ask her if he could go there. He needed to be somewhere that his family didn't know about, and a hotel would create a credit-card trail.

'Couldn't keep away?' she whispered, as he walked along the corridor to her apartment. She put her finger to her lips as he went inside. 'Carrie has just gone to her room. I don't want her to hear you.'

Joe rushed past her.

'What's wrong?' she said.

Joe took her hands in his and said, 'We need to talk.' He led her to the chair, so that they were sitting opposite.

'Joe, what is it? You're scaring me.'

'I need you to know that I felt something. I hope you did too.'

Melissa sat back and crossed her legs. Tears brimmed onto her eyelashes. 'This didn't take long, did it?'

'What do you mean?'

'The brush-off. The goodbye.' She wiped her eyes. 'Don't worry, this is for me, not you. Yes, I felt something, but now your ego has been buffed up, you're free to go.'

Joe leaned forward and took her hands again. He dipped his head to catch her gaze. 'This is not the brush-off,' he said. 'But I haven't been totally open with you; I should have been more honest. I'm sorry. It's difficult.'

'There's someone else?'

'No one else. That's not what this is about.' He looked directly into her eyes and said, 'I'm going to tell you things now that you won't understand. Or perhaps you will, I don't know, but I'm deadly serious.' He took a deep breath. 'You were right when you said I was devoting a lot of time to Mark's case, more than you'd expect for a burglary. I'm a good lawyer, but I'm not that thorough. I can promise you one thing though: I wasn't using you. I've surprised myself, but

I'm here now because I care about you. You've got to trust me on this.'

'Joe, just say it.'

His mouth was dry. He swallowed. 'Seventeen years ago, my younger sister was murdered. Followed down a woodland path not far from our home and strangled. It was on my eighteenth birthday.'

Melissa's hands gripped his tighter. 'Oh Joe, I'm sorry.'

'Your brother killed her.'

Melissa's mouth opened, her eyes widened. She dropped her hands and one went over her mouth. She turned away.

'Mark killed her?' A pause. 'Can you be sure?'

'Yes, I'm sure.'

Melissa stayed silent as she thought about what Joe had said, sometimes looking up as if she was about to say something, before realising that words couldn't make sense of what he'd said.

Eventually, she said, 'Tell me the story.'

So he did. He told her everything. What he'd done on his eighteenth birthday, and the secret he'd lived with ever since. His certainty when he saw Mark at the police station.

'This week has been the strangest week,' Joe said. 'It's the moment I've been waiting for, ever since then, but now it's arrived it doesn't feel like I expected. And now it's all gone wrong. I'm in trouble, Melissa.'

'What do you mean?'

'I followed your brother tonight. After I left here, my little sister Ruby told me your brother had approached her outside the school.' Joe blew out. 'Waiting for my other little sister, who's had to live in the shadow of what your brother did all of her life.'

'Why would he do that?'

'To taunt me, I'm guessing.'

'But why?'

221

'Because he's always known who I am.'

'You sound angry with me,' she said. 'Yes, he's my brother, but he's not me.'

'I'm not angry with you. I'm just angry. You don't have to apologise for him. Once I heard that, though, I waited outside his house. I was going to follow through with my threat, was trying to build up to it.'

'Threat?'

'To kill him.'

'You were going to kill my brother?' She shook her head violently. 'I don't speak to him, but he's still my brother, and still my parents' son. For them, and for your sake, don't do it. Joe, you're better than that. You don't have it in you. I can see it in your eyes, in your tenderness. You're a good man, I can tell. And my parents . . . ' She exhaled. 'You said you're in trouble. Have you . . . ?'

'No, I haven't. Your brother is still alive, but someone else isn't so lucky.' He got to his feet and went to the window. He watched the lights outside, the steady stream of cars on a distant road, the beam from a canal boat. 'I waited outside his house and I followed him. He went to a green in Worsley. I parked close by and watched him.'

'Why? What were you going to do?'

'I don't know. That's just it. I had no plan, no idea. I was just watching him. Except it wasn't him. It was his car and his clothes, but I hadn't seen him up close. When I got into the park, the man who I thought was your brother was dead. There was blood everywhere. I got some on me, on my clothes. I stepped in it, so there will be traces in my car. Someone might have seen me running away from the scene.'

'What, you didn't stay and report it?'

'I panicked,' Joe said, turning around. 'I know it's no excuse, but this is something new for me; you can't rehearse how you'd react.'

'So who was he, the dead man?'

'I have no idea, but I think your brother does. He must have sent him as a decoy.'

'What, you think Mark knew he might be killed?'

'He must have suspected it.'

Melissa thought about that for a few seconds. 'You can't go home. Stay here. Just for tonight.'

Joe was about to protest that it wasn't fair on her, but he knew she'd see it for the lie it was. He'd gone there for that very reason. He was in trouble and he'd turned to her for help.

Forty-two

Sam woke up and got straight out of bed.

'What is it?' Alice mumbled, her face buried deep in the pillow.

'Last night. The online chat on that site.'

Alice lifted her head. 'It's not even six o'clock.'

'Sometimes these things need a few hours to settle in, as if the sleep sorts it all out,' he said.

'Where are you going?'

'Online.'

Alice groaned and put the pillow over her head.

Sam reached down for his clothes, still on the floor from the night before. As he lifted his trousers, his phone fell out. A light was flashing.

It was a text from Charlotte: *Can you pick me up? My car's got a flat.* It had come in fifteen minutes earlier. That was an early start.

He called her. When she answered, he said, 'Something happened?'

'Didn't Brabham ring you?' Charlotte said, crunching on her breakfast.

'No, he didn't.'

'There's another murder.'

Sam pinched his nose and wiped his eyes. 'Give me thirty minutes,' and he clicked off. 'There's another body.'

'There's always another body somewhere,' Alice said. 'What time will you be back this time? Before midnight?'

He didn't respond but got dressed quickly. It was a sad reality that a dead body meant long hours. And they didn't get shorter when a suspect was found, because then the interviews went on and on, the time of day irrelevant.

Before he left the bedroom, Alice held out her arm. He bent down to her, and when she pulled him closer, he kissed her, the taste of sleep on her lips.

'I'll be back when I can,' he said.

Before he left, he looked in on Ruby. She was sprawled along the sofa. He made a promise to himself that he would spend some time with her, once he was able to grab some for himself.

The drive to Charlotte's house was spent trying to become more alert, the heat turned down low in the car, the blowers on, using the cold air to get rid of the last traces of tiredness. When she climbed in, the car was filled with perfume.

'Where am I going?'

'Worsley,' she said, and yawned.

'That's not in our division.'

'There are some similarities to our case apparently, so Brabham wants to check for a link.'

As he drove, Sam said, 'I think I got something about the website. I was thinking about it before I went to bed and my brain must have somehow sorted it out when I was asleep.'

'I'm interested,' she said.

'I received a reply from vodkagirl last night. We had a brief chat, and pretty quickly she wanted a picture of me.'

Charlotte smiled. 'You've been out of the dating game too long.'

'I don't understand.'

'Dating is all about photos now. If I chat to a bloke online, and I do, they soon get to wanting to see me naked. It's almost as if they're not bothered about meeting me but just want to stay in front of a screen all night, tossing themselves off.'

'And?'

'I tell them to get lost.' Then she blushed. 'Most times anyway. But even when I'm not interested, it doesn't stop the cock pictures from coming in.'

'But if you want to exploit someone, you have to get their secrets. Take Bruce from yesterday. He said vodkagirl wanted to know his darkest secrets, something to share.'

'Yeah, I got that, and I mentioned about the paedophile-hunter, the guy who lured them to a meeting with a camera.'

'But what if it's more than that?' Sam said. 'There was something else Bruce said. Vodkagirl had told him that a teacher had abused her, trapped her in a storeroom and tried to take her virginity. She said she was looking for someone to understand her feelings but described it as abuse.'

'And?'

'It was meant to turn Bruce on but also make him be a hero, by describing the teacher as her abuser. And what was Keith Welsby?'

'A teacher,' Charlotte said, starting to smile.

'That's right,' Sam said. 'Was that the demand? Kill my abuser and you can have me?'

'That's extreme,' she said. 'Who'd go for that?'

'A man who has desires burning him up so that he can't control them any more. Dreams of children. Like Henry Mason.'

Charlotte shook her head. 'No, it's too far. Murdering someone is a big step.'

'But what if vodkagirl has his secrets? What if he's sent things to her, pictures of himself, or disclosed things he should have kept to himself?'

Charlotte didn't respond straight away, until she turned to smile. 'I like it. So vodkagirl either blackmails Henry Mason into murdering Keith Welsby because of secrets he disclosed, or else persuades him to be her hero, and then she will be all his?'

'That's what I'm thinking.'

'And Henry Mason turned up to meet an underage girl, his duty done, and what he got was his own murder.' She frowned. 'One problem, though: who killed Henry Mason?'

'The person behind the profile. Who else?'

'Brabham won't be happy.'

'Why? Method and motive solved. We just need to find out who's behind the profile.'

'Because it stops the domino effect pretty quickly,' she said. 'No more big-time press conferences on this case, and it means this new murder will have nothing to do with ours.'

'Perhaps someone shouldn't have spoken to the press so soon.'

They parked close to the crime scene, in front of a restaurant that had been squashed into a low-rise building fronted in white pebbledash.

The area had been closed off for a few hours, the call coming in during the night, but a lot of the work had been held off until daylight to avoid the risk of contaminating the scene; a crucial piece of evidence could be hidden in the dark and be taken away on the sole of someone's shoe, like a cigarette butt or a piece of paper.

'Where's Brabham?' Sam said.

Charlotte looked around before she pointed to a cluster of people and the glare of a television spotlight. 'Looks like he saw the lenses and went straight over.'

Sam watched until the cluster broke up, the interview done. Brabham stepped away but he paused before he made his way to his squad. He was talking to a young female journalist, smiling and touching her arm, something more than a brief quote. As he moved on and she turned to watch, Sam recognised her:

Lauren Spicer, the young reporter who'd tried to get a quote from him a couple of mornings before.

'You were right,' Sam said. When Charlotte looked confused, he added, 'The young reporter got her scoop from Brabham.'

'But who's using who?' Charlotte said.

'That's their problem,' Sam said, as he looked around. There was a small cobbled footbridge that rose over the canal. Trees hung over the water further along, near to a large building with a fake Tudor front. A barge puttered along in bright reds and greens, with flowers spilling out of boxes on its roof, steered by a man in a wispy beard and denim cap, happy living in his cliché.

'It's a similar location,' Sam said. 'A local attraction to make sure the body will be discovered at some point, but quiet too. The houses nearby are the sort where people don't look out much, hidden behind high hedges. The road that passes is too far away to make for good eyewitnesses, and it's a major route to the motorway.'

'It's a park too,' Charlotte said. 'The local plods are probably called here most weekends in the summer, a magnet for those too old to stay indoors but not old enough for the pubs. So who would pay any attention to shouts and screams, except perhaps for a weary call to the local station?'

Crime scene tape was drawn in a wide arc around the green. Someone hovered nearby with flowers even though the victim hadn't been identified; wanting to be seen on the news, was Sam's guess. There was a small huddle of detectives in forensic suits at the edge of the crime scene tape.

Sam and Charlotte walked towards them. As they got closer, Sam said, 'So what have you got?'

One of the crime scene technicians pulled her hood down, her dark hair plastered to her head. 'A dead man in park and some sort of rendezvous,' she said. 'Stab wounds. Under the ear, the chest, a couple in the ribs.'

'The method is different, then,' Sam said. 'How long has he been there?'

'A few hours, most likely overnight. Rigor mortis has set in and the pool of blood has congealed.'

'Do we know who he is?'

'No, not yet. He was dressed casually. Hoodie and jeans. No flowers. It could be a feud over something. There's a hire car parked on the road just through there,' and she gestured towards the canal. 'The keys are in his pocket and it's been there all night. That's why it looks like a rendezvous, because he made a special trip. The local car hire place hasn't opened yet, so we can't get details of the hirer. Nothing obvious on his person.'

'Any sign of a struggle?'

'No, nothing. No other injuries apart from the stab wounds. My guess is that he was approached from behind and there was a frenzied attack. There are easier ways to kill someone, if that was the intention.'

Sam pointed at the brick monument and said, 'What is this thing? It looks like someone started to build a tower and stopped, so stuck a birdbath inside.'

'Built because they felt like it,' one of the nearby detectives said.

There were footsteps behind them, and as Sam turned, he saw it was Brabham.

'Let's not get any closer,' Brabham said. 'Not until we're suited up.'

Sam turned slowly on the spot, his hands on his hips. 'Why here?'

'The same reason as the other place, I suppose,' Brabham said. 'Quiet at night with good escape routes. Better than meeting in a pub.'

'But why this specific place, and the other place?' Sam said. 'It's got to be somewhere, I know that, but what if there is a reason for the meeting being here? When you choose a meeting place, it's a conscious decision, a thought process. It might be worth checking whether there is any link to these places. A history perhaps.'

'And if the domino theory is right,' Brabham said, 'the man there might be Henry Mason's killer.' He smiled to himself and said, 'One by one they fall.'

Sam suppressed his groan. Brabham had worked out the headline already. Sam was troubled, though, because he had to agree that there were some similarities with the Welsby and Mason murders. A man murdered in a frenzied attack when waiting around in a quiet and green area. It looked like Brabham was getting lucky, that he might be getting his dominoes.

Sam was happy about one thing, though: the more bodies there are, the stronger the likelihood that there would be a connection. It was little solace for whoever was carved up behind the forensic screen, but he'd just helped create a better chance of finding his killer.

Forty-three

Joe was unsure of his surroundings as he opened his eyes. He was in a large bed under a crisp white duvet, the morning sunlight brightening the wooden beams that crossed the bedroom ceiling. As someone stirred next to him, it came back to him. He was in Melissa's bed, fully-clothed, the disclosures of the night before draining them both. They'd spent the night talking until sleep had taken over, although it had been fitful. His mouth felt dry, his skin tired.

He reached across to move the hair from her face. He leaned in and kissed her. She smelled of warm clothes.

'I've got to go,' he whispered.

She stirred, her eyes barely open. 'Do you have to?'

'I'm sorry. I'll make it up to you.'

Melissa rolled over to look at the clock. She rubbed her face and yawned. 'Carrie will be up soon. She'll go straight into the bathroom. As soon as she does, sneak out. I'm not ready for the awkward questions.'

'Okay, will do.'

She propped herself up on her elbows. 'So what are you going to do today?'

'Follow your brother,' he said, stretching out, trying not to make a noise.

'And?'

'Just see what he's up to.'

'And if you can prove that he's responsible for any deaths?'

'I'll tell the police.'

'Are you allowed to do that? You're his lawyer.'

'At the moment, I'll be a suspect for last night's death. Right now, my needs come first.' He sighed. 'There are ways of doing it. Lawyers have been tipping off the police for years. Often just hints, whispers as to where they should direct their investigations, but a tip just the same.'

'I thought you were meant to help them, the criminals.'

'So did I, back when I first started out. I've learned the hard way that it's about making money, and there's no money to be made from crooks who don't get caught. No, we need them banged up just like everyone else does.'

She shuffled across the bed and put her arms round him. When she pulled him close, into her warmth, the smell of stale perfume, he wanted to stay there. If he did, he wouldn't have to face all the hurt.

'Just be careful,' she said, breaking the spell.

'Can I ask you something?' he said, his face buried into her neck, so that his words came out muffled.

'Yes, sure.'

'Have you ever suspected him of anything like this?'

She pulled away and looked him in the eye, her finger tracing small circles on his cheek. 'No, never,' she said. 'He's insignificant; no one would suspect him. That might be his disguise.'

'There's never been any police interest, even calls to see whether he knew anything?'

'No, nothing.'

'And another thing,' he said. 'Can I borrow your car?'

She smiled. 'Keys are on the side in the kitchen. Little black Alfa Romeo in the underground car park.'

He kissed her. 'Thank you. If I find anything out, will you help me?'

'What, help the police catch my brother?'

'No,' he said. 'Help the police catch a killer.'

She drew his head into her chest and held him one last time. 'If you can prove that's what he is, I'll do anything to stop him.'

Gina groaned and clasped her head as she rolled over in bed, the memory of the night before rushing at her. She needed to open her eyes more slowly. Her curtains were too thin to block out the light so the early-morning sun made her wince. She drank too much wine when she was alone, she knew that, but the events of the day before had made her hit the bottle a little harder than usual. Hangovers hung around longer than they used to, it was an age thing she knew, and she wanted to be clearheaded.

The walk across the bedroom was a weave. She grabbed a dressing gown as she made her way to the bathroom, and then dry-heaved over the toilet bowl as the effect of movement assaulted her.

She just about hung onto what she'd eaten the night before and straightened so that she could confront the mirror. Her hair was tangled over her face and her cheeks were flushed.

The light in the bathroom was unforgiving, bright spotlights in the ceiling, showing the wrinkles and creases she spent time hiding in her morning routine. The reflection wasn't a happy one. Her hands gripped the edge of the sink as she leaned in.

So this was it, the beginning of the end of her life. No job, just a long stretch of empty days ahead.

It was an uncomfortable truth that Gina had avoided by filling her days working for Joe and then relishing the downtime of the weekend. She'd told herself that she worked for Joe because of some desire to stay in the game, that she missed the world of crime when she left the police so much that she needed to work for a defence lawyer, but the truth was much simpler than that: she was lonely.

Not many people got close to Gina and saw the woman she became when she hung her suit in the wardrobe. Her life was uncomplicated, with no man to mess it up, but with complications came a busy life. Once she went home and the suit went away, all she had was a book for the evening, or wine and television, just marking time until the following morning. If she didn't work at all, what would she have?

It was quiet moments of reflection like that when her shield came down. If she collapsed in the house, who would find her? No one visited. She wrapped up her feelings as privacy, but it meant there was never anyone who called round just to see how she was. She'd accepted Joe's job offer to stop the way ahead being nothing more than decades of long nights alone.

Thoughts of the night before took her back to when Ellie was killed.

Not many killers got away from her when she was in charge of her own murder squad, so Ellie's death hung around her career like a stain. Knowing what Joe had seen might have changed things. Why hadn't she spotted that he was hiding something? He'd been so different to Sam, who'd been vocal and tearful and angry, wanting to get at whoever it was who'd killed his sister, but that changed into support for his mother. Gina had watched Sam grow up right in front of her, as he became the older brother, determined to cope. Joe had been different. He'd been withdrawn and quiet, lost in his own thoughts. At the time, she'd put that down to just how he dealt with things, everyone is different, but she'd been wrong all along and not spotted it. He'd been hiding a secret.

She leaned into the mirror again and grimaced. Her grey roots were showing where her hair parted. Lines puckered around her mouth and the creases around her eyes didn't disappear when the grimace ended. She pulled her robe tighter. She prided herself on her body but she didn't need the stark glare of spotlights to tell her that time was ruthless as it marched on.

She felt old, and she didn't want to. She still had a lot to offer.

Images of Joe came back to her from the night before, just flashes, the haze of alcohol making her wonder whether it had really happened like that, but she knew it was true. Joe was no longer the person she'd known. Now he was scared, in hiding, a prisoner of his mistake seventeen years earlier.

But he was still Joe Parker, the man she'd known ever since the day his sister died. Legally, he became an adult on the day Ellie was murdered, his eighteenth birthday, but Gina remembered the fresh face, barely shaving, and the long skinny legs, not yet fully adapted to his grown-up size. She cared about him. Did she really think he could have anything to do with a murder? No, of course not.

She went back to her bedroom to look for her phone, finding it under a pile of clothes. Scrolling quickly, she found Joe's number.

She'd made her decision. She needed to help him.

Forty-four

Mark Proctor was smiling as he walked.

It had been a good start to the day. He'd had a night to think about what to do, sitting on the roof, huddled against the cold. By the time the morning came round, cold and sharp, he'd worked it out. The day had improved when he got home and saw his metal box had been returned, left outside his front door. He'd wanted to cradle it, examine its contents, but instead he'd returned it to its place in his workshop – he'd look through it later. Now for a different plan.

He was a long way from home, in one of the villages close to the Yorkshire border. The house in front of him was large and made of stone, some Pennine grandeur in contrast to the grimy bricks of the council estate behind and overshadowed by the hills that rose in the distance. There were stone bay windows on either side of wooden double doors, the curtains open, showing off the large paintings of mills that adorned the furthest walls, celebrating what had built the towns but blighted the valleys.

Proctor paused for a moment. What he was about to do would change everything but he knew he had no choice. He climbed up the three stone steps that took him through flower-beds bordered by stone walls. He made his soles scrape noisily, hoping the noise had travelled inside.

He rang the doorbell and stepped back. It chimed through the house. He was going to enjoy this.

He turned around and looked into the valley. He wanted to

reveal himself like a showstopper, so he looked along the slate roofs that were warped through time, the houses in long rows. Remnants of history.

There was a delay before anyone answered. The door opened slowly.

Proctor turned around. He grinned. There was a man with thinning grey hair who kept his body behind the door, so that only the top of his head and scared eyes were showing.

The man's eyes widened when he saw him, and his fingers gripped the edge of the door a little tighter.

'Hello,' Proctor said, and grinned wider, his head cocked. 'I'm the man you were supposed to kill last night.'

Joe leaned against a fence in a small ginnel, where a line of wooden fences and trees made a snaking short cut that no one dared use. His hood was up, his hands thrust into his pockets. It made him look more suspicious, but at that moment anonymity seemed more important.

Proctor had gone into a house opposite, large and grand, three storeys, with a front garden that was terraced to the low wall at the front. The view behind was part-green, part-urban, wild Pennine slopes and downbeat housing. Cars streamed past constantly, and Joe hoped they provided enough of a distraction.

Joe had almost missed him. There'd been no car outside Proctor's house when he first arrived, so Joe was about to leave, unsure what to do, but then Proctor rushed back. He was driving a different car, a small green hatchback with a dent around one of the front light clusters, black tape holding in the glass. He'd rushed in, pausing only to collect something by the door, and stayed inside for around thirty minutes. When he came out again, he'd showered and changed, his hair still wet. Joe had followed.

Now all he had to do was wait to see what Proctor did.

*

Proctor walked along the hallway and into a kitchen at the back of the house, the man leading the way.

The kitchen was warm. There was a clothes rack over the hot plates of a yellow Aga, with socks and T-shirts spread out. There was an old square sink under a stone drainer and dusty hooks on the wall. It all looked reproduction, though, as if the man had ripped out whatever modern look had been adopted in the sixties and tried to take the house back to the grand old house it would have once been. The lure of original features trapped the house in time. Photographs adorned every cupboard: a child's smiling face, on holiday or at Christmas, some school photographs, a mother, proud and protective. Some of the photographs were old and faded by the sun that streamed through the large window.

Proctor's eyes narrowed.

The man shuffled as he walked, his shoulders slumped in an old sweatshirt and creased trousers.

Proctor sat down at the table. His chair creaked. The man went to the sink and grabbed a glass from the drainer, filling it with water from the tap. He stared out of the window and drank it slowly.

'People will comment,' Proctor said. 'What have you done? Called in sick, just not feeling up to it? Your first mistake, acting differently. Tell me, how did it feel? How were you when you got home? Scared? Or empowered, pumped with adrenalin, unable to sleep, filled with that sweet buzz of revenge?' Proctor laughed. 'And here I am.' He pointed to the drawer underneath the window. 'Is that the knife drawer?'

The man turned round and put the glass back on the drainer. 'What?'

'If you fancy another go, open it. I won't move. I'll just sit here and let you.' Proctor grinned. 'Watch out for arterial spray. It goes everywhere.'

'I don't know what you mean.'

'Oh come, don't be silly,' Proctor said. 'I guessed what was going to happen, so I sent a friend along, a quick hundred quid. Collect something and bring it back. He was just the courier service.'

The man looked down and gripped the edge of the sink. He said nothing.

Proctor reached into his pocket and pulled out a memory card. 'This contains the photographs I took. I parked further along from you and got everything.'

The man groaned and slumped to the floor. He sat back against the kitchen units. 'What do you want?'

'Money, of course,' Proctor said. 'This memory card is for sale, for the right price.'

'I haven't got any money, you bastard.'

'You should reign in your temper. I'm the man you were supposed to kill. I should be the one who's angry. Losing control means you make mistakes.'

The man didn't respond.

'And what about your friends? They'll never stop talking about it. Who would have thought it, Gerald a killer. It is Gerald, isn't it? Or do you prefer Gerry?' Proctor smiled. It was time to reel him in. 'So who set this up? The same happened to me. They had something of mine that I wanted back. We've been played, both of us. You'll get a message soon, asking you to meet her for your special treat. If you do, bang, you're next.'

'I've got nothing to hide.'

'You sure? I've got the pictures, remember.' And he waved the memory card.

'How much do you want?'

'Fifty thousand.' When Gerald scoffed, Proctor added, 'I want more, of course, but I've got to pick an amount you can get your hands on.'

'How the hell can I get that much?'

'Get creative.' Proctor winked. 'Just get a few credit cards

239

and you'll soon run it up. Withdraw the cash and give it to me. Sell your car and do the same. I'll enjoy sending these pictures to the police if you don't. It would create a ripple. I like ripples. You're a splash guy, I can tell.'

'What are you talking about?'

'Last night was just about that, nothing else. All you wanted was me. I bet it tortured you beforehand, all those years dreaming of it. And then there it was, the chance to get me.' Proctor shook his head. 'You've no imagination. Some people like to throw in a big rock and get off on the splash, the shock, but that isn't where the real enjoyment is. That's instant, thoughtless. No, it's the ripples you should search for. The splash is just the mechanism, but what follows is truly special, because the ripples affect everything they touch.'

'Just get to the point.'

'Which is why I would enjoy sending these pictures. I could sit back and watch your life being destroyed.'

'All right, I get it!' Gerald snapped. 'Wrap it up in whatever you want but it's just a sleazy blackmail plot.'

'We've all got bills to pay, Gerald, but I will do something else for you.'

'What?'

'I'll blame someone else for it, because you weren't the only person in the park last night.'

'How are you going to do that?'

'Give me something I can lay a trap with. The knife would be best.'

'I've cleaned it,' he said. Then his eyes widened. 'I wiped it off with a rag. It's in the garage, under something. I was going to bury it somewhere later, or burn it.'

Proctor grinned. 'Perfect.'

Forty-five

Joe checked his watch. Proctor had been in the house for nearly half an hour. Who else was there? One of Proctor's clients? Or was it an accomplice?

The front door of the house opened. Joe cursed and stepped backwards. He hid behind the branches of a laurel bush that were spreading through a hole in a fence. Proctor came out. He was whistling. He skipped down the stone steps and went to his car. He looked back up to the window, where a man was staring down at him. Proctor waved and then got into his car. The man in the window didn't move as he watched Proctor drive away.

A few minutes went by while Joe thought about what to do. Whoever was in that house seemed pivotal somehow, because Proctor had made the house his first trip of the day. And he'd lost Proctor, the sound of his engine long since faded into the steady drone of traffic noise.

The door opened again, and this time the man in the window was rushing down the steps towards a car parked further along, a red Jaguar, old-style.

Once the noise of the Jaguar disappeared as Proctor's had, Joe stepped out of the ginnel.

Now what should he do? Both Proctor and the man had left so there was no chance of Joe following. But Proctor had headed straight for the house, and whatever Proctor had visited for, it had made the man rush off. The answers must be in that house and Joe was in no mood to wait for events to reveal themselves. It could end up with Joe waiting on the wrong side of prison bars.

The street was busy with cars and buses, the sort of road that people drove along to get somewhere else rather than a destination in itself. No one would notice Joe walking to the house. There was a shale path running alongside it, a cut-through to the council estate on the other side, visible as brick blights beyond a line of concrete bollards. Joe thrust his hands into his pockets and headed for the path. He tried to look casual, his shoes scuffing the loose stones, but he was becoming conspicuous in his attempts. Just stay natural, he told himself, but what was natural in this situation?

He reached the back of the house without being seen and looked for a sign that someone else was in there, but everything looked dark.

The garden was bordered by a stone wall around six feet high. There was a gate under a stone archway. He pushed at it, but it just rattled in the frame, bolted on the other side.

Joe glanced quickly both ways and then launched himself at the wall. He hauled himself up, his feet pushing up on the uneven stonework and with his arms over the top. It scraped his stomach as he straddled it before he dropped onto the other side.

His shoes made a loud smack as he landed. He took deep breaths and sank to his haunches. Someone in the house next door would be able to see him if they looked out of the window. He waited for a shout but there was nothing.

The garden was a long rectangle, with a gravel path running between two brick planters, decking and chairs at the other end, pushed up against the wall. The chairs would give him another route out of the house if he were disturbed. He could vault the wall, using a chair to give him the help up, and disappear into the estate behind, where the intruder would be put down to some addict.

Satisfied that he hadn't been spotted, he ran along the path that bordered the garden until he was flat against the house. He leaned over with his hands on his thighs and sucked in air. This wasn't him, creeping around gardens. As he straightened, he knew that he was about to go a step further.

He walked slowly up to the back door, old and wooden, painted green, with flakes that pointed outwards like jagged fingers. There were small lattice windowpanes, dusty and cob-webbed, not double-glazed. Joe pressed his face against the glass to see how it was locked. The tarnished brass of a key stuck out of the lock. That made it easy.

Joe slipped off his jacket and screwed it into a ball before placing it against one of the panes. He closed his eyes for a moment, knowing that he was about to take the step that could end his career. But the stakes were higher than that.

The glass made hardly a sound when Joe punched his jacket, cushioning the blow but with enough force left to shatter the pane nearest the key. He reached in before he could change his mind and turned the key. When it clicked, he pushed at the door. It opened with a creak. The bottom of the door scraped on the broken glass. He stepped inside.

He'd crossed the line. All he could do now was keep on going.

He was in the kitchen. The glass crunched underfoot as he set off. He needed to find out more. He just didn't know what he was looking for.

The kitchen door opened into a hallway lined by old tiles, black and white squares and surrounded by a coloured border. The stairs ran from near the front door, by the entrance to the room that overlooked the road. There was a room at the back that looked out over the garden: a dining room.

Joe stepped quickly across the hallway and into the back

room. Sun streamed in through the French doors. It was a room to relax in, with a sagging chair in each corner. The walls were covered in pictures and photographs of a woman in her forties, with a teenage girl alongside. They were the most recent. The other pictures of them made Joe feel like he was winding back time as he turned; the woman became younger, slimmer, her hair longer, the girl became a young child and then a toddler. There were paintings stuck to all the surfaces, childlike, a small family group with the people drawn like rectangles, and a boat under a yellow circle of a sun. There were no pictures of the man, though.

There was a small desk in a corner, with the large monitor linked to a computer that was blinking a blue light underneath, the fans blowing lightly. There was nothing showing on the screen.

Joe went over to it and nudged the mouse. The screen flickered into a life. The desktop image was the same as one of the photographs on the wall, the woman and the teenage girl, hugging each other in front of the gleam of a reservoir. There was no password required.

Computers hold people's secrets, those dark places they visit when home alone, thinking that no one was watching. There is always a trail, though, even though it often takes an expert to find it, because no internet visit is invisible. Someone, somewhere, is always watching.

Joe went to the browser history first. It had been cleared. That might be routine. Or the man might be hiding something.

The email software was next. Joe was transfixed as it loaded in.

The inbox was full. The man was called Gerald King. A lot of it was rubbish. Emails from camping and angling sites, an astronomy site. It was mundane.

But there was one sequence of conversation that came from a sender titled only 'anonymous'. When Joe moved the mouse down, it highlighted a large number of messages. There had been quite some conversation.

He went to the top one first. It was a short message: **You got the wrong one.**

Joe went down the list, clicking as he went, his mouth opening wider as he read. He couldn't believe what he was reading.

He swallowed, his fingers trembling on the mouse. There was one with an attachment. Joe paused before opening the email, not wanting to see what he thought he might find.

It was a picture message entitled 'Katie'.

Joe groaned and closed his eyes as the image filled the screen. He felt the blood rush round his head, warming his cheeks.

The picture was of the same teenage girl as in the photographs, except this time she was lying on the ground. Her mouth was open in a grimace, faint bruises visible around her neck. Her eyes were closed, her shirt torn open, her small bra pushed up to show her breasts, her head against stone steps.

Joe had to clench his teeth to stop the bile rising. It wasn't the image itself – he'd seen plenty of crime scene photographs – but what he knew it represented. The murder of a teenage girl, strangled, the girl so full of life in the photographs on the walls so lifeless on the screen.

Joe was so engrossed in the image he hadn't heard the turn of the key, or the soft footsteps along the tiled hallway. He gasped as someone gripped his hood and forced his head onto the desk.

Forty-six

Sam was back in his car, the traffic streaming past, some of it slowing down so that people could look at the crime scene, the tape acting like an advertising banner. Was the killer in one of the cars, cruising past to enjoy his work? Sam glanced into the faces of those passing now and again, hoping to see something he recognised, like satisfaction, but he saw nothing more than intrigue.

He was searching the internet on his phone, his notepad open on his knees. It seemed an easier place to start than the police computer. Some of the uniformed police officers were watching him, especially the younger ones, in their eyes the hope that they'd end up on the Murder Squad. It was long hours and often unglamorous, but there is no higher reward than catching a killer. That moment of arrest beats everything, even though it's only the start of the journey, with a court case and potential pitfalls ahead. Sitting in his car close to a main road didn't seem like much, but it was the case coming together, and he relished that part of it.

He'd put the name of the grassy area into the search bar, and he found something sixteen pages in. Katie King, a schoolgirl murdered just over seven years earlier.

He clicked on the link and brought up an old newspaper article. It was lacking in detail, mainly an appeal for information. Katie had been at her boyfriend's house but they'd argued. She was fifteen, and the usual routine was that he'd walk her home. Not always the whole way, but at least so far that he could watch her until she turned into her driveway. That changed on the night she died. They'd fallen out over something trivial and Katie had stormed off. The walk home was a long one and it rained, so she took a short cut through the green. Her body was found the following day. She'd been strangled and her clothes partially removed. The article didn't say whether there'd been a sexual assault.

The most recent hit Sam could find was a fresh appeal for information three years earlier, but no sign that anyone had ever been caught.

Sam put his head back, frustrated. That was too remote a connection. Every park or open space in Manchester has probably had a murder at some point. Open spaces in the city attract killers because they provide privacy and darkness.

There was movement ahead. It was Brabham, walking towards him, tugging on his lip, looking thoughtful. It looked as though there had been a development. Sam stepped out of his car.

'I found something but it's too old,' Sam said, holding up his phone as Brabham came up to him. 'A girl killed here just over seven years ago. Katie King, but apart from that, nothing.'

Brabham put his hands on his hips so that his suit jacket splayed out. 'We've got a name,' he said. 'The hire car parked on the main road was hired out to a Mark Proctor. His occupation is listed as financial services.'

The space around Sam went quiet, like a door had been closed. He swallowed, his mouth suddenly dry, his hand reaching out for the support of the car. Sam knew the implications of what had been said; they rushed at him like a gale.

'Mark Proctor? Are you sure?'

Brabham looked surprised. 'You sound like you know the name?'

Sam was confused. He went as if to say something, but couldn't think what to say. He looked back towards the green.

'His name came up in relation to something else,' Sam said eventually. Unconvincingly. 'I'll go back to the incident room, try to find it.'

'Can you remember what?'

'No, not off the top of my head. If I go back there, it might trigger it.'

'You sure? I was going to Proctor's house. I wondered if you fancied coming along.'

'No, no, I'll need to do this,' Sam said, and climbed back into his car. 'It might be crucial.'

When he was back in the driving seat, he wiped his forehead as Brabham walked towards his own car. He was sweating. He looked back towards the green. It looked different, threatening somehow, the shadows created by the trees darker.

Oh Joe, what have you done?

Forty-seven

Joe gasped. The computer keyboard dug into his face, the desk banged against the wall. The man was screaming, not making any sense, loud in his ears. Joe pushed back using the edge of the desk. He needed to get away.

As Joe strained, the man's grip slackened, as if he was losing his balance. One more heave backwards and the man stumbled, so Joe kept on back-pedalling across the room, grunting with exertion. The room filled with noise. The clatter of a chair. The man's screams. A shout of pain. Two bodies stumbling, Joe on top.

A chair leg caught Joe in a rib, made him cry out, but he had no time to pause. The man was underneath him. Joe kicked back with his heel, catching the man on his shin, making him slacken his grip. Joe rolled away and scrambled to his feet. He leaned against the wall, panting from exertion.

He looked down at the man on the floor. He was holding his leg and lying in a foetal position. He turned to glare up at Joe. 'Who are you? Why are you in my house?'

'I'm the man who's leaving,' Joe said, and moved along the wall.

'Wait, don't!' the man said, and he rolled over so he could get to his knees. 'I'm not going to attack you,' he said, and there was defeat in his voice. He swallowed and closed his eyes. A tear escaped. 'Are you the police?'

'No, I'm just a man looking for answers.' Joe pushed himself away from the wall. He was wary of the man but he didn't seem dangerous. 'Are you working with Proctor? I saw him here earlier.'

The man opened his eyes and shook his head, incredulity on his face. 'No, not ever.'

'So why was he here?'

'I can't tell you.'

'I know what Mark Proctor is capable of,' Joe said.

'How do you know?'

Joe wondered whether he should tell him, but the picture that had been emailed and the photographs on the wall told him one thing: the man's daughter had been murdered.

'Mark Proctor murdered my sister,' Joe said.

The man's mouth gaped open. 'When was this?'

'Seventeen years ago.'

The man stayed silent, staring ahead, until he said, 'What was her name?'

'Eleanor. We called her Ellie. Proctor killed her on her way home from school, strangled her and discarded her like rubbish.'

'I'm Gerald King. That's my daughter in the photographs. Katie. Like your sister, killed and left as if she was nothing. Seven years ago now.'

'Tell me about her.'

'Loving, kind, sweet, trusting.' He wiped his eye.

Joe went over to the dining table and pulled out a chair. 'Don't sit on the floor, Gerald.'

He got to his feet and sat down opposite.

'How did she die?' Joe said.

'Katie had gone to a youth club with her boyfriend. She went every Tuesday. It was late April so it got dark fairly early, and it was dark when she left. I told her to call me if her boyfriend couldn't walk her, so that I could pick her up, but I'd been working late that night. She argued with her boyfriend. Katie didn't call me, she called her mum. I'd have left work to collect her, but Nicola, that's my wife, well, she'd been drinking. She'd started drinking more. Katie needed her less and Nicola felt a bit redundant, I think, so a glass of wine every night turned into a bottle. Katie rang home, her friends had gone on to a party so she was on her own, but Nicola couldn't collect her because she'd been drinking. So Katie walked home on her own. She never made it. Found on the green at Worsley. Strangled. Her clothes were all messed around with, her jeans round her knees, but the police said she hadn't been, well, you know ... '

The green at Worsley. Where the man was killed the night before.

Gerald paused to wipe his eyes. 'We should have been there for her, but we weren't.'

The guilt of those left behind, thinking that if they'd done things differently, their loved one would still be alive. God knows Joe knew that feeling well enough.

'Where's Nicola now?' Joe said.

'What do you think a drinker does if she blames her drinking for the death of a loved one? I can tell you: she drinks more.' Gerald looked at the ceiling and attempted to blink away the tears. When he looked down again, his cheeks were wet. 'We moved house so that we didn't have to see that place every day, but the hurt moves with you. So one day, she ended it. Hanged herself from the stair rail. I found her when I got home from work. I'd lost everyone then.'

Joe closed his eyes and let out a long sigh. This was getting too hard.

'So why was Proctor here?' Joe said.

Gerald clenched his jaw but didn't respond.

Joe remembered the email. *You got the wrong one.*

'It was you,' Joe said, aghast. 'You killed that man last night, whoever he was.'

251

Gerald stayed silent.

'Talk to me. I need to know.'

'What, so you can tell everyone what I told you and I go to prison for the rest of my life?'

'You did it because you thought he was Mark Proctor,' Joe said. 'I was following him for the same reason.'

Gerald looked at the floor. He was silent for a few moments before he said, 'He killed Katie. And he killed Nicola, in a different way.'

'Where did the email come from, with the pictures?'

'You saw it?' When Joe nodded, Gerald said, 'Someone who wouldn't give his real name. He told me he'd burgled Proctor and taken a box. There were things in it. Pictures, jewellery, newspaper articles.'

Joe's eyes widened. 'And?'

'He said he wouldn't go to the police because he couldn't go back to prison, and he hadn't been out long,' Gerald said. 'But he said what Proctor had done was wrong. Whatever bad things he'd done, it was nothing compared to Proctor. He wasn't prepared to come forward but he was giving me the chance to make it right. He reckoned Proctor would kill again, because people like him always do. The only way to stop Proctor was to kill him, and this person was giving me the chance. I've thought of nothing else for seven years. So when I got there, I couldn't stop myself. I lost it, just stabbed and stabbed until he stopped moving.'

'Why didn't you just tell the police and let them trace the emails?' Joe said.

'Because he said he would destroy everything if I did. There were other things there too. Some earrings, and some pictures of Katie not long before she died. I could have them if I killed Proctor, if I got rid of the man who took my daughter away from me.'

'How sure were you about this?'

252

'I asked him for proof. He sent me a picture of Katie's note-book. She carried one around with her because she used to pass messages in class. Just silly teenage girl stuff. I recognised her writing. Katie's notepad was missing. I asked the police at the time, because I thought it would have her final thoughts in it. Who she liked, music, just the daft things that made her the person she was. He'd kept it, like some cheap souvenir. I wanted it back and I couldn't stand the thought of him destroying it.'

'Something about this doesn't seem right,' Joe said. 'Could it have been Proctor you were speaking to all along?'

'I don't understand.'

'That has to be it,' Joe said, leaning forward. 'Who else would have access to those souvenirs? And why was he here?'

'Why do you think?' Gerald said. 'To taunt me, because I got it wrong.' He shook his head again. 'I killed the wrong man.'

'Just taunt?'

'And blackmail.'

'Whoa, that changes everything.'

'How so?'

'You're saying that you received emails that persuaded you that Mark Proctor is your daughter's killer. You were told not to leak the information but instead kill Mark Proctor. The wrong man was sent and you killed him. Then Mark Proctor comes here and demands money from you. How much?'

'Fifty thousand to begin with.'

'And who's the common person in all of this? I'll tell you: Mark Proctor. He's set you up to kill someone, and now he's trying to get fifty grand from you.'

'You think so?'

'It makes sense.'

Gerald thought about that for a few moments. When he spoke, his voice was quiet. 'So what do I do now?'

'You sit and wait, to see whether they work out it's you.'

'And if they do?'

'You've got problems.'

Gerald put his head in his hands. Joe thought he was crying, but when he looked up again, Gerald's cheeks weren't damp. He said, 'Why were you there, at the green? How do I know you aren't part of it, here to turn up the heat on me, advise me to pay out? You both get rid of some kind of enemy or rival, and you're here to play some kind of good-cop-bad-cop routine? You were looking at my emails. Were you here to delete everything, or take my computer, so the police can't examine it?'

Joe shook his head. 'No,' he said. 'I was there for the same reason you were: to kill Mark Proctor.'

Gerald put his head back and looked at the ceiling. He laughed out loud. 'So for once in my life I got there too early.' He shook his head. 'I should have just followed him, tried to stop him. I was sent other photographs too, proof of who was next, but I couldn't work out where it was or who it was.'

'Show me.'

Gerald went to his computer and located a file in his documents folder. He clicked on one of the thumbnails. An image came up on the screen.

Joe leaned in. It was a teenage girl in a school uniform, generic black trousers and white shirt. She was pretty, light skin and red hair, her demeanour serious.

'Do you know the school?' Joe said.

'I haven't looked that hard,' Gerald said. 'He only made contact a few weeks ago.' Gerald nodded towards the screen. 'So you think she might be the key?'

'I don't know,' Joe said. 'That's part of the problem. But if we can find out why he's chosen her, it might help us. We need to know more about Proctor. If we know the man, we might be able to understand him better and then work out his next move.'

'He told me he was going to blame someone else,' Gerald said. 'He took the rag that I wiped the knife with. He's going to do something with it. Plant it, I presume.'

'Shit,' Joe said. 'That will be me.'

'I'll tell the police it wasn't you.'

'How can I trust you?'

'Because I've nothing left to live for,' Gerald said. 'I've lost my daughter and my wife. I just exist, and now I've killed an innocent man. I don't even know if I want to get through today, never mind blame someone else for my troubles.' He reached out and gripped Joe's arm. 'Just stop him. Do whatever you have to do, but don't let him hurt anyone else. I'll be waiting here for the news. Once I know Proctor is taken care of, I'll hand myself in for what happened last night.'

'Thank you. I'll do that.'

Joe left the house, unsure of his next move. His uncertainty was resolved when his phone buzzed. It was a message from Gina: *Joe, we need to talk.*

Forty-eight

Sam had been walking towards the station when he'd got the call from Gina. He'd been unable to focus on his driving, almost went through a red light. His shirt collar felt too tight. Mark Proctor. Joe. They were both swirling around in his mind. As soon as he heard Gina's voice, he knew he needed to see her. He told her about a café a few streets away and headed for it.

It was a small boutique café that wouldn't have long left as a business. It aped the chain coffee houses but made a big play of being Fairtrade, the coffee varieties made trendy by being chalked onto a blackboard. The front of the café was made up of small tables in front of shelves filled with Italian food, like overpriced olive oil and pickled peppers, but there was a long conservatory at the back. Sam guessed the owners had been hoping to catch the lawyers and accountants and business leaders who wanted brunch on their way into the city. It wasn't that kind of town. The smart money kept on driving.

He had to wait almost an hour before Gina showed, the assistant behind the counter giving him long glances as he stretched out two coffees. He wondered whether Gina had changed her mind, but when she came in the determination in her eyes told Sam that whatever she wanted to say, she had few doubts about it. Gone was the usual suit, and in its place a long blue summery dress, her hair tied back in a clasp.

Gina came to his table with a large latte, and a black coffee for Sam. The caffeine wasn't helping him; it just made him edgier. He'd seated himself next to the toilets. It wasn't a pleasant place to be, even though the café was nearly empty, but there was less chance of someone sitting nearby.

Stale booze wafted across as Gina sat down. Her eyes looked tired and red. Sam hoped she'd been okay to drive.

'This isn't a social call, I take it,' Sam said. 'I'm having a busy day.'

'Anything but,' Gina said.

'So talk.' Sam wasn't in the mood for the usual pleasantries. He cared for Gina, his memories of how she'd been when still the cop in charge of Ellie's case inspired him, but the news about Mark Proctor had left him confused.

'Who's the man in the park?' Gina said.

'I can't tell you that,' Sam said, clenching his jaw.

'It's not Mark Proctor.'

Sam had been about to take a drink, but that made him pause. 'How sure are you?'

'Very sure.'

'What do you know about it?'

'Who do you think called the police in the first place?'

'That was you?' Sam said, confused, and then, 'How did you know?'

'Joe told me.'

The cup clattered as he put it down. He groaned and put his head in his hands for a moment, his fingers clutching at his hair.

'What's he done?' he asked.

Gina lowered her head to get Sam's attention. 'He told me he hasn't done anything.' As Sam looked up, she relayed the events of the night before. About how Joe had been following Proctor, and ended up following him all the way to the park, except he lost him. He went into the park and discovered the body, panicked and ran.

'Do you believe him?' Sam asked, but he sounded as if he didn't really want to hear the answer.

'Honestly?' Gina said, and then sighed. 'I don't know, which is the best I can do. I thought I knew Joe, but what I found out yesterday changed things. All I can say is that if he did kill someone thinking it was Mark Proctor, he knows he killed an innocent man, and Joe didn't look like a man who'd committed the ultimate sin. Just a man who knew things were looking bad for him and needed to work out how to sort it.'

'I'm going to have to come off the case,' Sam said. 'I don't know what help you want me to give, but Joe is going to be a suspect, the number-one suspect. I can't be seen to be helping him.'

'But you can if you're off the case?'

'I told you, I can't be seen to be involved. I know that sounds bad, that he's my brother and all, but I really don't know what to do. If he's killed someone, I can't lose my job over him. I'm not even sure I could speak to him again. Ellie was innocent. If that man in the park isn't Mark Proctor, then he was innocent too. Even Proctor might be innocent. What is the chance that Joe has got it wrong?'

'I know you can't be involved from within the case,' Gina said. 'Go to your inspector, tell him about Joe. Be upfront and look after yourself. Then let's find out the truth. About Joe, and about Mark Proctor.'

'And sell out my brother?'

Gina took a drink and looked deep in thought. 'What would you do if you found out Joe had done it, that he'd killed a man who had nothing to do with Ellie's murder?'

Sam thought about that. His first thought was that he'd turn Joe in, because catching killers was central to who he was; the horror of the crime outweighed brotherly loyalty.

But did it? Joe was still his brother. Being in prison wouldn't get the life back, and he'd seen enough killers escape justice through some technicality to know that the world still turns, lives still go on, that even the killer being behind bars goes just a short way to helping the family of a victim get over a death. Was seeing his brother locked up for life worth the small benefit it would achieve?

'I don't know,' he said finally, his voice quiet. 'I thought I did, but faced with it, I have no idea.'

'So don't tell them,' Gina said. 'Not yet. Tell them you know Mark Proctor, you can even mention Ellie, and people will understand. You can't have a biased investigation or else it gets torn apart at the trial. Work with me, for my benefit.'

'What do you mean?'

'I owe it to Joe to give him the benefit of the doubt, just for now. I don't know where I'm going to start, but I'm going to see what I can find out.'

Sam reached across and put his hand over hers.

Gina looked down at their hands and then up at Sam again.

'It's not just for Joe though, is it?' Sam said. 'It's for you, because I know Ellie's case still hurts you.'

Gina managed a smile, even though she didn't feel like smiling. 'There's more truth in that than you think.'

Sam took his hand away and drained his coffee. 'So where are you starting?'

'Ellie's case,' she said. 'I'm going to speak to an old friend on the squad, to see whether there's any chance of some new forensics.'

Sam shook his head. 'I spoke to someone yesterday. The case is dormant. It gets dusted down now and again, but nothing for a long time.'

'But if you called yesterday, you can bet someone is looking at it now,' she said. 'That's how it works with the cold cases: you look again whenever something new comes in.' She took another drink, the coffee making her more alert. 'Who's your boss?'

'Ray Brabham.'

'God, they rise so quickly,' she said. 'I remember him as a keen young detective. Fond of himself, so I remember, but he's smart. Why is your squad involved, though? The green at Worsley is on the other side of the city.'

'He thinks there might be a connection to our case.'

'I saw the paper. Domino Killer. What the hell?'

'That was Brabham's idea. A teacher was stabbed a month ago. The knife was found nearby, with a bloody fingerprint on it, but there was no match on our system. A first-timer. We got the match this week, though, when a man called Henry Mason was found bludgeoned in a park. It was his fingerprint. Both murders were on our patch.'

'And that's the domino effect? One falls into another?'

'Yeah, it's a stretch, but now there's this new murder. Another man in a park, Brabham couldn't keep away.'

'Except now it's dragged Proctor into it,' Gina said. 'Joe found the body after following Mark Proctor. Or, at least, who he thought was Mark Proctor.'

'And a car hired out to Proctor was found parked nearby. The keys were with the victim.'

They both sat in silence for a few minutes. The café was getting busier, the pre-lunch crowd coming in to pass the hours and stare at wicker baskets filled with artisan breads and organic fruit.

'What if the domino thing is right?' Gina said eventually. 'If it was supposed to be Mark Proctor last night, and that's who Joe thought he was following, wouldn't that make Proctor the man who killed Henry Mason? Each tumbles into the other. And Proctor was arrested the night Henry Mason was killed, if I've got the timeline right. Why this week? He's never been in trouble before but he gets arrested and then linked to a dead body, all in one week. And Joe was his lawyer. It's what brought them face to face. It's another coincidence, and when coincidences start to mount up, it usually means they are any-thing but coincidences.'

'What did Proctor say about what he was doing when he was arrested?' Sam said.

'Nothing. He kept quiet in the interview and told Joe virtu-ally nothing.'

'He broke into the police compound to steal his own car back,' Sam said. 'Did I read that right?'

'And set it alight,' Gina said. 'But why would he do that?'

'Because he's got something to hide?'

'What else can it be?' Gina said. 'There was something about that car that he didn't want the police to see. So here's the plan. You find out more about Proctor's burglary and what he was up to on the night. I'll speak to someone on my old team, see what I can find out about Ellie's case. We'll meet as soon as I can set something up.'

'No, I've a better idea,' he said. 'I want to go back to the scene of Henry Mason's murder. Meet me there, with someone from your old team.'

Gina thought about that, before saying, 'Give me some time. I'll call you when I'm ready.'

'It's a plan,' Sam said, and scraped his chair as he stood up. His day suddenly had a purpose.

Forty-nine

Joe sank back into a shop doorway as Sam left the café. The shop was closed, one of many shuttered up on the street; those still in business were mainly charity and bargain shops, the rows of despair broken only by payday lenders and book-makers.

Joe didn't watch Sam, he didn't want to risk a stray glance back alerting his brother; instead, he listened out for the sound of an engine. It seemed to be a long time coming, and he wondered whether Sam would suddenly appear in front of him, but eventually an engine turned over. He sighed in relief. He didn't know what Sam would do if he saw him but Joe didn't want the argument. He peered around the corner and watched Sam's car pull away, then stepped out and went into the café.

Gina was sitting with her hands round her cup. She looked up and smiled as he sat down, although it was filled with sad-ness.

'Thank you,' Joe said.

'I'm still angry with you,' Gina said.

'I know, and I'm sorry, I can't say it enough, but it's some-thing I've lived with for a long time.' He sighed. 'What did you tell Sam?'

'Just what you told me to say.'

'And what's he going to do?'

'He's going to look into the burglary some more, try to link it with Henry Mason's murder. I said I would find out more about any other killings Proctor might have been involved with. That means Ellie's too. I'm going to see someone from my old squad to get an update.'

Joe nodded and took a deep breath. 'What about me? Am I a suspect yet?'

'Sam didn't let on if you are, but you'll be on the list soon enough.'

A tetchy waiter came over and asked Joe for his order. He ordered an espresso – he needed the kick. 'Will you keep me up to date with what's going on?'

'And not tell Sam?'

'That's right. For now.'

'He's your brother. And Ellie's too.'

'I know, but he's a cop. If he thinks I've killed someone, he won't let me walk away from it.' Before Gina could say anything, he added, 'And I wouldn't walk away from it either. I know in my conscience that I didn't do it.'

'Good to hear.'

Joe's espresso appeared in front of him, and he took a sip before saying, 'And I know who did.'

Gina looked stunned. Her mouth opened as if she was about to say something, but she stopped herself, surprised. 'How? I mean, who?'

'I've been following Proctor again. He went to see someone this morning – Gerald King. He's the man. I had a look inside his house.'

'You broke in?'

'Do you think breaking and entering is my biggest concern right now?'

'So what happened?'

'He caught me, then he confessed to the murder in Worsley. Proctor knew he'd done it too, and he's got proof: photographs of Gerald running away. Proctor guessed he was being set up and sent someone along in his place. Just someone who needed a hundred quid more than he needed to know why he was waiting for someone. Now Proctor's blackmailing Gerald King. Fifty grand.'

'Wow!'

'Yeah, that's what I thought. Gerald has to buy Proctor's silence or else he sends the pictures to the police.'

'Proctor won't. He won't want the police anywhere near him.'

'Why not? They're going to speak to him because the victim used his car. What's he got to fear? They haven't got him for any other killings. In this, he plays the lucky victim, perhaps some remorse for the poor sap he sent along in his place.'

'But why did this man do it?'

'Simple: Proctor killed his daughter. On the same spot where the man was killed last night.'

Gina's face betrayed her shock at that, her mouth open, eyes wide.

'Proctor's been at it for years,' Joe said. 'Gerald was sent what he thought was proof. Pictures of a notebook belonging to his daughter.'

'But he got the wrong man.'

'He didn't know that. It was getting dark and he had to be quick, because Proctor is stronger than him; he couldn't afford a fight. What he got was all of his pent-up anger spewing out. Now? He's devastated. He just wanted revenge for his daughter. Her murder led his wife to kill herself. He was consumed by anger, hatred, but until he had the email, he had no focus, no target.'

'What if he'd said no, or reported it to the police?'

'The person behind the emails said he'd burgled Proctor and he had his daughter's things, because he'd stolen Proctor's box of souvenirs. If Gerald called the police, he'd get rid of everything. He had something Proctor wanted back, and there was a man who wanted his daughter's killer. All he had to do was arrange the meet. Gerald had never seen Proctor before, but he was given the choice over where to do it. That was where he made his mistake, because he made it too symbolic. The place where his daughter died haunts him.'

'But Proctor was suspicious, so he sent someone along in his place.'

'It looks like it.'

'What's Gerald going to do now?' Gina said. 'And why are you helping him?'

'Because he's a link with Proctor. I'm just following the trail to see where it ends. Gerald tried foul means and it went wrong. I'm going to try to keep him going for fair. We want to prove that Proctor killed our loved ones. For me, it's Ellie. For Gerald, it's his daughter.'

'And then what?'

'Gerald will hand himself in, for the sake of the victim's family. And I'll defend him.'

'Are you sure? How do you know he won't try to blame you, or just skip the country?'

'He's a good man deep down, just tortured by Proctor,' Joe said. 'And now Proctor is making it worse by blackmailing him.'

'What if Gerald kills him when they meet?'

'It's possible,' Joe said. 'But the look in his eyes told me that he's done with murder. He's not natural born, unlike Proctor.'

Gina frowned. 'It's a large amount to find. It would take some time to work out how to finance it.'

'I'm guessing that Proctor is confident he can sit this one out and wait for his cash. I want to make sure he gets that part wrong. We need to find out more about him.'

'There is one person I could ask,' Gina said. 'Mrs Proctor.

Let's see what she has to say for herself. She might just let something slip.'

'Good idea.'

'And you?'

'I'll wait to see what else turns up today. For the most part, I'm just trying to avoid the police.'

'I'll call you,' Gina said, getting up.

She paused as she passed him, then bent down to kiss him on the cheek. 'Stay safe, Joe,' she said, and then she was gone.

Fifty

Gina took a deep breath. She was outside Proctor's house. The driveway was empty and she'd spent some time watching the house for any sign of him. She hadn't seen any. No tall shadow in the windows. No, it was Proctor's wife she was after, hoping to get some kind of insight into the man, from the woman who knew him best.

Gina popped a mint into her mouth, the booze still strong on her tongue, and walked towards the front door, the sound of her heels drowned by the rumble of a passing bus. She'd gone home first to put on a suit. If she was going to play a part, she might as well look like it.

The house wasn't what she'd expected. It was large, once imposing and grand, but in what had become bedsit-land. The short concrete driveway was cracked in places and grass tried to assert itself. Gina fastened her suit jacket. She rang the doorbell and breathed out into the palm of her hand. Still bad. When the door opened, she smiled.

The woman in front of her seemed nervous, her eyes wide and darting from side to side. Her hair was cut short and simple and she was wearing a cardigan and trousers, greys and muted blues. She was a woman who didn't want to be noticed.

'Hello, I'm Gina Ross,' she said. 'I'm from Honeywells Solicitors.'

Before Gina had the chance to say anything else, the woman

put her hand to her mouth and said, 'Is it about the money? About Mark's accounts?'

That stalled Gina for a moment. 'Why do you think that?' she said.

'Are you here to sue us, to tell us we're going to court?'

'No, I'm not,' Gina said. 'It's about Mark's case, his arrest the other night.'

She looked confused. 'Arrest? I don't understand? The police were here earlier. They thought he was dead, but he's not, and now they're looking for him.'

'Can I come in please?' Gina said.

'But Mark isn't here.'

'You can still help me, though.'

The woman paused as she thought about that, and then, as if remembering her manners, she stepped aside. 'Of course, I'm sorry. Go through.'

Gina eased past her and looked around. She'd learned through her police career that a person's house was a barometer of their personality. So often she had been to houses with a BMW on the drive and yet holes in the furniture, as if all that mattered was how those outside the house perceived them. She'd been to untidy houses that were dirty through lack of care and substance misuse, and other times because the occupants' lives were too busy, with laughing children and chaos.

Proctor's house was different to that. It was quietly grandiose, in that it was bigger than they needed, with a wide and open hallway with rooms going off it, and a banister that curved upwards like a grand gesture. The contents didn't quite live up to it, however, with a stained pine dining table and bookcase in one room, and a stiff-looking sofa in another, straight-backed and purple. As Gina was shown into the main living room, there was nothing of warmth. The walls were painted light grey but weren't brightened by flowers or pictures. Instead, there were photographs in black frames of a young woman, a girl really, her arms round an older woman who bore a resemblance to Proctor's wife. There were no books or magazines strewn around, no cups on tables, nothing to suggest that it was a room where anyone relaxed.

'Call me Helena,' the woman said. 'Sit down, please.'

'Thank you,' Gina said, and sank into the sofa, the cushions insubstantial.

Gina was wondering if Helena was going to offer her a drink but she didn't. She sat down on the chair opposite but perched forward, her hands on her knees, her legs tightly together.

'I just need to know more about your husband,' Gina said.

'Why?'

'Because we're defending him. We need to know what story to present to the jury, or whether anything in his past can give him a defence.'

'What has he done?'

Gina tried her best at a sympathetic smile. 'I'm sorry, I can't tell you.' If she did, Helena would realise that Gina was going way beyond what she would do for a burglar.

'But is he going to court?'

'I don't know. Possibly not.'

Helena seemed satisfied with that. 'Mark's a good man,' she said.

'But you mentioned the money, his accounts?'

'I didn't mean anything by it.'

'So tell me about him,' Gina said. 'What's his story?'

'Why haven't you asked him?'

Gina leaned in, and Helena did the same. She was a follower, not a leader. 'You know what men are like. They keep things back to make themselves look good. Sometimes you've got to find other ways to help them.'

Helena smiled. The sisterhood thing had worked.

269

'A normal childhood, so he said,' Helena said. 'He grew up in Ancoats, although he doesn't see his family any more.'

'Oh, why's that?'

'He doesn't tell me so I've stopped asking. They didn't come to our wedding. I tried to find out about them, I wanted to invite them as a surprise, but Mark got angry when I told him I'd been trying.'

'Did you get to meet them?'

'Only his sister, Melissa. She was a little bit haughty, if you want my opinion, and I don't like to speak badly of people. Nothing obvious, but she'd been living down south and thought she was a bit special. As soon as I mentioned Mark, she scowled as if he was nothing but a bad memory. There was some big falling out, I know that much, but he won't talk about it.'

'Families are like that,' Gina said. 'Has he been in trouble before?'

'No, never. He has his business and works hard.'

'What sort of business?'

'Financial investments.'

'But you don't think he's doing very well?'

'Why do you say that?'

'You thought I was here to take him to court.'

'I know, I'm sorry. Some of his clients get angry when he can't pay them back quickly enough. One came here and started shouting, and I almost called the police, but Mark stopped me, told me that the customer is always right. He paid him in the end, but well . . .'

'Go on.'

Helena looked at the ceiling. Her chin trembled and tears brimmed onto her lashes. 'Please don't tell him this, but I found some accounts once, and they were different to his normal ones. I've seen those, the ones he sends to his clients, with balances showing how the investments are growing. These were different, just a handwritten log, and I recognised

270

Mark's handwriting. Like a list of names with dates and numbers alongside, and a running total.'

'Where did you find these?'

'He used to keep them in a blue metal box in the workshop, padlocked. I thought it was some kind of toolbox, for a drill or something, but I suspected something, so I looked inside. There were these logs, and other things; photographs and trinkets. I heard him coming so I had to put it away. I think he's moved the accounts now but everything else is still in there. It's been locked ever since.'

Gina felt a tremor of something significant. She tried hard not to give anything away, a skill honed through years of policing, where the killer questions are best coming after some indifferent casual ones, where you trap someone in a lie and then throw in the evidence that proves otherwise.

'Have you challenged him about it?'

Helena gave a small laugh. 'He's a man; he's allowed some secrets. It's how they are. It was none of my business.'

'Can you show me?'

'Why are you so interested?'

'Just curiosity,' Gina said. 'You made it sound interesting.'

'He's my husband,' Helena said. 'It would feel like betraying him.'

'Where's his workshop?'

'Just at the bottom of the garden. It's my father's old workshop really, but he's dead now, so Mark uses it.' She frowned. 'Spends all night down there sometimes. I don't know what he does. Reads books, I think, with his candles burning. He likes candles.'

'Don't you ever ask him?' Gina said. 'It seems so secretive.'

'It's where Mark goes to relax,' Helena said. 'I don't mind. A man needs to relax, don't you think? He works hard and he doesn't want me jabbering on about my day.' She blushed. 'I'm his wife. It's my job to serve him, keep him happy.'

271

Gina bristled but didn't say anything. She didn't want to get into an argument about conjugal roles.

'I'd seen the box before,' Helena said. 'I'd been curious, and one day he left his keys behind when he went out. I had a look.'

'Does Mark know you've looked inside?' Gina said, trying to sound casual, but she could detect the keenness in her own voice.

'I don't think so. He's never said anything. I'd just have to say sorry and hope he was all right with that.'

Gina was flooded by pity. For some reason, Proctor dominated this woman, kept her imprisoned by her own insecurities as he lived out his own sick fantasies.

The box was important though. Photographs, trinkets. It fitted with what Joe had said.

'Thank you,' Gina said, wanting to get away, to update Joe. 'You've been helpful.'

'Have I?'

'You have. I understand my client a bit more. That's very useful.'

'If you need any more information, I don't mind helping,' Helena said. 'Perhaps I ought to clear it with Mark first. I don't want to betray him. Not for all he's done for me.'

Gina wanted to grab Helena's arm and drag her out of the house, to urge her to get away, as far as she could. No more control. Be yourself. But she didn't. Instead, she said, 'Thank you for your time.'

'Are you going already?'

'Yes, I'm sorry. We're just so busy, but you've been a great help.'

She stopped, startled, when the door opened. It was Mark Proctor, smiling, confident and brash, walking into the living room and making Gina sit down again. She hadn't heard his car.

'This is a nice surprise,' he said.

'I just wanted to get some updates on your instructions,' Gina said, a flutter in her voice.

'So why are you leaving?' he said. 'After all, it's me you want, isn't it?'

Gina was uncertain but she realised quickly she had no choice. It would look strange if she didn't speak to him.

'Okay, thank you,' she said.

Proctor sat in the large comfortable chair. Gina got the message: it was his throne. She took her notebook out of her bag and a pen out of her pocket, to look the part.

'So what do you want to know?' he said, his hands held outwards.

'Just more about what you were doing at the time of the burglary,' Gina said.

Helena gave a small cough and said, 'I'll just make my husband a drink, if you're all right with that.'

So he had a title, husband, not Mark?

'What have you told Helena?' he said, once Helena had left the room, his gaze less genial, his tone sharp.

'Nothing. You're a client of the firm. Everything is confidential.'

'You just blurted out the word "burglary".'

'It was in direct response to your question?'

He pursed his lips as he thought about that, before saying, 'So what do you want to know?'

'About where you'd been on the night your car was stolen from the compound.' It was the only logical response.

'Why?'

Gina met his gaze. She'd dealt with people like him all through her career. She shouldn't be intimidated by him.

'Juries convict for the strangest of reasons, and just the whiff of suspicion can be enough. The allegation against you makes it sound like you were up to something. If you want to be believed in court, you have to show that you weren't.'

'Do I?' he said, his eyebrows raised. 'I thought the prosecution had to prove it against me, not the other way around? When did it change?'

'That's bullshit, and always has been,' Gina said. 'Once you get a judge to let it go to a jury, they can convict because they don't like the way you stand or smile.'

'And acquit because they just don't want to find someone guilty, even when they are?'

'Sometimes. Not here. The prosecution case will look complete and somehow you have to fight it off. So tell me.'

'Not yet.'

Anger started to bubble inside her. She wanted to rush him right then. He'd evaded her all those years ago and now he was enjoying her frustration too much. It was time to make him uncomfortable.

'I didn't think you'd help me,' she said. 'So I've been making enquiries on your behalf.'

'What do you mean?'

'Have you heard of ANPR cameras? The police have them in locations they won't disclose, but they clock and record every car that goes past. Really helps to narrow a suspect list down. I've still got friends in the police. It's easy for them to track down where you were with the ANPR cameras. I've already asked a friend to have a look, to see if we can build up a picture of your movements. If we can do that, we can show your night was an innocent one, and you are guilty of nothing more than being uninsured.'

Proctor breathed heavily through his nose and his eyes shone a little darker. 'There's no need for that.'

Gina leaned forward. 'Do you think you'll get away with saying nothing in court? Whatever I say to you, it will be nothing like the grilling you'll get in the witness box.' Her voice had taken on a keener edge. 'So enlighten me. Why would someone else steal your car when it's locked in a police compound?'

'Because people do stupid things. They make errors of judgement and forget about the fine detail.'

'Do you think that will be enough?' she said. 'Why would someone want your car so much that they'd take that risk, and then go on to torch it?'

'Perhaps some people have just got it in for me,' he said, glaring now. 'People develop irrational hatreds.'

'What were you hiding?'

'Who said I was hiding anything?'

'It'll be the first question on the lips of the jurors: why would he do it if he wasn't hiding something? What were you trying to destroy?'

Proctor sat back and jabbed his finger towards Gina. 'Your job is to check that the prosecution have done their job correctly. No one can make me talk. You know that, I know that. You want to hear the answers, I can see the desperation in your eyes, but I won't satisfy that. What will it cost me? A fine? A few hours of unpaid work for the community? That means nothing. Tiny ripples, that's all.'

'What are you talking about?'

Proctor leaned forward and his hands clasped together. He stared into her eyes. She met his gaze.

'Sometimes the ripples are more enjoyable than the splash,' he said. He cocked his head. 'Making no sense?' He smiled. 'I ought to think about getting a new lawyer. Perhaps you're not as good at your job as you think you are.'

Gina clenched her jaw in frustration.

Proctor gestured towards the door. 'If you've nothing left to add, it looks like our meeting has ended.'

Gina put away her notebook and pen. As she stood to leave, Proctor said, 'Don't feel bad. You can't expect everything to always go your way.'

She rushed out, almost knocking the cup out of Helena's hand, who was bringing in the drink.

'Goodbye, Helena,' Gina said, before rushing through the door.

As she stood on his drive, she took a few deep breaths to calm herself. She was angry. He'd been taunting her, her hands were shaking. She rushed to her car. Once inside, she called Joe.

He answered straight away. 'So what did you find?'

'A woman with no voice or authority, happy just to do whatever pleases him. I wouldn't be surprised if she knew something but chose to ignore it. The house has no character or warmth. But there was a funny thing.'

'Go on.'

'As soon as I arrived, she asked me if I was there about the money?'

'Did she say what she meant?'

'Kind of,' she said. 'Proctor's a financial investor, but he runs into problems with his clients sometimes. Helena said that he had a different set of accounts, hidden away in a metal box in his workshop at the end of the garden. I'm not surprised. Psychopaths are risk-takers but overestimate their own intelligence. He isn't going to be doing normal investments. He'll be running scams of some type. She said there were other things in there too. Photographs and odd things.'

'His memento stash,' Joe said. 'Gerald was sent copies of his daughter's notebook. But it won't be there any more. He was burgled.'

'There might be other things.'

'Stick to our plan,' Joe said. 'You're looking into any old cases. Speak to Sam.'

'Do I mention this?'

'No, not yet.'

'And what are you going to do?'

'I'm going to have a snoop around Proctor's workshop.'

Fifty-one

Sam rushed into the Incident Room, not wanting to waste any time. There was the packed silence of hard concentration. The latest murder hadn't been linked officially, but the possibility made everything more serious. The case could become huge – something momentous they would talk about when they got older. To their children and grandchildren, perhaps even to the television cameras: one of those true-crime programmes where just about any murderer gets a profile. Everyone looked up as if they were expecting Sam to give them an update from the new murder. When he went straight to his monitor, they went back to what they were doing.

Sam didn't meet anyone's eye. As much as their interest in him could be about updates, it could also be because his brother's involvement was getting deeper. Were his colleagues looking at him and wondering what he knew, whether he would share it? Sam didn't have many friends on the team. He was the quiet one by the window, the one who preferred to look for changes in behaviour patterns over knocking on doors.

He retrieved the list of registration numbers picked up on the cameras close to Henry Mason's murder site. He'd printed them out and folded them under his monitor the day before, waiting for some quiet time to start building a grid, working out the owners and separating them geographically, so that if nothing came up forensically they could quickly work out teams to visit each house.

He was looking for something different now; he was looking for Mark Proctor.

He logged onto the computer and went to the entries for Mark Proctor from a few nights earlier. The statements were on the system, everything done electronically, and he went to the arresting officer's statement. As he expected, Proctor's registration number was on there, the car seized and taken to the compound. He scribbled it down on the back of the papers and logged off. He grabbed his papers and headed for the door. He didn't want Brabham to come back to tell him he was off the team.

As he reached the doorway, someone shouted, 'Everything all right, Sam?'

'Just a line of inquiry,' he shouted back, as he darted along the corridor.

He got in his car and called Gina. 'On my way,' he said, and hung up.

It didn't take long to get to the park where Henry Mason was killed.

There was some twine wrapped around one of the gates. Flowers, Sam guessed, long since stolen. Gina was waiting on a bench just inside the park. Sam held up the sheets of paper as he got closer. 'Here's the list.'

'How close are the cameras?' Gina said. She didn't want to tell Sam about the visit to Proctor's house just yet. She wanted more certainty.

'There's one just as you come off the motorway,' he said. 'It gets them going off and on. It makes the ring road like a ring of steel. You can't get in or out without someone knowing about it. There's another on the way out of town. I got one from the road into Manchester from the next junction along.

If we know which junction he used, it will give us a better idea of his movements.'

'Have you gone through them?'

'No, not yet,' he said. 'I thought I'd wait to see how you were getting on.'

'Someone is coming here shortly. Someone I trust. He might have something for me.' She patted the bench next to her. 'Pull up some wood and make yourself comfortable.'

Sam sat next to her and pulled out the sheets of paper. 'This is from the camera nearest to here,' he said, holding up one sheath. 'If Proctor came from his house, he'd come past that way, but he's not stupid. He's avoided capture for a long time, and he hasn't done that by being predictable. I've got the lists from all the closest junctions and the ones in the towns on the way.' He handed over a scrap of paper with Proctor's registration on it. 'Let's get to it.'

The wind blew the pages as they both looked. Sam was looking for just the last three letters, because that was enough to memorise, and then he examined each entry if he came across it.

Each report ran to nearly a hundred pages, showing registration numbers and the times the vehicles were logged. The time span covered the evening rush hour so the traffic had been busy. Fifteen pages in, with the typed figures starting to blur in front of his eyes, he said, 'I've got it,' and tapped the sheet with his pen. 'Proctor came off the motorway and passed the camera just after seven.'

'Mingled in with the dregs of rush hour.'

'What time does it get dark?' Sam said.

'Just before eight.'

'He was getting himself in place nice and early. The attack was brutal, and because no one heard any shouting, I reckon Mason was taken by surprise. So Proctor was waiting patiently, and once it was dark, bang, hammer on the head.'

'I can trump that,' Gina said, and passed over the sheets of paper she'd been looking at. 'Just before nine thirty, his car was picked up on the camera at the next junction along. We've got him in the car, because he was stopped shortly afterwards, on the way home; so we've got him driving towards the murder scene and away from it.'

'We need more, though,' Sam said.

The sound of footsteps drew their attention, like the clip of leather soles. A man in a suit strode towards them.

'Is this your man?' Sam said.

Gina smiled. 'Yes. Tim Smith. One of the best detectives I've worked with. Just don't tell him I said that.'

As he got closer, Tim was panting. 'I can't stay long.'

'Good to see you, Tim. I take it you're not going to the gym much.'

He patted his stomach and grinned, a football of a paunch protruding over his belt. 'Can you tell?' He gave Gina the quick up-and-down. 'You're looking well.'

'Don't lie,' she said, and she tapped his wedding ring. 'I've got a hangover, I slept badly and my roots need doing. Did you get what I asked for?'

He looked at Sam, hesitant to answer.

'This is Sam Parker,' Gina said.

Tim frowned, as if he was trying to remember something, then said, 'You made the call yesterday, about your sister.'

Sam nodded. There was no point in denying it.

'You can trust him,' Gina said.

Tim paused for a moment, but when Gina raised her eyebrows, he relented and pulled out an envelope from his suit jacket. 'I did my best but I haven't got much.'

Gina reached out her hand, but Tim pulled the envelope away.

'What's it for?' he said. 'I can't do this if it's to help one of your clients.' Before Gina could protest, he added, 'This Proctor guy? You must have known I'd check out his most recent arrest? Honeywells is the name on the custody record. Joe Parker, right?' Tim nodded towards Sam. 'I know of Sam because of the call, but why are you working together?'

Sam and Gina exchanged glances, nothing more than twitches of eyelids and the slightest head tilts, but each knew what the other was asking: could they trust Tim? As far as Sam was concerned, if Gina did, that was enough for him.

'Full disclosure?' Gina said.

'Yes, full disclosure,' Tim said.

'Yes, Proctor's a client of the firm. And before you say anything, I'm not trying to get him off with anything. My boss is Joe Parker. Sam's brother. Ellie's brother.'

So Gina told Tim about how Joe was convinced that Proctor was Ellie's killer, and that he was somehow linked to other murders in the city.

'And Sam couldn't just find out about Ellie's case – or Proctor – without this subterfuge? It's all just a few clicks of the computer mouse away.'

'Come on,' Sam said. 'I can't go near anything to do with Ellie's case, and if we get Proctor for it, they might look at the computer trail. You're on the squad; you're entitled to look.'

'What you mean is that you'll do the same as searching the computer but in a way that won't get you found out?'

'It's not what you know, it's what you can prove,' Sam said. 'I'm not going to get you into trouble.'

'So you're trying to lock up your client, rather than keep him out?' Tim turned to Gina.

'Something like that,' she said.

Tim grinned. 'If only there were more defence firms like yours,' he said, and passed Gina the envelope. 'I can't let you keep them, but if you happened to make a note of what was on them, who would know?'

'Thanks, Tim,' Gina said, and pulled the papers out of the envelope.

As Gina flicked through them, Tim looked at Sam. 'Ellie's case was glanced over this morning,' he said, his voice softer. 'There's nothing that links Proctor in any way. I know we could do some speculative testing, to see if there is any DNA on her clothes we haven't detected before, but we're not going to get funding for it. You know how it goes now.'

Sam did know, but that didn't ease his frustration.

'So what are these?' Gina said.

'I went a bit deeper on Mark Proctor,' Tim said. 'I found something. Concern expressed about him from bereaved parents of murdered children. He'd got a reputation as a grief-junkie, someone who contacted families, usually just offering kind words. Some didn't want sympathetic voices, but others were receptive to them, used them as crutches to help them through. And Proctor was always there for them. He even married one.'

'What?'

'His wife's sister was killed and dumped in an alley that ran behind an industrial estate. Proctor turned up, like some self-appointed grief counsellor, and the victim's sister fell for his soothing words. Harry Neave was the SIO on that one.'

'I know Harry,' Gina said.

'Retired now.'

'It's okay, I know where to find him.'

Gina skimmed through the loose sheets. Four families had complained about Proctor, but one stood out amongst all of them: the Reilly family. They claimed that Proctor had known something the family hadn't.

'That's the one,' Gina said, tapping the piece of paper.

She reached into her handbag to get a piece of paper, and then scribbled down whatever details she could.

As Sam read it, Gina said, 'Has Proctor ever been arrested, or come close to it?'

'Apart from the other night, nothing,' Tim said.

'Let's see if we can change that.'

Fifty-two

Joe was sitting in his car, parked on the street further along from Proctor's house.

His mind was fixed on Proctor's workshop. If it was somewhere private, it might be somewhere he kept other secrets, the ones that haven't been stolen. Proctor kept keepsakes; the notebook belonging to Gerald's daughter told him that. There might be more.

He could tell Sam, in the hope that he could get a warrant, but he'd discounted the idea as soon as it came into his head. There wasn't enough evidence to link Proctor to anything at the moment, except that the dead man in Worsley had travelled there in Proctor's hire car? How did that implicate Proctor? If anything, it made him less of a suspect, because as far as the police were concerned it made him a potential victim. There was just some third-hand information that his accounts weren't what they should be and Joe's spark of memory. How could a detective on the Murder Squad hope to get a search warrant on that basis?

No, there had to be another way, and Joe knew that it involved him.

Joe dug into his pocket for his phone and called Gerald. When he answered, Joe said, 'You need to meet Proctor, to talk about the blackmail. Meet him in the city centre. I need some time with him away from the house.'

When Gerald agreed, Joe said, 'I'll know when he leaves, but let me know when he's with you. I need to know I've got some time.'

Joe hung up and waited. It was time for his second break-in of the day.

'So does Brabham know where you are?' Gina said, looking at Sam as he drove along the suburban road, looking up at the houses.

They were heading for the home of the family who'd complained about Proctor, that he'd been too intrusive, the family of murdered Zoe Reilly.

'I can just tell the truth if I need to, that I was looking at the camera records for the night of Mason's murder,' Sam said. 'He trusts me to do my job. He just hasn't worked out that I'm not doing it at the moment.' He came to a stop and straightened. 'Here we are.'

Gina looked past him, to a nondescript detached house built sometime in the seventies, if the wooden panels under the living-room window were anything of a guide. It was on a street of nearly identical houses, although the intervening years had cast some differences. A house on a corner was covered in ivy, and some sported extensions over the driveways.

'So this is the Reillys' house,' she said.

'Yes, I haven't been here for a while,' Sam said.

'You've been here before?'

'Did you see the path further along?'

'No, where?'

'Just before we turned right onto the street; the road came to a dead-end but the path carried on, along a bridge over a stream and then through the woods next to some football pitches.'

'No, I didn't notice that,' Gina said. 'You seem pretty familiar with it.'

'I arrested a flasher in his car once – some salesman who thought he'd found a quiet spot to look at pornography, or that was his excuse. Except he matched the description of a man who'd been seen hanging around in the woods, watching the kids play football. He denied it was him, and we couldn't prove it, but we spoke to all the people round here and gave a description of his car. He'll have found somewhere else, but he didn't come back here.'

'Why do you mention it?' Gina asked.

'Because Zoe Reilly was killed down there, in those woods.'

Gina was surprised. 'You know about the case?'

Sam raised an eyebrow. 'Do you know how Joe said he keeps a look out for any rapists or child molesters, because he would recognise the person who followed Ellie? Do you think I don't do the same? Whoever killed her may have killed again. Whenever a teenage girl is murdered, I take an interest. I am bound to, after Ellie.'

'But how would you know, if no one knew who killed Ellie?'

'I won't find out unless I look. Most come to nothing – it usually turns out to be a family member or someone close, like a neighbour or boyfriend. But I remember Zoe's case.'

'Because of the flasher?'

Sam nodded slowly and clenched his jaw. 'I paid him a visit. It was all off the books, just chasing up my earlier arrest, checking there'd been no repeat, that his rehabilitation had been successful. I told him about Zoe and how his behaviour could cause him to be looked at. He went pale, perhaps understood for the first time how much trouble he'd brought upon himself. He had an alibi, and produced enough evidence to satisfy me.'

'Did they get anyone?'

'No, they didn't,' Sam said, shaking his head. 'I know what it feels like in there.' He looked up at the house. 'It's more than

285

anger, because that needs a focus. It's bewilderment too, and frustration.'

'Let's go speak to them,' Gina said, and stepped out of the car.

Sam reached for his jacket, which he'd thrown onto the back seat. He took his time putting it on as he got out of the car, always looking at the house. Gina set off walking but paused to let Sam catch up. He was the one with the identification that would get them into the house, although Sam looked every inch a copper, from the greyness of his suit to the rigidity of his stride.

The front door opened before they reached it. A woman was standing there, dark brown hair flying around her face in the light breeze. Her mouth was open in surprise.

'Sandra Reilly,' Sam said, raising his identification. 'I'm DC Sam Parker, and this is Gina Ross.'

The woman swallowed and looked her lips. 'Is it about Zoe?' she said, her voice a croak.

'I'm sorry, I've no news,' Sam said, his voice softening, 'but could we speak to you?'

Mrs Reilly stepped away from the door. 'Yes, of course, I'm sorry. Come in.' She smiled, but it was a brave one, meant to disguise how she was feeling.

Sam and Gina walked from the short hall into a living room that looked like a tribute room. There was a large photograph of a teenage girl on the wall over the fireplace, and smaller ones in frames dotted around the room. It would be impossible to sit in that room without being reminded of Zoe.

She gestured at them to sit down. 'So what's this about?'

Sam started the questioning.

'This might sound strange,' he said, 'but do you remember a man who came to speak to you after Zoe was found. A grief counsellor.'

'Which one?' Sandra said. 'We spoke to a few, until we

realised that they didn't have anything to say that helped. There was no mystery to it; we have friends who did the same for us – gave us the chance to talk things over.'

'What about Mark Proctor?'

Sandra's eyelids flickered at the name. 'Yes, well, I remember him.'

'How so, out of all of them?'

Sandra sat down in a chair and looked out of the window. She stayed silent for a few moments. When she spoke, her voice was quieter, more reflective.

'This view hasn't changed,' she said. 'We've been here for twenty years. I was pregnant with Zoe when we moved in, and we had another little one.' A smile. 'Dominic. He leaves school this year, and soon it'll be just me and Ricky, my husband. We were so happy when we moved in. It seemed such a nice house. And it was, for so many years. I cling to this view.' And she looked towards the window.

Sam was transfixed. He knew Gina was looking at him, as if the despair he could feel balling tightly in his stomach was etched on his face. Sandra was describing his own mother in the years after Ellie died.

'Every day, this view is the same,' Sandra continued. 'A lawn. The curving tarmac. The neighbours heading out to work. And it used to be Zoe's view too. The same view but with Zoe as a small girl, playing with Dominic, dolls on the grass, a pink bike with tassels coming from the handlebars. Walking to school, each year taller, older, but the view never changed.' She let out a long breath. 'Then that final day. I watched her go. Just another day. She came back from school and was going to see a friend. I offered her a lift but she said she was okay. It was a nice evening, light and summery, and she was playing on her phone. She was always playing on her phone. I watched her go, I always did. She turned to wave at the bottom of the drive, and then she was gone.'

Sandra turned away. 'The view stays the same, and all I want is for it to include Zoe walking up the path, but it never will.' Her eyes narrowed as she looked at Sam and Gina. 'And you never caught him, whoever it was. I don't even have that focus.'

'Tell me about Mark Proctor,' Sam said.

'He knocked on our door one night. He was carrying leaflets from a charity, a bereavement service, said he'd been asked to come along. It was a month or so after Zoe had been killed. The police interest was dying down because there was nothing to report.'

'Did you ever check with the police whether Proctor had been sent by them?'

'No, I don't think we did,' she said. 'He was official, from a charity, so he said. And you can see how I am, needing to talk about it, to somehow understand it. And he seemed to know what to say, that it was about expressing ourselves, letting it all out, the usual stuff.'

'So why do you remember him so well?' Sam said.

Sandra frowned. 'It was just a gut feeling, and something he said.'

'Can you explain?'

'It seemed like he was enjoying it too much. He was supposed to be there for our benefit, a shoulder to cry on, but it was as if it was for his benefit. He wanted to see photographs and for us to tell him about Zoe as she grew up. He was showing too much interest, almost as if he wanted to make us upset. Ricky called him a grief-junkie. That's what he was, someone who liked all the drama and the pain.'

'But what did Proctor say that made you turn against him?'

'He mentioned a boyfriend we didn't know about.'

Sam and Gina exchanged glances. 'Unusual.'

'Yes, that's what we thought,' Sandra said. 'There's a large Pakistani community on the other side of the football fields.

288

The schools are always fighting each other, because the fields make a divide, schools on each side. Zoe was seeing a young boy called Khalid. I don't think it was anything serious, they met through friends. She didn't tell us because she thought we might object, and Khalid kept it quiet because he didn't know what his parents would say, their son going out with a white western girl.'

'And you found out through Mark Proctor?' Gina said.

Sandra nodded. 'He reckoned one of Zoe's friends had told him, but why would he get that involved? He was a shoulder to cry on, that's all. So I asked around. No one would admit to telling Proctor, but I found out where Khalid lived. I went to see his parents.' She sighed. 'They were lovely people. They'd heard about Zoe from the news and Khalid had kept it quiet, but it was nothing to do with them. They had no idea that Khalid had been seeing Zoe and, to be honest, I think they would have been okay. They were welcoming and kind but it didn't get us any closer to finding out who killed Zoe.'

'When was the last time you saw Mark Proctor?' Gina said.

'After I'd spoken with Khalid's parents,' she said. 'He was too controlling, as if he wanted to know everything. He shouldn't have known about Khalid before we did and, in the end, you learn to live with it. You never get over it, but just learn to accept that the pain will always be there.' There were tears in her eyes. 'Do you know when it's worst? When I forget about her. Not as in I've moved on, but if we have a night out or something, or a holiday, and there are moments when I'm laughing, having fun, and then it hits me, the guilt, the feeling that I shouldn't be happy like that because of Zoe. How can I enjoy myself as if I haven't a care in the world when Zoe is dead?'

'I've heard people say that before,' Sam said. He knew that Gina was watching him.

'So what is it about Mark Proctor?' Sandra said.

289

'Just some complaints we've had, and your complaint flagged up,' Sam lied. 'We're considering taking him off our list of approved counsellors.' He got to his feet. 'Thank you,' he said. 'Your information is very useful.'

Sandra didn't get up to show them out. 'So you've no news on whoever killed Zoe?'

Sam shook his head. 'I'm sorry.'

When they got outside, Sam let out a long sigh.

'You all right?' Gina asked. 'It seemed like she was talking about you, not just herself.'

'The pain is common,' Sam said.

'So how much more do we know about Mark Proctor?'

'Like she said, he's a grief-junkie. If he had something to do with Zoe's murder and he remembers the raw emotion in that house, he's got one hell of a souvenir.'

Fifty-three

Mark Proctor looked around as he approached Joe's apartment building. Deansgate was just ahead, a long stretch of cars and city-centre buildings. A hundred years earlier, the view would have been shrouded in smoke and fumes. Now, in the distance there were just glimmers as the sun reflected back from glass office blocks.

He turned away from the road and towards the front of the building. There were no police cars there, it was too early for that, but they would come eventually. It was Joe Parker he wanted to avoid.

He tried to think of how Joe would react if he'd been the one who'd killed the man the night before. He'd drive in quickly, panicking, blood on his clothes, the knife still on him, but he'd wipe it clean on a rag, just like Gerald had. He wouldn't think clearly so he'd make a mistake. The obvious thing would be to burn the rag, but his mind would be rushing too much. He would know one thing: the rag wouldn't be going into his apartment, it was too dangerous, but the knife would; you never leave a space in the knife block. He could clean the knife but the rag was just what it was, a rag, something you might leave in your car in case you needed to change a tyre. So he would get rid of it before he got to his apartment.

But if he was planting something, it had to be found. He

291

couldn't assume cleverness on Joe's part; it had to be his mistake. So what would the police do? They'd go through the bins. It was a large apartment block, and not enough space for individual bins for each apartment. No, there would be a communal bin, those large ones on wheels close to the exit, so people could drop stuff in before they left for work.

The entrance to the underground garage was ahead. It was high enough for a four-by-four but not high enough for a dustbin lorry, so the bins must be outside.

He tried not to look conspicuous as he walked, because planting evidence was no good if he was seen to plant it. He tried to make himself appear lost. He gazed up at the apartment windows, a mix of blinds and curtains, no balconies at the front. They were all facing the canals. The apartments on this side must be the cheap ones, where the only benefit was proximity to the city.

Then he saw it, the domed lid over a blue plastic tub on wheels, handles at the end.

He sauntered over, checking around as he got there, and lifted the lid just enough to drop in the bloodied rag. It wasn't much, but enough to deflect attention.

Proctor carried on walking, whistling as he headed for the footbridge and the scenic route into the city centre. He had an appointment with Gerald King.

'So what can we find out about Proctor's counselling service?' Gina said, as Sam drove on the motorway that encircled Manchester.

'I'll see if there's anything official, but I'm not expecting it,' Sam said. 'I wonder if it's just his little hobby.'

'But remember what Tim Smith said about Proctor's wife – her sister was murdered and Proctor ended up falling for her.'

'That won't be right, though, will it?' Sam said. 'If Proctor is some cold-blooded killer, some psychopath, he isn't going to fall for anyone. If he ended up with someone, it was for a reason. For people like Proctor, everything is a tactic.'

'Perhaps she was throwing out more grief than most and he found it intoxicating?'

'He's creating his own grief, that's his thing.'

'You have to think that Joe's theory is looking more credible now,' Gina said.

Sam nodded. He couldn't argue with that. 'So where now? Do you want taking back to your car?'

'What about the SIO in the case that ended up with Proctor getting married, Chief Inspector Neave? Or Harry, to me. He's retired now but I know where he lives.'

'And am I driving?'

'You're doing an okay job so keep going. Head for Ramsbottom.'

Sam did as he was told, flicking on the radio as he went, so that they would get any updates about the murder that were fit to broadcast. The greyness of the city was soon behind them as they headed north, the gentle green of the Lancashire hills in the distance, the Irwell Valley to their left as it cut through the sprawl of Bury.

Ramsbottom lay in the valley, below the road that headed towards the Lancashire mill towns that were the last pieces of industrial blight before the countryside took over, and everything was rural and ancient all the way to the Scottish border. The town was once just another mill town, its history built on cotton, the stone buildings blackened by smoke through the decades and forgotten when there was a push for modernisation in the sixties. It was reaping the rewards now. A clean-up and a steam railway had turned the small Victorian shop fronts and stone cottages into must-haves for the people who liked to work in the city but wanted to escape to the country at five o'clock every day.

They rumbled over a level crossing and turned left at the

sculpture of a fallen urn that served as a fountain, in front of the high splendour of the Grant Arms, where Dickens stayed when he was writing *Bleak House*. Harry Neave lived on an estate of newbuilds, in small cul-de-sacs that ran from a circular road.

When they turned in and parked up, Sam asked, 'Do you know Harry Neave well?' He glanced over at the house, wide with white pillars in the porch and sand-coloured brick, fake Tudor timbers attached to the first floor.

'Well enough,' Gina said, and climbed out of the car.

Sam was about to step in front of her as she marched towards the front door, but Gina held out her hand. 'He'll respond to me better than he will to you.'

Sam relented as Gina pressed the doorbell. The door was opened by a middle-aged woman with combed-back dark hair and an open-necked mauve shirt. There was a moment's pause before she smiled and said, 'Georgina, how on earth are you?'

Sam spotted the formality of Gina's full name.

'Lillian, you look well,' Gina said. 'Is Harry in?'

'At the end of the garden,' she said, and stepped aside to let them both in.

Gina led the way as Lillian went into the kitchen. 'Tea?'

'That would be lovely,' Gina said, and carried on through the house towards the door that opened onto the garden. As they stepped outside, she whispered, 'Lillian used to be a prosecutor. She and Harry are both retired now, but they were always a little above everyone else, if you know what I mean. Lillian came into the law late and reinvented herself, acquired a few airs and graces, and Harry modelled himself on something from a detective novel. They're decent people, though, and Harry was a good copper.'

They walked down some steps and along a path that ran alongside a neat lawn and beds overflowing with colour. There was a small fountain in one corner and a stone sundial in the middle of the lawn. They were trying to create a large country garden in a town garden plot. The view ahead made it worthwhile, though, straight down the Irwell Valley, the high buildings of Manchester just vague shadows. The sun shone as beams onto green hills in the far distance and the railway track snaked along the valley floor. Sam could imagine how pleasant it must be every weekend when the trains were running, blowing steam and noise into the air.

Harry Neave was sitting on a cushioned chair on wooden decking at the end of the garden. He turned round as they got close and a grin spread quickly.

'Well, well, Gina Ross. To what do I owe this pleasure?'

He was wearing a dark shirt and a paisley cravat, his grey hair slicked back. A small cigar was clamped into his fingers and his moustache was stained brown by it.

'I thought I'd see how retirement was treating you,' she said, and then pointed towards the view. 'It looks as though it's treating you just fine.' She turned to Sam. 'This is Sam Parker.'

Sam held out his hand to shake. 'I'm a DC,' he said. 'We're looking into a murder and we thought you might be able to help.'

'I'd be delighted.' Harry gestured to the two garden seats opposite. 'Sit down, talk to me. I know you're here about one of my cases, not for my expertise. Which one?'

'I don't know the victim's name but her sister was called Helena; she married a grief counsellor. The killer was never found.'

'The girl found behind the warehouses?' He nodded slowly, his smile gone. 'Yes, I remember that one. You always remember the ones you never solve. Adrianne Morley.'

Gina glanced across at Sam, knowing the truth of it. 'Did you have any suspects for it?'

'Not hard and fast,' he said. 'She'd been dragged into the bushes and strangled, but there was no sign of a sexual assault.

No clothes disturbed or semen anywhere. She had a black eye and a swollen cheek. It looked like she'd put up a fight.'

'It doesn't mean it wasn't a sex attacker,' Sam said.

'No, it doesn't, and there were a lot of things going on at that time. Inter-school stuff. Gang-fights, planned meet-ups to brawl it out. Adrianne had passed the exams for a good Catholic school outside the area and we wondered whether she'd been attacked when she was on her own, because no one recognised her, and it got out of hand.'

'What about her family?' Gina said.

'Not much of it,' Harry said. 'Adrianne lived with her older sister in the family home; her parents had been killed in a car crash. Pretty bad luck for her sister; she lost her parents and then her sister within a few years.'

'Do you remember the man her sister married? Mark Proctor. Some kind of grief counsellor.'

Harry took a long pull on his cigar as Lillian appeared with a tray of cups and a teapot, a small jug of milk to one side.

'Thank you, dear,' Harry said, as she placed the tray on the small table between them. It was as though Harry and Lillian had chosen to spend their whole retirement in a state of affectation.

Harry poured the tea, his cigar in his mouth, and once everyone had a cup he sat back and furrowed his brow. 'Yes, I remember him. Some good has come out of it, then. I used to wonder about Helena, whether she would go off the rails or something. A lot to deal with and she was only in her early twenties.'

'How was Proctor?'

'Friendly, quiet. We didn't recommend him. Came through some charity, I think.'

'Was he ever in the frame for Adrianne's murder?'

'No, not as I remember. He didn't come along until a few weeks later. The main focus was on the school.'

'Why the school?' Sam said.

'Rumours about Adrianne and a teacher, but nothing could be proven. We wrote it off as some crush.'

'Which school was it?' Sam said.

'St Hilda's,' Harry said. 'The Catholic school on the way to Uppermill.'

Sam felt a niggle of something. St Hilda's. The first victim had been a teacher there – until he was found stabbed to death near the canal, with Henry Mason's bloody fingerprint on the knife.

'That's the connection,' Sam said, leaning forward.

Gina looked at him quizzically. 'What is it, Sam?'

'The teacher who died a month ago, with Henry Mason's fingerprint on the knife – Keith Welsby. That's where he worked. Henry Mason is a posthumous suspect in that murder because of the fingerprint, and he wound up dead this week, with Mark Proctor fast becoming a suspect. Now the sister of Proctor's wife went to the same school. What do we say about coincidences?'

'That they're probably not coincidences.'

Harry looked down, deep in thought. After a few seconds, he said, 'That was the teacher.'

'Harry?' Gina said.

'Keith Welsby was the name of the teacher Adrianne had a crush on.'

Sam stood up. 'We need to go.'

'But you haven't finished your tea,' Harry said.

'Another time, I promise,' Gina said, joining Sam. She scribbled her number onto a scrap of paper she found in her pocket. 'Call me if you think of anything.'

He lifted up the paper and looked at it. He tapped it against his chin. 'I'd heard you'd retired.'

'I have.'

'It's hard to walk away from it, isn't it?' Harry said, and he chuckled. 'I might ring round a few people, all off the books.'

'Thank you, Harry, and look after yourself.'

They both rushed through the garden and then the house, Gina shouting her goodbye to Lillian as they passed through.

Once they were outside, Sam said, 'I'm going to the school, see what I can find out, but I'll have to go on my own. I'm sorry, but they keep records of visits like this.'

'I know; don't worry. Drop me off on the way. I'm going to try to find Joe. I don't want him doing anything stupid.'

As Sam set off, he felt the darkness descend on him. He was getting closer to finding out what lay behind his sister's murder, but it wasn't something he'd wanted to spend his life dwelling on. It had motivated his career choice but he'd long since resigned himself to the fact that he would never get an answer. He wasn't sure he was ready for the possibility that there might be answers after all.

Joe was the problem. He was in trouble. He had to do it for that reason alone.

Fifty-four

Proctor called the police as he walked away from Joe's apartment building. He went at a slow amble, not wanting to attract attention. His number would come up as withheld. When an operator answered, he said, 'I won't give my name, because I'm a neighbour, but I'm worried about a man in my apartment block. Joe, he's called. He's a solicitor. Joe Parker.'

'What's wrong, sir?' she said, over the faint clicks of her fingers on her keyboard.

'I saw him last night. He was dishevelled, with blood on his clothes, hanging around the bins outside the apartment block. He looked really, well, suspicious, I suppose.'

'Can you give me an address?'

'It's the apartments at Castlefield. I'm not telling you any more because I don't want him to know it's me. If it's nothing, I don't want him thinking I've got him into trouble. I'm just a neighbour, but he looked scared. I could see blood on his shirt, and he was wiping his hands.'

'We can get someone to speak to you later, if you—'

'No, I can't, sorry.' And he clicked off the phone. He smiled. Little ripples, the seeds sown.

He quickened his pace along Deansgate, marching past the small shops set into what were once railway arches and towards the crowds bustling around the designer shops and the large glass cube of a bank's Manchester office. As he reached St Ann's Square, he looked around: no one was following.

He scanned the corners of the square, an open space surrounded by shops and the Royal Exchange building, the solid stone of which had protected St Ann's Church from most of the blast of the IRA bomb in the nineties. It was busy with lawyers and office workers taking a slow lunch, mixed in with the shoppers drifting away from the retail complexes around the corner, pausing only to glance at the high-end jewellers and boutiques.

Gerald was further ahead, speaking on the phone. Proctor's stomach tightened. It wasn't through fear of how close he'd come to being a victim, because he'd never been close; he'd been one step ahead all the time. No, it was irritation, a tremble of anger at his impudence, that Gerald thought he was dim enough to wander into an obvious trap on some dimly lit patch of grass.

Gerald turned round as Proctor got closer, putting his phone into his pocket.

'Have you got any money yet?'

'I can't raise it that quickly,' Gerald said, his jaw set. 'It's a lot of money.'

'How much can you get?'

'Why are you so desperate for the money?' Gerald said.

'Is it about the money? Perhaps it's just about breaking you.'

'You did that a long time ago.'

'So when do I get it?'

Gerald put his shoulders back. 'You're getting nothing from me,' he said, his eyes filled with defiance. 'You got what you wanted. You're alive, and you've turned me into someone just like you.'

Proctor stepped closer. 'You'll never be like me.'

'Do your worst,' Gerald said, and prodded Proctor in the

chest. 'Go to the police, but I'm not letting you have your little victory.'

He turned to walk away. Proctor's anger rose quickly inside him, his cheeks flushing red. He stopped himself from doing anything. Not there. Nowhere so public.

Gerald turned. 'I failed last night. I won't fail again.'

As Gerald threaded his way through the crowds, Proctor stopped seeing him. Everything was blurred by rage, his blood rushing through his head.

Now was the time.

St Hilda's was an old Catholic school built in Victorian times. Ivy covered shiny red bricks and threatened to grow over the small windows that were dotted along the walls. It was in stark contrast to the glass and prefab that made up so many of the schools in the area. It protected itself behind high fences but, once the final bell rang for the day, the pupils were at the mercy of whatever the mean streets had for them.

Sam approached the entrance, a modern glass structure tacked onto the front, and, once inside, approached the hatch that constituted the access to those who worked at the school. He tapped on the counter but no one looked up until he coughed. Even then it took a while before anyone ambled over, a woman with glasses hanging from a chain. He had his identification ready.

'I'm here about Keith Welsby's case,' he said.

The woman took her time putting on her glasses and reading his identification card, before pointing to some chairs on the other side of the reception area. 'Sit over there and I'll get the deputy head.'

Sam did as he was told and studied the walls as he waited. There was a framed rugby shirt, a present from a former pupil who'd made it big, and pictures of the various heads of department.

Before he had the chance to take a closer look, the door opened in front of him and the woman he'd spoken to before beckoned him forward. 'Mr Bullman will see you now.'

Despite himself, Sam felt nervous, as if he were some errant pupil. He followed her into a long and dim corridor. There was a trophy cabinet along one wall and a wooden board with names of previous head boys and girls written in gold.

The woman knocked on the first door they came to, and swung it open when a 'come in' was bellowed from inside.

Sam went in and nodded respectfully. The door closed behind him. The man in front of him, Mr Bullman, stood to shake hands. He was tall and gangly, and his jacket rode far up his arms as he stretched his arm out. His blond hair had thinned to barely a covering.

'Thank you for seeing me at short notice,' Sam said.

'Anytime,' Bullman said, and gestured for Sam to sit down. 'An awful case. The pupils and staff here are struggling to come to terms with it. Keith Welsby was a much-loved teacher.'

'I don't need the press release,' Sam said, crossing his legs. 'Just some answers.'

Bullman's eyes narrowed. 'We haven't met before,' he said. 'Have they brought in some new detectives?'

'No, but I haven't visited the school before. I'm working on his case and looking for a connection with some other investigations.'

'Do they have any connection with this school?'

'That's what I'm trying to find out.' Before Bullman could bluster his way into a denial, Sam asked, 'Have there ever been any complaints made against Mr Welsby?'

A pause. 'We answered these questions before.'

'I'm just checking up on some new information.'

'There are complaints against teachers all the time. One of the hazards of the job. Kids make things up to deflect attention,

302

or parents misrepresent a meeting. You'll need to be more specific.'

'Of a sexual nature.'

There was a look to the left, enough of a pause for Sam to know that he was right.

'Why do you say that?' Bullman asked.

Answering a question with a question.

'The case I'm looking at may have some involvement with underage girls. Keith Welsby was a teacher of teenage girls, and single. There has to be a reason he was targeted. An angry parent or boyfriend?'

'Or just a random attack when he was in the wrong place at the wrong time? These things happen. Being a teacher may have nothing to do with it.'

'But that doesn't answer the question,' Sam said, meeting Bullman's glare.

'You're not dragging this school into this,' Bullman said, his voice rising a notch. 'We're the first choice for most parents on this side of Manchester. One of the best performing schools.'

'I'm not interested in the school,' Sam said. 'If I need to, I'll hang around the gates and speak to every pupil about Keith Welsby, get the rumours and the gossip. Once we have a few names, I'll speak to those girls, because their parents become suspects. But of course for every person I speak to, it's a new rumour, their parents finding out that Keith Welsby was a predator and that the school knew about it.'

Bullman's nostrils flared but Sam bored into his glare, let the silence grow until Bullman realised that there was no avoiding the question.

'If there is no link between this school and his murder, will you forget what I say here?' Bullman said.

'I can't make any promises.'

Bullman sighed. 'There were some concerns, yes. Nothing concrete, and no one made it official, but some of the other teachers said he was too familiar. Some of the year tens and elevens would go to his house for revision classes, and there were rumours of drink. And he liked it when the girls flirted with him.'

'But what about relationships?'

'Nothing we could prove. I know how it works, though. Teachers instil trust, and over time it becomes loyalty, so it's easy to conceal.'

'Any names of girls?'

Bullman shook his head.

'Do you remember the Adrianne Morley case? Around eight, nine years ago.'

'Of course I remember. It was a tragedy. For her, for her friends. Whenever a pupil dies, we remember. It was an awful case.'

'Was she one of Welsby's star pupils?'

'Did the police investigation turn anything up?'

'Please don't deflect, Mr Bullman,' Sam said, his impatience showing. 'I'm asking you what you know, not what the police know.'

Bullman picked up a pen and tapped it on the desk as he ground his teeth. He said, 'There were rumours. Unsubstantiated. Keith Welsby was a respected teacher.'

'Were those rumours mentioned by the school to the police at the time of her murder?'

'You can find the answer to that question by looking at your own records.'

'Did you say anything, volunteer those rumours?'

'No, I didn't,' Bullman said.

'Why not?'

'Because it was gossip, nothing more. This school had nothing to do with Adrianne's death.'

'And the school is all that matters?'

'Don't put words into my mouth, Detective.'

'I need to speak to a teacher or pupil who knew Welsby. Knew him well enough to know his secrets.'

'And if I say the school won't cooperate?'

Sam smiled, but it was bathed with insincerity. 'You know what I'll do. I'll put out a public appeal for former pupils of his to come forward with any information about his lifestyle.'

Bullman thought about that for a few seconds. He picked up his phone. 'Can you get Lucy Watson and bring her to my office.' He put down the phone and said to Sam, 'I've been making my own enquiries and was going to tell the police anyway. You might as well have it early.'

Sam raised an eyebrow. 'If you were forced.'

Bullman didn't respond, just sat in silence, his hands clasped together on the desk. Sam was prepared to sit it out. He wanted answers.

Five awkward minutes passed before there was a knock at the door. Bullman bellowed, 'Come in,' without taking his eyes from Sam. When it opened, there was a girl in a school uniform, blue skirt and V-neck jumper. 'Lucy, this is a detective looking into Mr Welsby's case. I'd like you to talk to him.'

'In private,' Sam said.

Bullman shook his head. 'If you talk to her in school, I stay in the room.'

Sam sighed. He knew he had no choice. 'Sit down,' he said.

Lucy went to a chair at the side of the room, a padded seat with wooden arms. She crossed her legs, long and slim, her brown hair straight and over her shoulders. She was elegant and mature, but in her eyes there was fear, still a little girl.

'I'm going to be in trouble and I don't want to be,' Lucy said. Her accent had no northern edges, perhaps she'd been taught to lose it, her parents hoping that some refinement would take her further.

'Just tell me about Mr Welsby,' Sam said.

She glanced over at Bullman, who nodded for her to continue. 'We were in love,' she said.

Sam didn't have to hide any surprise, because there wasn't any. He'd guessed the answer as soon as she walked in.

'So tell me about Keith.'

'He was a lovely man.'

'But you were a pupil of his.'

'I'm sixteen. Why should the law apply differently to him?'

Sam knew all the answers, that teachers held a position of trust and schools shouldn't be treated like somewhere to collect conquests, but he didn't voice his thoughts. It was time to let Lucy speak.

'How did it start?' Sam said.

'I was in his drama club. We put on a big performance every year. *West Side Story* this year; I was Maria. We rehearsed after school, and sometimes at his house. When you see people at home, it's different. They're more relaxed, you see the real man, and he was warm and kind.' Tears brimmed onto her lashes. 'It wasn't his fault. I started it. We were talking and it was late, sitting together on the floor, when I kissed him. I shouldn't have done it but the moment was right; I could see it in his eyes.'

'Were you sleeping together?'

'Yes.' She blushed.

'How many people knew?'

'No one, until he died. I told a friend, who told a teacher, who told Mr Bullman.'

Sam glared at Bullman, whose lips were pursed, fingers steepled under his nose.

'How long had it been going on?' Sam said.

'About three months.' She took a deep breath. 'He loved me. He told me so.'

And all the ones before you, too, Sam thought, but he didn't say it.

306

'Did he ever mention someone called Henry Mason?'

Lucy shook her head.

'Or that he was frightened of anyone?'

'No, nothing.'

'Is there anything about him that would cause someone to attack him?'

'No – he was so gentle,' Lucy said, and wiped her eyes. 'Are you going to tell my parents?'

'You're part of the case now,' Sam said. 'I have to. Don't think of yourself, though. Do the right thing by Keith. You might not know it, but you could help us find his killer.'

'Do you think?'

'I do.'

Lucy seemed happier with that. As Sam stood to go, she said, 'He was my first. He said it was important to him, because it showed that we meant something to each other.'

'I'm sure,' Sam said, and headed for the door.

Fifty-five

Joe put his phone away. Gerald had told him that Proctor was in the city centre. Joe reckoned he had thirty minutes to look around his workshop. He stepped out of his car and tried to close the door quietly, but the clunk seemed to echo along the empty street. He didn't want any curious neighbours checking to see whether it was a delivery van or some relative coming round for a chat.

His clothes were innocuous: jeans and a hooded top. Forgettable, that was the look he was trying to achieve. As he reached Proctor's home, he paused and tried to take in the building.

Most of the houses around had been turned into flats and bedsits. Joe had lived in accommodation like it when he first started out as a young trainee, living out of a studio flat in Salford that made his clothes smell damp. There would be at least one flat on every floor, and maybe more, every available space rented out. Proctor's house was different, because it was one of the few that was still a house, but that didn't mean it wasn't neglected and old. Paint flaked from the stone window sills and the door was faded with age.

He looked around. He couldn't see anyone paying attention, although whether anyone was watching him from the houses opposite was something he could only guess at. He cursed himself. He would attract suspicion as he looked around. He knew that from every shoplifting CCTV he'd watched, from every statement from store detectives he'd read. Looking around gives the game away but it was human nature too strong to ignore; know the risks to have the chance to back out.

But backing out wasn't in his plan.

He turned into Proctor's drive and went straight along the path at the side of the house. His head was down. Straggly rose branches snagged at his clothes. His steps echoed between the walls. He paused when he got to the corner.

Joe closed his eyes and took a deep breath. No one had come out.

He peered around the corner, ready to duck back, his fingers gripping the edges of the bricks. There was no one there. He let out a long sigh. His heart was thumping hard.

The garden was long, bordered by a high wall on one side. In better times, there would have been a neat lawn and beds teeming with shrubs and flowers, stone circles making stepping stones across the grass. Better times were a long way in the past, though. The grass grew long and was strangled by thistles, the stone circles like small interruptions, bald patches. The bushes around it overhung the lawn, making it gloomy, with weeds like a green tangle.

At the end, there was a building. It was the size of a small garage, with a sloping roof covered in moss and lichen. There was one window, dusty, a curtain on the inside. The walls were pebble-dashed but it was patchy and cracked.

He had one last check along the back of the house. There was a door, solid wood, no way to see who might be on the other side. He moved closer, looking around as he did. He couldn't see anyone. He had to start with the window.

His feet crunched on the stone patio as he crouched down, his back against the brickwork, his tongue flicking onto his bottom lip with nerves. He edged along slowly, his hands feeling his way, the stone sill getting closer. Once he was next to it, he closed his eyes and swallowed. He had to be ready to run if he was seen.

He rose slowly until he was standing, stretching and grimacing at the aches in his leg muscles, and let the room creep into view.

It was dim inside. It was a back room, with a dining table and a dresser. There were plates inside a glass cabinet, a dusty decanter and glasses. The room was empty. No one was watching.

He stepped away from the window and moved quietly to the garden. He tried to keep his footfall light, avoiding the paving stones and relying on the grass. It swished against his legs, the rustles loud as he went. When he got to the workshop, he looked back to the house. Still no one there.

The doors were large and wooden, painted green, but old and faded. He cursed. They were locked together with a shiny new clasp and large brass padlock. Gerald said there'd been a burglary. It must have been put on after that.

Joe looked around the door, hoping to see a weakness. He pushed at them. They moved against each other and clattered loudly.

He looked to the doorframe. It was rotten in places, the hinges rusted. He rattled the door again. The hinges rocked against the frame. That gave him an idea.

His took his keys from his pocket and used the end to scrape out the dust and dirt from the head of the screws holding the top hinge to the frame. Once done, he dug the tip of the key into the groove and pressed, turning slowly.

The screws had little purchase in the rotting wood, and once they began to turn it didn't take long to remove them all. Joe pulled at the top of the door and was able to make enough of a gap to lift his leg into and then squeeze his body in. He pressed his hands against the frame, his whole body jammed into the small gap, and pushed. As he pushed, the bottom hinge started to come away from the frame.

There was a tinkle as the hinge fell to the floor, followed by the loud scrape of the door as it swept over small stones.

Joe ducked inside and pulled the door closed again, panting through exertion as he leaned back against a wall. He was a burglar now, there was no getting away from it. He was trespassing; if he was caught his career would be over, he might even lose his liberty for a short while, but none of that seemed important. A memory of Ellie's grave came to him. He'd promised to do the right thing by her. That was driving him.

It was dark inside – a rag of a curtain at the dirt-covered window blocking out any light. Joe let his eyes adjust. There was a large black leather chair in the middle of the room, standing on a thick red rug, with small tables around the rest of the floor, large candles on each. There was a gas heater in one corner.

Joe used his phone to create some light and dust moved in the faint shimmer. He looked along the walls, hoping for some kind of display, a memento board that Proctor could gaze at all night, but there were just tools: rusted old shears, a strimmer with no twine, a dirt-covered spade. A wheelbarrow with dried cement caked on the inside. A lawnmower was propped up against the wall, a yellow toolbox was alongside, the lid open, screwdrivers spilled onto the floor.

There were some cupboards but they didn't reveal anything. Boxes of lawn-feed and weed-killer, unopened, and empty boxes that once held beer cans.

Joe was disappointed. He'd expected something more than Proctor's hideaway, for when he wanted to be alone.

There was a noise outside.

Joe crouched down and held his breath. It was the sound of a door and footsteps on the patio. He looked over to where he'd forced his way in. The door was pulled back to the frame, kept upright only by the padlock holding the loose door to the one still attached to hinges. Through the small gap, he could see the two hinges on the floor.

He shuffled across to the window, listening for the sound of movement outside. He waited for the heavy footsteps to get closer, or even to hear the soft thuds of feet on grass, but there was silence. He moved the curtain just enough to give a view. He lifted his head carefully, the wall in front of him getting lighter as he got higher, knowing that he was coming into view of whoever was outside. He swallowed.

It was a woman. Helena Proctor, Joe presumed. She was putting something in the rubbish bin and tidying up some loose twigs on the patio. If she looked along the garden, she would see that the doors weren't as they should be, and the hinges nearby. Joe's fingers gripped the sill as he watched, waiting for her to turn towards him.

She didn't. She put some more things into the bin and let the lid drop, then she turned and went back into the house.

Joe sat down and let out a long breath. Sweat coated his forehead. He looked at his hands. They were shaking.

He was just about to stand when he looked to the wall at the end of the workshop. There was a workbench, and at first Joe had thought there was nothing underneath. As he looked again, however, helped by the sliver of extra light brought in by the curtain that was still hanging open, he saw the gleam of shiny metal.

Joe scurried over. It was a metal box, the sort used to hold documents. He reached in and found the handle, pulled it towards himself. The clang of a padlock echoed as he brought it out. He couldn't get into it, but the way it was concealed, along with the padlock, told him that it must be important. He decided to take it.

As he made his way back to the door, he stopped at the tool-box and rummaged for a hacksaw. He grabbed one and pushed at the door, making a gap again, the wood screeching on stones once more, but he wasn't going to stop. Once outside, the cool breeze hit the cold sweat on his forehead. He jammed his back against the door to give the illusion of it being closed and threw the hinges into the narrow space behind the workshop.

He didn't look at the house as he rushed through the garden, the metal box and hacksaw swinging in his hand, and tried to look casual as he emerged from the driveway and then back towards his car. No one paid him any attention. He was waiting for a shout from the house, perhaps he'd been spotted, but there was nothing save the occasional noise of passing traffic all the way back to his car.

He climbed inside and started the engine straight away, the metal box on the passenger seat.

As he headed away, he placed one hand on the box. He'd taken a risk but he wondered whether the answers he needed were in there, the beginning of the end of his quest for justice for Ellie, an attempt to make good for all of his secrecy through the years.

His mind went to Gerald King and his daughter. That was the terrible flipside of his decision all those years ago; every murder after Ellie could have been a death prevented. For years Joe had been weighed down with the split-second decision he made on his eighteenth birthday.

He couldn't think of that. All he could do was try to make it right.

Fifty-six

Sam was back at the station. He had been hoping to sneak into the Incident Room and find out how the investigation was going, but as he got closer Brabham shouted, 'Parker!' and pointed to one of the rooms nearby.

Sam turned and went inside, waited for Brabham to join him. Brabham closed the door behind him as he came in and folded his arms.

'Sir?

'We've had the deputy head from St Hilda's on the phone, complaining about the attitude of one of my detectives, like he was acting out some maverick cop fantasy.'

Sam bit back his sigh. 'It wasn't like that.'

'So what was it like?'

'I was chasing a lead.'

'Which was?'

Sam wondered how much he should say, but then realised that he had to say everything or say nothing. It would all come back to Joe, but he couldn't help that.

'Can I sit down?' Sam said. 'It's a long story.'

Brabham paused for a moment, as if he preferred that Sam stood like a naughty schoolboy, but then pointed towards a chair. 'Help yourself.'

Sam sat down as Brabham leaned against a wall.

'I was looking into Mark Proctor, the man whose hire car

was used by the victim last night,' he said. 'You've gone with this Domino Killer theory so I went through the camera logs around the time Henry Mason was killed.'

'Explain.'

'You remember how you said one murder tips into the next, with Henry Mason's fingerprint at the scene of Keith Welsby's murder before Mason himself turned up dead? So it stood to reason that if your theory was right, whoever killed Mason might have been the victim last night.'

Brabham was nodding, his anger dissipating. Sam had gambled on stroking his ego and it had paid off.

'And?' Brabham said.

'Mark Proctor's car was in the area around the park where Henry Mason was found. A traffic cop stopped him for having no insurance and his car was seized. The thing is, later that night he broke into the compound and took back the seized car. That's pretty strange, because Proctor has no record, he's not the burglar-type. What he did next was even stranger: he torched it. Why would he steal back his own car just to set it on fire?'

Brabham frowned but said nothing.

'To get rid of forensic evidence?' Sam volunteered.

'I can see where you're going with that, but what does this have to do with St Hilda's?'

'There should be a link between Henry Mason and Keith Welsby because Mason's fingerprint was on the murder weapon, but we can't find the link. But if Proctor murdered Mason, what if there is a connection between Proctor and Welsby? Somewhere there has to be a link between these people. So what connects Proctor and Welsby?'

'You tell me.'

'Proctor's wife Helena went to the same school that Keith Welsby taught in, St Hilda's, as did her sister, and her sister was murdered a few years ago. It's her murder that brought

Proctor and his wife together. He was some kind of grief counsellor and had a habit of befriending the families of murder
victims. That's how he met his wife – Helena Morley as she
was then – by befriending her after her sister Adrianne was
murdered.'

'That's what they do, isn't it, grief counsellors? And how
does this link in with Keith Welsby or the school?'

'It seems that Mr Welsby liked the pupils more than he
should have done. I've spoken to Harry Neave, who was in
charge of the Adrianne Morley investigation, and there were
rumours that she was involved with Keith Welsby. Sexually.
Just rumours.'

'That makes it damn interesting,' Brabham said. 'A link
between the first and third murders. But what about Henry
Mason? He's got nothing to do with St Hilda's, so there's no
revenge motive there. You've got plenty of loose threads and
rumours but nothing to pull them together.'

Sam paused. He knew he'd come to an impasse, because if
he carried on, he would drag Joe into it.

'Sam?'

He closed his eyes and said a silent apology to Joe, but he
had no choice. He wouldn't be allowed to carry on with just
half the story. To get Proctor, he had to put Joe at risk.

'My sister was murdered seventeen years ago,' Sam said,
opening his eyes, trying to speak clearly, so that his thought
processes didn't come across as muddled. 'My brother is convinced Mark Proctor did it. He was following him yesterday,
and . . . ' Sam paused to take a breath. 'He followed him all the
way to the green in Worsley. Or at least he thought he did. It
looks like Proctor sent someone in his place. The victim on the
green? My brother found the body when he arrived and ran
away.'

Brabham's eyes widened. 'Why was your brother following
him?'

'Because my brother thinks Mark Proctor killed my sister.'

Brabham stood away from the wall and started to pace. 'What were your brother's intentions?'

Sam didn't answer. He could have said Joe had followed him out of idle curiosity, but it wouldn't stand up to scrutiny. He settled for silence instead.

'You're off the investigation,' Brabham said.

'I expected that.'

'Why didn't you tell me this earlier?' Brabham asked, his voice rising.

'I was trying to get everything in place first, so that I could be sure.'

'Sure of what?'

'Sure that my brother hadn't killed that man. And he didn't, I'm sure of it.'

'Jesus Christ, Sam!'

'I know how it looks.'

'Do you, really?' Brabham shook his head in disbelief. 'You have no idea how this looks. And there's another big problem.'

'Which is?'

'Proctor might be a suspect in the murder of Henry Mason, but he can't be a suspect in a case where he was supposed to be the victim. Your brother thought it was him and, if what you're saying is correct, he was lured to that park for his intended death. That puts your brother in the frame. Worse, maybe. He might be the next in the line, the fourth domino.'

Sam didn't respond. Brabham had reached the same conclusion he had.

'I've got one question to ask you,' Brabham went on. 'You have got to answer it honestly, because if it turns out you're wrong, you're done, over.'

Sam stayed silent. He knew what the question was before Brabham asked it.

Brabham stopped pacing and put his hands in his hips. 'Did

your brother kill the man last night, thinking it was Mark Proctor?'

'No, he didn't.'

'How do you know?'

'Because he's my brother, and I know him.'

Brabham's lips twitched as he thought about that. 'You're still off the case,' he said. 'If we catch someone, the defence will deflect onto your brother. If you're part of the team, the case will be thrown out. Too much bias, as it will look like the investigation was about clearing your brother.'

'I know that.'

'But if it wasn't your brother, who the hell was it? And why? And why the bloody hell should we bother?' he said, exasperated. 'If Proctor killed your sister, why don't we just let the psychopaths of Manchester kill each other until the chain breaks?'

'We could, but we won't, sir. We're cops.'

'I'm not bloody serious!'

Sam blushed. 'If Proctor was the intended victim, the poor sod last night was an innocent man, sent along by Mark Proctor in his place.'

'So who's behind it? Someone must be pulling all these strings.'

'What about Mark Proctor himself?' Sam said.

'But what about last night?'

'If Mark Proctor was supposed to be the victim, he sent his decoy to his death. Perhaps that was always his intention? It deflects us and makes him look like a victim. Did he have something on Mason and got him to kill Keith Welsby? Mason was chatting to an underage girl online, or at least someone he thought was underage. I'm thinking that he was blackmailed into it, that Mason disclosed secrets he couldn't bear to be revealed. Proctor got Mason to kill Welsby, and then Proctor killed Mason. The use of a decoy last night was just that, a decoy, not just for the killer but for us. If we keep on looking, we'll find a better link.'

'There's no *we* in this, Sam. You can't be near this investigation. Take a rest day. I'll get you reassigned until the case is finished, whichever way it goes. We have to look into your brother to clear him. Or,' and Brabham sighed, 'we have to look into him in case he's guilty and fooled you.'

Sam opened his mouth to object, but he knew it was pointless. Brabham had reached the same conclusion he had, that Sam was conflicted, because somewhere in this tangle of connected deaths his brother was a suspect.

As Sam got to the door, something occurred to him. 'We can at least solve our own case. Henry Mason's murder. If I'm right, Proctor was arrested after trying to dispose of forensic evidence. He won't have gone home. He might have been smeared in Mason's blood but no one noticed. Check Proctor's custody record for Mason's DNA. At some point, he will have touched it to sign it.'

Brabham smiled in response, but then jabbed his finger towards the door. 'You're off the case. Go.'

Sam turned to walk away.

Just before he was out of sight, Brabham called, 'I hope it works out for your brother.'

'Thank you,' Sam said. 'Me too.'

Fifty-seven

The air was still outside as Joe sat in his car on the edge of the moors.

He was on a gravel car park that overlooked the long spread of heather and grass, the spine of England, broken only by the occasional glint of water all the way to Derbyshire. He went there often, sometimes to walk, other times just to reflect, because it was timeless and peaceful. It was often shrouded in low cloud, or buffeted by winds that blew hard across the tree-less plateau, but today everything was still, as though the weather was being respectful to what he expected to find in the box.

He'd driven some of the way with his hand on the metal lid, unsure as to whether he wanted to see inside. Sometimes it was better to be left without answers. Could his imagination match Proctor's own sick fantasies? What was in there? Why had Ellie been chosen?

But he had to know, because there was his own guilt too. He'd felt the sharp stab when he saw the sorrow in Gerald's eyes, the pain inflicted by Proctor many years after Ellie's murder. Joe could have prevented that, and perhaps others, if he'd reported what he'd seen. How could he live with the true scale?

The padlock had already been broken, ten minutes with the hacksaw gaining him access, but he hadn't lifted the lid. He considered waiting for Gerald, but he hadn't called and Joe wanted solitude.

Joe lifted the lid slowly, putting off the moment of the reveal. It creaked. The light spread across the contents. He let out a long breath. His stomach rolled.

Everything was neat and ordered. Eleven envelopes, each with a description and a nickname. Was that because a name made them too personal? No, it was more than that, Joe realised, as he looked inside, because the envelopes were filled with photographs and newspaper clippings, like a collection of memories for each of his victims.

Ellie's envelope was near the bottom. Bile rose in his throat when he saw the nickname on the front: *Leggy fun*. That described her, but it was too personal and yet remote at the same time. It was Proctor knowing her, how she was, getting too close, but yet reduced to a description, not even a name.

Joe lifted out the contents carefully. There might be traces of Proctor on them, his DNA, or fingerprints on photographs, and they might be crucial. He placed them in the seat and put the box into the passenger footwell. His throat closed and tears welled in his eyes as pictures of Ellie appeared in front of him. Ellie walking home wearing large foam headphones, or hanging around near the shops, her arms folded over her chest, her legs crossed at the ankles, all teenage awkwardness and angst. In one, she was smoking, but it didn't look natural, the cigarette jutting out between her fingers as if she was just trying it out. In another, she was smiling. That was the Ellie he remembered. The laughing girl, annoying and fun and frustrating and endearing. He hadn't known at eighteen how much he'd loved her, but he understood it when she was gone.

Realisation hit him like a punch to the stomach. Proctor had been watching her. It wasn't random. But why Ellie? Were all his selections random, or was there a reason he'd chosen her, down to his own preferences or something different, a common link, a shared friend?

Then another realisation filtered in: even if Joe had followed Proctor when he set off after Ellie, there would have been another time. Something about Ellie had made him want her. She was always going to be his victim. He felt some of his guilt lift but it was replaced by some more, that it wasn't about making him feel better about himself. Or was it? Was this the whole point of it all, that it had never been about losing Ellie but about making himself feel less wrung out by guilt, because he wanted to make some right out of the wrong?

He moved the top layer of photographs and gasped.

The final picture was of Ellie lying down, her hair tangled in the leaves and soil, scrapes of red on her cheek where she'd hit the ground, but her eyes were closed, as if she was feigning sleep. But it wasn't sleep. It was Ellie as she lay dead, her last breath squeezed out of her moments before.

He didn't stop the tears this time. His cheeks became warm with them as he stared at the picture, his hands trembling. Proctor had photographed his dead sister as a trophy, so soon after her death that there must have still been something of her in there somewhere. Some sparks of life must have been detectable, her precious embers glowing, like dying sparks in her brain or the final slow crawl of her blood, her heart slowly coming to a stop. It can't have just ended like that, with whatever made her special extinguished. This picture was the epicentre, capturing the moment that everything became still, the ground under her no longer disturbed by her struggles, the pain now rippling outwards, about to hit her family, her friends.

There was something else too. She was wearing a necklace in the picture. He remembered it, a black inverted cross with a snake wrapped around it. Ellie liked it because her parents didn't. The disapproval was the whole point, but it provoked arguments. Joe couldn't remember it being returned to them.

He tipped up the envelope. Something slid out and into his palm: the necklace. Proctor's trophy.

He let the photograph slip from his fingers and stared out of the windscreen, everything blurred by his tears, the small metal cross digging into his hand. He needed to look at the other envelopes, had to know who else there had been. But not yet. He needed the silence more.

Fifty-eight

Gina was waiting for Sam by the canal. The afternoon was getting busy, young mothers walking their children home from school, kids playing around the steel fence that ran alongside the water. A blue barge cruised steadily towards a lock, but it wasn't one of the brightly coloured ones rented out by tourists. This was shabby, with a rusted bicycle locked to the back and a mongrel dog standing on the top. The town didn't even do idyllic canals well.

As he got closer, she pointed towards a pub that overlooked the canal, painted white with a line of England flags pinned to the sign. A black A-board at the front advertised the football matches that would be shown later that week, along with offers on cheap beer. It was dark inside and would allow them some privacy.

As Sam reached the doorway, he said, 'I thought you might have preferred somewhere a bit classier.'

'Surprisingly, that's hard to find around here,' she said. 'Anyway, it's dark and people won't bother us.'

They went towards a table near the back. It was quiet there, apart from a small group of people playing pool. Sam recognised one of them, and from the looks he was getting, the man recognised Sam; the perils of being a copper.

Gina went to the bar and Sam did his best to avoid the

glares from the pool table. He wasn't in the mood for an argument.

'So what have you got that's so urgent?' Sam said, as Gina came towards him, holding two glasses. Her drink was wine. Sam's was a pint of beer that was losing its froth too quickly. It was a pub for people who couldn't keep themselves away from beer during the day, but it didn't matter whether the beer was any good. By the time he took his first sip, Sam could see the pale brown of the ale through the thin veil of white at the top of the glass.

'Why are you drinking on duty? I expected you to ask for an orange or something.'

'Because I'm not on duty any more,' Sam said. When Gina raised her eyebrows, followed by a grimace as she tasted the wine, he continued, 'I had to tell Brabham about Joe and how he'd been following the man he thought was Proctor, and that Joe had been the person who found the body.' He shook his head and sighed. 'There just wasn't a way to tell the story so it made sense, because it was the link with Proctor that was important. If I didn't show it from last night, there was less of a link.'

'So you're suspended?'

'No, just on a rest day. I'm going to be reassigned.'

'Do you want to be?'

'Of course not. So tell me, what's so urgent?'

'I'm worried about Joe,' she said. 'He knows he will be a suspect but he's stopped answering my calls. It's time to tell you everything.'

'I'm not going to like this.'

'No, probably not,' Gina said. 'I went to see Proctor's wife earlier today. Joe knows about it, I told him, but I don't know what's happened since.'

Sam's jaw stiffened. 'Why didn't you tell me this earlier?'

'Because I'd promised Joe.' Before Sam could say anything,

she held up her hand in protest. 'I'm not playing any games here. I'm just trying to protect Joe, and at the same time get Mark Proctor. I'm juggling, not misleading, and there's more going on than just murder.'

'Tell me.'

'When I arrived, Proctor's wife asked if it was about the money.'

Sam frowned. 'The money? Sounds strange. What do you think she meant by that?'

'It sounds like he was running scams. She said he kept his accounts in a locked box in his workshop, and she said it contained other things. Joe was going to have a look in there but I haven't heard from him since.'

'What do you mean, have a look?'

'What do you think? Break in, of course.'

'He can't do that,' Sam said, shocked. 'That's burglary.'

'He's after Proctor. I don't think he'll care. I'll tell you something else, too: Helena Proctor wants to talk. Proctor came back as I was there and she clammed up. She shrank back; I watched her do it.' Gina gripped Sam's hand as if to emphasise the point. 'Get her on her own and find out his secrets. Ask about how he ingratiated himself with her. He's got some hold over her, but if you can break her you might just get something you can use.'

'Did you get anything from Proctor?'

'I pressed him on his car,' Gina said. 'I tried to play the tough defence lawyer part; you know, where you give your client a hard time so that he knows what to expect when he's in the dock. I've seen plenty of barristers do it, to see how the answers stack up, so they say.'

'Except you're a former detective giving it a go, not a trained lawyer.'

'The skills are the same. You know how interviews are: they're structured, creeping up on the suspect, question by question, with things being kept back, the rabbits in the hat, hoping to get a lie that doesn't fit with the secrets you're holding. Once everything is out there, they have to lie again to make everything fit. It's just the same for lawyers, except they don't have to be nice. Lawyers get to shout and harass and bark quick questions and get under the skin. If a copper did it, the interview would be thrown out for being oppressive, because it could lead to wrong answers. It doesn't seem to matter as much when you're in the witness box, that somehow the answers must be reliable, however hectored the witness is.'

'Because they've sworn to tell the truth, the whole truth and nothing but the truth. That's the theory.'

'Exactly,' Gina said. 'So I went at him, told him what to expect. Why would anyone else take the car back? Why would anyone else torch it? I put it to him straight: he could afford to pay the fine to get it back, so why pinch it to torch it? What is he hiding? What was he trying to destroy? I told him we'd have to tell the court what our case was, because the days of just saying "you prove it" are gone.'

'How did that go down?'

'Not a flicker. He sat back in his chair and looked smug, like he had the answers everyone else wanted to hear but he wasn't prepared to give them. At one point, he seemed like he was enjoying the game. He said that no one could make him talk, so he wouldn't, but my job was to check that the prosecution did everything correctly.'

'So we've got nothing.'

'That's wrong. We've got new access with Helena. Speak to her. And there's something else.'

'Which is?'

'I think Joe's right: Proctor did kill your sister.'

Sam blew out a long breath. 'What makes you so sure?'

'It was his eyes,' she said. 'No alarm or surprise or difficulty in being put under pressure. I was looking for a tell: a look away, a nervous lick of his lips, a widening of the eyes, but there was nothing. Cold and calm, but more than that. He was enjoying it. He said something, too.'

'Go on.'

'I was asking him about the car, about how everyone will wonder why he did it, and how he hasn't accounted for it. He said, "Sometimes the ripples are more enjoyable than the splash."'

Sam frowned as he thought about that, but nothing immediately came to him. 'And did he explain it?'

'No. He was going for enigmatic.' She leaned forward over the table. 'So what now?'

'You can't do much more,' Sam said. 'You're on the defence side, I'm the police. If we blur those lines, he'll suspect something. I'm going to speak to Helena, see if she really does want to talk.'

'And me?'

'Stick with me, if you want, wait outside. But keep calling Joe. We need to find him.'

Fifty-nine

The door knocked against the wall as Mark Proctor barged into his house. He was breathless, anger flushing his face. Gerald had stood up to him. He hadn't expected that.

He needed time to think, to consider his options. The police were getting closer because events were beyond his control. No, it was more than that. He'd let them get beyond his control. He was angry with himself.

He had to stay calm, be rational, think through his options. He needed money to get away, start again, create a false identity. Gerald had let him down and his own accounts were getting low; too low to run away with.

He could call the police, send them to Gerald's house, just for the cheap revenge, but the crucial forensic evidence? The bloodied rag? It was in a bin outside Joe Parker's apartment. Only some blurred photographs tied Gerald to the murder.

Another mistake.

As he went into the kitchen, to find himself some space, Helena came in. He didn't want that. He needed to be alone, away from her simpering.

'Are you all right?' she said. 'Where did you go?'

He didn't answer. Instead, he stared out of the window, his jaw set.

'Do you want me to make you something?' she said, getting closer. She put her hand on his arm.

He yanked his arm away. 'No, I don't want anything.'

Helena looked shocked as he turned round, her eyes wide, not used to his temper.

He groaned and turned away from her, willing her not to start with the tears.

As he was about to step away from the window, he thought he saw something. He wasn't sure what it was at first, so he looked again, his eyes scanning the garden. Something had changed.

Then he saw it. The workshop door was hanging open.

He pushed past Helena, making her stumble, and rushed to the back door, flinging it open.

He'd seen it right. The large wooden door was hanging not just open, but loose. Someone had broken in. *Not again!*

He was breathing hard as he ran across the lawn, panic clutching at his chest. He knew what he would find before he got there.

The door had been taken from its hinge, so that it flapped open like a wide lopsided gate. He didn't bother looking for his key. He just pulled hard on the wood. It scraped loudly on the concrete. His foot kicked a hinge screw. It tinkled on the floor as it bounced into the workshop.

He looked around, frantic, searching for something amiss. His tools were still there, so it wasn't a normal burglary.

He edged around the cement mixer and went straight to the corner, where his box was kept, returned only earlier that day. As he threw up the sheet that covered the small space where he stored it, he groaned. It was gone.

The sounds around him faded. He fell to his knees. All he could hear was the rasp of his own breath. His fingers clawed at the concrete floor.

There was a noise behind him. He turned. It was Helena.

'What is it? What's happened to the door?'

He swallowed. 'Someone's been in here.'

Helena looked around, confused. 'Has anything been taken?'

'Who was here?' he said, barking out the words, ignoring her question.

'Just the lady from the solicitor's, but you know that.'

He kicked out at the workbench. 'Fuck!'

'Mark, what's wrong?'

'Where did that bitch go?'

'I don't know, you spoke to her last.'

He pushed past Helena again, but with more venom this time, clubbing the side of his fist into her face as he went past. She cried out and sunk to the floor.

As he ran back up the garden, his car keys already out, Helena screamed after him, 'Mark, Mark!'

He wasn't stopping. He wasn't going back.

But he knew where he was going.

Joe drove into the courtyard outside his apartment block. He was checking for police activity, knowing that they wouldn't recognise Melissa's car.

There were two men he reckoned were police officers by a car, recognisable by the sharp crease in their trousers to the close crop of their hair, and two crime scene investigators in white paper suits rummaging through one of the large rubbish bins.

He thought about stopping and handing over the metal box, but realised that all it would do was give him a motive, although he guessed that they'd already worked that one out. He could implicate Gerald King, but he had that in his armoury if he needed to use it. Right then, he was more interested in going after Proctor.

He turned the car around and went for the exit again. He called Gerald as he drove, to make sure he was in. Once there, he wanted to be in and out as quickly as he could. Gerald was a murderer, whatever his justification.

Gerald looked pale when he opened the door.

'You all right?' Joe said.

'Just, well, you know . . . ' he said, and turned to walk back along his hallway. His shoulders were slumped, his steps slow.

Joe followed him into the living room. Gerald sat in a chair.

'I can't believe I met Proctor and let him walk away,' Gerald said. His eyes filled with tears. 'I let Katie down. I should have ended him but I was too scared of getting caught. But I deserve to be caught after last night.'

'I've only stopped by to give you this,' Joe said. He held out the envelope bearing the name of Gerald's daughter.

Gerald took it from him but didn't look inside straight away. Tears rolled down his cheeks and he made no effort to wipe them away. Instead, he said, 'Thank you,' and then reached into the envelope. He gasped as he pulled out a tattered blue notebook covered in scrawls and doodles, flowers drawn around the edges like a daisy chain. He held it like a precious artefact at first, his eyes wide and damp, disbelieving, but then he started to turn the pages.

Joe had looked before he'd arrived at Gerald's house. There was nothing they could use evidentially, but that wasn't the reason Gerald was looking. For him, it was about the touch of his daughter, her joy of life brought back to him. Tears were rolling down his cheeks as he turned the pages, reading her random notes, messages for her friends, shown in class perhaps, done at the back of class as the teacher faced the front. Short poems, some sketches. It wasn't a diary, but the thoughts of a teenage girl splashed over the paper, before the days of social networking and private thoughts shared to anyone with a mobile phone.

Gerald turned over a page and sniffed back some tears. 'Who's this?' He held up the notebook.

Joe hadn't gone that far into the book, but as he looked, a chill ran through his body.

It was a sketch of a man, just his face, a small flick of hair, the eyes just black dots. It was no artist's impression but the words underneath made it obvious: *Creepy guy*.

'Katie saw Proctor,' Gerald said, his voice just a whisper. 'She knew she was being followed.' He looke confused. 'Why didn't she say something?'

'Ellie was followed too,' Joe said. 'It was more than random. I'll never know if she knew.'

Gerald reached into the envelope and pulled out some newspaper reports. They were reports on the hunt for his daughter's killer, but they focused on the grief of Gerald and his wife. There were clippings from the various press conferences they did, and some magazine articles about them a year afterwards, showing Gerald and his wife shopping, the photographs sold on the helplessness on their faces, an ordinary couple trying to get on with their lives but every part of their sorrow etched all over them.

'It was never about Katie, or Ellie,' Joe said quietly. 'It was about us – about my parents, or you. It was our grief he enjoyed. My sister's death was just the event to set everything in motion. I've been trying to work it out, because they say psychopaths have no empathy with their victims. I can't work out whether that applies to Proctor or not. Does he just enjoy the chaos, and he's indifferent to the suffering, a psychopath to his boots? Or is it more complex than that? That he does feel empathy, our suffering, but he enjoys that suffering, that he needs to feel it to know he's alive, that he isn't a psychopath?'

'Don't humanise him,' Gerald said, through gritted teeth. 'You can't try to understand him because then you're halfway to forgiving him.'

'Or perhaps it's a way of allowing you to live a life?'

Gerald shook his head. 'No. I need this pain. The anger is the only thing that keeps me going. If I lose that, I've nothing.'

'You don't know that.'

'I killed a man!' Gerald shouted. 'Don't you get it? It's all right for you, because you can chase answers. Me? I've lost everything whatever happens, because I can't forgive myself for that. It makes me like him. No, I'm going to do one last thing. Kill Proctor. Kill the right man.'

Joe didn't respond. He'd carried those thoughts for so long, he couldn't protest at the wrongfulness of them. Instead, he reached across and tipped out the rest of the envelope's contents. Photographs of Katie. Like Ellie, they were of Katie hanging around, being a teenager, being collected by her mother.

And then there was the final photograph. Katie slumped against the stone steps of the small monument on the green, her eyes red from burst capillaries, her tongue protruding, grotesque and violent. Her clothes were rumpled and her notebook was on the floor next to her, spilled out of her canvas bag, kicked about as she fought for her life.

Gerald screamed. Joe turned away, he couldn't watch. He didn't want to intervene, Gerald would come to his own conclusion about his next step.

'I'm sorry,' Joe said.

Gerald pushed the photographs and clippings from his lap and instead went back to the blue notebook. It was as if he'd forgotten Joe was there.

Joe backed out of the room and closed the door quietly as he left the house. It was time for Gerald to spend time with better memories of his daughter. Whatever the future held was down to him, although Joe guessed that Gerald wouldn't simply carry on his life as if nothing had happened.

Sixty

Sam sat in his car, his eyes closed. Gina was with him, but they were both silent. Until that point Proctor had been a name only, some mention in a file, a threat on his brother's lips. Sitting in the car on the street where he lived made him real. He was a man, with a lawn and personal things visible through the window: photographs on the wall, ornaments on the sill, a NO SALESMEN sticker on the porch window.

'How long do we give it?' Sam said. He couldn't go to the house if Proctor was there. If Joe was right, he'd recognise Sam and clam up. It was Proctor's wife he wanted to see, after what she'd said to Gina, wondering whether she was there about the money. Proctor would control his wife; what she said, how she was. Sam couldn't let him do that, not if there was a secret to weasel out of her.

'There's no car,' Gina said.

'The longer we leave it, the more likely it is that he'll come back. He can't stay out all night. Have you heard anything from Joe?'

'He's not answering his phone,' Gina said. 'Let the daylight fade, so you can sneak around, check in the windows.'

Sam checked his watch. Eight o'clock. He wouldn't have long to wait.

They gave it another thirty minutes before Sam said, 'It's now or never,' and reached for his car door.

'Good luck.'

'I'm hoping I won't need it,' Sam said, and climbed out. A quick check along the street before he walked towards the door. No one was there.

He went to the window and peered through the small crack in the curtains. There was a woman sitting in a chair, her knees pulled up to her chest, looking deep in thought. No television on, no chat, no one else there.

He stepped away from the window and paused in front of the door. What was he risking by doing this? Why was he doing this? Helena Proctor would remember his visit and mention it, so any protest that he stayed out of the investigation would be left empty.

But Sam knew the answer. He was doing it for Joe. For his family. It was the reason he did everything.

Proctor's doorbell was a cheery chime. Soft footsteps could be heard on the other side before the door opened on a chain. A timid face appeared in the crack, just one side of her face visible. 'Hello?'

Sam produced his identification and held it up for her. 'Helena Proctor? I'm DC Parker. I need to speak to you about your husband.'

There was a pause, a couple of fast blinks, and then, 'Why? Who called you?'

That made Sam pause. It wasn't the response he was expecting. Something was wrong. 'Mrs Proctor, I need to speak to you.'

She closed the door as she rattled the chain from it. When she opened it fully, she looked at the floor and stepped aside. 'Please come in.'

That's when Sam saw her face properly.

Her right eye was swollen, her cheekbone an angry purple, her eyeball bloodshot. Her lip was cut.

Proctor had done this. There was no proof, but who else could it be? He thought quickly and realised he had a better reason to be there rather than some wild inquiry about dodgy accounts.

Sam stepped into a house that looked tired, as if there was no desire to update it. In the living room, the sofa and chairs sagged and the cloth was faded in places where the sun had been trained on them over the years.

Sam went to sit down and Helena sat on the chair opposite, closest to the fire, although it wasn't on. She perched on the edge of the cushion, her knees close together, her hands on her legs. Defensive, tucked in tightly.

'Mrs Proctor, I want you to tell me what happened to your face.'

'It's nothing. These things happen.'

'Like what?'

'I thought you were here about the burglary.'

'What burglary?'

'Someone broke into my husband's workshop this afternoon. They took the paperwork for his accounts.'

Sam tried not to react but he guessed that Joe had something to do with it. He'd crossed a line. Sam returned his focus to her injuries. If Proctor had caused them, he might be able to turn her against him.

'I'm here because someone heard shouting, as if you were in distress,' he said, trying to keep his voice soft and sympathetic. 'And now I see your face.' He shrugged. 'You can see why I'm here.' A pause. 'Did your husband do that?'

Helena looked down, some more quick blinks, nervous. 'I don't want to get him into trouble.'

'But if he's hitting you, he can't get away with it. Help me to help you.'

'No, it was my fault.'

'How so?'

'Because I should have looked after his things better. His workshop was burgled and I was in all the time.'

'That doesn't make it your fault, or that you deserve to be hit.'

'I'm sure he didn't mean it. He was angry, that's all, because of the burglary, with his accounts being taken.'

There it was again, more concern about his accounts than her own welfare. Helena had made some reference to money when Gina had visited, and for some reason it spelled trouble for her. All he had to do was let her speak and see what happened.

'Why would someone go after your husband's accounts?' Sam said.

Helena fidgeted. 'I don't want to get into trouble.'

'Why would you?'

She swallowed and shook her head, bursting to say something but prevented by loyalty to her husband. Eventually, she said, 'Should I get a solicitor?'

'Why? You're not under arrest. This is just a chat. And when I look at what he's done to you, I think you'll feel better for talking.'

Sam let the silence grow. There were no other sounds. No ticking clock. No shouts of children. Just the emptiness of a soulless house.

'I was worried this would happen at some point,' she said, after a long two minutes of nothing. 'I've told him but he won't listen.'

'What have you told him?'

'That people will find out and they'll come after him. They'll be angry, and they might not even bother with the police. Money makes people do crazy things.'

Sam thought back to the night before, the murder of a man mistakenly believed to have been Mark Proctor. Was it really about money? But then his mind flashed to Henry Mason. No, it was more than that.

Sam leaned forward. 'I think you'd better start at the beginning.'

After a deep breath, Helena said, 'There's a name for it. A Ponzi scheme or something.'

Sam tried not to betray his surprise but instead smiled sympathetically, as if Helena had confirmed what he'd always known.

'It wasn't supposed to wreck families,' she continued. 'He said it would work out, because people would still get their money back.'

'How long has he been running it?'

'Since before we met. Mark can be so charming when he wants to be. He talks so softly and sounds so kind, and people believe him. They gave him their savings – thousands of pounds – and he'd invest it for them. He gave them updates every year, and the investments sounded like they were doing really well, so when the policies matured they just invested again, rolled it over and over until they thought they were sitting on a massive amount. He looked after his clients. Visited them at Christmas, had calendars made up, and people recommended him. Whole families threw their money at him, cousins and uncles, and they think they're sitting on a fortune, just from his canny investments.'

'But any money he pays back is just from money given to him by new investors?' Sam said.

'That's right. There's no pot of money. He just has to keep them reinvesting all the time and he never has to pay it back, as long as new investors keep his own funds ticking over. I've told him, though, it's too big, that when it comes crashing down it will come down hard. People will be expecting a six-figure sum, their retirement plan, and all he will be able to say is that he'd taken their first investment and spent it, and just told lies about it ever since.' She shook her head. 'I worry that someone will hurt him. Losing money like that makes people angry. Or they might hurt me.'

Sam softened his voice. 'If you want to stay safe, you've got to help us.'

Helena wiped her eye. 'I'm scared. Am I in trouble? I told him not to, but he wouldn't listen.'

'Not if you cooperate,' Sam said. 'Tell me first: how did you two meet?'

He tried hard not to let the tension he was feeling show on his face. This was what he'd really come for.

Sixty-one

Joe drove through Manchester in a daze, not sure what to do.

Things were changing for Proctor. It wouldn't take the police that long to piece together his involvement in the murder of Henry Mason. How many other people break into a police compound to steal back a car, and then set fire to it? Proctor was in an end-game, demanding money, taunting Joe. He knew everything was unravelling. What would he do? Take off? Perhaps. Or was it about a final spree, his farewell hurrah, hurt those who've hurt him?

His thoughts swept back to Ruby. Family was his first priority.

The hills and open fields soon turned into motorway and an aggressive crawl all the way back into the city. He skirted away from the city centre and drove towards his mother's house, all the time checking his mirror for police cars.

As he turned onto the street, he went slowly, wary of a police presence. It was quiet. Some pensioners loitered around a metal gate, chatting the evening away, and further along a young mother pushed a pram, a faint glow of a cigarette over the child's head. A suburban scene, the day coming to an end. No one looked around as he crawled to his mother's house, no wary glances.

He bolted up the driveway, knocking and shouting out when he got through the front door. There was the sound of chatter from the back of the house. Was she alone? He walked through, his footsteps silent on the heavily cushioned carpet. As he turned into the dining room he saw his mother. She was alone, sitting in a cane chair in her conservatory, a film playing on a small portable television, the view of the garden blocked out by the reflection of the room in the glass. She looked up as he went in.

'Hello, Joe; this is a nice surprise.'

He leaned forward to kiss her on the cheek, her skin felt cold, and sat on a chair opposite. This was her favourite spot in the house, somewhere to reflect as she gazed over the garden that Joe's father had once tended so lovingly. At night, it was just somewhere she didn't leave.

'I'm not staying long,' he said. 'Has anyone been here looking for me, or called the house?'

'No. Are you expecting someone?'

He gave a smile of reassurance, partly out of relief. 'It's okay. Just checking.'

'Is Ruby with you?'

'She's at Sam's house. She'll be home soon.'

'Okay. Do you want a drink?' She started to pull herself out of her chair.

'No, stay put. Sit down. I need to talk to you.'

She sat back and looked more concerned. 'What is it, sweetheart? Are you all right?'

'Yes, I'm fine, it's not about me. It's about Ellie. Or, at least, after she was killed.'

Her look darkened and she seemed to slump in her chair. She glanced over at a picture of Ellie on the window sill, the colours faded from too much bright light. There were pictures of her in every room.

'What do you want to know?' she said, her voice quieter than before.

'I know the police were here all the time, and there were

people with the police who helped us, but was there anyone else who interfered? Did anyone offer you counselling you didn't want or who got too involved?'

She stared at the floor for a few seconds and then said, 'There were a lot of people showing an interest, but I don't remember much about that time. I was in shock, I didn't notice anything about the world.' Her hand went to her eye to wipe away a tear. 'If anyone had tried to help, I wouldn't have listened. I dealt with it myself, the hardest thing ever.'

'It was hard for all of us.'

'But she wasn't your baby, Joe; you can never understand. You think you can, but you can't.'

He didn't respond to that. He wasn't there to compete with her grief.

'There's something I've never told you before,' she said. 'I almost killed myself.'

That came at Joe like a punch. 'When? How?' His voice was hoarse.

'A few months after the funeral. Everything was supposed to get back to normal, but how can that be right? That's what I couldn't deal with, normal life. How could anything ever be normal again? The people who were supportive started to turn away, because what else could they say? So one day I walked to the motorway. It took me a couple of hours, but I made myself carry on, just thinking how I'd be free when I got there.'

'Mum, you don't have to tell me this.'

'I went onto one of the footbridges and looked out over the traffic,' she went on, ignoring him. 'I wanted to jump, to end my torment quickly. Do you know what stopped me? It wasn't thoughts of you and Sam, or your father, because all I saw then was more heartbreak ahead, that I couldn't stand it if something else happened to anyone else I loved; if it could happen to my lovely girl, then it could happen to you too.'

'What stopped you?'

'The other lives I'd ruin if I did it. The poor soul whose car or lorry would run me over, whose life would never be the same. The police who would have to scrape me up, knowing that however they tried to be strong about it, the sight would come back to them in the darkness. The person who had to break the news to you. And what if I misjudged it and killed someone, smashed through their windscreen? That person wouldn't deserve that. So I stepped back and came home. That was my worst day. I came home and told your dad that I wanted another baby. I wanted another Ellie. So we had Ruby.'

Joe swallowed. 'Do one thing for me then.'

'What's that?'

'When Ruby comes home, keep her safe. And you too. I want you to go somewhere, stay there until I tell you to come home, both of you.'

'You're scaring me.'

'Good,' he said. 'It means you'll do as I say. Call Sam. Ask him to help, but do it now.'

'And what are you going to do?'

'I'm going to try to sort this thing out.'

Sixty-two

Sam looked up at the framed photograph on the wall: a teenage girl in the arms of an older girl who was just recognisable as Helena Proctor, sitting on a bench overlooking the sea. The sugar-cube buildings in the background gave it away as a holiday shot. They were both laughing that carefree laugh, heads back, at some joke or other told by the person taking the camera. Now, Helena was quiet, sombre, as if that spark had been dimmed.

'That's my sister, Adrianne,' she said. 'She was killed when she was walking home from a night out.' She said it matter-of-factly, but Sam could tell that it was something she'd learned to do, to lock the pain away. 'Mark helped out with an organisation that looked out for the families of crime victims. The police did their bit but it was good to have someone separate from them. He was so kind. It's a cliché, that I ended up falling for him because I relied on him for support, like a patient who falls for a nurse, but I wanted to see more of him. And then, well, you can guess.'

'Tell me about your sister,' Sam said.

'Adrianne was a lovely, sweet girl. What else can I say? We weren't like close friends because she was nearly ten years younger than me, but she was my baby sister. I looked out for her.' Her expression grew sad. 'I had to. Our parents were killed in a car crash, because someone sold them a dangerous car, the pedals sticking, so it fell to me to look after Adrianne, and this place.' She gestured with her hands to the house. 'Or rather, I was supposed to.' A deep breath. 'However sweet she was, teenage years are hell and there's nothing new in that. That night, I didn't know where she'd gone. She was a handful; she would say she was going out and then there'd be the slam of the door. I'd question her when she got back, but there was always some reason why she couldn't tell me where she was going. There'd always be a party at the weekend, someone somewhere having a gathering, but why do these people let their houses get used like that? So yes, I lost control of her, but I'd had no lessons in being a parent. I was only in my twenties, wanted my own life, and due to—' She stopped to compose herself. 'Due to an accident, the job fell to me. Adrianne would be fine, or so I thought. I imagined us being best friends when she was older, and we'd laugh at how she tormented me, because that's what teenagers do.'

'I'm a policeman,' Sam said. 'I can't begin to tell you how many parents I've sat with who can't work out how their child ended up in a police station.'

'That was Adrianne all right,' she said.

'Tell me how she died?'

Helena took a deep breath. 'There was something funny about that night. Adrianne caught a bus and got off at a stop further along than she should have done. I've seen the footage from the bus, the police showed me. She was acting normally, but she went past her stop and waited for the next one. No one followed her. But why get off at the next stop? Why end up walking the way she did? It meant going down a long alley, past warehouses, a really long dark walk home.'

'What do you think about that?' Sam said.

'Putting off the argument when she gets in, I suppose, which makes me feel like it was partly my fault.'

Sam wondered whether the answer was something different:

was Adrianne trying to make it look as though she was coming from a different direction, covering up where she'd actually been, because she had a forbidden love? And was that forbidden love her teacher?

'Were there any suspects?' Sam said.

Helena's jaw tightened. 'No, none.'

'Did she have a boyfriend or anything?'

'Not that she told me about.'

'So you're no nearer to finding out who did it?'

'No, and that's the most difficult part.' She wiped her eyes and took a deep breath. 'Do you want to know about the burglary? It's happened before. I can show you?'

'Yes, I might be able to help,' Sam said.

She stood up. 'Follow me.'

As she took Sam along the hallway and through the kitchen, she said, 'Mark isn't a bad man. I don't know why he does it. He likes nice things, I suppose, or perhaps it's the thrill of it, every year wondering when it's going to collapse. I know it got a bit dicey a few years ago, when the banking crash happened, because people were getting worried and didn't want to renew, but he charmed them. Told them that the returns would be lower but now was a time to stay calm and hold their nerve. I heard him on the phone once. When the call ended, he was just normal, as if there'd never been a problem.'

They went into the darkness of the garden, their footsteps soft on the grass.

'And you'll say all this in court? Put it in a statement?'

Helena nodded. 'I don't want to get dragged into it, and I don't want people – his clients – to start coming here.'

They were heading towards a large building at the bottom of the garden, like a garage but with no driveway in front of it. When Helena reached the door, she moved it, making it creak.

'Someone took off the hinges,' she said.

Sam stepped forward to look and saw what she meant. The

347

double doors were hanging only from the right-hand hinges, both held together by a padlock in the centre.

He pulled on the door so that it opened like a wide gate and stepped inside. Helena reached round him to flick on the light switch.

'Has anything else been taken?' Sam said, looking around. It was like the inside of a garage, the walls filled with tools, but dominated by a large chair and deep rug. The air was cold and there was a slight smell of damp, as if the lack of warmth or air was taking over the carpet. There were candles on tables, spaced randomly, but they would not be enough to provide heat. Sam put his hand on the chair. The leather felt cold.

'No, I don't think so,' she said, biting her lip. 'He'll be angry about that, because he calls this his special place. There's a word for it: a man-cave. Men need somewhere to escape to, don't you think? It keeps them happy. Your man should be happy. I know that's old-fashioned, but it's how I feel. Mark loves it down here. Spends all his time here, on his own, reading, or sometimes just contemplating. It does look nice when the candles are lit. It used be my father's workshop. I'm glad that Mark's kept it special.'

She went over to a workbench and bent down to move the cloth that hung down over the edge. 'He kept his box of accounts here, but they're gone now.'

Sam looked under the table. There was nothing there. 'Do you want to make an official report?' he said, hoping that the answer was no.

'Not yet,' she said. 'I'll ask Mark.'

Sam reached into his pocket and produced a business card. 'If you need to speak to me about anything, will you call me? Let us do something about what he did to your face.'

Helena shook her head. 'It was an accident.'

'And is there any way I can contact you without Mark knowing?'

Helena gave him an email address. Sam jotted it down. 'It's on my phone, he doesn't use it,' she said, and she blushed.

Sam went to leave when Helena said, 'Will you do something else for me?'

'What is it?'

'See if you can find out if there's any progress in my sister's case. I know I won't get updates now unless something big is about to happen, but even something small might mean something.'

Sam smiled. 'I'll see what I can do.'

As he walked along the garden and back towards his car, he could feel Helena watching him all the way.

Sixty-three

'So how did it go?' Gina said, as Sam got back into the car outside Proctor's house.

As he set off, he said, 'Joe got the box from the workshop.'

'How do you know?'

'She told me the workshop had been burgled and took me down there.'

'So where's Joe? What's he doing with it?'

'I don't know,' Sam said. 'But there's something else: Proctor hit her. Her face is swollen and her eye looks bad.'

Gina was surprised. 'She wasn't like that earlier.'

'No, but since then someone has broken in and stolen his accounts, and it looks like it made him angry.'

'Will she make a complaint? It would give you the chance to look into Proctor properly. Get her away from him, get all of his secrets.'

'No, she wasn't interested in complaining about the assault, but she's worried about the money, scared it's going to come back to her somehow.'

'What's his scam?'

'Pyramid schemes, Ponzi schemes, call them whatever you like, but it sounds like she's been waiting all of their married life for it to come crashing down and she's scared she'll get dragged into it. You get that a lot with financial fraudsters: they dig themselves into a hole and it's the arrest that gives them the courage to start over.'

'That's a strange way of looking at it,' Gina said. 'Not having an alternative isn't the same as having courage.'

'I've seen the relief, though, because they knew the day was always going to come; we all put off the bad stuff, it's human nature. When they're forced to confront it, I've seen the weight come off them.'

Gina frowned at that but just said, 'How did you get her to open up?'

'She just did, almost as if she'd been dying to tell someone. Proctor has taken thousands from people, and even gets them to reinvest, although it's not really a reinvestment. It's just putting off for a few more years the news that Proctor has taken their money and spent it on cars and holidays. There's no proof there, though, and it makes it tricky if my brother has stolen the accounts. If Brabham finds out I was here, he'll be after me.'

'So why did you do it?'

'You know why. Justice for Ellie.'

'Go to the financial crimes unit then. Be a confidential informant, or whatever's the current buzzword.'

'That will take time, and there'll be nobody there right now.'

Gina looked out of the window as she thought about that. She was silent for a few streets and then said, 'I want the same as you, justice for Ellie. If Proctor has been hiding things all this time, we should have spotted him, because he was creeping around crime victims. But he must come across well, because he even got Helena to fall for him, a victim's sister. It's almost bloody romantic.'

'I'm not going to stop looking,' Sam said. 'We need something solid to link him. He's a fraudster who's plausible, a conman, but that's not the same as proving he's a murderer.'

'It makes him a good psychopath, though,' she said.

'How come?'

'Something you said earlier, about how fraudsters always seem relieved when they're caught. That won't be the case with all of them, and the ones who aren't relieved are the ones to worry about.'

'I'm sorry, I'm not following you.'

'I don't want to pull my experience on you, that's not fair,' Gina said, 'but I've met a lot more murderers than you have. Not all murderers are psychopaths, but the ones who are have recognisable traits: they're charming, plausible, persuasive, but remorseless; they have no fear of the consequences. Do those traits sound familiar with someone like Proctor?'

'It's pretty much how Helena described him.'

'Do you know what Ian Brady once said about serial killers?'

'I can't wait to hear this.'

'That what separates them from ordinary people is that they're brave because they live out their fantasies without any fear,' Gina said. 'He wrote a book about them, *Gates of Janus*. Not his own murders, but his warped insight into people who kill. What he didn't realise was that he got it the wrong way round, because for a psychopath fear of the consequences doesn't register. If there's no fear, where's the bravery? So what Brady said was just grandiose bullshit, and guess what: grandiose bullshit is another sign of a psychopath. Kind of ironic that rather than defining a psychopath, Brady just flagged up another trait he couldn't control in himself.'

'So are you saying that Proctor's financial frauds are a sign that he killed people?'

'Just that being a fraudster doesn't make him *only* a fraudster. Psychopaths are risk-takers. His scams sound like he lives his life taking risks, except he doesn't see them as risks in the same way most people do, because risk involves some fear of the consequences. Answer me this, Sam: if you were running his schemes, how would you be?'

Sam thought about that as they made their slow way through the city centre, to where Gina lived.

'I wouldn't be able to sleep at night,' he said.

'Through guilt for your victims?'

'Partly, or at least I'd like to think so.'

'There you go, another trait: a lack of empathy. He's taken a lot of money from a lot of people – perhaps people who can't afford to lose it – and he's spent it like it doesn't matter.'

'It's not just that, though,' Sam said. 'It goes back to what I said, that I'd be expecting everything to come crashing down at any moment. I'd be waiting for the knock on the door, for the rattle of handcuffs.'

'That's what Proctor doesn't feel; he couldn't possibly run scams like that for all those years if he did. Not all fraudsters are psychopaths, but a lot of bankers are.'

'So what do we do?'

'We keep digging. I'm going to see what else I can find out. If he keeps trophies, there must be other victims. Let me ask around about any unsolved murders and missing persons.'

'Good idea,' Sam said. 'I've still got some things I can be looking through. I'll call you later.'

They were both silent for the rest of the journey to Gina's house, each contemplating their next move. Sam knew what he would be doing: the No One Tells site. He reckoned he'd worked out the reason for the vodkagirl profile. He just needed to prove who she was.

When he pulled up outside her house, Gina said, 'I need to talk to Joe.'

'He hasn't been in touch with me.'

'If he does, get him to call me. I need to know how he's getting on.'

Sam smiled. 'Will do.'

*

353

The house felt silent when Gina got home. She'd started to notice it more recently; she was surrounded by familiarity, by pictures and trinkets she'd picked up over the years, but it was the absence of another human voice that she noticed the most.

She turned on the radio, feeling better when there were voices in the house. It was just some local station having a late-evening phone-in, but she enjoyed the inanity of it, even though it was just the sound of other lonely people hiding behind opinions to mask their real need to talk to someone else.

But she didn't hesitate for long. It was the vibrations of other lives she needed, not the words, and she knew her evening would become serious again. This was just a quiet moment before she got on the phone and rooted out all her old contacts, asking them to trace any old unsolved murders, or even missing persons. She needed to see whether Mark Proctor would show up somewhere else.

The wine bottle clinked as she took it out of the fridge and poured a glass. A fresh New Zealand sauvignon blanc, part of a case she'd received from a wine club. She knew she was drinking too much but she justified it to herself by calling it her little treat. Regardless, she felt like she'd earned it and took the glass upstairs to drink as she took a long bath.

She lit candles in the bathroom and let the hot water wrap around her as she lay back. The radio was still playing, and she enjoyed the way the gentle murmurs mingled with the soft lap of the water. The rigours of the day faded and she thought about the rest of the evening ahead. She needed the respite.

She was reaching for her razor when the radio stopped.

The electricity had tripped. It did that too often, ever since she'd had a new circuit board fitted, as if it was too sensitive to any variation. Plugging something in or turning on the oven could shut a circuit down.

She could wait until she finished her bath but the annoyance had spoiled the mood.

She stepped out of the bath and went back towards her bedroom, a towel around her, her hands feeling the walls as she got away from the candlelight in the bathroom.

There was a noise.

She stopped. It had come from downstairs. A metallic clunk. Gina held her breath and listened, waiting for it to repeat. There was nothing. It must have been outside, a gate clanging or something similar.

She threw off her towel and scrambled around her drawers for some clothes she could quickly throw on. Sweatpants and a T-shirt.

The house felt strange. Gina couldn't pin it down, but something wasn't right. It was as if she could hear someone's presence even though everything was silent. She stood stock still, listening out. Nothing.

The bedroom door opened with a creak as Gina moved slowly onto the landing. Her hand reached for the banister as she listened out again. Still nothing. There was some light creeping in from a streetlight outside, but it made shadows that shifted as she walked.

'Hello?'

Gina didn't know what made her shout. She was certain she was alone but some instinct told her she might be wrong. It was hard to define.

The top stair creaked like a crack in the darkness, enough to make her jump, and she put her hand to her chest, the fast rhythm of her heart fluttering against her fingers. Her breaths got a little faster as she descended, taking each step slowly. There was a door at the bottom that went into the living room and it loomed ahead like a trap. She stood in front of it, giving small nods, steadying herself.

The handle creaked as the door opened into the living room.

The moon at the back of the house shone silvery light along the room but it didn't make her feel any safer. Dust danced in the moonlight.

She could have gone out through the front door, but where would she go? It wouldn't make the electricity come back on. Gina peered through the living-room window. The lights were on in other houses. It wasn't a power cut. She thought about going to the house next door and asking for help from the man who lived there, just to lessen the menace she felt, but she dismissed it. That wasn't her way, never had been. She didn't play the little woman role, needing the big brave man to help her.

The garage was attached to the house and accessible through the kitchen. As she went through the living room, she told herself not to be so stupid. It was her home, she knew every inch. Nothing to fear in there. She found the drawer that contained all the junk, the half-used packs of batteries, the tin with reels of cotton inside, some food scales she never used, wooden skewers that had spilled out of the packet, and found her torch. She clicked it on. It worked.

She unlocked the door that led into the garage and stepped inside, swinging the beam around. It reflected back off muddy gardening tools and the treadmill that hadn't been used for a while. An upright freezer was silent. Gina shone the torch to the floor and moved slowly among the boxes she needed to get rid of and broken electric fans, her holiday suitcases piled up alongside. She stumbled against her cross-trainer and reached round so she could pull down the cover on the fuse box.

Gina frowned. The box contained a row of switches, each for a different circuit in the house. The sockets for each floor, the lights for each floor. She'd had to go to the box many times, because even a blown bulb could trip a switch. Whenever the circuit was tripped, a switch would be down, and sometimes it would trip the whole circuit and the larger red switch would be down too. The only switch that was down was the large master switch, so she couldn't work out which individual circuit had tripped.

She flicked the master switch upright and with relief she heard the house come alive again. The freezer in the garage hummed. A sliver of light appeared around the door back to the kitchen. The radio started to play. She should have turned on the light in the garage before she came in. She was still in darkness, only her torch lighting her way.

As she stepped backwards, looking down to see what she was standing on, all her senses went into overdrive. A prickle of fear shot along her spine. The hairs on her arms stood proud. Her chest tightened, her throat clenched.

The large garage door that opened upwards and outwards wasn't closed properly. A thin line of streetlight crept onto the concrete garage floor. It shouldn't be like that. She never used that door. It was always closed, her car left on the drive. Had she locked it, though? It wasn't linked to the alarm, which covered just the doors into the house. And the circuit board? No circuit tripped. Just the power turned off. As if someone had found their way into the garage and flicked off the power to entice her down there.

She swung the beam round in a panic, trying to move towards the door into the kitchen.

A face. Pale in the torchlight, eyes glaring, teeth bared.

She screamed.

Sixty-four

Sam's journey home didn't take him long, all of the traffic gone. As he swung his car into his cul-de-sac, the lights were off downstairs. Fear jolted through him, but he relaxed when he went inside and saw the light from their bedroom, just a blue glow of the television, fanning out across the landing.

He looked into the living room. Ruby was lying on the sofa, her head on a pillow, the television on but the volume set low. She was more interested in her phone. He tousled her hair. She looked up and smiled.

'I'll go check on everyone else,' he said, and tiptoed up the stairs, knowing that the doors to his daughters' rooms would be ajar. He looked in on each, as he always did, and the sight of them always made him smile, however his day had been. Nothing so innocent as a child asleep.

When he went into his own bedroom, Alice was propped up on her pillows. She was watching a reality show about some nonentities whose lives were chaotic enough to warrant being exposed to the world.

'Hi,' he whispered, not wanting his daughters to wake.

Alice smiled. 'How's it going?'

'Slowly. It feels like we're pulling everything together, but ...' He shrugged. 'These things are elusive.' He didn't mention that Brabham had thrown him off the case.

'Are you coming to bed?' she said. 'You've been working hard.'

'Not long,' he said. 'I just need to check something out.' And he held up the sheaf of papers he'd printed out at the station and brought into the house.

Alice just smiled and said, 'Okay.'

It wasn't okay, of course, Alice worried about how hard he worked, but this was different. This was personal.

He went back downstairs and spread the papers from the No One Tells site over the dining-room table. He made a coffee, knowing it was going to be a long night.

Something was troubling him, though, had been for most of the day. It was as if the answer was just out of reach, like a distant figure in the mist or faint scratches at the window. Was it in the papers, or was it something else, something more obvious, or something he'd heard but not processed?

The papers contained a long list of numbers and times but Sam had an unerring sense that the answer was somewhere in there. They were Sam's favourite type of clue: something methodical to work through, slow and steady, looking for patterns, a recurring number, something out of sequence.

Human behaviour is just that, behavioural; it follows patterns. When someone does something different, it stands out. Like someone taking longer to get home than usual or arriving to work late. A sudden spring clean of a house. Driving a different route. The papers from No One Tells were better than that, because they were incontrovertible, hard numbers, computer data revealing a fact that was hard to explain away.

Everyone who connects to the internet has their own specific address, a series of digits that tells the internet provider where to send the information. That's the IP address. Sam had worked on frauds where IP addresses were important, like fraudulent online auctions. He knew how they worked.

The data from No One Tells contained all the IP addresses

used by the vodkagirl poster whenever she logged onto the site. Or he, as Sam thought, if Proctor was posing as vodkagirl.

It's never as easy as that, though, because an IP address cannot identify the specific computer, just the internet address, so people who share the same wireless connection will share the same address. What is useful, however, is that the IP address can provide some geographical information, almost like an area code.

What Sam noticed straight away was that the numbers all seemed different, almost random. Either vodkagirl logged on in different places, like using public Wi-Fi in cafés, or, as Sam suspected, she used a proxy server. Using the internet leaves a trail, digital footprints showing your every move, but if someone surfs the net using a proxy site, the trail ends there. Vodkagirl was hiding behind someone else's connection, and there were enough internet proxy servers that were free and with no prospect of them ever giving out who'd visited their site.

Proxy sites provided people with privacy when they wanted to visit the darker corners of the internet with no fear of being found out. They were also the refuge for criminals, because they left no trace, which was why the authorities, particularly in the United States, ran some of their own. There was no better way to watch criminals than to get them to operate right in front of you.

Sam scanned the list quickly. There were hundreds of numbers, trawling through the list could take him all night, and for a moment he remembered Brabham's words, that he should leave the investigation alone. But then he thought back to Ellie, and that burn of her loss, still white-hot, made the effort seem worthwhile.

He booted up his laptop and did a quick internet search to find a site that would look up IP addresses. There were a lot, and most were prepared to provide some information for free, usually just the location of the internet provider's nearest connection, which could be within ten yards, or could be five miles away. If you wanted more, it cost, which was where they made their money.

He took a sip of his coffee, he needed to be alert for this, and then went to the list. There was only one place to start: the top. He typed the first IP address into the search engine, just a sequence of numbers separated by decimal points. When he pressed enter, it gave him a location: Seattle. There it was: the first proxy server. He'd been right: vodkagirl was hiding. He ran through it with a red pen and resolved to keep on looking. Sam was seeking the mistake, the time vodkagirl forgot to go through a proxy and used a home internet connection. If it provided a link with Proctor, it might be enough to persuade Brabham to go deeper.

It was going to be a very long night.

Sixty-five

Gina ran for the door into the kitchen. The man lunged at her, grabbed her sleeve. She yanked her arm away and threw the torch at him. She pushed at the door.

The light inside made her blink. She whirled round, to close the door and lock it, but he was too quick, too strong. He charged at the door, throwing Gina back, her head hitting the handle of a drawer on the other side of the kitchen.

She groaned, dazed, but she had to keep going. She scrambled backwards, getting ready to run for the front door. Fight or flight, that was the choice. Something told her flight was best, that noise was her friend. Just get onto the street. Shout, scream, anything to attract attention, so that the curtain-twitchers she hated so much would come to her aid.

The hard thud of a booted foot stopped her. It struck her hard in the face, delivered with venom, and her jaw cracked. Her world faded and Gina groaned as she fell to the floor again. The sound of the radio was more distant. The footsteps that came towards her were slow and deliberate. She opened her eyes and the view ahead was greyed out. She coughed, and then winced with pain as a stream of blood spewed onto the floor.

The pain sparked some alertness. She had to get out.

She tried to crawl along the floor but she was too slow. He grabbed her hair, making her yelp, the agony of her jaw making her dizzy. She tried to kick out, but it was weak, impotent.

He dragged her by her hair towards the living room, the slipperiness of the linoleum giving way to the burn of the carpet. She reached upwards and grabbed his wrists, to take the strain from her hair, the pain excruciating, but it just made it easier for him. Her sweat pants were dragged down her hips as she was pulled along the carpet, her sweatshirt rising up. She felt exposed, vulnerable.

The fireplace shuddered as she was thrown against it and she lay back, sucking in breaths, despite the pain as the air rushed in. The metal grate felt cold on the back of her head.

His boot smashed into her face again, catching her nose this time, and her head clanged hard against the grate. Blood sprayed in an arc.

Gina couldn't move now. Her head throbbed and she drifted in and out of consciousness. He pulled at her legs. The radio still played; sometimes she could hear it, and sometimes she couldn't. He dragged her by her feet. She was powerless to stop it as her head bounced along the carpet. Her ankles hurt, pushed up tightly against each other, but then she realised he'd bound them.

She took long breaths, her mouth open, the metallic taste of blood in her throat. Every part of her face roared with pain. Despite this, she swallowed and grimaced and said, 'What do you want?'

The words came out muffled and shards of pain made lights dance in front of her eyes.

He stepped forward and her eyes closed in recognition. She'd hung onto some vain hope that this was just a burglary gone wrong, or some sex attacker she could fight off, but she'd known all along who it was: Mark Proctor.

'Where's the box?' he said, snarling.

'Box?'

'You know which box. The one from my workshop. Where is it?'

'I haven't got it.'

He gripped her hair and pulled her head back. 'Answer the question,' he yelled, spittle flicking onto her cheeks.

'I don't know, I really don't,' Gina said, her eyes wide with fear, blood pooling on the floor beneath her mouth.

He considered that for a moment, his fingers still clenched around her hair.

'Is that all you want, the box?' Gina said, swallowing, grimacing. 'I can help you find it.'

'No,' Proctor said, letting go of her hair. 'I've come to balance the books.'

Gina tried to sit up but he reached out with the sole of his boot and pushed her back down.

'Okay, okay,' Gina said, sucking in air. 'What do you mean, balance the books?'

'It's what I do. Finance is all about balancing the books.'

'Not in your case,' she said. She gulped down some blood. 'Your books don't mean anything.'

'Oh, they do,' he said. 'It all depends on what the people looking at them want to see. Sometimes it's all an illusion. Or misdirection. Take this.' He gestured towards her. 'What do you think people will see? A burglar? A rapist?'

Gina's eyes flickered at that.

Proctor smiled, although the coldness in his eyes made it more of a grimace. 'You wish it was only that, don't you?' He knelt down and tugged at her sweat pants, eased them the rest of the way over hips, exposing her pubic hair and the tops of her thighs. 'I could make it look authentic, to throw them off the scent, because I've never done that. But you know that.'

'Know what?'

'That I've never raped anyone or abused anyone. I just made it look that way. I'm not one of those sickos. I can control what

I feel.' He reached out to touch her thigh, traced his fingernail along the skin towards her pubis.

Her stomach clenched.

He shook his head. 'Not my style.' He reached for the waistband of her pants and yanked them back up.

'So what is your style?' she said, nauseous from the pain and the taste of her own blood and the hard pounding of her heart.

Proctor straightened himself and went into the dining part of the room. He returned with a high-backed chair. He set it in front of her and sat down.

'Ripples,' he said. 'I told you earlier.'

Anger welled inside her, taking away some of the agony. 'Cut the enigmatic shit.'

His eyelids flickered in surprise but his tone remained the same, calm and measured. 'Think about it,' he said. 'Of the people you think I might have killed, were any raped? Assaulted? What about young Ellie Parker, your own case?'

Gina didn't respond.

'You know the answer: none. I'm no pervert who can't control himself. Do you think I couldn't get sex if I wanted? Look at me, I'm a handsome guy. An intelligent guy. No, I seek something more subtle. I'm an observer of the human condition.'

'You're a murderer.'

He shrugged. 'Labels, labels, labels.'

Gina closed her eyes. She didn't want to indulge his ego, because that was all it was, his need for admiration. She didn't want to give him what he wanted, but through the pain coursing through her, and the hatred for his invasion of her home, she knew that if he was talking, she was still alive. People might have heard her scream in the garage. Police cars might be on their way. One thing the exploration of his ego would give her was the most crucial weapon of all: time.

'Okay,' she said, opening her eyes, panting hard. 'I'll play your game. Why are you different?'

'I told you, it's all about the ripples. Nothing I've ever done was about an immediate need, the scream of my desires. They were just vessels, all of them.'

'You're not making sense.'

'I am, when you really think about it. You were a police officer for a long time, and you were after me, except you didn't know who I was. Where did you look?'

'Where else do we find creeps like you? The sex offenders register, as it grew. Local intelligence. Any sex offenders who'd moved into the locality.'

'You thought that little girl was a fantasy for me, something I couldn't control?' Proctor said, astonishment in his voice. 'That I liked the dirty pictures, but when that wasn't enough I moved onto the real deal?'

Proctor stood up and paced.

'Do I look like a cliché?' he went on. 'This is where you had it wrong. Most people are about the splash, the desire, the dreaming, then the release. But it's followed by shame, because they know they were driven by something they couldn't control. A need to be fulfilled, an explosion beyond their power.' He stopped pacing. 'I'm much better than that.'

'How?'

'Because the splash is over too soon. Don't you get it? The ripples are better, the shockwaves.'

'You did it because you enjoyed the distress of the families.'

He wagged his finger and grinned. 'You're catching on. I like to observe, to see how people are; people interest me.'

'You talk as if we're a different species.'

'You know, Gina, sometimes it feels like that, as if I'm looking at it from the outside. I can't help that. Like how a cat plays with a mouse. It doesn't want to eat the mouse. It's just a game. That's all this is, a big game, played out my way.'

Gina grimaced as she shook her head. 'No, it's not that,' she said, gasping. 'You're needy. You killed them because you're exactly like all the rest, because the victims are always the same; teenage girls, all unfulfilled potential. If it had been about the ripples, there'd be boys and women, and maybe even men. No, you're driven by what drives all the ones like you: you want young girls. But you despise yourself for it, so you build up a legend like this so you can make yourself sound better than the rest.' She spat blood onto the floor. 'It's just your imagination fooling yourself.'

Proctor stayed silent but his hands balled into fists, his fingers white with tension.

Gina stared at the ceiling. The voices on the radio still prattled away in the kitchen. At that moment, she craved the inanity of it, the loneliness she fought hard not to admit suddenly seeming beautifully simplistic.

'Who'll feel your ripples?' Proctor said. 'Who'll be there to weep at your funeral?'

Gina's eyes closed but tears squeezed out, wetting her cheeks. She tried to sniffle to stop them, but her nose hurt too much.

He stood over her. He blocked out the light so that all she could see was a dark outline.

'Hit a nerve, didn't I?' he said. 'This is the only ripple I get from you. A few tears. No one to miss you. No parents. No children. Probably a cousin or two, maybe a sibling, but they'll only show up to see if they get a share of whatever you leave behind.'

'Why would you kill me?' she said, her voice trembling. 'If it's all about what you leave behind, the chaos you leave, what purpose will I serve? Like you said, I leave no ripple, no trace, nothing to enjoy.' She took more deep breaths to combat the fear that was sweeping through her, adrenalin forcing back the pain. 'Just let me go.'

'No, I can't do that.'

'But why?'

'Because sometimes it's as cheap as revenge.' He shrugged. 'We all have our weaknesses. Do you think I didn't know Joe Parker was watching me yesterday? I know he saw me all those years ago, and I know he recognised me. He tried to disguise it, tried to claim it was a migraine, but I knew. When you've lived my life you have to be constantly alert. I asked for him, remember, so I was testing him, and then I knew. He was going to come after me. So why not discredit him?'

Proctor backed away and went to the dining-room table, watching Gina all the time. He rummaged in her handbag until he found her phone. He turned it on but it was protected by a passcode.

He raised it in the air. 'Tell me the code.'

Gina paused so he knelt over her and put his hand around her throat. He squeezed. Sweat broke out on her forehead.

She gulped and gave him the number. He put it in and smiled when the phone came to life.

'I followed Joe last night,' he said. 'He thought he was following me, but he hadn't planned on the decoy. So he was there when poor Greg was killed. What did he do? Call the police, the ambulance?' He shook his head. 'No, he drove here; I know that because I was behind him, but the police took a long time to get to the body. Why was that? My guess is that he didn't want you to call the police. But you did it anyway.'

Proctor went to Gina's call logs and then held up the phone in triumph.

'There they are. He called you, then you called the police. The timings are perfect. The police will think he came here tonight in a rage, angry at your betrayal, desperate for revenge.'

'No,' Gina said. 'He wouldn't do that. They'll know it's you.'

'But why would they? I'll call him when I leave here, and a call is so much better than a text. No record of the content, only that the call was made from here. He won't dare call for

368

help, the police are looking for him, and he'll want to be the hero too much. He'll rush up here and leave his traces everywhere.'

Gina's breaths came fast now. 'What will you do to him?'

He cocked his head. 'Him? Nothing. The system will take care of him, when it accuses him of your murder.'

He threw the phone onto the floor and lunged at her. He put both hands around her throat. Her eyes bulged as he squeezed. His teeth were bared, spittle flicking onto her as she bucked and thrashed, but her bindings made it too hard to get away.

The pain in her chest was like a deep burn as she fought to suck in air. She tried to shout out but she couldn't. Proctor's eyes bulged, his face contorted with effort.

The room went hazy and blurred. She felt hot as she struggled, her clothes twisting round her body.

The light hanging from the ceiling seemed to move, except she knew it was still. She tried to focus, hoping to defeat the clouding of her brain as Proctor squeezed the air from her body, but she couldn't fight nature. Her mind flew back through her life. A happy childhood. Some failed romances. First kiss. Last kiss, too far in the past to remember it properly. The people she arrested, like a fast-moving mugshot gallery, mixed in with the victims she left behind. Tearful, scared, angry.

It started as a white dot. Tears wet her cheeks but she didn't feel them. Another cough. A shiver. The dot grew, as if she was advancing towards it, the dot becoming a circle, a bright light.

There was a noise. Someone banging on the window. Proctor slackened his grip. Air rushed back into her and she gasped and coughed.

Proctor turned towards the noise. Some long-forgotten training kicked in and Gina jabbed out with her bound feet, catching Proctor on the knee, making him shout in pain.

There was another bang on the window, louder this time,

more frantic. There were shouts. Proctor scrambled backwards, looking for a way out.

As the front door opened, Proctor got to his feet and limped towards the door at the back of the house. He clicked open the patio doors and the noises from outside rushed into the house.

Gina lay down again as her neighbour rushed to her. His arms enveloped her and he pulled her to his chest, comforting her.

For a moment, she wanted that human contact, but then she thought about Proctor and where he might go next.

She looked up and nodded towards the bindings round her ankles. 'Stop hugging me and get me a fucking knife.'

Sixty-six

Joe kept checking his rear-view mirror as he drove to Melissa's apartment, nervous of the police stopping him, but there was just the evening traffic, a mixture of late shoppers and young men cruising. Melissa looked tired when he got there, as if the news about her brother had been on her mind all day, re-arranging how she saw her life. Her skin appeared drawn and her eyes were red, as if she'd spent some of the time crying.

Joe rushed past her and held up the metal box. 'I got it.'

When Melissa didn't respond, he said, 'You all right?'

Melissa exhaled and sat down. There was a half-empty glass of wine in front of her. 'I'm not going to like this,' she said. Then she apologised. 'I'm sorry, I know it's worse for you. What is it?'

'Like I thought, his box of souvenirs. Dead girls.'

'How many?'

'Eleven. Not all dead. The more recent ones are all missing persons. He must have found he enjoyed their misery more.'

Melissa swallowed and put her hand to her mouth. 'Eleven?' she said, her voice barely a whisper. She closed her eyes and said, 'Are you sure they're all down to Mark?'

'I found pictures of my sister,' Joe said. 'He'd stalked her, photographed her, as if he'd singled her out, but why would he do that? But there was one picture of her that makes it certain. It was Ellie on the floor, taken before the police arrived, because she was still wearing the necklace we hadn't known she was wearing on the day, one never returned to us by the police. And the necklace was in the envelope.'

He reached into his pocket and dangled the necklace from his finger.

'It was as if I could see her pain, even though her eyes were closed. She didn't look at peace. She looked contorted and frightened, and it's something I wish I hadn't seen. And I can't remove it from my head now. So yes, I'm sure.'

'But how has he got away with it for so long? Eleven? That's inhumane. A slaughter.'

'Look out of your window,' Joe said, pointing towards the lights of office blocks and apartment buildings. 'Look at all the counties you can see from here. Hit that motorway just a couple of miles away and you're in West Yorkshire, or Lancashire, Merseyside, and South Yorkshire just over that way. He travels around, county to county, knowing the police forces don't share information well. All those different police areas within forty-five minutes from here – less probably – so easy to avoid having them linked. A few years ago, some of the forces didn't even use the same computer systems.'

Melissa leaned forward to take a drink of wine. 'I've been trying to get things straight in my head, thinking back through his life, at least what I know of it, looking for clues, answers. Things that had no importance back then now seem magnified, things I haven't told anyone.'

'About Mark?'

She nodded.

'You can't blame yourself.'

'But I'm a part of it, don't you see. I know it doesn't make me responsible, but it makes me wish I'd seen it so I could've stopped it.'

Joe put the box on the floor and sat down opposite. 'Talk to me.'

Melissa went to the fridge and returned with the bottle and

an extra glass. She poured Joe a glass of wine and topped up her own. She ran her finger around the rim of the glass before she started talking.

'Our house was cramped. There were three of us children, but I was the only girl, so Mark always had to share with my other brother, Dan. He was older than Mark by a couple of years and used to bully him. When I was really small, I'd lie in bed and hear Mark crying, or the sound of a fist being struck, or Dan taunting him. It was different for me, because I was in my own little cocoon, the baby sister, my bedroom all pink and fluffy. As they got older, Dan became a bit of a lad, going out boozing, but when he was home he would be getting at Mark all the time. When I was around ten I realised that Mark was a little different. He'll have been around nineteen then but he was a loner. He used to disappear for hours at a time and not tell anyone where he was going. I remember Dan teasing him that he was going off to his den, his little hiding place.'

'How did you get on with him?'

'Really well, which is why this is so upsetting. I can't believe it. When I got older and started getting upset over boys and stupid stuff like that, he was always there for me. He'd listen to me, comfort me.' She shook her head. 'I can see it now. I understand.'

'What do you mean?'

'Something he once said.' She took another drink. 'I'd split up with someone, just a boy who broke my heart but was soon forgotten about, because that's what being a teenager is about, strong reactions. Mark was great. He made me drinks, checked on me, let me talk about this boy, whose name I don't even remember now. Then I met someone else and it was all forgotten. Mark was angry with me. He said I was selfish, that I only ever noticed him when I was sad and ignored him when life was back to normal.'

'This is all about attention?' Joe said. 'I can't believe it.' He laughed, short and bitter. 'No, I can believe it. That's the whole damn point. He was Mr Anonymous, picked on by his older brother so he used to find secret places where no one could hurt him. No one noticed him until they needed him.'

'We should have spotted that we were damaging him.'

'No!'

Melissa looked shocked.

'Don't make it your fault,' Joe said. 'Big brothers pick on little brothers, it's part of life. Little sisters can ignore them. Families are complicated, but most people get through it all somehow. For your brother, it just went a different way. Doesn't Carrie ask about her uncle?'

'Sometimes, but I just say we don't get on. One day she might understand, but she's too young to know, just fourteen, and that was even before I knew about all this?' She pointed towards the box. 'You have to take it to the police. Let them deal with it.'

She was right. Those were the thoughts he'd had as he stared out of the windscreen on the moors, not really looking at anything, just letting his thoughts wash over him, like whether he could carry on being a lawyer, or whether Proctor was worth giving it all up for. The photograph of Ellie dead on the ground told him that his career would mean nothing if he didn't get justice for her.

'I want to understand it first,' he said.

'No, please, Joe. Do the right thing.'

'How much do you think the police will do? So he takes an interest in murdered teenagers? He's a grief counsellor, the perfect cover, wouldn't you say? Some defence lawyer like me will say it.'

Melissa didn't respond.

Joe put his hand on the box. The contents were precious.

'There is one more thing,' Joe said. 'There's an extra envelope. It has no press clippings or death photograph.'

'What, someone who might still be alive?'

'That's my thinking. He's been watching someone.'

'There's someone to save.'

'Only by stopping your brother.'

'So take this to police.'

She was right again. He could save the girl by killing Proctor, but he didn't want to do it that way. Joe had seen the pain in Gerald's eyes, the knowledge that he'd ended a life. However much Proctor deserved it, Joe didn't want to live his own life with torment like Gerald's for company. He'd take the box to the police, but he'd find the girl too and warn her in case the police can't act. For Joe, it was personal. It was about doing for this stranger what he hadn't done for Ellie.

Joe lifted the metal box onto the wooden table between them. Melissa was leaning back in her chair, uncertain, both hands clasped around her wine glass.

'I'm not sure I can do this,' she said.

'This is your brother in here,' Joe said, putting his hand on the box. 'If you thought you knew him, this might be where you find out you didn't know him at all.'

'But somewhere in there might be some blame for me, something I should have noticed.'

'You can't blame yourself. I carry more blame than you, because I could have said something that might have caught him earlier. This box is like something I let him do.'

Melissa stared at the box for a few seconds more and then said, 'I need to know.'

'Are you sure? This will rewrite your childhood, make you see everything differently.'

'Show me. I need to make sense of it all.'

Joe opened the lid and reached in. He produced an envelope with Ellie's name on the front. He let the contents fall onto the table without looking. 'This is my sister.'

The pictures of Ellie landed face up. Melissa leaned forward, transfixed by the images, eyes wide. She picked up the first one. It was Ellie outside the local shop, puffing gingerly on a cigarette. Melissa traced her finger on the image. 'I can see her soul in that picture,' she said. 'She looks so alive, a girl trying to become a woman.'

'She was doing just that,' he said. Then he pulled out the press cuttings, scattering them onto the table. 'This was his real thing, though. It wasn't about the murder; it was about the effect it had on everyone else. His grief counselling was just a way of wallowing in it. Why do you think he killed your cat? Because he liked the cruelty? No – it was because he liked your distress. And I bet he tried to be more supportive, to be there for you. But it was just about getting close so that he could feel your pain.'

'Are people that calculating?'

'I've been a defence lawyer for long enough to know the answer is yes. And do you know what else strikes me?'

'Go on.'

'No one noticed him. He was the quiet one who took himself off to his own little private space. Your other brother was the go-getter, the lad around town, and you, well, you're the little princess, daddy's girl. What was he? The quiet middle one, ignored by all. These murders are his own little force field, his impact on the world. A desperate little man, obsessed with being noticed, except he's found a different way, where only he knows what he's done. A very solitary pursuit.'

'And I played a part in it.'

'Don't dwell on that. I played a bigger part. I could have said something back then, about the man I'd seen follow Ellie. If he'd been caught, all these girls would still be alive. I let him stay free. I carry the guilt. You weren't to know. I was.'

'That's a lot to carry around.'

Joe reached into the box and drew out more envelopes. 'Every one of these is partly down to me.'

'It's not a competition,' Melissa said. 'Let me look. Who else is there?'

Joe handed Melissa a few more envelopes. They all contained the same thing: stalking photographs, a death shot, then press clippings. There was always something from the body – an earring or a necklace or a pen – anything that was a part of the real person. Melissa thumbed through them in silence. She shook her head occasionally, her eyes showing a mix of horror and disbelief, each death shot bringing an involuntarily widening of the eyes.

When she'd finished, she put them face down on the table and covered her eyes. 'I can't believe this,' she said.

'And there's the one I told you about,' Joe said. 'The envelope that's less full than the rest, with no clippings or death pictures; just the stalking pictures.'

'Show me.'

Joe passed over an envelope that was thinner than the rest. It contained the pictures that had been sent to Gerald King, of the girl from the school he couldn't identify.

Melissa lifted the flap and reached in.

As she looked through them, she went pale and let the pictures slip from her fingers onto the floor.

'Melissa? What's wrong?'

She put her hands over her mouth. They were trembling violently.

Joe bent down to retrieve them. As he did so, his gaze landed on a photograph frame on the wall unit behind Melissa. He hadn't paid it any attention, not consciously, but the girl in the photographs had seemed familiar as soon as he'd seen them. Now he knew why. There were pictures of her all around the room.

The girl in the photographs was Carrie, Melissa's daughter. And Proctor had been stalking her.

Sixty-seven

Proctor gripped the steering wheel and screeched, his teeth bared, his wild.

'Shit!'

It was all going wrong. Gina Ross. Joe Parker. All of his past racing forward to mock him. He couldn't let that happen. He should have killed Gina. He'd meant to, but he'd taken too long, had wanted to make her suffer before she died. That wasn't how he did things: it was about the effect, not the act. Normally he killed quickly. With Gina, it had been about revenge, about emotion. He'd let it get out of control.

One last act, that's all he needed. He was leaving, he didn't know where to, but he needed to make one final wave, something that would leave his stain long after he was gone.

Carrie. It was always leading to this.

Melissa had shut him out. He wasn't going to allow that. He'd had to watch his niece grow up without knowing him.

He shook his head angrily, even though there was no one else in the car.

No, it wasn't that. It was growing up without *noticing* him. Her uncle, Melissa's brother, everyone's rock.

It was Thursday, he knew where she went. The youth club. He'd watched her there before. He'd always known it was coming to this. He'd just been waiting for the right time. It had arrived.

He checked his watch. She'd be leaving.

He drove quickly towards Ancoats, the shadowy blocks ahead shutting out the lights from the city centre.

The youth club was in a restored church. He thought he was going to be late, people were spilling out onto the road, teenagers hugging goodbyes. Some were leaving in large groups, others climbed into waiting cars, and there were those who skulked home on their own. The quiet ones on the edge of everything. Like he'd been. He wasn't on the edge any more.

He slowed as he drove past the end of the street and looked down towards the church. He couldn't see Carrie.

He could drive round the block. She had to be nearby.

Then he saw her just ahead, picked out in his headlights, wearing jeans and a T-shirt, her long hair flying in the light breeze. Ginger and luxurious, just like Melissa's.

Carrie was with just one other person, a girl smaller than she was.

There was no time to make a plan. With no one else nearby, the youth club some way back, he had to move quickly.

He swerved to the side of the road, thumping his front wheels onto the kerb, making Carrie and her friend turn around and back up towards a wall, fright on their faces.

He jumped out of his car. 'Carrie, I'm a friend of your mum. Come quickly. There's been an accident.'

Carrie looked uncertain. 'What do you mean, an accident?'

'Your mum's at the hospital. I've come to collect you.' He stepped closer. 'We can't waste any time.'

Her friend stepped forward. 'No, don't,' she said. 'Call your mum first.'

'There's no time for that. Come now.'

Carrie looked at her friend, who was shaking her head. Carrie held up her phone. 'Just let me call her.'

He was losing control of it. Carrie was tall and athletic. He

379

couldn't let her make the call. She'd run away and he wouldn't catch her.

He reached into his pocket and produced a knife, the blade long and jagged, one he kept in his car to use against girls like Carrie. He lunged forward and put it against her neck. She screamed but he clamped his hand over her mouth.

'Get in my car. Now!'

Carrie's friend screamed but he didn't stop. He pressed the point of the knife into her throat, pushing in the skin and drawing a large drop of blood, before pulling her towards his car.

'No, please, don't,' Carrie said, sobbing, but she didn't resist or try to run away.

Small punches landed on his back. It was Carrie's friend, but she wasn't strong enough.

There were shouts further along the street, people from the youth club spotting what was going on. He had to be quicker.

He opened his car boot. 'Get in.'

'No, no, I can't. Please don't.' Her face creased in tears as her friend ran down the street.

Proctor hit her with his fist, connecting with her jaw. She grunted and crumpled and dropped her phone. He forced her into the boot, lifting her ankles in as he slammed the boot lid, pausing only to collect her phone.

He looked along the street. People were coming towards him, some running.

He jumped into the car and stamped on the accelerator. There were bangs on the rear door as people reached him but he was able to get away, exhaust fumes filling his rear-view mirror as he glanced behind him.

He'd done it. He let out a long breath.

Now for the finale.

'Where is she?' Joe said to Melissa, looking around the room, his gaze catching photograph after photograph showing the girl from Proctor's envelope. Some were posed school pictures; some were less formal photos: Carrie laughing with friends and or hugging Melissa.

Melissa was panicking. Her hands trembled as she tried to steady her phone. 'The youth club,' she said. 'She goes there every Thursday. Has done for a couple of years. It's just somewhere for the kids to hang out.'

'And it's a pattern, easy to follow,' Joe said.

She pressed Carrie's details in her contact list and muttered her name to herself. The phone rang out. 'She doesn't always answer,' Melissa said, her voice deep with anxiety. 'We argue about it all the time; I tell her that I need to know where she is.'

'We'll go there now. You keep calling. Check her social media. I'll drive.'

Melissa ran for the door, pausing only to slip on some shoes and grab her keys. They rushed out of the apartment, pacing as they waited for the lift.

'It's not far,' Melissa said as they ran to her car.

'You keep phoning her and direct me.'

Joe climbed into the driver's seat. Melissa was still trying Carrie's phone, but without success.

'Where am I going?' Joe said.

'To the main road. Go right. About half a mile, just behind a small supermarket.'

Joe sped off, the engine loud between the high mill buildings. Melissa was calling Carrie's number again. 'Why won't she answer?'

'Won't her friends be with her? She might be fine, just talking or whatever.'

'You don't know teenagers,' she said. 'Their phones are bolted to their hands.' She threw her own phone into the footwell. 'Fuck!'

There was a small supermarket ahead, Joe ignoring the speed limits. 'This one?'

'Yes, down there.'

There was a building next to a small church further along. Light spilled from an open doorway, catching the barbed wire along the gutters and the small crowd outside. Melissa was out of the car even before Joe had come to a stop, running straight into the cluster of teenagers jabbering at each other. Cars were arriving behind them, parents getting ready to collect.

'Carrie?' she shouted, pushing through the crowd.

Young teenagers looked round at her. Some backed away. Others giggled. Some hid the glowing ends of cigarettes in their palms.

'Carrie!'

A girl stepped forward. It was Wanda, one of Carrie's friends. She was crying. Her nose was bleeding. 'Someone took her.'

Melissa grabbed her by the arms. 'When? Who?'

'I don't know,' she said, trying to back away. 'A man. He put her in his car and drove away.'

'Hey!' a woman said, pulling at Melissa's arm. 'Leave her alone.'

Joe stepped between them, to stop a fight starting. 'We're just looking for Carrie. She's gone missing. We're sorry.'

The woman let go of Melissa, scowling, but recognised the panic in her eyes.

Melissa set off towards the youth club building, up a concrete wheelchair ramp and into a narrow corridor, before bursting into an open hall with wooden flooring marked out as a basketball court.

'I'm looking for Carrie,' Melissa shouted.

There were two adults, a man wearing a vicar's dog collar and a woman in her fifties, along with a small group of older children. The man looked at the others and said, 'We've called the police. Are you her mother?'

'Who's taken her?'

382

'I don't know. A man in a car. He hit her.' He stepped forward. 'I'm sorry. We're all sorry. I don't know what else to say.'

'Did you get his registration number?'

'It happened too fast.'

Melissa called 999 and shouted information about her brother down the phone. When she hung up, she ran for the door, but when she got outside she realised she had no idea where to go.

Joe headed for the car. 'Come on, to Mark's house. We'll start there.'

His phone buzzed. It was Gina. 'Gina?'

'Proctor's been here,' she said, hoarse and breathless. 'He tried to kill me.'

'Have you called the police?'

'Yes, they're on their way.'

'Where did he go?'

'I don't know, Joe, but you've got to find him. He's settling old scores.'

'Are you all right?'

'Just find him.'

Joe hung up.

Melissa was already in the car, staring into space, her hand over her mouth, trembling. 'Not Carrie,' she said, almost to herself, as Joe climbed in.

Once he was in the driver's seat, he tried to call Sam. His phone was engaged.

'Shit!'

People had to move out of the way as Joe floored the accelerator, some swearing at him. He didn't care. He had to find Proctor. He hadn't saved Ellie. but he sure as hell wasn't going to fail Carrie.

Sixty-eight

Sam was pacing, his phone ringing out, waiting for Charlotte to answer.

He had something. Tremors of excitement rippled through him. The IP addresses had been the key.

The first hit had come quickly, close to the bottom of the first page, where an IP address came back as the south of Manchester, the first one outside of the United States, away from the proxy servers. He'd highlighted it in green and carried on until a second Manchester hit came along, pinpointed on a map by a small icon, the same area as last time. He'd flicked back through the paper sheets excitedly, knowing he was onto something, looking for the green highlighter. When he found it, he'd checked the numbers and grinned.

The same IP address.

He'd almost smacked the table with excitement. From then on, he'd been looking for a specific number, skimming the pages, until he'd found eleven more. The coincidence of the numbers was too great; they had to represent a specific location.

But he'd known he needed more than that. He had to link vodkagirl's IP address to Mark Proctor. Then he'd remembered something: Helena Proctor had given him her email address, an email account her husband didn't know she had.

He'd sent her an innocuous message, asking her if she'd

located any other evidence of his accounts, and then chewed his nails for five minutes until a reply came in. It had been short: *No, nothing, not yet, but I'll look tomorrow. Sorry.*

That hadn't mattered. He had what he wanted: something from the Proctor household that would show up his IP address.

A quick internet search had taught him how to find the IP address in an email, hidden in a long list of commands when he viewed the message header.

The same. The IP address had been used to log into the No One Tells website using the name vodkagirl, who'd had some contact with the victim of the murder in the park, Henry Mason, whose bloodied fingerprint was found on the knife that killed Keith Welsby, who was known for becoming too familiar with pupils, and had worked at the same school that Helena Proctor's murdered sister had attended.

That was it, the umbrella that somehow kept everything close. Or was it a circle, everything looping back round to the start? Whatever it was, he'd made the connection to Mark Proctor.

But what about a motive? The man he'd met who'd exchanged messages with vodkagirl had said it seemed like a big tease in order to obtain some kind of confession.

The vodkagirl identity was just about getting men to confess their darkest secrets. If you cast the net widely enough, there'd be men out there with secrets they didn't want revealing. Would that be enough for them to kill if they thought there was a risk that their secrets might come out?

But why would Proctor want Keith Welsby dead? The case was all about Proctor creating grief so that he could revel in it. Why would it matter who his wife's sister had been sleeping with?

Perhaps Welsby had been looking into Adrianne's murder, keeping up the hunt long after the police investigation had gone quiet. Had he tracked down the killer, realised that it was Mark Proctor and paid with his life in order to keep him quiet? The No One Tells site was used like an auditioning process. Dangle the thought that vodkagirl was really an underage girl wanting an adventure and you attract people with all the secrets. Once you've got the secrets, you've got the power: kill Welsby or your secrets will come out.

But that would take a long time, and if Welsby knew Proctor had murdered Adrianne, time was not on Proctor's side.

Sam wondered if it was something more basic than that, something Proctor had not factored in: had he grown to love his wife and blamed Welsby for allowing him to kill Adrianne? That's how psychopaths are: they blame other people.

But what dirty secret did Proctor have on Henry Mason that made him kill Welsby?

And then Sam remembered the flowers. It was more like a date than a final handshake on the job being done. Had vodkagirl offered more reward than just a lid on his secrets? Henry Mason was waiting at the park for a liaison, flowers in his hand. He was expecting to meet an underage girl for sex. What had vodkagirl said? Kill my abuser and you can have me? Take my virginity? Had that been enough for Mason?

What he'd met instead was a hammer wielded by Mark Proctor. Vodkagirl had served her purpose. Proctor had used the fake profile to get Mason to kill Welsby, and then he'd killed Mason to destroy the trail. By posing as an underage girl, he'd guaranteed that Henry Mason wouldn't mention her or the meeting and covered his tracks properly, except Proctor didn't cover them well enough. He didn't always go through the proxy server.

Sam had felt like punching the air. He'd got Proctor.

But why kill Henry Mason at all? The link between Proctor and Keith Welsby was clear enough, but there was no clear link between Proctor and Mason? Henry Mason was never going to talk, and Proctor exposed himself by killing Mason. There had to be something else.

And what about the murder the night before, the body Joe had found in Worsley? Proctor had done everything he needed to do in order to avenge the murder of his wife's sister. Why one extra?

Then he'd realised why: deflection. As Brabham said, how could Proctor be the killer when he was supposed to be a victim? The simplicity was clear.

But if Proctor had acted to somehow get vengeance on the person his wife blamed for her sister's murder – the teacher who was too much of a coward to make sure his schoolgirl lover got home safely – why now, after all these years?

Sam's thoughts had returned to Henry Mason. Was there something more to this? Then he'd remembered something. Helena Proctor felt responsible for her sister's death because she was the substitute parent, bringing up her sister after their parents died in a car crash. She blamed it on a faulty car. Henry Mason sold cars.

He'd called Charlotte. He'd asked her to look into the crash and whether there was any link with Henry Mason. He'd been waiting for her to call back but his impatience had got the better of him.

Charlotte answered.

'Sorry, Brabham was here,' she said, excitement in her voice.

'Tell me.'

'I didn't speak to Mason's widow. I looked at Helena Proctor. Or Helena Morley, as she was then.'

'Go on.'

Charlotte paused. Sam knew he'd put her in an awkward position; she couldn't be seen to be helping him.

'You can take all the credit,' he said. 'It's important.'

'You were right,' she said eventually.

He grinned. 'Tell me.'

'I've got the report in front of me,' Charlotte said. 'A husband and wife were killed in a car crash. The daughter, Helena Morley, reckoned the car had been glammed up to get through a sale, because there were problems. The brakes were sticking and the accelerator. They were killed on the motorway, crashed into a bridge support when the husband swerved to avoid a queue of traffic. No proof that the car was faulty; it looked like he'd noticed the queue too late. Sold to them by Henry Mason. Helena gave Mason grief for a few years, writing letters and hanging around outside the showroom. We warned her off but she carried on. He took out an injunction against her in the end because we didn't act quickly enough. That stopped it.'

'Oh, you little beauty,' Sam said, almost shouting. 'They're all linked.' He laughed. 'Proctor's cleaning up for his wife. I don't believe it.'

'But why would he do that? It doesn't make sense.'

'Guilt,' he said. 'Perhaps after all this time, somewhere in his twisted soul he's discovered a heart. He's grown to love her, in his own way. Maybe he always did, so he deflects his guilt.'

'I'm not following.'

'Psychopaths blame others, never themselves, often portraying themselves as the victims. It's a classic sign. Has he convinced himself that he's not really to blame, that it was all the teacher's fault for letting Adrianne go home alone, that it was Welsby's fault for letting Proctor get his way? And the car? If Henry Mason hadn't sold Helena's parents that dodgy car, they'd still be alive and might have kept the reins a little tighter on Adrianne. He's killing the people he blames for letting him kill Adrianne.'

'I've got to speak to Brabham,' Charlotte said.

'Do that. Say you found it, I don't mind.'

Sam clicked off. He put his phone against his chest. They were nearly there.

His thoughts were interrupted by the shrill ring of his phone. It was Joe.

'Joe?' he said. 'Where are you?'

'Proctor's kidnapped his own niece,' Joe said, breathless. 'Carrie. Fourteen years old. He's been stalking her and now he's taken her.'

'I'm on it,' Sam said.

'There's something else, too.'

'What, for Christ's sake?'

'Proctor attacked Gina, tried to kill her. He's getting revenge. Keep Ruby safe.'

'Shit!'

Joe clicked off.

Sam grabbed his coat and ran for the door. He remembered how Gina had been over Ellie's death. He owed her.

Sixty-nine

Proctor looked around and the memories flooded back. He wasn't prone to sentimentality, but it was hard not to think of all the years that had passed. The view wasn't the same, much of what he'd known had been bulldozed away, but there were enough remnants to allow his mind to fill in the gaps. He was in his favourite place, and he knew it might be his last time there.

It was the solitude he remembered. All of his childhood spent in the company of someone else, his older brother Dan, a bullying ever-present. Night after night, or so it seemed, he'd be picked at, prodded and teased. So he'd craved the quiet spaces, loved walking to find them, those quiet places on the towpaths or in old abandoned buildings. A few hours alone, watching people, dreaming of letting them know he was there. Well, they knew now.

And he knew something else, too: if he was saying goodbye, he had to make sure people remembered him. For so long, it had been about his effect, the ripples he sent out, the quiet man enjoying what he did, how he relished that no one knew, even when he was among them. Not any more. If this was his curtain call, it was time to be noticed. This was about the splash.

One more look around. There was no one on the street and no one looking out of a window.

He opened the boot of the car. Carrie was curled up in it. Her cheeks were drenched with tears and her eyes opened wide as

Proctor leaned in for her. Despite her desire to get out of the cramped space – he'd heard the thumps in the boot as she'd tried to stretch out to relieve the cramps – she shrank back as he got near her. He grabbed the rope that was in the corner of the boot and bound her wrists together, before yanking her hard. Her upper body hung over the bumper helplessly, so he pulled harder until she tumbled out of the car. She grunted when she landed on the concrete.

'Stay quiet,' he said, jabbing her in the ribs with his foot. He reached into the boot again and found a rag. It was dirt-covered and smelled of oil, but it would do.

Carrie tried to shuffle under the car. He grabbed her ankle and made her screech in pain as her T-shirt rode up and her flesh scraped across the loose concrete.

Proctor knelt down. Carrie cowered against the car bumper. He wrapped the rag around her head to make a gag, pulling it hard. He lifted her chin with his finger and moved a strand of hair that was stuck to her forehead. Her skin was damp with perspiration and he felt his heart rate increase. The feel of her skin was like static under his fingers.

'Be a good girl,' he said. 'You're going to come with me and you're going to do exactly as I say.' His fingers strayed to her neck and traced her jawline, felt the slight bump of a mole under her chin. 'I've killed people, Carrie, you have to know that. Girls your age too.' He held up his hand to quell the wail that was building. 'If you want me to let you live, you've got to do as I say. Do you understand?'

There was a long period of silence before she nodded.

'Good. We're going to walk in there together.' And he gestured towards the building behind her. 'I've still got the knife so don't get brave. You don't want your mother to find you like that, bleeding out on the pavement. If she loves you, she'll do what I say, and you'll be home soon.'

Carrie nodded again.

Proctor knelt down and grabbed her under her arms, pulling her to her feet. He pushed her forwards and she stumbled to her knees, wincing in pain. When he lifted her again, a thin stream of blood ran from her leg where small stones stuck to her skin.

He moved a piece of metal security fencing and took her inside.

He had to be careful as he walked her forward. The floor was littered with loose bricks and stones, jagged pieces of metal scattered around, the slow crumble of a building no one used anymore. There was talk of redevelopment, but the building work had ground to a halt in recent years.

There were stairs in the corner of the room. Thin light came in from the street lights, but it was murky, the windows thick with dirt. The world outside seemed distant. His footsteps were loud scrapes that echoed through the building. The floors were mostly intact but as he looked up he could see to the top floor, gaps allowing a clear view.

Proctor led Carrie to a tall metal pillar and sat her down. He knelt down next to her. Small insects scurried away as a cobweb got tangled in her hair.

'You're going to stay here for a few minutes and then we're on the move again.' There was plenty of slack on the rope so he tied it around the pillar, pulling it tight.

Carrie's whimpers turned into sobs but he knew she couldn't move.

He took out Carrie's phone. The screen was cracked from where it had fallen to the floor but it still worked. 'Shall we make a phone call first? Your mother needs to know where you are.' He stroked her hair. 'Then later, we're going to have some fun.'

He dialled Melissa's number. As he waited for it to connect, he thought about what he could do. He was making it up as he went along, no real plan in place, but he had to make it have impact. This is how he would be remembered.

Seventy

'Who's Gina?' Melissa said. 'What's going on?'

Joe stared out of his windscreen in disbelief. He clenched his jaw. Anger surged inside him.

'She works for me,' he said, a crack in his voice. He swallowed to keep back the tears; part anger, part distress. 'No, more than that. Back when Ellie was killed, Gina was the senior officer in charge of the investigation to find her killer: your brother. She's been in my life ever since then in some way or another.'

'And my brother has just tried to kill her?'

'He's saying goodbye.'

'What do you mean?'

'For the first time, whatever life he's built is coming unstuck. He killed a man on Monday night, for reasons no one knows. Then last night he was supposed to be the victim. He's been found out. He must know his souvenirs have been taken. He can see all his secrets leaking out. So he's having one last strike back at the people he sees as his enemies. Gina, for being the person who used to hunt him. Or perhaps, somewhere deep down, because he'd wanted Gina to catch him, to stop him, but she failed, so he blames her for turning him into what he is. And he's hitting back at you, too, for shutting him out of his family, for humiliating him.'

'Don't make it about me! He's got my daughter!'

'I know, and I'm not. He's always known this moment

would come. So he's having one last kick-out at those he blames. Maybe he blames me, too, because he knows he was seen. I could have stopped him. Psychopaths do that.'

Melissa put her head back and covered her face with her hands. 'What about Carrie? Where do we start?'

'His house.'

As Joe drove, Melissa called her ex-husband. She tried to stay calm, just a tremor to her voice giving her away, but she ended up throwing the phone into the footwell. The cover came off the back and the battery sprung loose.

'He thinks it's my fault,' she said, tears streaming down her face. 'Because I made her stay in Ancoats, because he thinks it's too damn rough for Carrie, and I should have kept a proper eye on her. He can't blame me for this. It's not fair.'

Joe reached across as he drove. She gripped his hand. Her jaw was set, her gaze determined. She needed her daughter back.

After a journey that seemed to take too long, they turned into Proctor's street. The police were already there, two marked squad cars parked outside, the lights still turning so that the street was lit up like a nightclub.

Joe pulled up alongside the kerb. 'Wait here.'

'No, I'm coming with you.'

'Please, stay here,' he said, more sternly this time. 'We don't know what's going on in there. Please let me check it out.'

Melissa didn't respond. She understood the unspoken truth, that her daughter's body might be further along the street. She just couldn't bring herself to acknowledge it. Instead, she turned her head to look out of the window.

There was no one with the police cars, although lights were on inside the house. Joe walked onto the drive. He swallowed. His heart was beating hard, his mouth dry, his mind still reeling from the call about Gina, but he was sickened most by the thought that Proctor had taken another child.

Joe walked straight into the house. There were voices coming from the living room. Male voices. Hectoring. Distorted conversations came from police radios.

Joe pushed at the door. As it swung open, three uniformed officers turned round. There was a woman sitting down in a chair, her face bruised.

'Helena?' Joe said.

'Are you Mark Proctor?' one of the policemen said, advancing towards him, his finger going to the button on his radio.

'No, I'm his lawyer,' Joe said, realising it gave him a reason to be there. 'What do you want with my client?' He spoke with an authority he didn't feel.

The officer looked back at the woman in the chair, who just shrugged. She'd only met Gina.

'It's too early for you,' the officer said.

Joe stepped forward and whispered to the officer, 'Can I speak to you privately?'

The officer put his head back and rested his hands on his equipment belt. Joe didn't drop his gaze until the officer relented and pointed towards the door.

Joe went out first and walked along the hallway towards the kitchen. The officer followed and then stood with his booted feet apart, his arms folded across his stab vest. The air was filled by the sounds of his uniform: the jangle of his equipment, the thump of his boots, the rustles of his jacket.

'This isn't what you think,' Joe said.

'You don't know what I think.'

'I do. You think I've come here to interfere.' The officer stayed silent so Joe pointed towards the breast of his stab vest. 'Any bodycam whirring? I'm not telling you anything if it's going to be recorded.'

The officer shook his head. 'No, it's not.'

Joe exhaled and leaned back against the kitchen work surface. He looked at the floor, working out how much he could say, until he remembered about Carrie. It was no longer about Ellie or any of the others.

'Mark Proctor murdered my sister many years ago. He's murdered a number of people.'

The officer's brow creased. 'What's your name?'

'Joe Parker?'

'Any relation to DC Parker?'

'Sam's my brother.'

The officer relaxed and leaned against the counter opposite. 'How can you represent scumbags like him, if he killed your sister?'

'Another time,' Joe said. 'Proctor has kidnapped his niece. I'm with his sister, the girl's mother. '

'That's why we're here,' he said. 'We got the call but he's not here.'

Joe was interrupted by the sound of someone rushing into the house. 'Joe?' It was Melissa.

'In here, in the kitchen,' he shouted.

There were footsteps, quick and urgent. She was holding her phone in the air. 'I put my phone back together,' she said, her voice coming in gulps. 'He'd left a message. Mark, he needs money. If he gets it, he'll let her go.'

The officer clicked the button on his radio and began to call it in, providing the latest information, more urgency in his eyes at the sudden realisation that he was in the eye of the storm.

'Did he say where he was?' Joe said.

'No, but he was outside. And I could hear her. She was crying. Oh God, I could hear how frightened she is.'

'Pass me the phone.'

She handed it to him. The line was still open, the answer machine telling him to press 2 to hear the message again. He pressed it.

After a few seconds, Proctor's voice came on: 'Hi, Melissa. It's me, Mark, the brother you turned your back on. Well, times have got tough for me. I need help. I need you to come in for me, to remember that you're my sister. I need money. A lot. A hundred thousand. I know your husband can get his hands on it. You think I haven't kept an eye on you? I know about your family, and I know he can release the funds. I've seen the cars he drives, the places he goes to. Get me a hundred thousand and I'll disappear, you'll never see me again.' A few deep breaths, as if he was exerting himself. 'A little incentive. Say hi, Carrie.' High-pitched sobs, muffled and indistinct. 'There you are, Melissa. Do it for me. Or for her. Either way, I don't care. Just do it. Transfer it into my account.' He reeled off a sort code and account number. 'I'll know when it's gone in. Goodbye, Melissa. Stay safe.'

The call ended.

Joe rushed past the officer and back into the living room. 'Helena, where does Mark go?'

'I don't know what you mean,' Helena said, startled.

'You know him best. He must have somewhere quiet he goes to when he wants to be alone, somewhere different to his workshop.'

Helena shook her head. 'I wish I could tell you, I really do,' she said, tears in her eyes. 'We have our own secrets, let each other live our lives. I don't know as much about Mark as I thought I did.'

'Nowhere comes to mind if he was hiding out somewhere?'

'No, sorry.'

Joe turned round, despairing. Melissa was standing there, ashen, her hand over her mouth, tears running down her face.

The officer who'd gone to the kitchen stepped forward and put his hand on Joe's arm. 'Go home, Mr Parker. Both of you. Someone will be there soon to stay with you, but you can't do anything here.'

Joe knew he was right. He went past him and took Melissa's hand. 'Let's go,' he said, and led her out of the house. There were hard times ahead.

Seventy-one

Sam ran from his car and towards Gina's house, the small cul-de-sac now filled with police cars and white vans. There was movement all around him: the crime scene investigators arriving, setting up perimeters; uniformed officers knocking on doors to reassure people.

He'd been there earlier, giving Gina a lift home, and it had seemed so safe, just a suburban block on a family estate. When he returned, the lights on inside seemed so much more menacing.

There was an ambulance outside the house, the back doors open. As he got to it, he looked inside. Gina was lying down.

'Gina?'

She lifted her head. 'I'm all right, Sam.'

He stepped into the ambulance. Her cheek was swollen. 'What happened?'

'Mark Proctor tried to kill me.' Her voice was hoarse. She closed her eyes as tears welled up. She swallowed and grimaced.

Sam went to her as if to hold her hand, to be some comfort, but she shook her head. 'No, Sam. Thank you, but I'm not going to let him beat me. I'm strong enough to get over this.'

'Did he . . . ?'

'No, he didn't rape me, if that's what you're thinking. He wanted to kill me, that's all. At least you've got an excuse to arrest him now.'

'We should've realised you were in danger. I let you go in there alone.'

'I go in there alone every day. You're not at fault.'

Sam looked out of the rear door of the ambulance. Neighbours were watching from nearby windows, some gathering on doorsteps further along. Brabham appeared.

'Gina?' Brabham said.

'In here,' she shouted.

Brabham scowled as he leaned against the ambulance. 'Who's behind it?'

'Mark Proctor,' she said.

Brabham glanced at Sam, expecting some kind of *told you so*, but there was no room for that.

'You should have told me,' Brabham said to Gina.

'I was going to,' she said. 'We just wanted to get things straight first.'

'We've been looking for him all day.'

'And my brother,' Sam said.

'Where is he?'

'It wasn't Joe last night,' Gina said. 'I know who did that. There was a girl killed on the same spot seven years ago – Katie King. Her father killed the man last night. Gerald King. He's your killer.'

Brabham's mouth fell open.

'So you can forget about arresting Joe and help him instead,' Sam said. 'He's with Proctor's sister, Melissa. Proctor has taken his niece, Melissa's daughter.'

'I was just getting up to speed on that. There's someone on their way, but we've got more people looking for him.'

Gina sat up when she heard that. 'What do you mean, he's got his niece?'

'Just that. He snatched her outside a youth club.'

'Do you know what car he's driving?'

Brabham shook his head. 'He burnt his own out and left the

399

hire car at the scene of the murder last night, so my guess is another hire car. We'll got someone speaking to the airport places, because they'll be open and be able to access the databases.'

Sam put his head back and let out a long breath. 'What now?'

It was Gina who spoke. 'We'll find him.'

'You're not fit,' Brabham said.

Gina ripped off the device attached to her finger that measured her pulse and clambered off the stretcher. She pushed past Sam and shouted for Brabham, grimacing at the pain in her throat. 'You're not my boss,' Gina said, and then to Sam, 'Give me your car keys or drive me to Joe.'

'You can't, after what you've been through.'

'Try and stop me,' she said. 'Where's your car?'

'Round the corner.' Sam pointed.

Gina set off running. 'Come on!'

'You can't go,' Brabham said, grabbing Sam's arm.

Sam looked after Gina, who was hobbling round the corner. 'I've waited seventeen years for this,' Sam said. 'I don't care what it costs, I'm going.' He pulled his arm away.

Sam ran around the corner, where Gina was waiting.

'Are you sure you're up to this?' he said.

'You're not the only one who's waited a long time for this. Now drive.'

Sam unlocked his car and jumped in, Gina alongside.

'Mark Proctor,' he said, his tone determined, his eyes fixed in concentration. 'We're coming for you.'

As Melissa opened the door to her apartment, silence greeted them. Joe hadn't met Carrie yet, she'd always been out or in bed when he'd been round, but the atmosphere seemed much more hollow. There were echoes as they walked.

Melissa was walking quickly, frantically, and she went straight

400

into Carrie's bedroom. She collapsed onto her bed and pulled the pillow around her face.

Joe watched from the doorway as she sobbed. He felt impotent, helpless, and swathed in guilt; Melissa's brother might be behind it all, but Joe had helped bring it back to Melissa. Everyone since Ellie somehow came back to him. He'd had the chance to do something about Mark Proctor and hadn't.

He turned away and went to the window in the living room. It was a view he was unaccustomed to, different to the comfort of his own apartment. Here, the water seemed so much more threatening. It ran brown and murky under low bridges, the towpath lined by piss-soaked narrow passages as it cut through a dark and open wasteland. The lights of Ancoats were like a perimeter, everyone locked away, the undeveloped centre always threatening. Was Carrie out there among the lights, or was she trapped somewhere in the darkness, scared at the noises of those who ventured out at night? Was Proctor with her, or was he somewhere else so that he could keep one last secret, one final bargaining chip?

It seemed so bleak and desolate out there, despite the lights from the apartment blocks. It was brighter on Melissa's side of the canal, with restaurants and a pub close by, but still it was more shadow than light.

He checked his watch. Still no sign of the police.

Joe went back into the bedroom. He didn't know what he was going to say. He felt as though he should apologise for the chain of events he'd started, but as he watched Melissa hug the pillow, tears making the cloth wet, he realised that it wasn't about him or his guilt. Right then, it was about Carrie and Melissa.

He climbed onto the bed. He put his arm over Melissa's body and pulled her into him. Her hand gripped his and placed it against her cheek.

He had to get her through this somehow. He owed her that much at least.

Seventy-two

Proctor walked back to where he'd left Carrie.

He'd been sitting on the canal bank, watching the reflections of the streetlights. He didn't know what lay ahead and he needed some time to reflect. He wanted Melissa to know that she could have found Carrie if she'd looked harder. It was no longer about escape, he knew that wasn't going to happen. It was about what he left behind.

It was quiet by the canal. The largest mills were closest to the water, so that it made the streets dark and somewhere to avoid at night. As he walked past the pub nearby, the Thursday night crowd was getting rowdy. There was a band playing Irish music. He thrust his hands in the pockets of his leather coat and dipped his head. Not far now.

He looked up at the building where he'd left Carrie. It stood as a shadow, two four-storey blocks of brick and blacked-out windows, connected by high steel walkways. He checked whether anyone was there – no one was watching – and pushed at the security fence. As he stepped through he was enveloped by darkness. His favourite place, where no one could see him. No one could hurt him.

He moved slowly through the yard, to keep his footsteps quiet, and then into the building itself. However hard he tried, he couldn't stop the echoes. There was a flutter of wings somewhere, disturbed by the crunch of his shoes, and above all of it, soft whimpers coming from the small space under the stair-well. Carrie was still there.

He pulled his phone from his pocket and shone the screen towards her. Carrie's pale skin reflected back like a ghost. Oh, how he loved her complexion, the family trait. Strawberry hair and skin like glass.

He knelt down in front of her. Carrie shrank back, her hair sticking to the cobwebs on the wall. He reached out for her hair and let out an involuntary sigh. As he ran it through his fingers, he imagined how Melissa would react. Her grief, her agony. The excitement surged through him.

He closed his eyes. It was too easy to mistake it for passion. It was something very different. He had to think of something else and control it. That wasn't why he'd taken her. He took deep breaths through his nose. He pressed his knuckles into the grit on the floor, needing the pain to distract him.

By the time he looked at Carrie again, he'd calmed himself. He knelt down and untied the rope from the metal pillar so that just her wrists were bound. Carrie's chest was rising and falling quickly, her eyes wet and scared. He slipped his arms under her body and lifted her. She was tall but still skinny, light enough to lift.

He grunted as he straightened. Her body felt damp, her T-shirt moist through perspiration. She couldn't wrap her arm around him to help him take the strain, so he had to do it all himself. Her ribcage dug ridges into his arms.

His first footfall was loud on the stairs as he took her to the floor above. Each step echoed and threw up dust. More cob-webs trailed across his face as he got higher. He was heading for the top floor; he wanted a good view for his farewell.

He had to put her down for a rest after two flights of stairs. He was gentle with her, though, laying her on the ground so that she didn't hurt herself. As he fought to get his breath back, he went over to the window, wiping some of the dirt away so that he could see through. All he could see was the orange glow behind the dark shadow of the building opposite. That was where he needed to be.

The remaining flight of stairs was easier. He stood in a large doorway, the double doors that once protected it long gone. He was looking across the walkway that connected to the next building. The steel was worn in places, cracks showing, the lattice of the bridge revealing the drop below. There would be no surviving if he fell, just a long drop onto broken-up concrete and then eternal darkness.

He threw Carrie over his shoulder, fireman's-lift style, and began his walk across.

The bridge clanged as he went and it moved in the brickwork, so that it bounced as he walked. He had a brief look down, into the darkness, but it made his vision swirl. Instead, he focused straight ahead, to the approaching doorway, lit deep blue by the light that filtered in through the opposite windows.

Carrie grunted as he put her down, dropping her more roughly than he'd intended. He grabbed the rope around her wrists and pulled her across the floor. She bumped over small stones that were dotted around until he threw her against the wall. He stood over her and saw that her T-shirt was ripped. Her bra was showing. Small, clean, her skin unblemished.

He turned away. Not that.

There was a mattress in the corner, with a sleeping bag inside a rolled-up plastic sheet. He shuffled Carrie onto it. Damp and mildewed, he couldn't keep out the rain and the cold, but it had been new when he'd brought it in a few years earlier. It was where he spent long evenings watching; he could see people but they couldn't see him.

He went to the window and moved the piece of slate that covered one of the small panes, the nail that held it in place scraping on the tile as he moved it. Moonlight came in, making

Carrie's skin glow. He had a better view now, across to Melissa's apartment building, with her window on the corner.

He clenched his jaw. He'd miss this. He'd thought of this moment for so long, but it wasn't supposed to be like this. It was where he spent so much time, watching her. He'd seen everything from his position. Melissa and Carrie enjoying each other's company, both of them wandering the apartment as they relaxed. He'd watched Carrie grow, from the little girl running around to the young woman she was now. Just like he'd watched her mother. He'd even seen Joe Parker the night before. That hurt.

And he could see Melissa again. On Carrie's bed, Joe with her, distress obvious from every contortion of her body.

Ripples.

Now it was time to bring more pain.

He went to the hole he'd knocked in the roof some months before. A pile of bricks in one corner served as a step. He pulled out the tarpaulin and climbed up, grabbing the edge of an oak beam, his head emerging through the gap, his face illuminated by moonlight. The rest was effort, pulling himself upwards, his face red, until he could lie flat on the tiles, panting from the exertion.

The roof had three peaks, so that he could lie between two and let his body be submerged by the shadow. It gave him the sounds of Ancoats and the cool of the night. And an uninterrupted view of Melissa's apartment. It was different to being inside. Being on the roof felt like they shared the same space, the same piece of air.

He watched Melissa for a few minutes. She wasn't doing much, just lying on the bed, Joe Parker's arms around her. That wouldn't find her daughter.

It was time to say hello again.

He pulled out Carrie's phone and dialled.

*

Melissa's phone rang, making them both jump.

She pushed away from Joe and grabbed it from the bedside table. She held it up. It was showing Carrie's name.

'Hello?' she said, her voice frantic.

When Melissa's eyes closed, Joe knew who was on the other end. He whispered for her to put it on speaker.

'Where are you?' Melissa spat out the words.

'Don't rush me,' Proctor said. He was speaking quietly, his voice almost drowned out by wind in the microphone. He was outside.

'Bring her back,' Melissa wailed. 'I don't care about the others. I don't care where you go. Just let Carrie go and run. That's all you have to do.'

'So get the money. I can't go anywhere without money.'

'I don't have that sort of money. No one does.'

'What about your lawyer friend, Joe Parker. Ask him.'

'I just want her back. Please, Mark, please.'

'So that's a no? I didn't realise there was a price you wouldn't pay for Carrie. Who gets all the blame now, sweet Melissa?'

'Wait, wait!' She wiped her eyes. 'Talk to me, Mark, it's been a long time. We can sort this thing out.'

'What's this, the big reunion?' Proctor laughed. 'It's over for me, I know it. Either you get the money for me somehow, so I can run, or else it ends now. But I'll make some noise before I go.'

'Don't hurt her, please.'

Proctor went to say something but stopped. Music came through the phone, like a sudden burst, and the noise of people. He clicked off.

Melissa curled up on the bed, her arms across her stomach, grimacing as if in pain.

'We need to focus,' Joe said, trying to take the phone from her.

406

'I just want my baby back.'

'So we need to find out where he is. He clicked off when there was a noise.'

Melissa looked at him. 'I don't know what you mean.'

'He hung up as soon as there was a noise, as if he was worried it would give him away. He's somewhere busy.'

Then something occurred to him. He went to the window and looked out, but all he could see was his reflection. 'Turn off the lights.'

Melissa ran to the switch and plunged the room into darkness.

'He knows I'm here,' Joe said. 'He mentioned me.'

'He must have heard you in the background.'

'I didn't say anything, I was too busy listening. No, it's something else. I think he can see us.'

Melissa rushed to the window to join him. They scoured the darkness ahead but it was all just that, shadowy brick blocks and the moonlight on the murky ribbon of canal water.

'Where?'

'His place, where he goes to be alone. He had somewhere as a child. Why not somewhere as an adult?'

'But why so close?'

'To watch you, Melissa. Don't you see? You're the sibling who rejected him.'

'You mean he's been watching us the whole time?' she said, her hand over her mouth, trembling.

'He couldn't just find somewhere to take Carrie and observe you without going there before. It's too convenient, too quick.'

'He might be in a car.'

Something occurred to Joe. 'Get the photographs he's taken of Carrie.'

'Why, what for?'

'There's something we should have spotted.'

Melissa ran through to the living room and came back with

the envelope they'd looked at earlier in the day. Joe closed the blinds as Melissa turned on the lamps.

She pulled out the photographs and scattered them across the bed. 'What is it?'

Joe picked up one, a shot of Carrie walking along the pavement in her school uniform, a brick wall the backdrop.

'I knew it,' he said.

'What, what?'

'Look at the angle,' Joe said. 'It's from on high, looking down, like a vantage point. This wasn't taken from a car or van. And she's in her uniform so it must be on her route to school.'

Melissa picked up another one. 'This is the same. And it's got the canal in the background. I can see the towpath.'

She went to the window as Joe clicked off the light again. They both peered around the blind, looking for something, anything.

Joe opened the window.

'What are you doing?' Melissa said.

'That sudden burst of noise made him hang up. If he's watching close by, the sound must be close too.'

They sat on the bed in silence, straining to hear something above the light drone of traffic and the occasional chatter of conversation.

Then it came back. A sudden burst of music, people shouting.

'It's the pub,' Melissa said, gripping Joe's arm. 'They have a band on every Thursday.'

'He's so close,' Joe said, scanning the buildings nearby, trying to see something in the darkness. 'There!'

'Where?'

'Top floor of that building. It's all dark but there's a glint in the window. It's faint but it's something moving.'

Melissa ran for the door, Joe just behind.

They were going to get Carrie.

*

408

'Shit!'

Proctor threw the phone off the roof, gritted his teeth as it sailed through the air, landing with a smash as pieces were strewn over the road. The pub was too noisy. He cursed his bad luck. Why then, when he was talking? The sounds might place him.

He looked across. The light had gone off in Melissa's apartment. *Shit!*

His shoes clattered on the tiles as he scrambled across the roof and dropped down into the hole. Dust flew as he landed with a thump. Carrie was on her knees in front of the window, her wrists against the broken windowpane, rubbing the rope against the jagged edge. Her bracelet twinkled in the moonlight.

She looked round and yelped when she heard him. She dropped back to the floor and shuffled to the wall, shrinking back.

He rushed at her and slapped her across the face, a loud crack in the night. He was breathing hard. He had to stay in control. *Don't make mistakes.* But his anger was growing, becoming harder to check. He grabbed the rope around her wrists and dragged her across the floor, grimacing, enjoying it too much. Carrie shrieked in fear and pain, muffled only by the gag. He clamped his hand over her mouth, making her cheeks puff red.

'Shut up! Now!'

She whimpered.

He yanked her to her feet and pulled her towards the hole in the roof. It was hard work. He lifted her over his shoulder and put one hand on the roof edge, the other arm over Carrie. He was panting through exertion and tried to clamber up on the same pile of bricks he'd used before. It was too hard. He was going to have to push her up and hope she landed properly.

He got her shoulders through the opening and then put his own shoulder underneath her. With a heave, Carrie dropped over the lip and tumbled down the tiles. Proctor couldn't see her but he heard the clatter of her body against the roof. He paused to listen out for how it ended, whether there was a muffled scream as she went off the edge, but there was nothing.

Proctor hauled himself back through the hole, the breeze cooling the perspiration speckled across his forehead. Carrie was slumped in the crevice where the two roofs sloped and met, her ankles over the edge. He took a few deep breaths and then slid down to join her. As he got close, he had a glimpse over. A long sheer drop, too dark to see the ground.

Carrie was trying to shuffle herself along, snakelike, to get away from it. He grabbed the rope and helped her, pulling her into the middle. He sat her upright. She put her head back against the roof and tried to suck in air around the gag, soaked from saliva.

He sat opposite and leaned back against the tiles. He let out some long breaths before he chuckled to himself. 'This is where you say that you can see your house from up here.'

Carrie tried to swear but the gag muffled it. She stamped down on a tile in frustration. It cracked.

Proctor leaned forward. 'You need to stay quiet and calm,' he said. 'You don't know how much I've looked out for you. I've seen you grow, Carrie, watched you from up here. But for one of us, it ends today.'

Carrie closed her eyes and sobbed. As Proctor watched, a thin trickle of piss tracked its way down the tiles, her jeans soaked.

'Just let me go,' she tried to say around the gag.

He turned away, disgusted.

It was never meant to work out this way. He was going to come for Carrie at some point, he'd always seen her as his finale, but it was meant to be in his time. He would come back into the family, be there for his poor bereaved sister as she tried to come to terms with her loss, the ripple to beat them all. It might be enough to satisfy whatever drove him so that it wasn't there any more. But this was wrong, all too soon. All he could do now was hurt and take the blame.

He saw something and gasped.

Melissa and Joe Parker were running out of the front of her building. From the direction of their sprint, both of them looking up, they'd worked out where he was.

'She's coming for you,' he said, and he grabbed her by the rope again, pulling her towards the edge.

Carrie wriggled against him, tried to scream, kicked against the roof tiles, but it was no use. Once Melissa was out of view, running along the side of the building, he hooked the rope that bound her wrists over a drainpipe that protruded above the lip of the roof.

'What will always torture her is that she wasn't quick enough,' he said. 'She'll replay it, year after year, the time wasted on her bed, how she couldn't get up here fast enough, or get past me, because your end is like sand in a timer.'

He grunted with effort as he pushed at her. She slid closer to the edge, her eyes wide, screeching through the gag. She tried to dig her heels into the slates but it was pointless. He strained with effort until her legs were hanging over the edge, her feet kicking uselessly in the air, nothing beneath them but a long fall. He gritted his teeth and gave her a final push.

Carrie's body thudded against the side of the building. The rope around her wrists that he'd hooked around the drainpipe had worked.

He looked over.

She was hanging by her arms, only the bindings around her wrists supporting her. The ground was a long way below. She tried to dig her feet into the brickwork but there were no gaps to give her a toehold. She was like a worm on a

411

hook. As she struggled, the drainpipe creaked, the long metal screws scraping in the mortar. One of her shoes came off and took an age before it bounced against the ground a long way below.

'If she loves you, she'll get past me,' he said. 'But she'll need to be quick. Trying to cut through that rope must seem like a really bad idea now.'

And with that, he was shuffling back across the roof before dropping back into the roof space.

It was time to say hello to Melissa.

Sam and Gina were close to Ancoats. Gina was swallowing hard, still in pain from where Proctor had throttled her.

'Why would Proctor set fire to his car if he knew how it looked?' Sam said.

'Was that as bad as leaving it in the police compound covered in blood traces?' Gina said. 'What would the police do when they found out his car had been nearby and it was in their compound, and they knew who'd been driving it?'

'But it drew attention to himself. He could have gone back in the morning with his insurance and reclaimed it, got it cleaned of whatever needed removing.'

'He was panicking. For all of his superiority, it was blind panic, because he wasn't the one in control.'

Sam's phone rang. He looked at the screen.

'It's Joe,' he said.

Sam clicked the answer button. 'We're on our way,' he said. 'Sit tight.'

'He's here!'

'Who?'

'Proctor, he's here.'

'Joe, where are you?'

Gina looked at him, detecting something in Sam's voice.

'Outside Melissa's apartment,' Joe said, breathless.

'What are you doing?'

'No time,' Joe said. 'Just get here.'

'Where, Joe, where?'

'Some kind of abandoned warehouse in Ancoats, opposite Blake Mill, Melissa's apartment block. An Irish bar nearby.'

'We're nearly there,' Sam said.

'Get everyone here!'

The line went dead.

'Proctor?' Gina said.

'He's in an old warehouse near Blake Mill.' He tossed her his phone. 'Call Brabham. He's in the contacts list. Tell him where we're going.'

Gina thumbed through his contacts as Sam accelerated along the main road towards Ancoats. He overtook other cars and made ones on the other side swerve to avoid him. The sound of Gina talking merged with the roar of his engine and the occasional blast of a horn.

'Down there,' Gina said, pointing to a narrow street.

Sam skidded into it, his back wheels swinging outwards, his engine loud between the brick walls on either side of the street.

The view ahead opened out, just the dark empty space of the canal basin ahead, dots of apartment windows further away.

'It must be round here,' Sam said, craning forward, Gina doing the same.

He turned left so that the canal was to his right. Large dark blocks of stone were ahead, turned into silhouettes by the brightness of the apartments further along.

'There's the Irish bar,' Sam said, pointing, slowing down.

Gina gripped his arm. 'Shit, there,' she said, and pointed.

Sam slammed to a halt as he saw what Gina was pointing at.

There was a young girl high off the ground, her arms hooked around something, swinging against the wall of a warehouse, her hair wild in the breeze.

Gina made another call, 999, and barked instructions. They

413

stared out of the windscreen for a few seconds in disbelief, praying that someone else had called the fire service and that a long ladder would arrive any moment.

No blue lights flickered nearby, no sirens wailed in the distance.

Neither of them said anything as they ran from the car.

Joe ran hard alongside the building, Melissa with him, looking for a way in.

'Do you think she's here?' Melissa said, between gasps of breath.

'Where else?'

It was a warehouse, last used for printing supplies. The bricks were dark and old, replaced in places, left to fall away in others, with grilles and boards over most of the windows. Two metal gangways joined the top two floors, visible only by their silhouettes against the night sky.

'How do we get in?' Melissa said, banging frantically at the bricked-up doorways.

Joe looked around, trying to see some kind of entrance, but then at one corner he saw a kink in the security fence that blocked off the yard.

'There,' he said, and ran over, Melissa behind.

The security fence was just a row of metal screens connected by overlapping brackets at each end. One of them had been pushed away so that it was only joined at the bottom, capable of being pushed to create a gap.

Joe put his shoulder against the screen to move it. It screeched on the cobbles on the other side. When there was enough of a gap, he held it so Melissa could get through. Once inside, the world beyond the yard seemed to be shut out. Everything was dark, the outline of the roofs the only thing visible.

Joe grabbed Melissa's hand and they both edged forward as

they tried to get their breath back, reaching out with their feet to sweep for hazards. There were loose stones, small metal brackets, discarded bottles. The ground was uneven, with cobbles breaking free from where they'd been fixed for over two hundred years.

Joe was looking for a way into the building.

'There,' Melissa said, and pointed to a darker shadow in the corner of the yard.

They both ran towards it, their feet skidding sometimes on loose stones, but they wanted to get inside. Any shreds of light were swallowed up as they went into the doorway. Their footsteps echoed.

Joe put out his hand. His eyes tried to adjust to the darkness but it was impossible. The windows were blocked off by metal screens so that there was not even the faintest glimmer of light to cling onto.

'Mark, please!' Melissa shouted.

They both listened out. Nothing came back.

Joe reached out with his feet, his arms out, stepping forwards, Melissa holding onto the back of his shirt. He was waiting for the sound of sudden movement, the blow, grimacing in the darkness, nerves making his insides churn, but he had to keep moving forward.

He jumped. Something against his face. He let out a breath. A cobweb, hanging from the ceiling.

'Mark!' Melissa shouted again. Still nothing.

Something fluttered, the sudden noise of wings loud, fast like whistles. A bat, probably, perhaps more than one. Melissa yelped. Joe's heart thumped. Sweat dripped into his eye.

His foot hit something. A wall, or something else? He reached out. A wooden block, then another. Stairs.

'Let's go up,' he said.

The steps creaked as they climbed slowly. Their hands trailed along the wall at one side, damp and dirty, coarse in places, slick with moisture in others. They felt the space around them open up and there were specks of light, some of the windows merely blacked out and with the street light showing through, creating faint outlines. The air was less damp than on the ground floor.

'Carrie! Mark!' Melissa shouted again, but still nothing.

'Listen out,' Joe said, and put his arm across Melissa.

There were no sounds.

'They can't be on this floor, we'd hear something.'

'But how big is this place?' Melissa said.

'Big, but I still think it's up.'

They crept through to the next floor. Still silent. The air felt colder. There was more light, like a fan across the floor.

'There,' Joe said.

There was a large opening, like a huge open door, and beyond it a metal bridge joining onto the next building, so that employees could carry cloth between the buildings without going down the stairs, from the days when they were locked in once the shifts started.

'That must be the building overlooking my apartment,' Melissa said.

'Where we saw something,' Joe said, and set off towards the bridge.

As they got to the doorway, Joe looked down. They were only three floors up but already it looked too high. Each floor had high ceilings so that the bridge was a long way from the ground, just a dark hole beneath them, the building opposite shutting out all light. The bridge was around twenty yards long, with another one above it, connecting the top floors of the buildings, but it seemed to stretch into the distance.

Joe stepped onto the bridge and it dipped. He gripped the rail as the air was filled with the sound of metal moving against stone. His feet clanged as he moved slowly, the bridge swaying with every step, bouncing as he got closer to the centre. The metal felt like it was flaking under his shoes. All he could do was look straight ahead and keep moving.

It seemed to take an age to get across, Melissa still on the other side, but the colossal shadow of the opposite building eventually swallowed him up.

There was no way in. The entrance doors were closed off. He pushed at them, frustrated, but they just banged against the frame.

He looked up. He'd have to try the gangway above.

'We have to keep going up,' he said.

Melissa turned, she wasn't prepared to wait for him, so Joe ran back across, ignoring the sickening bounce of the bridge, until he was back inside the darkness of the building.

Melissa found more stairs and ran up them. Joe rushed to catch up, stumbling as he twisted his ankle on a piece of brick he hadn't seen. When he joined her at the top of the stairs, he was looking across at an identical metal walkway, except this time there was an opening on the other side. He could see into the building and some of the streets beyond.

Joe pushed past her and went first.

'I'm not the little woman, and I want my daughter back,' Melissa said.

'And if this bridge isn't safe, there's no kids to grieve for me,' Joe said, and stepped forward. 'Wait until I get across. If I make it, you know it's all right for you too.'

It moved when he stepped onto it, as though the stone supporting it was crumbling. Joe's stomach lurched and he gripped the rail, but he kept on moving forward. It was in a worse state than the bridge below. Some of the metal was cracked, as if it was rusting through, but Joe wasn't going to stop. He stared forward and kept on marching, the night filled with the sound of metal grating against stone and the creaks as it bounced.

Joe paused at the doorway. The room was better lit, with the

417

light coming in through a broken window and a large hole in the roof. He listened, tried to hear something over his own deep breaths. There was a noise, something banging on the roof.

He looked up and stepped forward.

Joe didn't see the brick coming.

It smashed into his cheekbone, knocking him backwards onto the walkway. He banged his head on the rail. The weight of his falling body knocked out one of the metal panels in the side of the bridge. It seemed a long time before it clanged onto the ground.

His head tilted backwards, nothing to stop the fall of his body. He strained to lift himself but everything seemed to take too long. The stars were just swirling dots. The sound of his hands on the metal walkway seemed muffled, his heartbeat loud in his ears, but he grabbed the rail and slid back onto the bridge. He groaned as he rolled over. There were footsteps behind him, moving quickly.

Instinct kicked in. Joe rolled to one side and a brick smashed against the rail. Fragments peppered his face and grit went into his eye, the pain bringing him round. He looked up. There was someone standing over him, arms out from his body, tensed and angry. Mark Proctor.

Joe kicked upwards, the gasp of pain from Proctor loud and satisfying. Proctor bent over in agony so Joe lashed out again, his boot catching Proctor in the face, making him rock backwards.

Joe got onto all fours, sucking in air. There was blood on the back of his head, he could feel it matting his hair, but he wasn't backing down. This was his moment.

Melissa shouted, 'Where's Carrie?'

Proctor got to his feet. He laughed, blood running from his mouth. His eye was swelling, a fractured eye socket perhaps, but he bared his teeth in anger, unbowed. 'Little Melissa. It's been a long time.'

Melissa ran across the walkway. It bounced as she ran, the air filled with loud clangs. She scrambled over Joe and flailed towards Proctor, her blows wild and angry. Proctor punched her face and she went down hard, groaning, lying on the floor just inside the doorway.

Proctor turned as if to go back towards Joe but his attention was distracted by a noise, like bangs on the roof, the sound of someone struggling: Carrie.

Joe got to his knees and ran at Proctor. His shoulder thumped into his stomach, a rugby tackle, his legs driving hard, forcing Proctor backwards, unbalanced. As Proctor landed, winded, Joe pushed himself off and headed for the hole in the roof. Melissa had lifted up her shoulders and blood pooled onto the floor.

Joe hauled himself upwards.

The height was dizzying. The orange streets seemed a long way below. He tried to stay steady in the join between two roofs. He couldn't see her. The tiles felt slippery. They made loud cracks as he moved across the roof, his arms out to balance himself. He tried not to think of the height, but he felt sick with every slip as he went.

'Carrie!'

His shout was loud and bounced between the buildings a long way below. There were blue flashing lights in the distance, coming from two angles. Sirens wailed. Help was on its way, but it might be too late for Carrie.

Then he saw it. A drainpipe. It was sticking out above the roof edge and was moving. As he listened, it clanked against the brickwork.

Joe threw himself forward, clattering onto the tiles. He scrambled towards to the edge. He gasped and closed his eyes when he got there. The view below swirled, it was so high, the street lights moving as if they were caught in a high wind. He had to fight that. Carrie was hanging from the drainpipe, her body swinging. She was looking up, petrified, a soaked and filthy gag around her mouth. The drainpipe was leaning away from the wall, as if her weight was pulling it out.

Joe shuffled further forward, taking deep breaths to fight the nausea of the drop, and reached over. His shoulders and chest were over the edge. He banged into the drainpipe and it creaked. Mortar dust drifted onto Carrie, making her blink and grimace. He couldn't stop. He reached down and grabbed her under her arms. He strained as he pulled her towards him. He tried to push his legs against the roof tiles, scared she would drag him forward, send them both over. She cried. The muscles in his arms felt about to give up the fight.

He shouted as he strained, and then her bound wrists cleared the top of the drainpipe. He had all of her weight. He tried to inch back and bring her with him.

Carrie banged against the edge of the roof, her face on the tiles, her body still over the edge. She was wriggling, scared, trying to pull herself forward. She was soaked in sweat and it made her slippery.

'Keep still,' Joe gasped.

He roared as he pulled her back one final time, his shoulders straining, his teeth bared. She cried out in pain as the edge of the roof tiles dragged along her stomach, drawing blood. That didn't matter, she was coming up.

She flopped forward onto the roof tiles as Joe fell backwards, drained, panting.

Carrie's eyes were filled with fear, cheeks stained by dirt and tears. Joe hauled himself onto his knees, sucked in lungfuls of air and reached forwards to pull at her gag, bringing it below her chin. Her mouth curled into a sob.

'No time,' Joe said.

The sirens got closer. Joe looked. Blue lights were colouring the buildings around.

He pulled at the knot on the rope around Carrie's wrists. The rope was thick, making it easier. Once they were free, Carrie threw her arms around him and sobbed into his shoulder. He let her stay like that for a few seconds, her ribs against his arms, her arms skinny and frail. For a moment, he wished it had been like this with his sister, that he could have rescued her and had this moment with her.

There were noises behind them. Proctor's head appeared through the hole in the roof. Carrie tried to scramble up the tiles to get away, but Joe gripped her hand.

'Stay behind me,' he whispered. 'Get off the roof when you can.'

Carrie nodded.

Proctor hauled himself up and then stood with a foot on each roof slope, his feet wide apart. He was holding a large knife.

'It ends now,' Proctor said, and he moved towards them.

Roof tiles cracked under Proctor's heavy footsteps. He was just a few feet away. He lashed out with the knife.

Joe leaned backwards. Carrie scrambled away. They were close to the edge again. Joe sneaked a look back and his breath caught in his throat.

Proctor was moving towards him. 'You're frightened, just like your baby sister,' he said, sneering.

Joe tensed.

Proctor grinned, his eye swollen. 'She enjoyed it, I think. She thought it was a game at first, sweet Eleanor. I had her secrets, because I'd watched her. Not so sweet, you know.' He swung out with the knife again. 'I liked how she struggled against me. Do you know she cried?'

Joe closed his eyes. He couldn't listen to this. He understood what Proctor was doing. Proctor knew his days were done. He was trying to make Joe go with him.

'You must have guessed, though,' Proctor said, his tone mocking. 'I could see the confusion in her eyes, that her brother was just behind her. So where was he? He'd save her,

her big brother Joe. But no, you were a coward, not wanting to follow me. So she pushed against me as I killed her. I like to think I gave her a good time just before she went.'

Joe rushed at him. His feet skidded and clattered on the tiles but he wasn't going to stop. Proctor lashed out with the knife and it felt like a punch to his side, but Joe kept on going, lifting Proctor, pushing him backwards.

Then they were falling, the roof gone, air whistling through his hair.

The landing came hard. They'd fallen through the hole in the roof. Proctor screamed, drowning out the loud crack of his rib. Dust flew. The knife clattered across the floor. Carrie scrambled down behind them, sobbing, and then ran to Melissa, who was trying to stand, still dazed.

Joe scrambled towards the knife, now close to the top of the stairs, glinting in the faint light.

Proctor rolled onto his front. 'Is this how you dreamed of it?' he said, gasping, spitting blood. 'All those years thinking of me, of what I'd done to little Ellie. How does it feel?'

'Melissa, go,' Joe said, panting, exhausted. 'Take Carrie home.'

She didn't say anything, just hugged her daughter.

'Go!' Joe shouted and grabbed the knife. He held out the blade, his teeth bared, blood on his chin.

Proctor got to his knees and took a deep breath. Then he laughed, his head thrown back. 'What are you going to do? Kill me?' He laughed again. 'You'd spend your life in a cell.'

There were more shouts behind them.

'Oh look,' Proctor said, glancing backwards. 'Got the whole fucking family here now.'

Joe looked over Proctor's shoulder to see Sam and Gina on the other side of the metal walkway.

'Put the knife down,' Gina shouted, her voice hoarse.

'It's over,' Joe said to Proctor, and he grimaced. He looked down at his jumper. There was a small tear at the side and the wool was dark and slick. His own blood. Adrenalin was keeping away the pain but how long could he last?

The sound of sirens became deafening.

'I should have fucked her,' Proctor said. 'Not her.' And he gestured towards Gina. 'No, your sister. I'm pretty sure I'd have been her first.'

'Don't listen to him, Joe,' Gina shouted, getting closer, the metal bridge making loud clangs as she walked across. Sam was with Melissa and Carrie, trying to lead them away.

Joe didn't pay them any attention. He was replaying that day again. Ellie walking. Proctor waiting. Flashes of memory coming to a head in an abandoned warehouse in Ancoats. His long-held promise to himself: to kill the man who murdered his sister.

And the man was right there.

Proctor turned towards the doorway as the police cars outside came to a stop.

'Maybe not,' Proctor continued, stepping closer to Joe. 'There was a moment, just a moment, when I thought she was enjoying it. Just the way she pushed against me. Took away some of the enjoyment, if I'm honest. Had to press that little bit harder.'

Joe dropped the knife, it clattered on the floor, and ran at him. His hands went around Proctor's throat. He pushed backwards. Proctor's feet skidded on loose stones, his hands flailed at Joe. But Joe wouldn't be stopped.

He propelled Proctor towards the open doorway, to the metal walkway, until Proctor banged into the railing, leaning backwards.

Proctor gasped but grinned, his eyes bulging.

Joe pushed him harder, towards the blackness beneath. Proctor was unbalanced, one foot off the ground, over the edge, not resisting hard enough. Someone was shouting but

423

Joe paid no heed. He was locked into the memories of Ellie, of all those years of wanting this moment. Proctor's fingers were trying to find Joe's eyes but Joe dipped his head, got closer to Proctor, felt his spittle on his cheek. The bones in Proctor's neck were brittle under his grip so he squeezed tighter, felt the sweet rush of revenge as Proctor gasped louder for breath, his eyes starting to roll.

Joe didn't see the blow coming. Another brick, thrust in hard between his shoulder blades. He yelped in pain and his hands loosened around Proctor's neck.

Proctor dropped onto the walkway, gasping, clutching his throat. He crawled towards the safety of the warehouse. He collapsed onto his stomach, moaning, breathing hard.

When Joe looked round, it was Gina. She dropped the brick.

'I didn't do it for him,' she said. 'I did it for you, Joe. You can't be like him.'

The warehouse on the other side of the walkway became filled with torch beams and shouts, the sounds of heavy police boots.

'Over here,' Gina shouted. She pointed at Proctor. 'There. He's the one.'

The bridge bounced as three police officers ran across. Proctor didn't move as they took hold of him.

Joe hung his head. His breath came hard. He felt cheated, that had been his chance, but as his anger subsided he was left with just one truth: his hunt for justice for Ellie was over.

Seventy-three

Joe was driving. Sam was doing all the talking, cajoling Helena Proctor, wanting her to find out what she could from her husband. Helena wasn't saying much; just polite agreement, her hands toying with the handles of her handbag.

They were heading for Forest Bank, the prison where Mark Proctor was being held until his trial. It was new and plush, along a road that ran past a country park. It could be mistaken for a new office complex if it wasn't for the high concrete wall that surrounded it.

This wasn't an official visit; it was just about Sam and Joe getting answers. Two weeks had passed since his arrest and Mark Proctor hadn't spoken to anyone. He'd stayed silent in his police interviews and even during the court hearings. Joe had been there for the first appearance, where the court clerk had become frustrated, even threatened Proctor with contempt if he didn't give the information required. That had drawn a slight smile from Proctor. Joe knew what it meant, that his problems were too great to worry about that.

Joe got some satisfaction from that, knowing that Proctor saw everything ahead as bleak.

Joe looked into the rear-view mirror. Helena was staring out of the side window, her bag on her lap. She'd been married to one of the worst serial killers in the history of the north, preying on teenage girls for years, and one of the victim's turned out to be her own sister. Helena had a lot of things to work out for herself and Joe guessed it could take her some time.

'Will you be all right?' he said.

Helena looked forward and nodded, gave a faint smile. 'I'll be fine. I just want him to know that it's goodbye.'

That sounded reasonable, although Joe was surprised that her anger wasn't greater, as if she still bore some feelings for her sister's killer.

Joe pulled into the car park opposite the smoked glass of the entrance and stayed silent as Helena got out to make the lonely walk. She was dressed smartly, as if she wanted Proctor to know just what he'd let go, in skirt and heels, her handbag now over her shoulder.

As they watched her, Sam said, 'She must feel so cheated, knowing what he did. He'd been in her bed all these years, comforting her, when all the time he'd been the killer.'

'Like we've found out, a grief-junkie,' Joe said. 'Helena must have been the biggest prize of all, someone he could watch every day.'

'What I can't understand is that he must have had some feelings for Helena,' Sam said. 'People like Mark Proctor don't have feelings, not in the same way that we do, but he took Helena's revenge. He persuaded Henry Mason to kill the teacher who'd been molesting her sister and then he killed Henry Mason himself, revenge for selling the car that killed her parents. That's pretty smart. Perhaps it was his way of making amends for what he did.'

'You're being too kind,' Joe said. 'Something doesn't fit well with me. The man killed in Worsley was meant to be him.'

'The perfect distraction. There might be a reason why Proctor sent that man along, or perhaps it didn't matter who was chosen, but you have to admit that his death makes you doubt Proctor's part. What better defence can there be than to claim himself as the victim?'

'I understand your case theory, but when I saw Proctor in court, he looked confused. There's something we're not getting, I'm sure of it.'

'That's just his arrogance,' Sam said. 'He assumed he was too clever for us and can't work out how he got caught.'

'Are you sure you've got enough?'

'We got lucky. My hunch about the custody record was right: Henry Mason's DNA is on the page where Proctor signed it the night he was arrested for stealing his own car back. For the first time, Proctor had panicked. He'd been caught in the act and it trapped him. The link with the IP address does the rest, because it shows that Proctor was in contact, luring Mason to his death, posing as vodkagirl. We have a motive, revenge for the death of Helena's parents, and it's enough to keep him inside for now, along with Carrie's abduction.'

'You must be the real hero, coming up with the DNA and IP stuff.'

'It doesn't feel like that,' Sam said. 'And we want more, because I want him to pay for everything. Yes, we've got the photographs and souvenirs but they don't prove direct involvement in Ellie's murder. His defence lawyer might squirm Proctor out of that.'

'Perhaps if they find the bodies of the missing girls, there is nothing a defence lawyer can do,' Joe said.

'Yes, maybe.'

Joe frowned. 'Something isn't quite right, though.'

'What do you mean?'

'I just don't get that Proctor was being so gallant, getting revenge for his wife. He killed Adrianne. How could anyone be as cruel to Helena as that?'

'Perhaps somewhere he saw it as redemption,' Sam said.

'It didn't do Gerald any good.'

Sam didn't answer that. When the police went to Gerald King's house, they found him hanging from the same stair rail his wife had chosen, his daughter's notebook on the floor beneath him, the last thing he'd held.

Sam watched Helena disappear into the prison entrance and asked, 'How's Carrie?'

'They're taking it slowly, but she's a strong kid.'

'And Melissa?'

Joe smiled. 'Taking it even more slowly.'

'But there's still something to take?'

'It's weird that something good should come out of all of this.'

'You think a lot about her.'

Joe didn't reply. Sam's smile told him that he didn't need to.

Helena walked over to the table where Mark Proctor was sitting. She'd left her bag in the locker in the reception area and fought the urge to fold her arms across her chest self-consciously. She wanted this to be her swagger. This moment had been a long time coming. Other prisoners looked at her as she walked, wearing red bibs over grey sweatshirts, except those awaiting trial; they got to wear their own clothes. The bibs were still compulsory.

The room was comfortable, she hadn't expected that. Blue carpets and chairs, the prisoners separated by small tables. There was a corner with playthings, so that the prisoners' children could find some joy in the formality of the meeting. Prison guards stood around the edge of the room, with keys on silver chains looped onto their belts, their clip-on ties smart over pressed white shirts. She glanced up at the cameras mounted on each wall, looking for the passing of contraband. She doubted they would record sound; there'd be too much of it.

Proctor watched her all the way, a half-smile on his lips. When she sat down, he said, 'Go on, get it out of the way. You hate me? There's a queue for that.'

Helena put her knees together, her hands on them, poised. She tilted her head. 'Is that why you think I'm here?'

'Isn't it? Or is it that you're divorcing me? Fine. Get your solicitor to send a letter.'

She shook her head. 'That isn't why I'm here. I want to tell you things.'

He rolled his eyes. 'I hurt you? Yeah, well, these things happen. What do you want to know? How your baby sister cried and pissed herself as I squeezed the life out of her?'

Helena blinked and looked down, took in a breath to compose herself.

'Are you miked up, hoping for a confession?' he scoffed. 'So predictable.'

Helena looked up again. 'The confession is from me, you murdering prick.'

Proctor's smile twitched. 'What do you mean?'

She smiled, but it was thin and mean, her eyes glaring. She spoke quietly and slowly. 'I've got four words for you, and I want you to remember them every morning you wake up in your cell, when you try to work out how it all went wrong for you.'

He cricked his neck.

She leaned forward and spoke in a whisper. 'I did it all.'

He went as if to say something, but stopped. He put his head back, confused. He leaned forward, his arms on the table. Helena leaned back. 'What are you talking about?'

'It was all down to me,' she said. 'You need to know that.'

He frowned. After a few seconds, he said, 'You're not making any sense.'

'I've known about you for some time now. This was about payback.' She raised her eyebrows as she spoke with a snarl. 'Nice little Helena wouldn't do that, would she? Sweet invisible insignificant docile servile little Helena? No, not her. That's what they'll think.'

429

Proctor folded his arms, his jaw set.

'I found your box,' she said, spitting the words out. 'Did you think I could watch you disappear to my father's workshop and not wonder what you were doing? There were other rooms you could have used, but it was always down there, in my father's special place? You were so secretive even though it was so cold. So I went looking and I found it.'

He swallowed. 'The box was locked.'

'I know. I had a new padlock ready, exactly the same make,' Helena said. 'I scuffed it up so that it didn't look new. All I had to do was replace the padlock and put the new key onto your key ring. I did the swap when you were in the bath and waited until you went out. I used my spare padlock key, because they always come in pairs.'

'This is bullshit.'

'Is it? You might not know but I can get a little obsessed about things. But you wouldn't know that, because you never really noticed me. Tell me: were you the one messaging Henry Mason, making him spill his dirty little secrets?'

He didn't answer.

'So if it wasn't you, who else could it have been?' she said.

Proctor paled.

'I saw everything. My sister, you bastard.' She took a deep breath through her nose, tried to blink away her tears. 'You murdering fucking bastard. I saw her pictures, how she died. And all those other sweet things too, those young souls.'

He folded his arms. 'Bullshit. You'd have gone to the police.'

'That wouldn't be enough,' she said, her fist clenched, fighting to stop herself from banging the table, knowing it would bring the guards over. 'You'd walk away from it all and I wasn't having that. It wouldn't stop you either.' She crossed her legs. 'So I used you. I had my own demons to exorcise.'

Proctor shook his head. 'No, I would've known.'

She scoffed. 'Would you? Or maybe you didn't see past the

430

little woman act? Didn't you ever wonder why it was *that* teacher?'

'So, he'd been fucking your sister, and for that you wanted him killed? And I'm the bad guy?'

'It's not just that he was fucking her,' she hissed, leaning forward, gripping the edge of the table. 'Don't you get it? He let her go home alone, a child, because protecting himself was more important. He couldn't be seen with Adrianne, so she stayed on the bus for the extra stop, so that she came back to the house a different way, so no one would know where she'd come from. And you were waiting.'

'That was down to her,' he said. 'The same routine every time. I used to watch them, but you know that, if you've seen the pictures. She loved the back of his car. He didn't love her back, though. Why didn't he come forward to help the investigation?'

She slammed her hand onto the desk, unable to stop herself, making a guard look over. 'So now you understand.'

He shook his head in disbelief, gritting his teeth. 'You know what, for the first time in my life, you interest me.'

'I don't need your admiration. You're weak. How easy was it to get you to kill Henry Mason, all over your little box of dirty secrets, your treasured memories?' She blinked away tears. 'My little sister, reduced to a souvenir. I guessed how much you'd want it back. Remember the burglary, when it went missing? So easy to stage. I just threw a few things around and moved the box to somewhere you couldn't find it. I knew you'd do anything to get it back. You think you're so clever but you were predictable. I knew you wouldn't call the police. You didn't even bother with an insurance claim. And do you remember the blackmail that made you kill Henry Mason?'

'"Kill him or the box goes to the police", the messages said.'

'No, *I* said,' and Helena slapped her hand against her chest

431

in emphasis. 'You kill the man in the park and it goes no further, that's what I said, because we'd have something on each
other. Simple.'

'So you were sending me those messages?'

'Right in front of you, and you thought I was just looking at
the internet or going on that quiz app I like.'

'But you weren't so clever, because you didn't mask your
internet address enough,' he said. 'Some of those messages will
come back to you.'

'No, Mark, not to me. To you. Don't you get it? That was my
back-up plan. Whenever you were in the house, I didn't use a
proxy server. I made sure it would all come back to you.'

'But you wanted Mason dead. Why am I the bad guy?'

'Because he killed my parents when he sold them that death
trap.' She stood up and leaned over the desk, jabbed her finger
towards him. 'I had a good life before you came along, before
that car came along. I never told you his name because when
Adrianne was taken away,' and she raised her hand, 'no, when
you took her away, Henry Mason seemed less important, and
my hatred was focused elsewhere. But he sold them a car that
my father drove into a bridge. It was faulty, it must have been.
He'd told me the pedals felt strange. Without that car, my sister
wouldn't have had just me, and she wouldn't have sought out
a new father figure, like Keith Welsby. And she wouldn't have
come across you. We'd still be a happy family. I was only
twenty-four. It wasn't my job to look after her.'

'And you didn't, did you?' Proctor said, sneering. 'This is
what it's all about, that you let your sister down and you're
trying to make it everyone else's fault.'

A guard shouted over, 'Sit down!'

'But I got Mason's secrets,' she said, ignoring him. 'Like you,
he was sick, liked them young. Sometimes he paid for it, I
watched him, so I knew how young he liked them, and other
times he looked for it on the internet. He put a link on his

432

Facebook page, No One Tells. It wasn't there for long, but I saw it.'

'I said, sit down!'

'You remember all that weight I lost last year?' she continued, ignoring the guard. 'You never noticed me, did you, but it dropped off. I set the trap, and sometimes being skinny enough to show your ribs is enough to convince someone you're a child. He never got my face, though. And the things he shared with me.' She shook her head. 'I had enough to ruin him. Pictures of very young girls, some he'd even taken himself.'

'Please, miss, sit down.'

'He told me stories too, things I could prove, from when he used to work in a children's home,' Helena went on, oblivious to the guard. 'He thought I liked hearing about it, and I did things for him, on the webcam, a skinny body eager for him, but with the camera too low to see my face. I videoed him. Just a camera out of view but pointing at the screen. But I didn't need to blackmail him into killing the teacher in the end. He thought with his cock, you see. So I promised him that if he killed Keith Welsby, he could be my first time. I made up some lies about Welsby so it sounded as though he deserved to die, a teacher who'd raped a friend but she wouldn't come forward. That's what I learned about people like him, that they don't see it as abuse. They try to twist it as something the girl enjoys.'

'And then you got me to kill Henry Mason,' Proctor said, nodding.

The guard started to walk over, impatience showing in his stride.

'Like the papers said, dominoes, that's all it was,' she said. 'Mason kills Welsby, and you kill Mason when he turned up to claim me, and then someone kills you. Who'd suspect the grieving widow, a victim once before? And I get rid of everyone. You included.'

433

'But why did you give the box back to me?'

'Because you hadn't been killed!' Her hand slammed the desk again. 'I wanted it back in your workshop, so I could interest people in it, hoping they'd do something with it, take it away and work everything out. I couldn't know anything; that was the point.'

Proctor glowered, a deep pink hue to his cheeks. He'd been trumped. That hurt the most.

'So you chanced upon Gerald King,' he said.

'I didn't want him involved. I'd hunted around on the same site I used to trap Mason, because the trap was the same, someone eager and underage. I wanted secrets, enough to make someone act, but they were too hard to find. They were mostly cowards in the end, wanting an internet thrill, nothing more. So I gave the honour to someone who deserved it: Gerald, one of your victims. Because that's what he was to you. It wasn't really about his daughter. It was about the misery you could spread.'

'But I didn't die.'

'No, and that's something I've got to live with, but you made that happen.'

The guard put his arm across her. 'Sit down or leave.' All other conversations drifted into pauses as everyone turned to watch.

'You weren't that clever, choosing that spot,' Proctor said. 'Didn't you think I'd suspect something?'

'Gerald was insistent. It was symbolic.'

'And what if he hadn't gone through with it? I'd still be alive.'

'There'd be someone else. I was prepared to wait. In the end, you trapped yourself. I got lucky. They linked it to you and even found a motive.'

'Miss, please!'

Proctor's fingernails tapped on the table surface before he

slammed his hand down, unable to control his anger. 'You're a killer, just like me.'

Helena stepped round the guard and slapped Proctor hard across the face, the crack of her palm on his cheek turning everyone silent. 'I'm nothing like you!'

The guard grabbed her around waist and tried to pull her away.

'You come here to lecture me about morality,' he said, standing up, his eyes wide with rage. 'You're no different.'

'You're the one in a cell, not me,' she screamed, and kicked out at the table.

The sound of footsteps was loud. Firm hands grabbed her by the arms and pulled her away. Another guard grabbed Proctor and pushed his head down to the desk.

'The police will find the others soon,' she shouted, as she was led towards the door.

'Others?' he said, muffled.

'Yes, the others. I know where they are.'

She hit the door hard as she was pushed through.

The last word she heard him shout as she was propelled towards the exit was 'Helena!' The word was filled with anger and confusion and the knowledge that she'd won. That would torment him. That was her prize.

'Here she is,' Joe said.

Helena was walking towards them, her finger under her nose as if sniffling, but when she climbed in there was no sign of tears.

'You all right?' Joe said.

She straightened her hair. Her cheeks were red. 'I will be,' she said.

'Where do you want to be?'

'Just take me home. I need to pack.'

Joe and Sam exchanged glances.

'Where are you going?' Sam said.

'I'm selling up. I can't live there any more, too many memories of my sister, and of Mark and all of his lies.'

'Where will you go?'

She thought about that. 'Somewhere hot. It's time for a new start. I might even change my name, so that I can disappear. I need to put all of this behind me. There's nothing for me here except bad memories. I want to go and never be found again.'

'I can understand that,' Sam said. 'Well, good luck, I suppose. You'll come back for the trial, though?'

'Yes, of course.' She frowned and leaned forward, put her hand on the back of Sam's seat. 'This sounds stupid,' she said, 'but my father's workshop ...'

Joe looked at Sam. He remembered the workshop. The candles, the damp feeling in the air.

'I was thinking about it before I came up here,' she said, 'and about the girls they never found. Well, Mark spent all of his time in there and I never understood why. The floor is really uneven, you see, as if someone has been digging in there and refilling it, but why would they do that? Then I think about the ones they've never found ...' And she shuddered.

Joe knew straight away what she meant. They were in the workshop, buried. He thought back to it. The candles, randomly spaced. He got it now. The candles weren't there for light. They were markers, little flickering souvenirs of what lay beneath.

Sam pulled his mobile from his pocket. He dialled a number and whispered into it that he needed to meet at Helena's house.

As Joe watched in her in the rear-view mirror, Helena looked out of the side window, her handbag on her knees. She looked composed, almost content.